Frontiers Past and Future

Frontiers Past and Future

Science Fiction and the American West

Carl Abbott

University Press of Kansas

Published by the

University Press of Kansas

(Lawrence, Kansas 66045),

which was organized by the

Kansas Board of Regents and

is operated and funded by

Emporia State University,

Fort Hays State University,

Kansas State University,

Pittsburg State University,

the University of Kansas, and

Wichita State University

Library of Congress Cataloging-in-Publication Data

Abbott, Carl.

Frontiers past and future : science fiction and the American West / Carl Abbott.

p. cm.

Includes bibliographical references and index.

ISBN 0-7006-1430-3 (alk. paper)

1. Science fiction, American—History and criticism. 2. Alternative histories (Fiction), American—History and criticism. 3. American fiction—West (U.S.)—History and criticism. 4. Western stories—History and criticism. 5. Frontier and pioneer life in literature. 6. Literature and history—West (U.S.) 7. West (U.S.)—In literature. I. Title.

PS374.S35A23 2006

813'.0876209—dc22 2005027616

British Library Cataloguing in Publication Data is available.

10 9 8 7 6 5 4 3 2 1

The paper used in this publication meets the minimum requirements of the American National Standard for Permanence of Paper for Printed Library Materials Z39.48-1984.

CONTENTS

PREFACE

This book is an exploration of overlaps between writing about the American West and writing about the American future. On the first side of the equation is the solid territory of frontier and western history, descriptive writing, and regional fiction. On the second side is speculative fiction whose authors have used ideas about the western past and present to help them think about the future. Substantial and insightful bodies of analysis have developed as guides to each territory—the fields of western history and western literary studies on one side and science fiction criticism on the other. I understand that I may have sacrificed some depth by trying to span the gap between these different intellectual realms, but I hope that my bridge allows some interesting views and vistas not possible from each side alone.

I have been a regular reader of science fiction since I was in the fourth grade and discovered the juvenile fiction of Robert Heinlein. I can tell you exactly where I was when I first read Heinlein's *Rocket Ship Galileo* (1947), *Space Cadet* (1948), and *Red Planet* (1949). Andre Norton's *Star Man's Son: 2250 AD* (1952) was scary but her *Star Rangers* was exciting, and the series of science fiction novels for young people published by Winston from 1952 through 1956 whetted my appetite for the adult books of Isaac Asimov, Poul Anderson, and many others. Since then, science fiction has been my major recreational reading. I have tried to keep up with new and interesting authors and with the more consumer-oriented criticism. From this base of familiarity, I have looked for science fiction narratives that start with an understanding of the historical present and work forward from that understanding with care for logic and plausibility.

The majority of evidence comes from science fiction novels written and published in the United States since the 1940s. Novels allow the fullest development of ideas, sometimes in a series of several books with continuous action or with common backgrounds and premises. Novels are accessible in libraries and in new and used bookstores for readers who want to follow up on my arguments. In addition, much of the best and most ambitious pulp magazine writing of the Golden Age of the later 1930s and 1940s were serials and novellas that were later expanded into books. I supplement science fiction novels with shorter fiction from magazines and anthologies, with movies, and with television shows. As a check on my personal knowledge, because hundreds of science fiction novels appear each year, I have also considered the appropriateness of all the novels that have won the annual Hugo and Nebula awards. Hugos have been conferred by fans at Worldcon, the major annual science fiction convention, since 1953, and Nebulas are given by the Science Fiction and Fantasy Writers of America (formerly the Science Fiction Writers of America) since 1965.

For help with the paragraphs about space cowboys, many thanks to participants on the H-West Internet discussion list as moderated by Elliott West. J. R. "Jones" Estes helped to run down many references and introduced me to some knowledgeable friends. For suggestions about books, movies, and television shows to consider, thanks to those who commented on versions of my ideas as presented at the Western History Association, the Western History Workshop at the Autry National Center, the University of London conference on Metropolitan Catastrophe, the Newberry Library's weekly colloquium series, and the colloquium series of Stanford University's Center for the Study of the North American West. I also appreciate the comments of a number of writers who have been willing to answer e-mail queries about their work, particularly Kim Stanley Robinson, James Gunn, Greg Bear, and Melissa Scott.

My writing has been facilitated by a sabbatical leave from Portland State University and by a summer research fellowship from the Oregon Council for the Humanities. A different version of Chapter 4 has appeared in "Homesteading on the Extraterrestrial Frontier," *Science Fiction Studies* 32 (July 2005): 240–64, and portions of Chapters 3 and 5 in the "Falling into History: The Imagined Wests of Kim Stanley Robinson in the Three Californias and Mars Trilogies," *Western Historical Quarterly* 34 (Spring 2003): 27–48.

Frontiers Past and Future

Introduction: Launching Pads

History is the trade secret of science fiction, and theories of history are its invisible engine.
—Ken MacLeod, preface to *The Star Fraction* (2001)

Future History

Science fiction is about the future, and the kinds of futures that its writers depict are conditioned by the ways that they understand the past and present. Every story about a possible future—whether ten years or ten centuries out—is a projection of some aspect of human history. The story may extrapolate the consequences of a recent social or technological development forward into the next decade, or it may envision the decline of the Roman Empire reenacted on a galactic scale. In either instance, the concepts that the writers deploy and the behaviors that they imagine derive from their experience of the present—and from their knowledge and interpretation of the past.

Readers have long known that the problems and worries of the day quickly find their way into science fiction: stories about technology as a cure for economic depression in the 1930s, nuclear holocaust stories after 1945, stories responding to the Vietnam war and feminism in the 1960s and 1970s, environmental disaster scenarios in recent decades. These connections are a staple for science fiction criticism, which pursues the lines of influence and argument among politics, social change, and fictions of the future. Writer and critic Samuel Delany has argued that "SF is not about the future. SF is in dialogue with the present. It works by setting up a dialogue with the here-and-now, a dialogue as rich and intricate as the writer can make it." Thomas Disch writes that "science fiction is not about predicting the future but about examining the present."[1] Those who ignore the past, in other words, can have no conception of the future. My goal is to discuss this dialogue, to examine how the ways in which we remember and talk about the past make it possible to imagine and express many American and global futures in science fiction narratives.

Fewer analysts have examined ways in which science fiction writers incorporate their conceptions of the past into depictions of the future, although historians well know that to engage the present is invariably to engage understandings of the past. In this book, I explore one way in which common understandings of American history figure in stories about the universe to come. For many writers of American science fiction, the exploration and development of the American West has been a fertile source of ideas and models for future centuries.

In choosing to focus on projected narratives of the American West, I've selected one of many ways in which historical thinking figures in visions of the future. An equally interesting discussion could address the idea of imperial fortunes and cycles of civilization in stories of multiplanet empires and galactic civilizations that decay at the core and face challenges from their hinterlands and frontiers. A different book could explore the ways in which science fiction writers have looked to the Rome of Suetonius, to the warring states of Renaissance Italy, or to the tenuous feudal polity of the Holy Roman Empire as models for imagining the politics of future societies.

I look at the use of narratives of American westward expansion because it is the history that I know best. I want to explore the ways that science fiction writers have thought about and used this western history, particularly their growing tendency to acknowledge the complexity of the historical western experience by imagining ambiguous futures. I am also interested in the other side of the relationship: What does the appropriation and transmutation of the western past suggest about the influence of older and newer approaches to writing about that history? There are seamless connections: the extension of western narratives into imagined futures means that historians and science fiction writers are both engaged in interpreting the past of the American West.

Science fiction—for my purpose—can be understood as a variety of history. It is imagined and undocumented, to be sure, except in the words of the fiction itself. But much science fiction operates within the essential constraints of historical narrative. It makes its characters and events believable by placing them in larger social settings. It speculates about the chain of changes that might lead from any present to any future. It explores how specific innovations in technology or alterations of culture might affect the ways in which people think, understand, and behave.

To start with a working definition, science fiction is a genre of popular writing that sets its stories in scientifically plausible futures that may be as close as tomorrow or as distant as far millennia. Science fiction's settings and projections of the future have to be scientifically or technologically conceivable. They may project the use of known technologies, such as interplanetary rocket ships and computer-mediated virtual realities. Or they may use gimmicks that have at least a toehold in theoretical science, such as faster-than-light communication using tachyons or interstellar travel through the complexities of a folded universe. In a definition proposed by critic Kingsley Amis, "science fiction is that class of prose narrative treating of a situation that could not arise in the world we know, but which is hypothesized on the basis of some innovation in science or technology, or pseudo-science or pseudo-technology, whether human or extraterrestrial in origin."[2]

It is important to stress that science fiction is rooted in knowledge that is available at the time of writing. Writer Samuel R. Delany has emphasized that science fiction must be "in accord with what we know of the physically explained universe." Joanna Russ has asserted that it has to be true to known facts and processes. Robert A. Heinlein, another writer who is otherwise far removed from Russ's and Delany's values and aesthetics, similarly argued that science fiction cannot blithely contradict things that are known to be true about the world at the time of writing.[3] This baseline knowledge includes scientific explanations of natural processes. It also extends to the nations, societies, cultures, and economic systems within which people live their lives.

In this sense, science fiction is concerned with projecting possibilities, not predicting probabilities. We now know that science fiction writers of the 1940s and 1950s usually got the 1980s and 1990s wrong. There are no helicopters in every garage, no space cadets in training on Venus. However, the mismatch of speculation and later reality does not invalidate the enterprise. Nor does it destroy the value and interest of well-wrought stories, as long as the author was true to the baseline starting point.

How far to stretch from the known into the unknown is the author's choice. It is helpful to think of a continuum from careful projection or extrapolation (conservative in assumptions) to speculation (freer in assumptions). A science fiction writer might project the tendency for Americans to live in gated communities, or the development of a market for human organs for transplants, or the tendency for teenagers to live their lives online. Writers might also speculate about the technological interventions needed to enable humans to live their entire lives as Martians, social changes that produce a stable anarchist society, mutations that create a subset of superior humans (a very popular option), or—in contrast—a time when dolphins and chimpanzees have acquired the capacities and status of intelligent beings. Whatever the specific venture into the unknown, science fiction expects that an author will systematically work through the implications and impacts of the central change that she or he has introduced.[4]

We should pause to note that science fiction writers can also use the genre techniques to extrapolate and write forward the past as well as the present. An *alternate history* is a fictional thought experiment about a historical turning point: What would have happened if every western European had perished from the Black Death? What would things be like if the Confederate States had won independence in 1865 or the Axis powers had won World War II? What if Charles Lindbergh had been elected president of the United States in 1940? In all such cases, the author has to think historically about the different ways in which a particular culture, economy, and political system might have been able to change, as well as the strength of cultural and institutional inertia.[5]

In defining my own approach to science fiction, I follow writer Kim Stanley Robinson, who explicitly defines science fiction as historical in character—as articulated narratives that can be seen as anchored at their origins in "real" times and circumstances. "In every science fiction narrative," he writes, "there is an explicit or implicit fictional *history* that connects the period depicted to our present moment." Readers can assume that a plausible sequence of events might lead from our present to the events in the story and can observe how the writer varies the assumptions behind those events. Science fiction writer and critic Norman Spinrad similarly argues that science fiction plays with "the mutability of history and world-lines" while relating "the past or present milieu of the setting to the extrapolative principle."[6]

Robinson's argument about the historical nature of science fiction has deep roots in the field. Robert Heinlein and magazine editor John W. Campbell were close associates in shaping modern science fiction. In May 1941, Campbell declared in an editorial in *Astounding Science Fiction* that science fiction novels were "historical novels laid against a background of a history that hasn't happened yet." Two months later, Heinlein reminded an audience of fans and writers about the centrality of historical change: "There won't always be an England—nor a Germany, nor a United States, nor a Baptist Church, nor monogamy, nor the Democratic Party, nor the modesty tabu, nor the superiority of the white race, nor aeroplanes. Any custom, technique, institution, belief or social structure that we see around us today will change, will pass."[7] In his own early work, he offered examples of the ways in which some of those changes might occur, developing a timeline for the "history of the future." In the manner of a history textbook, the timeline divided the next two and a half centuries into distinct periods and imagined the interactions among technological, political, and social developments.

When Robinson and Campbell and I call science fiction "history" or "historical fiction," we are drawing attention to the fact that science fiction stories are about the societal ramifications of change. Science fiction writers think historically when they envision path-dependent futures. Let one thing change, be it technology or custom, and other things start to change as well, and trickles of difference merge into a cascade of history. Whether a story is set ten years or ten centuries hence, the writer has to have some sense of how the world of the story got to be as it is. As Edward James puts it, "Sf writers have to construct new histories, of our own world or others," in order to provide a context for the specific change on which they want to pivot their story and a framework for thinking through its impacts.[8]

If readers are wondering where the spaceships and ray guns come in, my interest is in stories that *use* engineering and scientific applications and inventions, but not in stories that are *about* the devices. Science fiction writer Isaac Asimov offered a useful distinction among science fiction story types: gadget stories, adventure stories, and social stories.[9] In effect, the sequence describes levels of complexity, from stories that can be set in a single scientific laboratory to stories about the social context in which that laboratory functions and the sort of society that might emerge from its discoveries and developments.

Here is where strangers to science fiction often make the mistake of confusing the gizmo with the genre. Margaret Atwood is a case in point. Although her novel *The Handmaid's Tale* (1986) is a chilling extrapolation of cultural trends that are driven by changes in the techniques and technologies of reproduction, she has denied that it is science fiction. Science fiction, she says, has to be "filled with Martians and space travel to other planets, and things like that," whereas her novel should be termed "speculative fiction." Not long after, however, she reviewed a new book by science fiction writer Ursula K. Le Guin, whom she admires, and then differentiated between "science fiction proper (gizmo-riddled and theory-based space travel, time travel, or cybertravel to other worlds, with aliens frequent);

science-fiction fantasy (dragons are common; the gizmos are less plausible, and may include wands); and speculative fiction (human society and its possible future forms, which are either much better than what we have now, or much worse)." Her intent, of course, is to divide a genre with a "downright sluttish reputation" from work characterized by "accomplished and suggestive intellectual play."[10] In other words, someone who approaches science fiction from the viewpoint of "serious" writing is likely to draw class distinctions in which an aristocracy of literature reigns over a proletariat of popular paraliterary forms, a few of which have learned enough proper manners to be allowed into the house.[11]

In fact, Atwood is one of many writers who have published science fiction without the label. Much near-future science fiction appears as mass market thrillers, such as the science extrapolations of Michael Crichton. However, writers with high literary ambitions have long written stories that fit the definition of science fiction even though they are edited, marketed, reviewed, and understood outside the genre. Rudyard Kipling wrote technologically based science fiction in "With the Night Mail" in 1905, and E. M. Forster did the same in "When the Machine Stops" in 1909. George Orwell's 1984 (1949) and Anthony Burgess's *A Clockwork Orange* (1963) are both frightening social extrapolation that depend on changes in technology. John Barth's *Giles Goat-Boy* (1966) is both technical and social science fiction. Walker Percy's *Love in the Ruins* (1971) takes place in a projected near future. Don DeLillo's *Ratner's Star* (1976) develops from the science fiction premise of the search for extraterrestrial intelligence.[12]

The emphasis on science fiction as thought experiments about historical possibilities separates it from many of the books and videos that sit on the "science fiction" shelves in your nearby library, bookstore, and video rental outlet. In particular, science fiction is not fantasy, a genre with its own rules and clichés. The division is relatively clear, although many writers can, and do, work successfully in both categories. Science fiction deals with a universe we could live in; it hasn't happened, but it might, just conceivably. Fantasy deals with worlds we can never inhabit. Carl Malmgren draws the distinction in this way: Science fiction is concerned with the transition from the known to the unknown, fantasy with the contrast between the real and the unreal.[13]

Science fiction thus is not happy tales of talking animals or white witchcraft, like much children's literature from the entertaining adventures of Dr. Doolittle to the justly admired Harry Potter books. It is not vampire tales, whether by Bram Stoker or Anne Rice (there goes *Buffy the Vampire Slayer* [1997–2003], I'm sorry to say). It is not didactic and moral tales set in imaginary lands such as Narnia or on purely allegorical planets. C. S. Lewis's moralizing space tales are on the bubble: The protagonist flies to Mars in *Out of the Silent Planet* (1938) in a poorly described spaceship, but he gets to Venus in *Perelandra* (1943) with the supernatural assistance of a cosmic angel and fights evil scientists in *That Hideous Strength* (1945) with the help of a resurrected Merlin and his magic.

Nor is science fiction the same as imaginary sword, sorcery, and swashbuckle adventures. It is possible, with enough explanatory tissue, to craft science fiction narratives in which there are technical and sociological reasons for characters to live in lofty castles, ride horses, wrap themselves in woolen cloaks against the chill north wind, fight skillfully with pointed weapons, and endlessly replay the intrigues of the House of York and the House of Lancaster. But most of the multivolume "chronicles" of such-and-such a hero or thus-and-such a realm are fantasies that often use pseudomedieval settings because readers have ready-made mental images of castles and dungeons.[14] So keep a keen eye out for tapestries, high-spirited steeds, and climates that blow very hot or very cold but remain conveniently within the range suitable for humans.

The adventure stories that are sometimes called "space opera" or "planetary romance" are a fuzzier category. Many, many novelists and screenwriters place human beings on a distant planet in a far future and then let the characters do really fun things like rescue princesses, fight with light sabers, and blow up battle stars.[15] It is possible to have space operas in settings that are conceptually extrapolated from the present, and I include them among my possible texts. It is also possible to set superficially similar stories in a fictive time and place without any such connections, or any explanation of why the inhabitants seem to be human beings who speak English (often presented as "Anglic," to suggest the passage of time). Although fans and publishers often group historically rooted science fiction and space opera as a single genre because of common themes and tropes, writer Pamela Sargent distinguishes the subcategory as "science fantasy."[16]

Some comparisons may make the distinctions clear. Kenneth Grahame's *The Wind in the Willows* (1908) and Richard Adams's *Watership Down* (1972) are creative and often pointed fantasies. In contrast, H. G. Wells's description of the perversion of medical technology in *The Island of Dr. Moreau* (1896) is science fiction. The contrast is similar with projected utopias: Samuel Butler's *Erewhon* (1872) and Austin Tappan Wright's *Islandia* (1942) are utopian fantasies set in fully imaginary lands. Ernest Callenbach's *Ecotopia* (1975) is a less imaginative book but stakes its affiliation to science fiction by positing a plausible chain of events from the troubled present of the 1970s to a superior future. In the world of televised adventures, the original version of the nearly unwatchable *Battlestar Galactica* (1978–1980) was space opera whose humans and aliens adventured in a free-floating future. The very well-done *Babylon 5* (1994–1998) was science fiction. Despite human-acting aliens (including a nasty specimen who's a dead ringer for the emperor Caligula) and physically impossible space battles with the entire galaxy at stake, its story line takes politics seriously and reaches back to connect to a possible twenty-first-century future.[17]

Expansionist Adventures

Like a slowly growing river, science fiction has many sources. Some scholars cite utopias from the Renaissance and earlier as important predecessors (with Plato as a proto–science fiction writer who presumably perceived only a faint shadow of the science fiction idea). Others trace its origins to satirical writers, like Jonathan Swift, who invented distant lands or sent characters to the moon for satirical intent. Critic and writer Brian Aldiss has argued vigorously that the most important ancestor is Mary Shelley's *Frankenstein, or The Modern Prometheus* (1818) as the first self-conscious effort to imagine the effects of a new technology.[18]

For the writers I highlight in this study, a more immediate predecessor is Jules Verne and the amazing expeditions he sent his characters on. Many of Verne's books depend on Earth-bound exploration first, technology second. *Five Weeks in a Balloon* (1863) and *Around the World in Eighty Days* (1872) are travelogues and travel adventures and *The Mysterious Island* (1875) nearly so. *Journey to the Center of the Earth* (1864) is fantastic, but requires no social or technological transformations. *20,000 Leagues under the Sea* (1869), with undeniable technical glitz, depends on scientific extrapolation for its premise but not its plot, leaving *From the Earth to the Moon* (1865) as a somewhat lonely example of "pure" science fiction.[19] His publisher's collective title for Verne's many volumes was "*Les Voyages extraordinaires.*"

Nineteenth-century Europeans loved to read about fictitious adventures in exotic but real places—Africa, the Arctic, the Pacific, the Outback, and, of course, the American West. The middle-class literature of the British Empire teemed with colonial adventures. One of the most popular children's books of the era was R. M. Ballantyne's *The Coral Island: A Tale of the Pacific Ocean* (1858). This story of boys cast away in the Pacific and surviving on their wits in the style of *Robinson Crusoe* went through innumerable printings and remained high on the "best books" lists of British children well into the twentieth century. Ballantyne provided a familiar context for Robert Louis Stevenson's *Treasure Island* (1883) and served as the foil for William Golding's *Lord of the Flies* (1951). Ballantyne's work was a prototype for other adventures on the margins of the European world, from Canada's northern forests to Australia's great desert.[20] Well primed by such adventures, Europeans were a ready market for Wild West shows in the 1880s and 1890s. German readers devoured Karl May's westerns about Old Shatterhand, and other western American heroes adventured in French and Norwegian.[21]

Whether these adventure stories were for children or for adults, they helped map the far reaches of growing empires and functioned as a form of colonial claiming. In part, they were a direct response to the newly competitive European imperialism that followed the wars of 1861–1871. France turned outward after defeat in Europe, newly unified Germany and Italy sought their own colonies, Russia plunged deeper into central Asia, Japan and the United States jumped into the game, and Britain scrambled to protect its interests in Asia and to grab more pieces of Africa. Authors drew on the reports of explorers and scientists, nonfiction travel accounts, and geographical magazines for background, redressing the material for popular consumption. Typical of other countries, the British imperial adventure confirmed rather than challenged the values of the late Victorian era: whiteness was good, European civilization was good, migration to the colonies was patriotic, manliness was excellent, but sometimes needed to be tested against non-British adversaries or against nature itself (as Antarctic explorers Robert Falcon Scott and Ernest Stapleton were to do).[22]

Tales of imperial adventure varied across the spectrum, from popular entertainment to serious literature—just as American science fiction would do a century later. With more thoughtful writers, ironies take hold. Kurtz gains wealth in the interior of Africa but loses both soul and life in Joseph Conrad's *The Heart of Darkness* (1902). In *Nostromo* (1904), Conrad shifted focus from the European colonizers to their colonial descendants in a fictionalized South America. Here European models lead the creole elite astray and both imperial capitalism and liberal European-model revolution fail. Rudyard Kipling's great novel *Kim* (1901) narrates the exciting adventures of an Irish youth in a very colorful India, depicting the colonizers as sterile, mechanical, and uninteresting, the colonized as fascinating, spiritual, and revitalizing, even at a time when their daily lives were being scripted by British overlords.[23]

For writers whose goal was a rousing adventure rather than the exploration of character and culture, the expansion of geographical knowledge was a challenge to be met by making up places. As imperial nations divvied up most of the real world and global corporations exploited increasingly isolated resources, adventures of European expansion began to feature unknowable or impossible locales. Travel romancers around the turn of the twentieth century invented undiscovered islands in the wild ocean, hidden Antarctic valleys conveniently heated by volcanism, cave cities, and unexplored plateaus in Amazonia, and then peopled them with atavistic animals or unexpected colonies of surviving Phoenicians, Vikings, Israelites, and Crusaders.[24]

Turn-of-the-century adventure fantasies are still fun (if readers can partition off the books' racism). A key figure was British writer H. Rider Haggard, a contemporary of Verne. *King Solomon's Mines* (1885) and *She* (1887) helped set off an explosion of novels about lost races or lost places.[25] One of the most successful follow-ups was Arthur Conan Doyle's *The Lost World* (1914), in which an eccentric British scientist discovers dinosaurs surviving on an isolated mesa in South America. Indeed, Robert Fraser pinpoints *The Lost World* as "the point at which quest romance merges with two related forms: detective and science fiction." The best-known American versions are the African adventures that Edgar Rice Burroughs began with *Tarzan of the Apes* in 1912. Later examples of the extraordinary earthly voyage include the movie *King Kong* (1933) and the novel *Lost Horizon* (1933), James Hilton's tearjerker about Shangri-La.[26]

Once the imperial adventure or quest romance was freed of real settings, it was easy to transpose the adventures to other planets and sun systems. Writers pioneered science fiction by shifting the focus from *lost* races and places to *new* peoples on *new* worlds, writing the fantastic forward rather than sidewise or backward in time. Edgar Rice Burroughs began two long, successful series, one about Tarzan in Africa and the other about John Carter on Mars, in the same year, 1912. He followed with additional book series set on Venus and in the supposedly hollow interior of the Earth. Pamela Sargent explicitly sees the whole category of space opera as an extension of the search for unexplored places. It is "the kind of writing that uses all the props of science fiction—spaceships, advanced technology, aliens, and the rest—to tell stories that seem to be our culture's version of adventure tales in exotic places. They can't be set in unexplored and unknown regions of Earth any more, so they're set in other parts of the universe instead."[27]

As it developed from the early pulp magazine "scientifiction" of the 1920s to the complex genre of the twenty-first century, American science fiction has continued to look to future times and other places. The mission of the starship *Enterprise*, remember, is "to explore strange new worlds, to seek out new life and new civilizations." Most common is a future in which humans are pushing beyond the limits of the Earth to the moon, the planets of the solar system, to other suns and systems, through the galaxy and beyond . . . also in which humans are shaping a future Los Angeles, future San Francisco, future West, future Pacific world.

Romances and Westerns

With this background, it is easy to see science fiction as a variety of romance, the large and venerable category of fictions about characters who venture to the edges of danger, the margins of society, the boundaries of known traditions. Whether quest stories, war stories, spy stories, lonely-house-on-the-moor stories, or other variations, romance has a taste for the wild, irregular, and adventurous. Martin Green points out that such stories are often structured around "the idea that all human societies have a center where their laws are promulgated and revered, and a frontier where they are partially ignored, but where the law-making power fights life-or-death battles." He continues that the dichotomy can be "imaged as a campfire around which people cluster and a fringe of darkness where dangers lurk. . . . [as] capital cities versus national frontiers . . . [as] the city's daytime and official activities versus its criminal nightlife."[28] The aesthetic of the romance is that of the sublime rather than the beautiful, the awesome spectacle rather than the well-wrought object. The "sense of wonder" that science fiction fans seek and praise is another way to describe the grandeur, astonishment, and inspiration of the sublime.[29]

Scholars of American literature have firmly established the romance as a central tradition running through two centuries of American fiction. Men in wild nature, settlers on frontiers, heroes and heroines confronting unexpected challenges—these are the topics of novelists from Hawthorne, Cooper, and Melville to Faulkner and Hemingway and closer yet to Peter Matthiessen and Cormac McCarthy.[30] The American romance has juxtaposed old and new worlds, or near and far worlds, highlighted the men and women who travel between such worlds, and grappled with the implications of conquest, settlement, or progress.[31]

More specifically, American science fiction lies at an intersection where the imperial romance or adventure story meets the American "Western" and western American regional fiction more generally.[32] Indeed, the American version of the colonial adventure is the frontier story, written in different versions from the life of Daniel Boone and the novels of James Fenimore Cooper, through dime novel adventures, and into its modern Western form with Owen Wister's *The Virginian* in 1902. As present-day genres, Westerns and science fiction exist in uneasy companionship in the world of popular reading. Each has its devotees who consume every Western or science fiction paperback they can find but ignore the other category. By my count, Rosauer's supermarket in Hood River, Oregon, where I shop on the way to my weekend cabin on Mount Hood, displays equal numbers of both types (although crowded to the side by truck, car, motorcycle, hunting, and fishing magazines).

Westerns and science fiction share substantial parallels beyond their position on display racks. An obvious similarity is the importance of the physical setting. Critics across the board agree that landscape is a central player in avowed Westerns and western regional literature alike. Jane Tompkins asserts that the desert is the typical setting for Western novels and movies because its openness places human beings directly in nature. The landscape, she continues, is not just a backdrop but also an active element in western novels and movies: "the physical world comes first. . . . in between the apocalyptic moments of creation and dissolution the landscape sends a multitude of other messages, messages that seem as true and incontrovertible as the mountains and plains. It is the genius of the Western that it seems to make the land speak for itself." Mary Lawlor adds a social as well as personal dimension, writing that "The frontier was typically construed as a border zone that harbored mystery and danger, but that ultimately opened onto a plentiful, inviting space. . . . The wide, figuratively horizontal plane featured in such prospects gave material form to the ideals of democratic possibility so central to U.S. national culture from its beginnings."[33]

Science fiction prominently embodies both of these ideas. Science fiction extends western openness to infinity, from cold desert surfaces of the moon or Mars to the wide-open spaces of entire galaxies, making the western plains and desert actually as well as metaphorically boundless and extending their possibilities and dangers to the ends of the imagination.[34] Unlike in the Western, however, this physical setting can not simply be described or evoked. It has to be consciously introduced and sometimes highlighted. Settings that are unseen and unseeable places or time-places (like future cities) can never be assumed in the way a contemporary novelist can assume Monument Valley or Montmartre. If they match established genre conventions, future settings can sometimes be sketched only briefly. But frequently the description of strange new worlds is part of the fun. Along with other types of enjoyment they may take from their reading, science fiction fans like to be awed by high mountains and massive waterfalls unknown on Earth. Many of us enjoy the vicarious fun of hip-hopping around low-gravity asteroids and clearing at least small buildings with a single bound. We want to see stars swirling thickly around the galactic core and world-spanning cities that cover entire planets.

Very often, moreover, the science fiction setting or "landscape" plays the same sort of active role that Tompkins finds in the Western. Science fiction is a genre where new lands act as antagonists in the plot, delivering strange disasters and challenges to the human characters. To understand and cope with these challenges is to advance the plot (or to save one's own life). Technically oriented science fiction writers such as Poul Anderson spend much effort in the physical aspects of world-building, taking care to consistently describe the astrophysics, geology, meteorology, and biotics of imaginary planets according to known physical laws. At the extreme of Hal Clement, who used science fiction to explore puzzles of unearthly ecology, the imagining of settings on planets of great mass or of great cold is the primary goal of the fiction. More common, for our purposes, are the many books whose action is driven by the demands of adapting to life on the moon, Venus, Ganymede, or new planets around new suns. These are settings where earthly habits need to be forgotten fast and the principles of new ecologies quickly understood—or else the moon or planet itself strikes out to kill. The problems are not different in essence from the way that Willa Cather framed the challenges of initial settlement in *O Pioneers!* (1913), where the land "seemed to overwhelm the little beginnings of human society that struggled in its sombre wastes."[35]

Krista Comer, whose interest is the literature of the twentieth-century West, extends the point about the importance of the natural setting to western regional literature outside the Western genre. "Landscape is the single most telling signature of western identity," she argues. "Countless western narratives . . . take up landscape and/or nature (not the same thing, to be sure) as defining parts of western, and counterwestern, experience. Critics do so too. Big country, big sky, majestic mountains, mystical desertscapes, rough ranchlands, clean rivers, and fresh rejuvenative air symbolize that which is deeply, truly western, including, again, counterwestern."[36] She goes on to examine how women have conceptualized the rural and urban spaces of the modern West in ways that may differ from the masculine assumptions of cowboy and outlaw stories. This is a question that also concerns such western science fiction writers as Ursula K. Le Guin and Octavia Butler, who have tried to imagine futures with different gender relations and opportunities.

Spaciousness implies movement, and much writing about the American West—travel writing, nature writing, and fiction—has also been about *entering* the landscape. Lewis and Clark kept meticulous journals of exploration. Francis Parkman followed the Oregon Trail westward. Mark Twain reported on travels through Nevada and California in *Roughing It* (1872). Cowboys have ridden into the high country, pioneers have crossed the wide Missouri, naturalists have hiked through new landscapes. As Wallace Stegner writes, "look at any book that is western in its feel . . . and you will find that it is a book not about place but about motion, not about fulfillment but about desire."[37] Science fiction has the same preoccupation with going there and getting there and with the technologies that make such movement possible. Ask the nonfan (Margaret Atwood?) about science fiction, and she will say "space travel"—not space dwelling, or planet settling, but the process of travel itself. *Star Trek* is about "the *voyages* of the starship *Enterprise*," and its impulse engines, warp drive, dilithium crystals, and transporter room are inescapable elements in every show. And more broadly, much science fiction is a search for places to start over, for new "geographies of hope," to borrow another Stegner phrase.

To move into and across "empty" spaces, finally, is to occupy and claim those spaces. The undertext of the American western is the advance of civilization through contests with nature, native peoples, and nasty outlaws. This theme of continental expansion encompasses the dominant national myth of the United States, and it serves as the American equivalent of European imperialism and imperial adventuring. Science fiction similarly deals with the outward spread of Earth-based peoples and cultures. In its details, it helps to normalize the idea of different futures and make the coming centuries semifamiliar territory that its writers and readers have tentatively named and claimed.[38]

Connected Stories, Seamless Centuries

This is a book about connected stories. The narratives through which we understand the past—particularly the past of western North America—provide some of the most powerful and lasting ideas and models for speculating and writing about the future. My intent is to show how one important set of ideas and values weaves itself through much science fiction writing, and to argue that the ways that science fiction uses these ideas are more interesting than might appear at a quick glance. This book does not claim to offer the only, or the best, way to read American science fiction—just one fruitful way.

One way that the stories of past and future connect is through the overlap of fictional genres. As just discussed, there are important similarities between science fiction and the fictions of the American West. Work marketed as science fiction includes versions of expansionist romance. It also includes variations on the formal Western, which is this country's own variety of imperial fiction. Science fiction, especially in its formative years of the 1930s and 1940s, was an obvious form of romance with a penchant for isolated protagonists, stress on the power of the individual mind and will, and dependence on strange or mysterious situations. As the genre has become more sophisticated, it has maintained this tendency to place individual characters on the margin between civilization and wilderness, the known and the unknown, the familiar past and the endless future.

Another connection is the shared subject matter between western historians and science fiction writers. The topics that attract western historians have frequently been adapted for future stories. As the following chapters will show, there is science fiction about mining frontiers and homesteading, about the urbanization of the West and its ties to the Pacific world, about the massive engineering that makes inhospitable lands livable, about the ways in which individual settlers come together as conscious communities. Historians now emphasize the "unbroken past" of the American West, meaning continuities of development from the eighteenth century to the twenty-first century. Science fiction takes these same ongoing concerns and processes and projects them into coming decades and centuries. In effect, many science fiction writers are imagining an "unbroken future" in which new frontiers evolve in continuity with the old western frontiers.

A third connection has to do with answers as well as questions. Over the last half century, historians have deepened our understanding of western America. There is still a frontier narrative, but there are also stories about borderlands and racial interaction, about capitalism and class struggle, about global connections and contexts, about cities and city people, about the challenges of accurately learning the environment. Science fiction writers who see the future in terms of the western past have been participating in the same process. Their stories also have grown nuanced, tempering optimism with the understanding that every change brings unexpected consequences. In effect, historians and science fiction writers have converged on the same understanding that both the past and future are complicated places. By identifying and examining some of these connections of genre, subject matter, and approach, I hope to advance the ways in which we think about both the American past and its future.

1 Never Final Frontiers

Is this how it was a century ago, she wondered, when the women, the night before, lay ready for sleep, or not ready, in the small towns of the East, and heard the sound of horses in the night and the creak of Conestoga wagons ready to go. . . . On the rim of the precipice, on the edge of the cliff of stars. In their time, the smell of buffalo, and in our time the smell of the Rocket. Is this then how it was?
—Ray Bradbury, *The Martian Chronicles* (1950)

This mission, cloaked in technology and driven by both greed and desire and something as old as the species—it, too, was part of an unstoppable exploring impulse that had conquered an entire planet, and now was starting on a second one. "Wagon Train in Space," some wag had described an old sci-fi TV series. An apt description for them as well.
—Gregory Benford, *The Martian Race* (1999)

Space Cowboys

Space cowboys are hard to avoid. Scan the oldies stations on your car radio and you're likely to hear the twang of Steve Miller's 1973 hit "The Joker," in which the singer claims the multiple personalities of gangster of love, Maurice, and space cowboy.[1] Space cowboys are also front and center in the movie of the same name. In *Space Cowboys* (2000), Clint Eastwood, Tommy Lee Jones, and James Garner—all remembered from roles in movie and television westerns—play retired astronauts brought back for a final ride into space. Space cowboys are implicit in *Armageddon* (1998), in which Bruce Willis plays a roughneck oil rigger from Texas who saves the Earth from an onrushing asteroid. And the imagery is inescapable in *Star Wars* (1977): Luke Skywalker grows up on a ranch under the rim rock, has his first adventure in a dusty frontier cantina where aliens are stand-ins for Mexicans, and links up with the loner Han Solo, who plants his cowboy boots on the control console of the *Millennium Falcon* and whom director George Lucas has characterized as—we knew it—a space cowboy. The short-lived television series *Firefly* (2002), set five centuries into the future, used a country-and-western-style theme song. Its first aired episode began with the trope of postwar drifters in a dusty saloon, with the "Independents" standing in for the disillusioned Confederate veterans of so many western films, leading quickly to a barroom brawl and a train robbery.

Space cowboys are the liftoff for this book, which is about the ways much of American science fiction imagines the extension of the American West into the future. The stories that any group tells about its past condition the ways that group thinks about the future, and for Americans, western narratives are especially powerful. We have long projected political and cultural hopes on the West in forms that range from geopolitical boosterism to communitarian experiments. Because such stories of the West are so dominant in the American imagination, they echo and re-echo in imaginative writing about the future. Science fiction can be an extension of this western discourse, reinscribing the hopes and fears that shaped stories of the nineteenth- and twentieth-century West onto settings that stretch even more broadly across space and more deeply into time. A substantial portion of American science fiction is based on ideas, tropes, and narratives that are rooted in understandings of a western regional past and present.

The connection at first seems straightforward. Americans like frontiers as zones of adventure and possibility, and the western half of North America is the favorite. Despite the prominence of Daniel Boone, books like *The Last of the Mohicans* (1826), movies like *Drums along the Mohawk* (1939), and efforts to dramatize the frontier of eastern oak and sycamore forests, the trans-Mississippi West grips the national imagination most strongly. Perhaps its visual openness, compared with the thick natural forest cover of the East, makes it easier to envision heroes at work. Perhaps the West is more popular because Colt revolvers shoot faster than Kentucky rifles. Perhaps because it came later in time, it is closer to the borderland between memory and history.[2] Whatever the reason, the word *frontier* to most Americans means prairies, deserts, the Rocky Mountains, and maybe the frozen North. In turn, the whole range of the experience of western America, from the Great Plains to the Pacific Ocean—cowboys, miners, homesteaders, engineers, Wobblies, community builders—has provided templates for imagining future frontiers. The result, in a substantial body of American science fiction, is a seamless connection of centuries, a set of stories that links the nineteenth and twentieth centuries to the twenty-first century and beyond.

The western stories that animate science fiction come from our common fund of historical knowledge. They come from grade-school history classes and sophisticated historical scholarship, from detailed empirical accounts and cherished national myths, from mass market fiction, films, and television shows—all of which are embroiled with the ideology and metaphor of the frontier and with the imaginative function of the West as a last, best place. Taken together, these stories and ideas that connect frontier, growth, and opportunity shape many of the habitual ways in which Americans understand and talk about their national experience. They are hardy and enduring, and they are highly impervious to challenges from evidence.

The western American past features in science fiction in three ways. The first is through imitation and direct borrowing from the Western, that distinct genre of novels, movies, and imagery that revolve around cowboys, outlaws, lawmen, and other strong individuals set against the large, seemingly empty West of the nineteenth century. The second is the metaphorical use of the frontier and frontier imagery to link the positive values of westward expansion to future situations and stories. The third, and the focus of my attention, is the rewriting of specific narratives of western history and development such as mining rushes, homesteading, and landscape engineering.

Historians who examine these future narratives will be struck by parallels to changing understandings of western history. Since the 1980s, many historians of the American West have emphasized the continuities of development across time and geography, placing the far western frontier within a context of continuous European-American expansion and finding common issues and problems running from the eighteenth century through the twentieth century. By placing these same concerns in stories of the future, science fiction extends these continuities into the twenty-first century and beyond. Just as historians have tried to introduce more actors and more concerns into the simple story of westward movement, we can see a parallel development from frontier science fiction to complex stories of future regional change.

It Looks like Arizona

The great-grandfather of American genre science fiction was Edgar Rice Burroughs, who launched a very successful series of stories about Mars with the serial novel *Under the Moons of Mars* in 1912 (later issued in book form as *A Princess of Mars*). Burroughs opens with the hero, John Carter, taking refuge from a pursuing band of Apaches in an Arizona cave, falling into a trance, and awakening on Mars, where he faces enough exciting adventures to fill a total of ten volumes. Burroughs's Mars stories transplanted the clichés of exotic adventure fiction from the American West to the planet Barsoom. Bad guys now came in bright colors and sometimes had extra arms, but they rode the equivalent of horses, wielded lances and rifle equivalents, and roamed the dusty planet like western Indians.

Burroughs was the first of many science fiction writers to appropriate the settings and tropes of western fiction. Much of the pulp magazine science fiction of the 1930s and 1940s directly adapted the conventions and plots of the popular Western (sometimes by writers who worked in both genres). Science fiction fan Wilson Tucker coined the term *space opera* in 1941 in direct imitation of the already recognizable genre, the horse opera. A decade later, editor H. L. Gold (a New Yorker through and through) tried to buck the trend by pronouncing that his new magazine, *Galaxy Science Fiction*, would publish no Westerns disguised as science fiction. Gold's comment, however, came in the same period in which one pulp writer supposedly took a western story, changed only a few crucial words, and sold it to *Amazing Stories*.

Because new planets are often imagined as places of grand vistas and wide-open spaces, the landscape of the West has provided an easy source for sketching the appearance of new places. Since Burroughs launched John Carter's adventures, readers have come to expect Mars to look a lot like Arizona, or Death Valley, or perhaps an airless North Slope of Alaska, in part because such comparisons simplify the writer's task and make it easy for readers to envision unseen planetscapes.[3] When Chesley Bonestell painted vast, colorful, and detailed moonscapes and planetscapes for *Colliers* and other mass market magazines in the 1940s and 1950s, he worked in the tradition of western landscape painters like Thomas Moran and Albert Bierstadt, as well as many cover artists for science fiction magazines who adapted the same imagery.[4] Bonestell turned to space art after a career as a Hollywood artist, and the classic movies *When Worlds Collide* (1951) and *Forbidden Planet* (1956) featured the same southwestern locations that so conveniently served western film producers. *Star Trek* beamed Captain Kirk, Mr. Spock, and Dr. McCoy down to dozens of planets that look exactly like Griffith Park in Los Angeles, where many of the shows were shot. Three decades later, the skilled and sophisticated writer Kim Stanley Robinson likened Mars to the California desert, Monument Valley, and the Painted Desert in his award-winning Mars trilogy. It is "a Utah of the imagination."

Characters look like "a weatherbeaten sodbuster" and a scientific outpost like "a desiccated café in the Mojave."[5] Conversely, Americans have often used the analogy of the lunar surface to convey the strangeness of western landscapes. Western novelist Owen Wister in 1885 thought that Wyoming looked "like what the scenery on the moon must be."[6] Tourists today can visit the Craters of the Moon as a National Monument in Idaho.

Star Bridge (1955), by James E. Gunn and Jack Williamson, opens with both scenery and action straight from the dustiest of western novels and movies. The hero is Alan Horn, a name that would fit any cowboy. This gun for hire is fleeing pursuers across the plains of North America on his way to Sunport, where the vastly powerful Tubes short-circuit Einsteinian relativity and connect Earth to the capital of the oppressive Eron empire. In the first two pages, the "tired buckskin pony" drinks at a spring behind a "looming mesa." A buzzard circles on the wind. There is a canteen on the saddle horn, dust stirred from the horse's hooves and caked on its lathered sides, a "heavy unitron pistol" slung under Horn's shoulder. His "hard, grey eyes" search "the hot, cloudless sky." "I think we've lost them, boy," he whispers as he pats the tired flank of his mount (the hope is too good to be true, of course). For another 65 pages, until Horn takes a wild Tube ride to Eron and lands in the midst of a galactic revolution, the setting remains southwestern—reddened desert sun, canyons, cliffs, campfires, boot marks, and jackrabbit tracks in the red dust.[7]

Writers have continued to import the figures of western popular fiction into more recent science fiction, although they have had to think hard to keep the model fresh. John Jakes, best known as the author of historical novels about the movement westward from the Appalachians, imagined a sophisticated galactic bureaucrat forced to cope with a planetary culture that evolved as a sort of super-Texas in *Six Gun Planet* (1970). In effect, the protagonist is a version of the tenderfoot or outsider who comes west and learns to stand up to the local toughs and bad guys. In John Boyd's *The Andromeda Gun* (1974), an alien finds itself uneasily coinhabiting the brain of a nineteenth-century gunslinger.[8] Ben Bova's recent solution was to make one of the twelve multinational explorers on the first Mars expedition a Navajo who is trying to balance the mystic wisdom of his grandfather against the scientific rationalism of his culturally assimilated college professor father (UC-Berkeley). When he first steps onto the new world, he forgets his NASA script and exclaims "Ya'aa'tey" to his own surprise, the annoyance of mission control, and his parents' embarrassment.[9]

High Noon, with its simple, dramatic structure, is another favorite for writers who want to reuse or retool the settings and tropes of western fiction and movies. In the movie *Outland* (1981), Sean Connery is a special investigator sent to uncover the reason for high mortality among mine workers on the moons of Jupiter. He finds the locals ground down and cowed by the corrupt mining corporations and decides to fight for justice. Like Gary Cooper, he ends up confronting the bad guys alone as the people he's come to help cringe in the shadows.

The climax in Melissa Scott's novel *Trouble and Her Friends* (1994) is also *High Noon*–ish, although with a twist. Scott modeled the book on the discussion of the essential elements of western fiction and movies in Jane Tompkins's *West of Everything* (1992). She sees her book as a direct reworking of the classic Western around the idea of a cybernetic frontier, but one that queries the genre by using two lesbian computer hackers as the protagonists, rather than a single laconic hero. At the showdown in cyberspace, Trouble stalks the town bad guy through a virtual western Main Street townscape in a confrontation copied directly from western movies. By slipping into the virtual realm of computers, she finds a "dirt road and sunlight and flat wooden buildings, a double line of them along the single road, the only road today. . . . The Mayor will be waiting there—And then she has the image, belatedly, the grade-B western's final scene, and she grins in spite of herself, wishing her icon remade as she could remake it, given time, and starts walking, slow and easy, hands at her side, up the dusty road." Her opponent comes to face her clad in black under the "false sunlight burning down out of a dust-white sky." Trouble and her companion Cerise complete the image by pulling on new icons: "a gunfighter's silhouette, battered ten-gallon hat and loose cap-shouldered duster," one with a white hat and one with a black.[10]

Even Scottish-born Paul McAuley, presumably with limited personal investment in western myths, is another recent writer who has undercut the trope. In his far-future Mars, the first settlers from the United States and Tibet have been pushed aside by the Chinese, instead surviving as mounted drovers who push herds of yaks to market. One of the cowboys rescues the hero Wei Lee from an attacking dire wolf with one sure shot: "A pony and a rider were silhouetted against the red sun. The pony reared on two legs, and then it was galloping down the ridge. . . . He leaned on the front grip of the high, square saddle of his bay pony. A short-barreled rifle rested in the crook of his arm. With his free hand he pushed up the brim of his black felt hat: a lean dark weathered face, with bright blue eyes and a white smile."[11]

Wagon Trains

"Space: the final frontier." Is there any American who has not heard this phrase? Who has not encountered the starship *Enterprise* boldly going "where no man has gone before" (rewritten as "where no one has gone before" for the 1990s)? Gene Roddenberry, the creator of *Star Trek*, had been the lead writer for the 1950s television western *Have Gun, Will Travel* before he sold TV executives on the idea of a new show that he characterized as a sort of "wagon train to the stars."[12] He may have been recalling Robert Heinlein's novel *Farmer in the Sky* (1950), in which colonists travel from Earth to Ganymede in the *Mayflower* and the *Covered Wagon*, or the same author's *Tunnel in the Sky* (1955), which offers a glimpse of pioneers heading through an interstellar gate to a new, empty planet. They travel in "boat-tight Conestogas" led by a wagon boss on "a Palomino mare, lovely as a sunrise" and dressed like a don of old California. Ray Bradbury's story "The Wilderness," included toward the end of *The Martian Chronicles* (1950), similarly begins in Independence, Missouri, and gains evocative power by depicting interplanetary migration as a repeat of the Oregon Trail. Women whose husbands are already on the red planet speculate about their new life as they wait to follow: "Is this how it was a century ago, she wondered, when the women, the night before, lay ready for sleep, or not ready, in the small towns of the East, and heard the sound of horses in the night and the creak of Conestoga wagons ready to go. . . . In their time, the smell of buffalo, and in our time the smell of the Rocket. Is this then how it was?"[13]

Heinlein and Bradbury imagined their future wagon trains in an era when many other Americans were seeking literal and metaphorical replacements for the frontier that had presumably vanished with the advance of civilization and spread of modern machinery.[14] When he accepted his presidential nomination in Los Angeles in 1960, John F. Kennedy situated himself as "facing west on what was once the last frontier," and acknowledged that some might think that the frontier was over. Instead, he proclaimed that Americans stood "on the edge of a new frontier—the frontier of the 1960s—a frontier of unknown challenges and perils. . . . I am asking you to be new pioneers on that New Frontier." JFK may not have gotten very far in exploring this New Frontier, but the image had far more resonance than its predecessors and successors. Harry Truman's Fair Deal, Dwight Eisenhower's Dynamic Conservatism, and Lyndon Johnson's Great Society all mired in the complications involved in trying to alter social and economic relationships in a mature society. "New Frontier" suggested escape from those same social snares: an adventure in the Peace Corps, a venture to do good in city slums, a race into space against the Soviet Union.

One such replacement frontier was aviation. Pilots and promoters in the first decades of flight repeatedly presented their endeavors as pioneer work on the "sky frontier." Aviators were brave, brash, young, and nearly all male—an elevated reprise of California's Forty-Niners. It was almost impossible not to equate the U.S. Air Mail Service of the 1930s with the Pony Express.[15] From such thinking about the dangers, excitement, and loneliness of flying in frontier terms, it is an easy transition to framing the challenges of flight beyond the atmosphere in the same way. Indeed, "rocket plane" flights by gutsy test pilots in the 1950s were an important step in developing the technologies for orbital space shots and then the space shuttle.

Spacefaring as part of a New Frontier also took resonance from the idea that science and technology themselves are frontiers. In 1945, Vannevar Bush, the head of the wartime Office of Scientific Research and Development, issued *Science, the Endless Frontier*. In requesting the report, President Franklin Roosevelt evoked the western image with the statement that "new frontiers of the mind are before us." Bush answered with similar language. "The pioneer spirit is still vigorous within this nation," he wrote. "Science offers a largely unexplored hinterland for the pioneer who has the tools for his task. The rewards of such exploration both for the Nation and the individual are great."[16] Popular imagery and imagination of space exploration in books and movies in the 1950s and 1960s provided part of the context in which politicians such as John Kennedy made space exploration a major government enterprise.[17] NASA played off the same popular connection of past and future when it used the frontier metaphor to add appeal to its budget requests and named its extraterrestrial survey craft to recall the sagas of earthly exploration: *Mariner*, *Viking*, *Voyager*, *Pioneer*.[18]

At the same time that NASA was curtailing its manned space exploration after the sixth and final *Apollo* moon landing in 1972, Gerard O'Neill was preparing his manifesto for settlement on the High Frontier. His proposal for permanent orbiting habitats around the Earth as a way to leap beyond the resource constraints of a single planet nicely combined adventure, science, and environmental worry, as well as the idea that frontiers nourish democracy. Much of his writing is devoted to detailing the engineering necessary to build space islands capable of supporting populations in the millions, but he has also articulated a political agenda: "The opening of a new high frontier will challenge the best that is in us . . . the new lands waiting to be built in space will give us new freedom to search for better governments, social systems, and ways of life."[19] Science fiction writers quickly adopted O'Neill colonies as part of the consensus future, allowing them to invoke orbiting habitats with a few phrases rather than devoting effort and words to detailed description.[20] The combination of frontier hopes and engineering speculation motivated the Planetary Society, cofounded by astronomer Carl Sagan in 1980, as well as the more recent Artemis Society, which advocates renewed human exploration and settlement on the moon, and the Mars Society, which urges manned missions to Mars.[21] In January 2004, President George W. Bush advocated a program to return human beings to the moon and to land them on Mars. Invoking the spirit of Lewis and Clark and the inherent American impulse to explore, he said, "Mankind is drawn to the heavens for the same reason we were once drawn into unknown lands and across the open sea. We choose to explore space because doing so improves our lives and lifts our national spirit."[22]

It is a short step from research frontiers, blue-sky engineering proposals, and presidential speechwriting to the proposition that science fiction is based on a continuation of the pioneer experience that Americans value so highly. Gary Wolfe points out that important anthologies of the 1950s bore titles such as *The Space Frontier*, *Beachheads in Space*, and *Frontiers in Space*. It is therefore no surprise that readers expect space exploration to "work" like the nineteenth-century frontier. In the 1940s, for one example, Robert Heinlein wrote frontier comparisons into the background of stories about the future solar system as a way to give special power and poignance to the adventure plots.[23] In "The Long Watch," a military officer on the moon chooses death by radiation in order to dismantle atomic bombs and prevent a mad general from nuking the Earth. As he dies: "He was not alone; there were comrades with him—The boy with his finger in the dike, Colonel Bowie, too ill to move but insisting that he be carried across the line." "Logic of Empire" describes the reinvention of indentured servitude as the way to get a labor force for plantations on Venus. In a colony of escaped debt peons, the man in charge rules strictly but fairly in a way reminiscent of "the apocryphal Old Judge Bean, 'the Law West of the Pecos.'"[24] Heinlein also harked back to the prophets of a manifest destiny for the United States. One of his early characters is Rhysling, the blind poet of the spaceways, known through the solar system for his poem "The Green Hills of Earth:"

The arching sky is calling
Spacemen back to their trade.
All hands! Stand by! Free falling!
And the lights below us fade.
Out ride the sons of Terra,
Far drives the thundering jet,
Up leaps the race of Earthmen,
Out, far, and onward yet—[25]

The High Frontier metaphor operates even more concretely to support programs of planetary settlement. A book about a Mars landing by the experienced and respected science fiction writer Gregory Benford, for example, is framed with the ideas of explicit manifest destiny and renewal of the *American* frontier. A group of privately financed American astronauts race a Chinese-European team to be the first to land and return from Mars. The $30 billion prize, put up by a consortium of Earth governments, is a twenty-first century version of the competition to invent a chronometer for measuring longitude. The Americans overcome technical and environmental challenges but realize that they need to split up to survive. As the married couple on the team decide to stay behind for an extra three years, Benford brings the story full circle. The heroine sees herself as part of the "unstoppable exploring impulse that had conquered an entire planet, and now was starting on a second one."[26]

Robert Zubrin, a committed propagandist for manned Mars expeditions and settlement, has made the connection with even less subtlety. He followed his nonfiction arguments with a science fiction novel about a first Mars landing. The book's purpose is to sell the metaphor of high frontier as reality. At the climax, the expedition historian, who has decided to stay on Mars and help to form the first Martian family, passionately invokes the American western heritage and regenerative capacity of the frontier as the justification for the huge cost of planetary exploration.

> The American frontier created a stage where the actors could make up their own parts and their own script. We became the most creative nation in history, because we could see the infinite potential of the human mind, if only it's given a chance.
>
> Now, though, we're slowing down. . . . It's become much harder to find a place where we can try new things, so fewer new things get tried. . . . We don't build new cities any more, and so we've begun to think of ourselves not as the builders of our country, but as mere inhabitants.
>
> Our frontier has been gone too long, and now our nation is losing its spark. We can't let that happen. Here on Mars we have a chance to open a new frontier that can breathe life back into our civilization.[27]

New Western Stories

Wagon trains in space, arching skies, and thundering jets are fine as far as they take us, but the western past provides more than a simple metaphor of courage and triumph. Science fiction has grown to include more complex and interesting versions of the future in which costs and ambiguities of the frontier experience are acknowledged or made central. For examples that will be discussed at length in later chapters, two very interesting trilogies from the 1980s and 1990s build these costs into the basic structure of their narratives. Kim Stanley Robinson's books about the settlement of Mars make the environmental costs of pioneering and settlement a central point of debate among his characters. Pamela Sargent's trilogy about the human settlement of Venus pivots on the ways in which migration, pioneering, and the construction of new communities burdens women and children and creates gaps between generations and classes. Robinson, Sargent, and many other writers explore the processes of community making and the painful transition from adventure to everyday life as their characters try to create cultivated gardens rather than faring far to find a wilderness or an Eden.[28]

These books, along with many others I'll be dealing with, surround the protagonists with dense supporting casts comprising people who have their own goals and points of view, thereby mirroring the constraints on real historical actors. Characters tussle with the ambiguities and compromises of politics. The theme of continuity is everywhere as each generation deals with an ever more complicated and historicized present. In these and many other examples of more complex science fiction, understanding emerges from the dialogue among characters and the continually changing settings they find themselves in.[29] Time and again, these settings are understood and presented as new variations on older American experiences of exploration, resource development, and settlement.

My argument is that some of the most influential work in American science fiction needs to be understood as American writing that probes the meaning of the nation's past as well as its future. Science fiction certainly examines universal human experiences, as many literary critics point out, but many of the standard topics that science fiction writers visit and revisit—new worlds, space, technology, aliens—are directly part of the American western experience.[30] For this reason, much of the crucial work within the science fiction genre that speculates about the American future is deeply dependent on an understanding of the national and regional past. Many science fiction authors find it natural to use the stories that Americans tell about the development of the West and write them forward for places and times yet unknown.

Among literary scholars, Gary Wolfe and David Mogen have taken the lead in analyzing the ways that popular understandings of the western American frontier pervade American science fiction as myth and metaphor. Wolfe has commented on the extraterrestrial future as a direct extension of the national fascination with the western frontier as

> an arena for the kind of heroic individualism that increasingly seemed to be disappearing in the urbanized and industrialized East. With the closing of that frontier, the popular audience sought promises of yet new areas to explore, and science fiction gained popularity as a kind of literature which not only offered new frontiers but did so without sacrificing the technological idealism that had equally come to characterize industrial America. Science fiction offered its audience both the machine and the wilderness.[31]

In so doing, the genre has suggested one way to reconcile the conflict between the machine and the garden—economic growth and pastoral renewal—that Leo Marx identified as a central tension in American culture.[32]

Mogen takes the discussion a step further. He contrasts science fiction that rigorously extrapolates past and present trends in technology and social relations with more loosely constructed stories that make symbolic and figurative use of the same past. He emphasizes the power of the western frontier as a source of analogies, metaphors, and thematic myths (such as the ability of the American Adam to start anew or the power of regeneration through violence). He finds that the historic West figures little in extrapolative writings but, as the preceding discussion suggests, very prominently in the work of writers such as Ray Bradbury, who invoke the frontier as analogy while skipping lightly over practical connections of present to future.[33]

On close examination, however, the notion of a single frontier experience fragments. *Frontier* and *West* as general concepts have evocative power, but the historical frontier was constituted from multiple and changing processes and narratives, each of which manifests and expresses part of the larger story. Americans have constructed not a single story, but a powerful set of stories to explain how their nation expanded across the western half of North America and to describe the sorts of societies that the expansion created. My goal is to take the discussion the next step by examining the multiple and often conflicted stories that Americans have developed behind the facade of "frontier." Sometimes these stories are optimistic. Sometimes they have been dystopian. If we consider how they continue to interact and shape visions of our future, we may be helped toward a better understanding of options and possibilities for our present condition.

Although the terminology is now a bit unfashionable, historians of North America have often written about "frontiers" in the plural—fur trading frontier, mining frontier, lumberjack's frontier, cattleman's frontier, farming frontier, urban frontier. With the emphasis on the development of distinct sets of resources, the practice dates back to Frederick Jackson Turner in the United States and Harold Innis in Canada. Indeed, Turner, in his famous essay on "The Significance of the Frontier in American History," described the European American settlement of North America as a series of stages. "The United States lies like a huge page in the history of society," he wrote in 1894. "Line by line as we read this continental page from West to East we find the record of social evolution. It begins with the Indian and the hunter" and follows with "the trader, the pathfinder of civilization," then with ranching and "sparsely settled farming communities," and finally with "the manufacturing organization with city and factory system."[34] This sequence indeed sketches the elements of change in many regions of North America: the identification of natural resources and their initial exploitation, the expansion of settlements and corporate organization, the growing social and economic complexity of cities that coordinate regional empires and begin to create their own sources of wealth. If we add the experiences of labor union organizers, civil engineers, federal bureaucrats, utopian colonists, Asian and Mexican immigrants, hippies, and modern survivalists to those of explorers, mountain men, and Forty-Niners, we have many of the narratives that underlie and explain the national ideology of abundance.

Each of these frontiers has had its own internal logic that traces a distinct narrative, and each of these narrative frameworks manifests or expresses one part of the encompassing myth of frontier renewal. Each specific story—such as the narrative of homesteading by families and small communities—has served as a template for many works of science fiction. The result is bodies of fiction that link concrete aspects of nineteenth- and twentieth-century America to the twenty-first century and beyond. We can approach any of these interconnected narratives with an eye for commonalities and contrasts in treatment. We can explore how science fiction reproduces and adapts ideas found in nineteenth- and twentieth-century fiction and civic discourse about the economic and political possibilities of the West. In so doing, we can see how the ways in which we remember and talk about the past of the American West make it possible to imagine certain futures and difficult to imagine others.

We can also read science fiction in the light of recent changes in the academic study of western American history. The past twenty years have brought the rapid emergence and intellectual success of the so-called new western history. Traditional history of the West emphasizes the distinctness of the frontier as place and stage of development. In contrast, the findings and argument of new western history can be summarized as continuities of development from the eighteenth to twenty-first century across the supposed chronological barrier of the ending of the frontier; the convergence of many peoples arriving from every direction; the conquest of indigenous peoples and the landscape itself; the dominant role of capitalism; the conservation of cultural norms carried from Europe, eastern America, and other homelands; and the determining power of communities rather than individuals. This work also highlights the dependence of supposedly self-sufficient pioneers and present-day westerners on the federal government, the contrast between the region's rural image and urban reality, and the internal tensions of a multicultural and multiracial society. Taken together, these arguments delineate a western America whose future has always been contested among different groups and goals, with the popularly understood westward movement only one strand among many. In short, newer western history is about historical and moral complications rather than mythic simplicity.[35]

Science fiction writers have been active, if indirect, contributors to the dialogue through which Americans have slowly been accepting a history that is more complex than a simple epic of "winning the West" through "undaunted courage."[36] A growing body of science fiction has interrogated and complicated this popular history and thereby reinforced the message of recent western historiography. The newer understanding recognizes, in the words of historian Elliott West, that the American West has "a longer, grimmer, but more interesting story" that encompasses not only the full range of virtue and vice but also the voices of many disparate peoples—Navajo and Cheyenne, Chinese and Filipino, Hawaiian and French Canadian, Yankee and Mexican, Italian American, Finnish American, African American, and many others.[37] Of particular importance to the concerns of science fiction, western historians now view western North America as one of many Eurocentric colonial realms or settlement regions whose counterparts are Argentina and New Zealand, Australia and Kenya, Siberia and Brazil. There is now a large and exciting body of historical scholarship that offers comparisons across different margins of European-American expansion and imperialism. In this framework, exploration of similarities and differences among historical settlement frontiers and the imagined frontiers of science fiction is an easy and natural step.[38]

Science fiction has increasingly been raising the same sorts of concerns about the costs and contradictions of expansionism. In ways similar to new western historiography, it questions and complicates the popular western story. If there is a single recurring theme in the more recent science fiction that I explore in this study, it is historical and moral complexity rather than mythic simplicity. The relationship is one of convergent evolution rather than direct intellectual influence from university classrooms to the writers' laptops. To swipe a turn of phrase, historical writing and science fiction—whether in the 1950s or the 1990s—have come out of something in the same intellectual soil, out of the same American effort to probe the past in order to maintain a critical hope for the future.

Most commercial science fiction offers three elements. The first is a story line or plot revolving around a dilemma or conflict; typical are standard adventure stories and family sagas familiar from the long traditions of literature. The second element is an extrapolation or speculation that makes the plot intellectually interesting, and on which the bulk of critical analysis has focused. The third element is a backdrop setting, or backstory, against which the action is placed. In *Star Wars*, for example, the plot involves young people claiming their rightful place in the world; the extrapolation includes the technology of light sabers and the mind-bending powers of Jedi knights; and the backstory is the existence of a multispecies empire with lots of English spoken, like the British Empire in 1900.

Although I will pay attention to story lines and character development, I'm also interested in social extrapolation and the background within which that extrapolation is placed. In words familiar to science fiction fans, I'm interested in "world building" and the themes and assumptions from which the social dimensions of new worlds are constructed. One of the challenges and pleasures of science fiction is the need to read actively and to meet the author halfway in constructing the world setting. As Tom Moylan writes, knowledgeable readers "quickly realize that the 'setting' of the text is where the primary action is"; they learn to pick up clues about the strange world of the book as a traveler might become familiar with a foreign land.[39] I am interested in new and compelling settings and stories that draw on the narratives of the American West, but I am equally interested in the repeated use of the same basic setting, such as the common assumption that our solar system's asteroid belt will become the home to self-reliant prospectors.

The organization of this book mirrors both the Turnerian sequence and the complicating arguments of recent historians. In the order of chapters, I trace a version of the Turnerian procession—miners, engineers, farmers, community builders, city dwellers. Within each chapter, I start with simpler or more optimistic visions and move toward more complex and often less celebratory understandings of the past in the future. In so doing, my discussion moves from obvious and straightforward ways in which western narratives are written onto the future to more ambiguous and questioning stories that reflect Americans' increasing ambivalence about aspects of their past. I will note some of the ways in which the tropes of western fiction are used and recycled in science fiction, and I hope to offer some insightful readings in individual books and stories, but my central interest is in narrative content rather than literary method.

"Beyond Alaska" introduces science fiction texts that take the solar system as a proving ground for explorers, adventurers, and lone wolves.

Here are the individuals or individualists of the high frontier, its explorers and mineral prospectors and construction workers. The solar system here is an object for the traditional masculinist narrative of the frontier—with the interesting addition of female protagonists in recent years. Many of the stories I highlight give their characters few self-doubts; they are actors rather than thinkers. But also in parallel to the North American mining frontier, the era of the lone wolf fades into industrialized mining and clashes between organized workers and absentee corporations. Labor warfare against "the company" is as common as battles against the airless elements.

The West has been the land of many small beginnings, but from the start it has required Americans to mobilize capital and expertise on a large scale to facilitate resource development through dams, bridges, and water diversions. It is also the place where engineering has combined with the needs of research to create the Big Science of atomic energy production and astronomical observatories. "Science Projects" is about the transplantation of big dreams to new settings, and also about the way in which science fiction writers understand and project the enterprise of science itself, as it has evolved from individual tinker-heroes to massive public enterprises.

"Johnny Appleseed, John Wayne, and High Homesteading" examines these same high frontiers becoming homes, bringing the sweeping stories of terraforming down to (new) Earth. New planets promise pastures of plenty for settler families. The science fiction of homesteading adds women, children, and sometimes aliens to the man's frontier. It often accepts the positive goals of community making, but it understands that there are complications and costs. Science fiction writers explore these costs both through down-to-planet stories about high homesteading that stress the challenges of learning the land and the dynamics of families adapting to new lands.

After settlement comes the creation of community institutions and government. "Frontier Democracy" examines the complications of maturing societies as mapped onto the particularly American themes of democracy and disillusionment. The American West has required cooperation even as it has seemed to exalt extreme individualism. Californian Josiah Royce in the nineteenth century saw the possibilities of forging a better society from the necessities of cooperation on the frontier, an idea amplified by Frederick Jackson Turner. The focuses for this chapter are settler revolutions in places like the Moon and Mars, future versions of the very American practice of writing constitutions, and efforts to depict utopia as a process of community making.

Since the classical era of *polis* and *civitas*, challenges of civic life have been most formidable in large cities, which bring together millions of individuals with different goals, interests, cultures, and languages. The American West was an urban frontier from its first European settlement, grew around cities as economic organizing centers, and remained the most metropolitan of American regions at the end of the twentieth century. Just as California has been a metaphor for the American future, the West's premier cities of San Francisco and Los Angeles do heavy duty for science fiction as representations of future communities, the topic of "On the Urban Edge." In their contrasting depictions we find the continuing importance of place for western fiction as well as see manifestations of the problems and possibilities of the urbanized society that lies before the twenty-first century.

Consideration of metropolitan California leads easily into the imagining of a Pacific world. The West has always symbolized the national future, and at the turn of the twenty-first century, westerners appeared to be honing the cutting edge of a new information age. Old and new visions of a Pacific future form the underpinning for a group of novels often grouped as "cyberpunk" and "nanotech" speculations. By drawing out possibilities from new information technologies, both electronic and biological, they depict a world that pivots on the Pacific nations and functions under the control of giant corporations. The result is an updating of the American expectation of a Pacific destiny, but in the form of cybernetic anarchies and autocracies. "Information Everywhere" looks at the science fiction take on the postmodern world of space-time compression, where there may be a partial loss of regional identity and therefore a partial end to the story of westering America.

The concluding chapter returns to the big question of "Americans, Our Wests, and Science Fiction." Science fiction is inherently historical in its conception and sensibility, because to tell a science fiction story is to construct a narrative that weighs the consequences of change. Just as we gain new insights when the narratives of our past western history become more complicated, we also benefit when thoughtful science fiction can help us understand the complexity, costs, and promise of our national vision. The tensions that science fiction explores are those that remain ongoing concerns of the American nation—the tension between individual freedom or even heroism and the necessity for cooperation; the possibilities and limitations of growing and building ourselves out of social and economic dilemmas; the effects of technological change on national fortunes and on the interactions of classes and races. Over the seamless centuries, these are questions that play out in mainstream literature, civic discourse, historical scholarship, and science fiction alike.[40]

2 Beyond Alaska: Sourdoughs, Lunies, Belters, and Other Tough Guys

The moondogs seated at the tables—most of them male—were a lean and sullen bunch, with hard faces reminiscent of West Virginia coal miners and oil-rig operators from the Alaska North Slope.
—Allen Steele, *Lunar Descent* (1991)

It's the toughest kind of frontier, specially in the Belt. All the riches come down here.
—Eric Kotani and John Maddox Roberts, *The Island Worlds* (1987)

Out in the Belt

Gregory Benford's short story "Dark Sanctuary" (1979) starts with a burst of action.[1] Far into the depths of the asteroid belt, a laser has just targeted methane ice prospector Rosemary Jokopi. As she dives for cover inside her one-person ship and slams against its airlock bulkhead, she knows that in the belt, "you either have fast reflexes or you're a statistic." Waiting breathlessly for another hit from the unseen attacker, she crawls through the tiny ship to the bridge—"a fancy name for a closet-sized cockpit" (145).

Who's at the other end of the laser? Methane ice from the belt is a valuable commodity. It can be sent sunward in long, looping orbits to reach the moon and Earth-orbiting cylinder habitats much more cheaply than water can be boosted out of Earth's gravity well. The result is intense competition, a code of cooperation (rock rats always answer a distress call), and fierce defense of property: "Prospectors shoot at you if you're jumping a claim. . . . Prospecting by yourself is risky enough without the bad luck of running into somebody else's claim. At once I wished I wasn't such a loner" (146).

It turns out that Jokopi has stumbled on a huge alien craft lurking in radio silence in the belt, and the rest of the story involves some problem-solving about its character and intentions. The central tension of a lone brave prospector pushing into the unknown, however, remains. As Jokopi muses, "Belters aren't scientists. They're gamblers, idealists, thieves, crazies, malcontents. . . . Once you've grown up in space, moving on means moving *out*. . . . Nobody wants to be a groundpounder. So Belters are the new cutting edge of mankind, pushing out, finding new resources" (152).

"Dark Sanctuary" is a bit off track from Greg Benford's more common fictional themes (he is known for realistic novels about the practice of everyday science in the near future, and for a series of cosmos-spanning books that project a far future for humankind). However, the story neatly encapsulates assumptions that many science fiction writers have shared about life in the middle reaches of the solar system over the next few centuries. In this commonly described future, it will be the lure of mineral wealth that draws pioneers and prospectors to the cold corners of the solar system. Beyond the ore-hiding mountains of the lower forty-eight, beyond the glaciers and forests and frosty oil fields of twentieth-century Alaska, lie the airless worlds of the moon and the asteroid belt. They are lonely, desolate, and rich in minerals. Brave, resourceful, hardy, and sometimes foolhardy men and women search these vast reaches for the big bonanza that will make them rich and free them from the numbing isolation of tiny lunar rovers and cramped exploring vessels.

But there's a catch: the political influence and economic stranglehold of Skycorp, or ASTEX (Asteroid Exploration), or some other name for "the company." In one western state after another—California and Colorado, Arizona and Montana—the necessity and power of capital transformed individual prospector-entrepreneurs into industrial wage workers within twenty or thirty years of the initial mineral strikes. If we trust the science fiction imagination, we'll see the same processes at work in the future with prospectors, miners, and spaceport workers growing restive under the thumb of Earth-based owners and their allies in big government. When the economic system begins to clamp down on the rugged individuals, the option is to organize and fight back as workers.

This future has been shared and shaped by three generations of science fiction writers. Jack Williamson described it in the 1940s, Robert Heinlein developed it in the 1950s and 1960s, Larry Niven built it into his "Tales of Known Space" in the 1960s and 1970s, Allen Steele and C. J. Cherryh revisited it in the 1990s. The projected solar system is a proving ground for explorers, adventurers, and lone wolves. The cold, airless reaches of the solar system reproduce the imagery of the mining frontier as a rugged, heroic frontier. "Alaska" itself serves both literally and metaphorically as the transitional time-place between the nineteenth and twenty-first centuries. The presentation has grown more elaborate with the decades, but the outlines remain the same. They derive from the experience of western mining frontiers generally, from the real and imagined experience of the far north more particularly. Beyond the forbidding environment and fierce individualism of Alaska lies a future frontier where even more isolated men and women cope with even harsher conditions in their struggle to survive.

In the next section, I explore some of the reasons why Alaska keeps reappearing as a metaphor and reference point for science fiction texts about future mining frontiers. Alaska is a place where extremes of environment begin to suggest the dangers of space. The dark cold of northern winter, where the very air is dangerous, previews the dark, cold vacuum of space. Indeed, in one example of reality imitating imagination, NASA since the 1990s has been funding research at Haughton Crater on Devon Island in the Canadian Arctic as a way to test possibilities for Mars exploration. In addition, popular culture takes Alaska as the most recent of American frontiers—and one that is still active, where pioneering and rugged individualism are ongoing opportunities. For readers and writers in recent decades, it has the resonance of experience rather than history and seems a natural prelude to stories of these coming centuries.

In the next two sections, I examine the ways in which the common narrative of the mining frontier has been adapted for stories of the future. As with the usual understanding of Alaska itself, science fiction initially treats the airless frontier as the place for rugged, individual men to battle the environment and solve technical problems ("Rock Rats, Wildcatters, and Freerunners"). However, most western mining regions passed quickly from the era of self-reliant prospectors to an era of industrialized mining and labor-management conflict. Science fiction versions of radical labor organizing and resistance by working men to bureaucrats and bureaucracies is treated under the heading "One Big Union."

In the last section, I take a different angle. An examination of two science fiction novels written forty years apart adds questions of gender to those of class. In Jack Williamson's *Seetee Ship*, women are spirited sidekicks of the male heroes. In C. J. Cherryh's *Heavy Time*, they are depicted as equals who transform "man's work" into "pioneering work." The change reflects the feminism of the 1970s, with its insistence on opening careers to talent, and the more specific reanalysis of the western development narrative with attention to women as adventurers, pioneers, and settlers.

The Simple Flag of a Last Frontier

Sometime in the 1950s, a brightly colored advertisement in the Sunday comics section of the *Dayton Daily News* offered to sell me a SQUARE INCH OF ALASKA! I was perhaps eleven years old, and I bit. I bought. I eventually received a deed to my very own piece of the frontier, soon tucked away and lost to some later housecleaning. Fifty years later, wealthy Americans put money down to reserve a spot on the first commercial voyages to the moon, an act with more than a little resemblance to my minuscule claim on a distant landscape.

If twentieth-century Americans had not had Alaska conveniently tucked away in the far left corner of their continent, they surely would have invented it to ease their way through tumultuous decades of war, economic transition, and cultural change. The final line of "Alaska's Flag," the Alaska state song, lays claim to the "last frontier." At least four generations have envisioned the far northwest as a last frontier where pristine nature promises the chance for a new start and a renewed life. Alaska has been imagined as a northern testing ground that separates real men (and dogs) from the pack. *The Great Alaska Train Adventure*, a 1996 travelogue and documentary, sums up the common image when its sales pitch claims that "a whole different way of life exists in Alaska, one suited for those self-reliant types willing to turn their backs on much of the rest of society and tough it out through the brutally cold winters and remote locales."[2]

Other movies set in Alaska play with three variations on a theme: rip-snorting sourdoughs, dogs against the wilderness, and men against the wilderness. The classic "Alaska movie" is *North to Alaska* (1960) with John Wayne ("Big Sam McCord") and Stuart Granger as tough sourdoughs who've struck it rich in the Nome gold rush at the start of the twentieth century. A sampling of more recent films offer big scenery and tough characters (or tough scenery and big characters). On the dog-story rack at the video store are *White Fang* (1991), in which man and dog bond in the tough environment of the gold rush, and *Balto* (1995), an animated story of a heroic sled dog who brings medicine to Nome in 1925. Both animals—significantly for the image—are part wolf. On the adventure rack are *The Edge* (1997), one more "men against savage nature and themselves" story, and *Runaway Train* (1985), a movie that is almost pure movement and scenery—a *Great Alaska Train Ride* without a conductor or engineer.

When *Alaska* magazine proclaims that its editorial mission is "exploring the last frontier," it is following a tradition that traces back to the late nineteenth century and the travels of John Muir and Jack London. Muir voyaged up the Inside Passage in 1879 and again with tycoon E. H. Harriman in 1899. Visiting a region that had so far attracted few Americans except army explorers and Presbyterian missionaries, he found a land of new possibilities for individual and national renewal. His descriptions, which were not extensively published until the 1890s, were so enthusiastic that the Northern Pacific Railroad used some of his material for a travel brochure.[3]

London made much of his career out of his experiences and observations during a visit to the Yukon-Alaska mining district in 1896–1897. Most familiar is *The Call of the Wild* (1903), which starts on the old frontier of California and takes its story northward. London and later writers of Alaskan adventures, such as Rex Beach and James Oliver Curwood, were imperial in their vision, but Susan Kollin makes the interesting argument that they were also nascent environmentalists who saw a *resource* frontier to be managed as well as exploited. Arising at the same time that cults of manliness and Arcadia were interacting with the practical conservation of the new United States Forest Service and National Park Service, their work represents a "greening of American expansion."[4] For one example, Elam Harnish in London's *Burning Daylight* (1913) advocates a Progressive style of resource conservation—an understanding of the Alaskan experience that makes an early link to the "scientific" dimension of science fiction.

Alaska was a twentieth-century favorite because it was contiguous, American, and simple—and so big it seemed empty. Other extracontinental possibilities for expansion and adventure, in contrast, were much more complicated. Africa in the late nineteenth century was contested among native Africans, Europeans, and Arabs. The American Henry M. Stanley, for example, had to mobilize a substantial expedition to travel across Africa, and he encountered Arab armies along the way.[5] South Africa might have made some claims as a new California, but its multigroup conflicts were too complex for American engineers and investors to deal with. Latin America had high mountains and deep forests, but it also had touchy, independent governments. Australia already had its own outbackers. Even the South Sea islands, despite the images conjured by Herman Melville and later Margaret Mead, were scarcely *tabulae rasae* as British, German, French, and U.S. navies jockeyed for coaling stations. And few Americans harbored romantic notions about the Philippines after the bloody suppression of its independence movement.

Alaska, in contrast, was a huge canvas waiting to be painted. The inconvenient fact that Canada shared the far northwest was easy to ignore. So were the claims of native peoples, who were too scattered to loom very large in the imagination (not to mention minimized by the common assumption that Indians were in the process of vanishing). Alaska was a blank on the map for solitary twentieth-century Americans to fill with their adventures. Certainly the early American image of the far north was one of hearty, determined, adventuring individuals. The classic photographs of the Klondike gold rush, reenacted in Charlie Chaplin's *The Gold Rush* (1925), show *individuals* toiling like a long row of ants up the Chilcoot Pass. There is no community endeavor in the image, just one weary and determined prospector after the next.[6]

By the second half of the twentieth century, Alaska took on the role of a symbol as much as a place. Men of my father's generation, shaped by the 1930s and 1940s, dreamed of the new Alcan highway as a road to adventure, a mental escape even if circumstances never quite worked out.[7] Arthur Miller played on the understanding of Alaska as a "site of possibility" in *Death of a Salesman* (1949), in which Uncle Ben tells the family that "opportunities are tremendous" throughout the northern territory. Alaska glimmers as escape for characters as different as Dolores Haze in Vladimir Nabokov's *Lolita* (1955) and Coach Pepper in Larry McMurtry's *The Last Picture Show* (1966). It is the true wilderness against which the Atlanta office workers of James Dickey's *Deliverance* (1970) measure their own attempt to recover the primitive in the southern Appalachians.[8] In short, as John Whitehead points out, Alaska remains for many Americans an "untransformed West" that is envisioned to be more like the nineteenth century than the twentieth or twenty-first.[9]

At the end of the twentieth century, Alaska still served as uncharted, dangerous territory. Jon Krakauer's *Into the Wild* (1996) explores the death of lone wolf venturer Chris McCandless who came to Alaska to find isolation in uncharted territory. Because there were no blank spots on the map by 1992, McCandless's solution was to throw away his map and transport himself generations into the past, only to perish as the metaphorical wilderness proved all too literal.[10] Philip Fradkin's *Wildest Alaska: Journeys of Great*

Peril in Lituya Bay (2001) links the dangers of the past to the dangers of the present, finding nature as unyielding today as it was to earlier Alaskans. As William Lang writes, the issue at Lituya Bay is "nature's dimensions and powers . . . welcoming one moment and terrifying the next."[11]

Alaska has meant space: elbow room for neo-pioneers, vast distances to support spiritual quests and personal challenges. It means extremes of cold and distance that validate it as a testing ground of danger and adventure. Review the titles of "Alaska books" from the last quarter century: *Coming into the Country . . . Going to Extremes . . . Arctic Dreams: Imagination and Desire in a Northern Landscape . . . Yukon: The Last Frontier . . . Saga of a Bold Land*. Their titles draw readers with images of distance and harshness, even when the stories they actually tell are complicated by the *Exxon Valdez* oil spill, the presence of wage workers, residents' fondness for government subsidies, and battles over environmental change.

Nevertheless, the intertwined images of escape, challenge, and re-creation remain strong, with Alaska as a setting where the modern has penetrated only part way. Seth Kantner's novel *Ordinary Wolves* (2004) uses a young man caught between two cultures to contrast Anchorage as a foothold of civilization with a far northern village. T. C. Boyle's 2003 novel *Drop City* revisits the frontier story with simultaneous cynicism and sympathy. He follows a 1970 commune from Sonoma County, California, to Alaska, where members learn the skills of survival on the edge of civilization, in part from real outbackers who have committed to a life in the wilderness. While blissing out in California, they see a Charlie Chaplin movie ("something about Alaska—was that possible?"). When the county authorities run them off their farm, their alternative is Alaska:

> No rules . . . no zoning laws, no taxes, no county dicks and ordinances. You want to build, you build. You want to take down some trees and put up a cabin by the most righteous far-out turned-on little lake in the world, you go right ahead and do it and you don't have to go groveling for anybody's permission because there's no-fucking-body there—do you hear me people? Nobody. You can live there like Daniel Boone, like the original hippies, like our great-grandfathers and great-grandmothers—off the land, man, doing your own thing, no apologies.[12]

Alaskan scholar Judith Kleinfeld, another Daytonian turned Alaskan, offers a social scientist's gloss on Boyle's fiction. She has collected the stories of new Alaskans for whom the myth of the north has remained potent.

They carry images of Alaska from films and adventure books and deliberately avoid challenging the myth. Even high-ranking scientists prefer the romance to the facts, she argues, and the myths animate their lives into reality. In her positive evaluation, the "frontier frame of mind" that has motivated so many people to try Alaska becomes the script for creative, interesting, and generous lives.[13]

The quirky television show *Northern Exposure* (1990–1995) simultaneously depended on and undercut the Kleinfeld frame of mind. The show's creators populated a small Alaska town with traditional escapees like bush pilot Maggie O'Connell, seeking freedom from debutante life in Grosse Pointe, Michigan, and storekeeper Ruth-Ann Miller, who packed all her possessions into a station wagon in 1971 and headed north from Seattle, never to return to the lower forty-eight. For both characters, Alaska offered the challenges and satisfactions of independence. The major characters also included Maurice Minnifield, an astronaut turned land speculator. He sees the northern frontier as "acres of opportunity" but also the closest he can come to revisiting the high frontier. He turns his palatial log-cabin home into "Tranquility Base," with themed rooms devoted to Chuck Yeager, Buzz Aldrin, Wally Schirra, Alan Shepard, and Jim Lovell.

Maurice Minnifield is a character in tune with the assumptions of many science fiction writers, for whom the lonely reaches of the solar system reproduce the imagery of Alaska as a heroic frontier. On the airless moon, among the distantly orbiting asteroids, in the empty interstices of interplanetary space, men and women vie against the elements and the void. The societies of Luna and the belt are marginal to the power centers of Earth, and there are few other people to get in the way of Lunies and Belters going about their business, or to save them from life-threatening perils—no wolves or bears, but plenty of errant meteors and malfunctioning equipment.

The inhospitable environments of the moon, planets, and asteroids repeat and magnify the challenges of the north, as do the constrained spaces of permanent artificial satellites. Science fiction writers depict heroic individuals and small groups of men and women pitting themselves against the demanding environment and against tyrannous regimes on and off the surface. The standard depiction of the asteroid belt between Mars and Jupiter is similar, as writers frame this vast realm as a literally trackless wilderness where explorer-prospectors face danger and earn fortunes by discovering a mineral bonanza.

Rock Rats, Wildcatters, and Freerunners

It's lonely out among the asteroids. Science fiction writers commonly assume that asteroid belt culture is based on grinding isolation. The typical Belters of the coming centuries will be prospectors who spend long months arcing through the voids in single-person or two-person ships, confined with their hopes and misgivings. Think of month after month of close quarters in a doubleship as a future version of winter in the snowbound Klondike cabin in Charlie Chaplin's *Gold Rush*, another life support bubble surrounded by a deadly environment. When not in their ships, Belters are bouncing over the surface of jagged asteroids in fragile spacesuits that cut the individuals off from anything except their readouts and the sound of their own breathing.[14] The psychological pressures that result lead to disastrous inattention, to deep eccentricity that stamps someone as a poor-risk partner, to psychosis. Here is a quick description of the miner ship *Trinidad* in C. J. Cherryh's *Heavy Time*: "You spent three months breathing each other's sweat . . . so tight and lonely you could hear each other's thoughts echo off the walls. . . . The Belt was lonely and tempers got raw. Two men jammed into a five by three can for months on end had to give each other room—had to, that was all."[15]

The small ship and the psychological pressures that result are common elements the authors use to construct a distinctive Belter culture. Belters give their base camps on larger asteroids names like Rock City and Grubstake, in self-conscious imitation of the western American frontier. They are often fiercely independent (writers with libertarian views sometimes use asteroid belt settings to promote their open-market, antiregulation ideology). Belters are impatient with those who don't share the same hardships, and they fear the gravity wells of large planets as both physical and metaphorical traps.[16]

In this shared future, the lone prospector appears first on the moon and inner planets. In *The Moon Is a Harsh Mistress* (1966), set in 2076, Robert Heinlein describes a society whose foundation was mining deposits of water ice but where lucrative strikes are becoming scarce. He has "an old time drillman" talk about the problems of finding water: "today you have to listen farther out or deeper down to find ice."[17] Prospecting for water is also the central occupation for most Martian settlers in John Barnes's *The Sky So Big and Black* (2002), although here too, good deposits of subsurface ice are growing harder and harder to find. The implied image matches the Rocky Mountains and Great Basin of the mid-nineteenth century, when prospectors combed Colorado, then Idaho and Montana and British Columbia and Nevada and Oregon, for silver ore and traces of gold.

Like the participants in historic mining rushes, these are highly mobile men and women. In *The Moon Is a Harsh Mistress*, the "frontier society" of the moon rises up to free itself from the oppressive Earth, gaining economic and political independence. But after the battles, things seem too settled. The water miners are finding fewer and fewer deposits; even on an independent moon they face a future as wage workers. The option is emigration. The last passage in the book reads: "Since the boom started quite a few young cobbers have gone out to Asteroids. Hear about some nice places out there, not too crowded. My word, I'm not even a hundred yet."[18] In an early book for teenage readers, Heinlein described the effect when news of a big new discovery of fissionable materials in the asteroid belt reaches Mars: "Haven't you heard of the Hallelujah Node?. . . Three fourths of the sand rats on Mars are swarming into town. . . . They're stocking up for the Asteroids and kicking in together to charter ships." The demand for the right tools and supplies skews the Martian economy in ways similar to the impact of the Forty-Niners on San Francisco and the Klondikers on Seattle.[19]

The goal for most prospectors is the asteroid belt. The belt is in fact a vast, largely empty torus between the orbits of Mars and Jupiter. It centers roughly 250 million miles from the sun (160 million miles from Earth). Within this great donut of space, which stretches tens of millions of miles across, are the elliptical orbits of hundreds of thousands of rocks that circle the sun in a constantly changing dance, courtesy of the perturbing gravity of Jupiter as it sweeps by to the outside. A few of the rocks might be big enough for substantial settlements, on their surface or tunneled beneath it. Most are smaller, grading down from miles across to hand-sized chunks and dust. Their numbers are huge, but the distances within the belt are even more vast. The pilot of a prospecting ship in the belt would have much in common with navigators in the uncharted Pacific, voyaging for days or weeks between one island and the next.

Belt-based fiction is premised on the availability of enormous wealth. A mining frontier needs saleable minerals, so it is assumed that some of the asteroids have commercially valuable deposits of raw metals or fissionable materials. The prospector's challenge is to ignore the swarms of useless silicate rocks and locate those with a big payoff. The prolific writer Ben Bova also invokes the wealth of the asteroids as the prologue to an adventure about prospectors battling the Earth-based company:

> Millions of chunks of rock and metal float silently, endlessly, through the deep emptiness of interplanetary space. . . . They contain more metals and minerals, more natural resources, than the entire Earth can provide. They are the bonanza, the El Dorado, the Comstock Lode, the gold and silver and iron and everything-else mines of the twenty-first century.[20]

The men and women who seek this wealth are "rock rats" and "wildcatters" and "freerunners."[21] They are fiercely independent prospectors who may run in the red for years, piling up debts for fuel, oxygen, water, docking fees, and ship repairs while hoping for the discovery that will clear the books and make them rich. In port at larger asteroids they spend their ready cash on booze, drugs, sex, and vid stims while waiting for the dockyards to get their ship ready again: "There were just enough really big finds to keep the stars in the prospectors' eyes. They kept doggedly searching for the one asteroid that would allow them to retire in wealth and ease."[22]

The assumptions have spread beyond science fiction itself. Mary Doria Russell, a "serious" writer from outside the genre's traditions, uses a science fiction plot to examine issues of theology and faith in *The Sparrow* (1996). Part of the background are asteroid scavengers in the standard mode of lone prospectors: "Aussie wildcatters had gone from rock to rock, hoping to make the one big strike that would pay off the equipment mortgages they owed to Ohbayashi and set them up for life. Ninety-nine out of a hundred wildcatters went broke or crazy or both and abandoned their last asteroid with the equipment in situ."[23]

Rough democracy among equals complements fierce independence and impatience with outsiders. Like the early mining districts through which Colorado and California prospectors regulated their property rights in 1859 and 1860, the men of the wide spaces have their own codes of behavior. There are hijackers and dangerous rivalries among desperate prospectors, especially in the early wild days, but the miners commonly maintain their own law. Eric Kotani and John Maddox Roberts posit asteroid belt vigilantism: "The Kill On Sight net was universally respected in the lawless, courtless far reaches of the outerworlds."[24] Jack Williamson's asteroid miners agree that "the rock has to be inhabited and marked, you know, to keep the title clear."[25] C. J. Cherryh assumed that prospectors would share a commitment to mutual aid, even in the face of increasing bureaucracy and company regulations. Robert Heinlein's Belters in *The Rolling Stones* (1952) may look a scruffy lot, but they practice a rough-hewn democracy that values every person for his positive contributions.

In a classic story from 1951, Isaac Asimov described similar self-regulation among the Martian Scavengers.[26] These are the crews of two-person ships who wait between Earth and Mars to salvage the "shells" that serve as the booster stages of Earth-to-Mars rockets. The nested shells contain the water fuel and are discarded as the fuel is used. They drift along the Earth-Mars route, and Scavengers patrol the spaceways, rope them with magnetic lines, brand them, and send them spiraling down to Mars for metal salvage. With "gaunt, cheek-sunken" faces, Scavengers look like men battered by the desiccating cold of the Arctic. They are largely asocial loners who stay out for six to nine months at a time: "Usually you had to change partners each trip and you could stay out longer with some than with others." They are fiercely competitive, but they also share a basic set of values and comradeship and an agreed upon set of rules to keep the competition honest. A sighting of a shell is a "strike" that needs to be "roped," or taken under control. If the shell is roped within a scavenger's customary territory, it is his, no matter how much the team who first spotted it may grumble.

One Big Union

In Kim Stanley Robinson's early story "Coming Back to Dixieland" (1976), a bunch of "slageaters," or miners from the asteroid belt, Jovian moons, and Uranian moons get their big break by playing old-time jazz in an amateur night battle of the bands. The story centers on their efforts to hold their band together to win the competition and get a four-year performing tour of the solar system. In their world, that's the only way off the Jupiter Metals mines payroll. "When this thing is over," says one of the miners in a pessimistic mood, "they going to send us back to the rocks to work and work, every third shift, till some equipment catches you or some tunnel collapses."[27]

Robinson's miners are beaten down by the company, but they have one unusual escape route. For other miners and construction crews, there's no escape. They're angry. They're organizing on the moon. They're organizing on Mars. They're ready to take on the bosses and the company goons. They're in open rebellion against the dead hand of Earth. This is the common story for writers who want to explore what happens as the mining frontier matures. The industrialization and corporate control of prospecting and mining on Mars is the background story in the Sean Connery action film *Outland* (1980) and the Arnold Schwarzenegger action film *Total Recall*

(1990). It's a subplot in the *Babylon 5* television series (1994–1998) and a central feature in John Barnes's novel *The Sky So Big and Black* (2002). It's the conflict between moon-based workers and the home planet that drives the action in Heinlein's *The Moon Is a Harsh Mistress* and Allan Steele's *Lunar Descent* (1991).

The evolution from self-reliant prospecting to the deeply riven mining industry is also a story of the American West from the late nineteenth century. Between the 1860s and the 1890s, the individual prospectors who swarmed to Colorado, Idaho, and Montana organized themselves into the Western Federation of Miners, which leaders like Big Bill Haywood transformed into the Industrial Workers of the World in the early twentieth century. In Cripple Creek, Colorado; Coeur d'Alene, Idaho; Butte, Montana; and Bisbee, Arizona, miners of gold, silver, copper, and coal fought against powerful corporations and often against the power of government exercised through the National Guard. In a parallel process, science fiction envisions the rugged, independent-minded workers on the new mining frontier as organizing to fight the repressive hand of Earth-based corporations and bureaucracies.

The moon is a frequently posited battleground. As the first territory beyond the stratosphere to be settled, it is also the first to experience the transition from frontier to economic colony. Life on the moon is an alternative to a mundane existence at the bottom of the Earth's gravity well, but an initially open mining economy gives way to manufacturing as the mines play out, as Larry Niven describes as background for *The Patchwork Girl* (1980). The strip mines that have made lunar cities rich have begun to give out. Meanwhile, the mining frontier flourishes further out, in the belt, creating diplomatic tensions between Lunies and Belters that complicate the solution of a lunar murder mystery.[28]

For some, a growing society of domed or subsurface cities brings its own sense of confinement best remedied by moving on. In Robert Heinlein's good-natured juvenile novel *The Rolling Stones*, the choice to move on is a happy one. The Stone family represents the three generations of the lunar colony. Wisecracking grandmother Hazel Stone was one of the original founders. Her son writes scripts for space opera serials and his wife is a physician; their four children are all precocious in one way or another, quick to learn calculus and eager to see the solar system. Even now, decades after first settlement, "The moon is still an outpost, a frontier," but it's getting crowded. Says Hazel in her best Daniel Boone imitation:

"Luna is getting to be like any other ant hill. I'm going out somewhere to find elbow room, about a quarter billion miles of it." So they get a good deal on a used spaceship and set off for a year "on the road," first to Mars and then to the belt. It's there that the fifteen-year-old twins Castor and Pollux take a whirl at prospecting, but they quickly see that so much money has to go for the necessary equipment ("special suits, emergency shelter, keyed radioactive claiming stakes, Geiger counters, prospecting radar, portable spark spectroscope, and everything else needed to go quietly rock-happy") that turning a profit is unlikely. At the end of the book, the Stones are having so much fun that they decide to keep going to the moons of Jupiter. If *Star Trek* is a "wagon train to the stars," the analogy for the Stones is "Winnebago to the Belt."[29]

But most workers, of course, can't simply buy a spaceship and take off. They are stuck on the wage worker's frontier. Even in the nineteenth-century United States, independent pioneer farmers and ranchers were a minority among harvest hands, railroad construction crews, miners, loggers, and mill workers. Men without families and communities followed the cycle of crops and performed the stoop labor in California wheat fields and Colorado sugar beet fields. Other footloose laborers built and repaired railroads and cut down trees during the summer. In the winter the same men drifted into cities, spending their wages on cheap rooms, liquor, women, and gambling along Denver's Larimer Street district, in Portland's Burnside district, around Seattle's Pioneer Square, and other skid rows. These were men who had both the freedom and the need to join Coxey's Army of the unemployed in 1893 and the Industrial Workers of the World in the early 1900s.[30]

The evolution from the individual frontier to the wage workers' frontier is the underlying premise of *The Moon Is a Harsh Mistress.* By 2076 the moon's population has reached two million men and one million women. Lunar society is governed under a Lunar Authority set up under UN auspices but now largely independent. By the time of the book, several decades into settlement, a complex economy of retailing, services, and hydroponic farming has grown, but the moon remains a frontier society that originated in water mining. The water allows Lunies to grow grain, which feeds overpopulated Earth, with very unequal terms of trade.

The plot—which tells of a successful war of lunar independence—condenses the historical change from prospectors to labor organizing to revolutionary cell in the space of its second major scene. The hero is sent to spy on a labor meeting, listens to the complaints of individual prospectors, and ends up recruited into a revolutionary cadre before the night is over. The revolution starts with "as non-political a people as history ever produced."[31] It ends with an alliance among the separate lunar cities who win by using a sentient computer and the political savvy of the revolutionary leader to outsmart the stronger home planet, giving the workers a victory that they deserve.[32]

Allen Steele, in several novels and short stores written during the 1980s, offers a more fully developed picture of the first space frontier as a world of hard-rock miners and hard-drinking construction workers. Orbiting power satellites, an O'Neill colony, and a moon base are imagined as Virginia City or Dawson or the North Slope: "It was well known that life in Olympus Station was monotonous: sleep, eat, work, and not much else. People often compared the wild nightlife in Skycan to that of Deadhorse, Alaska."[33] The stations, of course, are controlled and managed environments, but the moon itself is a physical frontier that carries the implications of challenge and renewal. It is regeneration through wildness. As one character muses, the comforts of Earth cannot compete with elemental experience. They are attractive, "Unless, of course, you've really been in the wilderness. Such as having walked on the moon. Once you've been there, the frontier never lets you go."[34]

Steele sets his novel *Lunar Descent* on the surface of the moon in a company town, where a few hundred miners work under the thumb of Skycorp. Workers who sign a contract to work on the moon sign up for two years straight, because it is too expensive to send "moondogs" back and forth: "On the Moon you're there for keeps till the job is over or unless you're fired."[35] Life is hard work punctuated with illicit home-brewed booze. In the outback, miles from the base, there is even a desert hermit, Honest Yuri, a mad artist and scavenger/packrat who has decided never to leave the moon.

The company, worried about shrinking profits and thinking about selling out to a Japanese competitor, puts the squeeze on the miners, withholding promised bonuses and upping production quotas. Discontent boils over into a spontaneous general strike. The base administrator joins in, demonstrating the sort of solidarity between workers and local business owners that often marked western mining towns. Studies of mining towns such as Butte and Anaconda, Montana, and Cripple Creek, Colorado, have shown the strong ties between the miners and mill workers on the one hand and the merchants and professionals who served their needs on the other. The connection extended to politics and labor action, with unions speaking for the interests of the working-class community as a whole and the local middle class taking the side of strikers rather than the corporate elite.[36]

Also in parallel to the western American experience, the company enlists the American military to break the strike. The governors of western states in the late nineteenth and early twentieth centuries were often in the hip pockets of corporate moguls, calling out the National Guard to harass strikers, arrest labor leaders, and break the union. In *Lunar Descent*, the threat is the First Space Infantry of the U.S. Marines. It was created to prevent hostile takeover of the American moon bases by foreign powers, but it is ready to do the bidding of big business. Because the strike is illegal, "We could have the posse come down on us in a matter of days," warns one of the lunar leaders.[37] Indeed, the Marines seize the base after the moondogs put up a spirited resistance (but it turns out that the miners win anyway through brilliant computer hacking and unlikely financial maneuvering that gives them control of the entire company). The gimmicky happy ending draws on the long science fiction tradition of clever technical solutions for social problems, but Steele's larger goal remains: to describe a realistic frontier that contains far more roustabouts and wage workers than explorers and mountain men.

Seetee Ship and *Heavy Time*

Jack Williamson's *Seetee Ship* and C. J. Cherryh's *Heavy Time*, written forty years apart, illustrate the longevity of basic premises about the future of the asteroid belt—and the growing complexity of its treatment. Williamson's treatment is typical of the Golden Age science fiction of the 1940s, with clear heroes and villains involved in a plot that turns on a technical gimmick. Cherryh adds two sorts of complications. First, she emphasizes the nuances of bureaucratic and organizational infighting, in contrast to Williamson's unrealistic and essentially romantic picture of power politics. Second, she introduces tough women who define their own purposes and carve out their own spheres of action.

Williamson, a pioneer of American science fiction, directly placed himself in the frontier tradition. Born in Arizona in 1908 and raised on a New Mexico ranch, he calls his father a pioneer and himself "a typical frontier son" who internalized the classic narrative of the American West and recognized himself in "the limitless freedom of the space frontier" when he encountered space opera in *Amazing* magazine in the late 1920s. He sold his first space adventure story in 1928 at the dawn of the modern American genre. He continued his writing career through the Golden Age of the 1940s and beyond, increasingly collaborating with other writers such as James Gunn and Frederick Pohl. The western desert chapters of *Star Bridge* (1955, coauthored with James Gunn) were largely his writing and drew directly from his New Mexico roots. He designed a "rousing opening that would begin in mundane earthbound circumstances and expand into the far reaches of the galaxy."[38]

Williamson wrote three stories about the asteroid belt for *Astounding Science Fiction* in 1950, which he published under the name Will Stewart, and fixed them up into the novel *Seetee Ship* in 1951. It is pure space adventure. The scientific premise is the existence of antimatter ("contraterrene matter" or "c.t.") that is adrift in the belt and releases enormous energy when it collides with regular matter. Rick Drake, "a lean young giant with bright blue eyes and bronze-red hair," is a newly trained engineer who returns from college on Earth hoping to realize his father's dream of harnessing seetee for peaceful power. The powerful Interplanet Company has put down an asterite independence movement and is squeezing the rock rats out of business. It wants to harness seetee for a superbomb. The action is driven by these rival goals, embodied in Drake and in an officer of the High Space Guard, and complicated by the necessity of resolving the confusions introduced by a mysterious alien ship.[39] Hovering on the sides of the plot are nasty German-Martians and deceitful Russian communists from the Jovian moons, whose efforts to take over the High Guard are thwarted by Drake and the steadfast officer.

The plot is simple: Drake returns from school on Earth with his new degree, goes to work for Interplanet at its headquarters on the large asteroid Pallas, falls in love with the niece of Interplanet's boss in the Mandate, finds himself in rivalry with an ambitious military officer, leaves Interplanet to help his father's quest for seetee power, and falls into a series of adventures as Rick and the officer find common cause in fending off a communist mutiny among the High Space Guard while solving the mystery of an alien ship that has suddenly appeared among the asteroids.

Williamson's belt is a decidedly American future. The choice of villains (who speak awkward European-accented English) and the dilemma of military versus civilian uses of science directly reflect the concerns of the late 1940s, but the description of the setting repeatedly invokes the images of the western frontier. The capital city of Pallasport is "a new, gaudy, flimsy town of rootless adventurers" where rock rats sell their thorium ore to Interplanet representatives. The belt is a "new frontier of high space" whose miners are "tough pioneers." They defy meteor storms and the drifting seetee to explore and settle down to raise their families. Dedicated and resourceful Rick Drake "had learned in childhood to love the dark challenge and the splendid promise of this wild new frontier, and the feel of it now awoke the call of space in him, as old as his life and as strong as anything he knew."[40]

Helping to advance the action are two women who can best be described as plucky sidekicks. Drake's coworker Ann O'Banion was a childhood friend with whom he used to play games of spaceman-and-pirate. This former tomboy may hold a modest job as an administrative assistant, but she has the guts to call the bluff of the High Space Guard when the cards are down. Karen Hood, the High Commissioner's niece, arrives with twenty-seven pieces of matched luggage, but she catches on fast to the tensions between Interplanet and the rock rats, and she's gutsy enough to defy the authorities to help Rick escape Pallasport. She comes to the belt to escape the social restrictions of her upper-class upbringing and realize her own potential, as she tells Rick during a quarrel:

> I'm here because I like it. . . . I could have stayed home in Solar City. . . . I had money of my own—and plenty of chances to marry more, thank you. But I don't care for penthouse parties. . . . If you think this frontier town is too rough for women, you don't know what you're talking about. . . . I'm working hard to make my own way. I like it here. I like the people—even their blunt talk.[41]

To live happily ever after, the characters pair off. Tall, beautiful Karen Hood makes it clear that she is waiting to be won by the bashful Rick Drake, no matter the social gap. The Guards captain, who turns out to be an honest fellow, wins over the feisty Ann O'Banion. They are both strong women, but they end up standing by their men in the most clichéd version of adventure stories. They're strong when they need to be, but that strength turns out to make them more attractive mates rather than giving them true independence—the wives standing in the ranch house doorways as their husbands gallop off into the dusty distance to catch the rustlers or track down the train robbers.

If *Seetee Ship* is easy to pigeonhole as midcentury space adventure, C. J. Cherryh's *Heavy Time* is not. "Adventure" hovers in the background of the action like a half-suppressed fear and breaks out only in a chaotic climax that leaves the most sympathetic character dead and the other protagonists as survivors but not winners. The book makes demands on its readers. It begins with a moral dilemma that is never fully resolved, and all of the characters act from doubt rather than certainty. The story jumps among multiple points of view, following the thoughts as well as the actions of the characters. It is fragmented and ambiguous in ways that show the author's sophisticated understanding of both narrative technique and historical interpretation.

Cherryh, born as Caroline Janice Cherry in 1942, abandoned a career as a teacher of Latin and classics when her science fiction writing career took off in the mid-1970s. She is skilled at thinking through future changes in human societies and at imagining how nonhuman cultures might interact with humans. These cultural speculations are grounded in a style that focuses on the internal thoughts and fears of her flawed characters. At the same time, more than a dozen of her books are embedded in a systematically imagined Alliance/Union future for which she reworked the classic science fiction themes and tropes of interstellar trade, intrigue in spaceport bars, genetic engineering, war between multistellar empires, and confrontations between humans and aliens.[42]

Heavy Time is set in 2323, at the beginning of the Alliance/Union chronology. Although the putative time is more than a century after *Seetee Ship* (2190), both deal with the same midfuture in which human beings have had several decades to explore the solar system and develop new societies with growing differences from Earth; an equivalent temporal setting might be the three centuries of changes after the Jamestown settlement. The two books share many of the same basic assumptions about belt society. The belt is a place of escape from the thick restrictions of Earth society. Women have opportunities in the belt that they don't on older planets. The common language is English. There is mounting tension between independent miner/prospectors and the monopolistic company that runs the economy, conflicts that are manifested both in the distinctions of social class and in political intrigue. The space navy hovers behind the company and props it up.

But the political world of *Heavy Time* is much more complex than the situation of *Seetee Ship*. ASTEX, Asteroid Explorations, runs the belt as a subsidiary of the all-powerful Earth Company. The heart of the economy consists of huge space stations with metal processing factories that require a large industrial labor force and layers of middle managers. The factories consume ore from metal-rich asteroids that are spotted and tagged by small prospecting ships and routed to the refinery stations using the gravity well of Jupiter to control the speed and direction. At the refineries, the asteroid chunks are turned into ingots and foam steel to help Earth build its fleet for a war in progress. Over the years, many of the prospectors have become ASTEX employees, but the company charter requires that it also deal with the remaining independents, or freerunners.

Freerunners are in a bind. They depend on the Belt Management ("Big Mama" in their terms) for navigation charts, docking rights, and laser-assisted acceleration, but ASTEX thinks they're a nuisance. They cut into profits, they are constantly reshuffling their two-person crews of pilot and "numbers man" or navigator, and they attract misfits who don't follow rules. The company keeps imposing new regulations, assigns them the least promising sectors, slaps liens on their bank accounts, and sometimes cheats them outright. When old-timer pilot Morrie Bird and hotshot numbers man Ben Pollard rescue a greenhorn prospector whose ship has been mysteriously holed and whose partner has been killed, they know they're in for grief.

Cherryh makes her readers work. She dribbles out the background exposition in scattered paragraphs and quick allusions that may or may not be explained in later chapters, and only at the end is she forced into the long expository monologue that is the bane of science fiction. She also writes from multiple, interior points of view—Bird and Pollard, the rescued spacer Paul Dekker, pilot Meg Kady, navigator Solheila (Sal) Aboujib. Everyone has fears and doubts, everyone worries about what to say and still gets it wrong, everyone sizes up the situation from her own self-interest, even when she's trying to cooperate. Readers gain much of their understanding of the larger political and economic context by contrasting the multiple points of view of different oppressors and oppressed, mirroring the way that many recent historians stress the multiplicity of stories and understandings of the American West.

Heavy Time imagines the world of the belt from the bottom up. The class system is clear, with different decks in the space station for different folks. Company employees have cushy clubs and free booze, while everything on 8-deck comes from the automat. Independent spacers who find themselves on company decks are shown the way to the transit stop by firmly polite cops: "ASTEX didn't want a spacer walking on their clean deck, fingerprinting their beige painted walls. He understood the rules. He didn't even spit on the floor."[43]

Cherryh's characters know that they are embedded in a corporate-governmental bureaucracy. Williamson presented the political setting for *Seetee Ship* through impassioned speeches about ideals and dialogues among folks at the top. Rick Drake, fresh out of school, lunches with the High Commissioner in the third chapter (he's Karen Hood's Uncle Austin, to be sure) and has access to the rest of the belt leadership. In contrast, Cherryh's protagonists must deal with mind-numbing paperwork required by clerks and midlevel functionaries "who tested high in, so he had heard, Company Conformity." To get along, you need to be polite to the paper pushers and fill the blanks on the forms with just the right words. You need to know who's open for a bribe and how to trade information for information with an old acquaintance: "You learned what bought what from whom: some were cheap and some cost more than a freerunner could possibly pay, but you always kept track of your old classmates and, on call, you did favors . . . because favors got you favors."[44]

The physical environment of the station is more fully imagined than in the science fiction of Williamson's era. There's no gimmicky "paragravity," but rather a quick description of the way spacers move in the low gravity of the decks—a bit like snagging a ski tow. The range of entertainments matches the physical capacities of prospectors adjusting to weight, mostly new vids, lots of beer, and better food than could be carried into the void. "Heavy time" refers to the requirement that spacers spend a certain amount of time on the high-gravity decks of the station so that their hearts, kidneys, bones, and joints do not deteriorate from too much time in null gravity: "Mostly you worked out til you were about to drop, if you had to wrap your knees in bandages and pop pills like there was no tomorrow," all with the goal of getting down to 2-deck where gravity was .9 *g*, "that was as heavy as spacers lived."[45]

Cherryh's women are tough and determined, weary and wary. The belt means an adventure for Karen Hood in *Seetee Ship*, but it is a desperate grasp for a new life for Meg Kady, an anticompany activist from Sol Station with an attitude, a rab haircut, and a criminal record for smuggling. For Corazon Salazar, who dies in Dekker's accident before the story begins, it was a way to escape the heavy thumb of her powerful Mars-politician mother.[46] Meg Kady and Sal Aboujib, a belt-born renegade who has rebelled against her family, aggressively control their own sexual lives (they choose who sleeps with Bird and who with Pollard) and plan further ahead than their partners. They manipulate the men around them and carve out as much independence as possible. Nevertheless, they are still dependent on the professional judgment of men: Do they have the skills to take out a leased ship on their own as pilot and computer operator? Would a ship owner sign one of them as his partner for his own run? Their lack of full control over their fates chafes painfully.

In one of the most interesting passages, Kady recapitulates the concept of cultural hegemony and cooptation of radical movements after Herbert Marcuse's *One Dimensional Man* (1964) as she reflects on failed protest efforts. Now thirty-five years old, she was an anticorporate agitator, or rab, at Sol Station in her twenties. In 2315, Earth Company broke up the movement by firing into a mob outside company headquarters; now it has domesticated and marketed the rab style. "The rab got themselves shot to hell in '15 and here we got these damn synthetics swaggering around with the company label all over. The plastics don't know what we were. They turn us into clothes. Into *corp*-fad. Damn young synths make the music without the words."[47]

Out of these multiple experiences and points of view, *Heavy Time* presents a compelling vision of the divergent evolution of Belter culture and Earth culture. Although he has been decades in the belt, Morrie Bird is an immigrant from Earth, while Ben Pollard is Belter born. Some of the differences are in the details of experience: "Talk to Ben about Shakespeare—Ben'd say, What shift does he work?. . . Say, I went up to Denver for the weekend, and Ben'd look at you funny, because weekend was another thing that didn't translate. . . . Ben didn't really want to know; he couldn't spend it and he wasn't going there and never would and that was the limit of his interest." "Couldn't spend it" is the key. Belters have to pay for everything, even the air they breathe, and learn to deal with everyone in a pecuniary relationship. "If you want to figure Bird," Meg tells Sal, "you seriously need to understand, blueskyers don't know what short supply is. They don't think by the numbers: air's free and they got nothing but heavy time, so they give it away—they give it away even if they haven't got it, because it's their pride, you see?"[48]

The result of clashing cultures is the moral dilemma at the center of the book. By regulations, Bird and Pollard have a claim on Dekker's ship because it was out of control when they found it. Pollard sees the claim as a simple right and Dekker as a failure to be written off and out of their lives. Bird accepts half ownership when the claim is upheld, but he feels an obligation to help Dekker regain his mental stability and to get reestablished—motivations that Pollard finds totally inexplicable. As with many moral dilemmas, they're both right. Taking the ship is kicking a man while he's down, but Dekker comes out of his disaster dangerously angry and unstable. His accident, it turns out, is the result of ASTEX malfeasance, and its uncovering triggers a workers' revolt, a coup by Earth Fleet, and Bird's own death in the ensuing riots.

This ambivalent ending illustrates the way in which science fiction writers have begun to question as well as repeat the narratives of the American West. They borrow stories and situations and use the patterns of the past as templates for imagining the future, but that adaptation and treatment has been growing more complex over the last half century, reflecting some of the ways in which Americans have slowly been reevaluating and revaluing their legacy of continental expansion. Fifty years ago, the mining frontier seemed to offer a simple model for the future. As with the common view of Alaska, science fiction initially treated the airless frontier as the place for rugged men to battle the environment and solve technical problems in one more variation on the story of man against the wild. The characters are future versions of Forty-Niners, Pike's Peak gold rushers, and Klondikers.

In recent decades, however, science fiction writers have complicated the story by introducing issues of class and gender. Some have turned to the decades after the big bonanza, when self-reliant prospectors turn themselves into militant workers to resist corporate and bureaucratic oppression. Allen Steele, for example, reinscribes the western wage workers' frontier on the moon. The asteroid belt of C. J. Cherryh still provides a personal escape hatch where individuals can hope to make their fortunes, but it is no longer a *simple* frontier. Jack Williamson, writing more than fifty years ago, acknowledged the possibility of labor-management conflict but subordinated the problem in the uniting force of patriotism. There's no such out for Cherryh's freerunners, whose terms of freedom are narrowed by the power of the company. Her protagonists are flawed or ironic as well as heroic. Women increasingly appear as equals who transform "man's work" into "pioneering work." In effect, science fiction is elaborating the history of the future in ways that parallel the expanding range of questions that western historians now ask about the western American past, allowing Americans to think about the dilemmas of their national experience even while enjoying a good read.

3 Science Projects

The red rock and sand are all under water
that we ourselves pumped out of the ground
drowning what little we knew at the time
of this place as it was in the air
like gas burned off in a welder's fire.
—Kim Stanley Robinson, "Vastitas Borealis" (1999)

The mind-tour had been filled with great spectacles interspersed with images of individuals who seemed to have no life apart from their obsession with the Venus Project. Wadzia had not mentioned the drain placed on Earth's limited resources by more than four centuries of support for the Project.
—Pamela Sargent, *Venus of Shadows* (1990)

Flying Saucers

The Wanderer (1964), a Hugo-winning novel by Fritz Leiber, begins on the night of a lunar eclipse. Paul Hagbolt, a public relations specialist for the U.S. Moon Project, and Margo Gelhorn, fiancée of an astronaut, head north from Los Angeles on the Pacific Coast Highway for good viewing. Not far from Vandenberg Air Force Base, where the moon program is based, they come on a small group of flying saucer enthusiasts who have gathered for an oceanside symposium, on the theory that an eclipse might be a time when saucers reveal themselves.

Boy, are they right! At 11:02 P.M. Pacific time, a huge yellow and purple sphere pops out of hyperspace somewhere outside the orbit of the moon. Lighting up the night sky, the huge mass of the Wanderer triggers earthquakes, volcanic eruptions, and huge tides that sweep over all of Florida, much of the San Fernando Valley, and every other low-lying part of the Earth. Meanwhile, the inhabitants of the new planet casually dismantle the moon to fuel their traveling world. While the "saucer students" struggle to reach safety above high tide in the Santa Monica Mountains, the creatures of the Wanderer abduct the PR man and a moon-based astronaut for a bit of interspecies sex and indirect apologies (the planet is actually inhabited by a bunch of extraterrestrial juvenile delinquents on the lam from the cosmic authorities, and they didn't think to check the Earth for intelligent life before their catastrophic arrival). The cosmic cops turn up in their own planet for a laser battle before the Wanderer and its pursuer zip back into hyperspace, leaving behind a moonless Earth.

The Wanderer is a deftly written variation on the story of the unidentified flying object, detailing a series of adventures that eventually bring together true believers, ordinary West Coast citizens, and federal scientists. Reports of UFOs and complex speculations about federal government cover-ups of alien contact have been a recurring subtext in American popular culture since the cold war. UFOs can pop up anywhere—France, Portugal, Vermont, Brazil—but they are deeply linked with the American West. Kenneth Arnold kicked off the UFO era on June 24, 1947. While flying his private plane across the Cascade Mountains, he spotted nine fast-moving, disk-shaped objects off the shoulders of Mount Rainier. Reporters turned the objects into "flying saucers" and triggered nearly a thousand similar reports of fast-moving lights and objects within the year. Saucer-shaped spacecraft quickly became a Hollywood staple in movies such as *The Day the Earth Stood Still* (1951). My own first-grade imagination, not totally occupied by Dick, Jane, and Spot, made flying spacecraft out of the large disk-shaped light fixtures that hung from the classroom ceiling in Galbraith School, Knoxville, Tennessee.

In the years since, reports of flying objects have come in waves, fueled by periodic "eyewitness" magazine articles and books. Many Americans first assumed that unknown lights and objects were experimental aircraft or weapons, either American or Soviet. As the decades wore on, claimants such as George Adamski began to report their abduction by aliens who were sometimes nice and sometimes nasty (Adamski's Venusian friend Orthon wanted to keep earthlings from blowing each other up, but the phrase "alien probe" quickly became medical and sexual shorthand).[1] Folks who are not willing to accept explanations of weather balloons, optical refraction, and other human or natural causes now assume that UFOs are extraterrestrial.

For a region so thoroughly explored by fur trappers, prospectors, cowboys, and sheepherders—not to mention more recent naturalists, bone hunters, forestry students, petroleum geologists, hunters, anglers, day hikers, cross-country skiers, and backpackers—the American West still feels big enough to remain a convenient reliquary for the unknown. There is a cottage industry in the Pacific Northwest that is devoted to proving the existence of the Sasquatch.[2] As Thomas Pynchon notes in *Vineland* (1990), the same tangled landscape houses thousands of acres of illicit marijuana plantations, for "half the interior hasn't even been surveyed . . . ghost towns old and new blocked up behind slides that are generations old and no Corps of Engineers'll ever clear, a whole web of logging roads, fire roads, Indian trails for you to learn. You can hide, all right."[3] The campy film *Tremors* (1990) posits giant killer worms in the Nevada desert—a far more saleable location than, say, Illinois cornfields. The visitors in *Close Encounters of the Third Kind* (1977) zoom around a diverse American landscape, but they choose photoscenic Wyoming to land their very large saucer and pick up Richard Dreyfuss. And the federal government, as many Americans think they know, recovered the bodies of extraterrestrials from a saucer that crashed near Roswell, New Mexico, on July 2, 1947.[4] Since that time, the government has presumably preserved the humanoid bodies, as well as other aliens, at Area 51, a portion of the Nellis Air Force Bombing and Gunnery Range north of Las Vegas (how else to explain tighter security and strange atmospheric lights after 1989?).

The constantly proliferating versions, variations, and offshoots of the Roswell tale, including the television series *Roswell* (1999–2002) centering on teenage aliens, assume the existence of a large, powerful, and growing military-science establishment that is housed both overtly and secretly in the wide western spaces. Conspiracy theorists start with real examples of concealed military science—the Manhattan Project and the unpublicized side effects of atomic tests, early missile tests at White Sands, New Mexico, the tunneled complex of the North American Air Defense Command beneath Colorado's Cheyenne Mountain, advanced testing of spy planes and stealth aircraft at isolated bases in Nevada and California—and imagine them extended in purpose and expanded in size. The special effects blockbuster *Independence Day* that hit the theaters on July 4, 1996, for example, depicts Area 51 as a vast set of underground labs, hangars, and other facilities all prepared to deal with alien spacecraft and pilots.

Far-fetched as it may be, the Roswell myth and its cousins are a conceptual stepping stone from the very real role of big—and sometimes secret—science and large-scale engineering in the development of the American West to the imagination of parallels in future centuries.[5] The next section, "Manhandling the Planetscape," reviews the role of applied science and engineering in remaking the American West to be hospitable to the customs and culture of eastern Americans and Europeans. The challenges and problems in adapting the arid West to agriculture and urbanization are a direct prelude to imagining the terraforming new worlds—that is, transforming their climates and ecologies to be friendly to humans. "The Ethics of Terratransformation" and "Tyranny and Terraforming" then examine the ways in which science fiction has used future engineering to address two of the basic ethical questions that have arisen out of efforts to manhandle the earthly environment. One question is whether it is morally acceptable to choose such interventions—to bend continents and worlds solely to the service of humankind. The other is about the human costs of intervention: is it necessary for individual goals and freedom to be subordinated to the goals of larger political entities in order to make massive changes on the landscape?

Manhandling the Planetscape

The twentieth-century West was a natural home for the big and often clandestine science projects that created the nuclear age. The nation's nuclear era began in secrecy on the sagebrush plains of Hanford, Washington, and the isolated mesa of Los Alamos, New Mexico. The wartime facilities established the idea that the federal government would and could devote huge sums of money to secret science, and that the spacious West was the best place to hide such secrets. The demand for thousands of nuclear warheads during the cold war built an atomic West around research, design, and production. Lawrence-Livermore Laboratory in California explored the edges of nuclear physics, the National Reactor Testing Station in Idaho dealt with power production, and Sandia National Laboratory at Albuquerque took on the responsibility of the production engineering of nuclear bombs. The Hanford Reservation in central Washington produced plutonium, the Rocky Flats facility on the outskirts of Denver turned the plutonium into triggers for thermonuclear bombs, and the Pantex plant at Amarillo, Texas, manufactured nuclear weapons. The bombs topped Titan missiles in underground bunkers in Arizona and Minuteman missiles clustered in subterranean silos in Montana and the Dakotas.[6]

Las Vegas became an especially eager atomic city with the 1951 opening of the Nevada Test Site sixty-five miles north of town. Atomic Energy Commission workers played host to thousands of scientists, engineers, and military men during each series of test shots to evaluate nuclear "devices" from the national laboratories. New subdivisions soon stretched northwest to serve the test site's daily commuters. The Chamber of Commerce provided up-to-date schedules of tests and gave out road maps that marked the best vantage points. The 1953 yearbook of Las Vegas High School, the Southern Nevada Telephone Directory, and the official Clark County seal all featured mushroom clouds. Even after the Limited Test Ban Treaty of 1963 moved testing underground, the test site continued to account for nearly 10 percent of the workforce in southern Nevada.[7]

In one set of historical consequences, the rise of the atomic West was an important contributor to the growth of a regional economy driven by the interacting development of science and engineering for military applications, the expansion of the armed forces, and the aerospace and electronics industries. The scientific-military-industrial complex has dominated the growth of California, Washington, New Mexico, Colorado, and Alaska for two postwar generations. Three states—California, Texas, and Washington—together received more than 33 percent of all prime military contracts by the end of the 1950s, Alaska was little more than a federal defense colony, and another dozen western states were also heavily dependent on defense dollars.[8]

New waves of defense spending during the Vietnam war and the Reagan administration reinforced the connection between applied science and the West's growing educational and information industries.[9] Stanford Industrial Park in 1951 was the first planned effort to link the science and engineering faculties of major universities to the design and production of new products. It was the first step in the evolution of Silicon Valley as the seedbed of the electronics and computer industries and played a role similar to that of UCLA and Cal Tech for aerospace industries.[10] The shared market for these early electronics companies was the rapidly evolving market for guided missile systems, which were remaking the American strategic and tactical arsenals.

Big science, however, damaged landscapes at the same time that it made the fortunes of universities, cities, and corporations. Because the Great Basin is a land of sharp light and long vistas, the photographers have been among the most insightful commentators on the physical changes. Peter Goin has used pictures and text to document the results of hundreds of atomic tests in *Nuclear Landscapes* (1991). Peter Hales has explored the origins, development, and sometimes painful results of the nuclear communities in *Atomic Spaces* (1997). This recent interest in contemplating some of the West's most devastated areas fits within Patricia Limerick's argument that historians should give as much attention to the physical evidence of failure—such as abandoned mining works—as they do to stories and places of success.[11]

The atomic-age West is an injured region, as the photographers and essayists make clear. Utah ranchers and townspeople downwind from Nevada test sites developed abnormally high cancer rates. Residents of Grand Junction, Colorado, and other communities near the Four Corners unknowingly built houses and schools on radioactive tailings. At Hanford, tens of billions of dollars are being spent for the safe disposal of radioactive liquids that have been sitting for decades in rusting tanks, ponds, and trenches within a few miles of the Columbia River. The ten square miles of Rocky Flats, which came close to becoming an American Chernobyl in 1969, has a future for antelope and prairie dogs but not people.[12] Even with only partial cleanup, New Mexico salt deposits are receiving contaminated materials from Rocky Flats and other sites. In a multistate contest from which the Department of Energy eliminated all eastern states, Texas and Washington managed to fight off a high-level radioactive waste repository now destined for Yucca Mountain, Nevada (with Nevadans now much less enamored of the nuclear age, despite projected spending in the tens of billions of dollars).

An emphasis on undoing the impacts of nuclear weapons development is a recent shift of attitude, for atomic energy also figured into engineering dreams about reshaping the landscape. Find it hard to draw natural gas from deep pockets in western Colorado? Organize Project Rulison to shake things up with a subsurface fission explosion in 1973. Thinking about a new canal through Central America? Why not propose to blast through with atomic explosions—likely to be far quicker than the grinding steam shovels that George Goethels had directed in Panama in 1906–1914, but luckily not implemented. Need a trial run for a canal? Let Edward Teller take the lead in pushing Project Chariot, an Atomic Energy Commission scheme to dig a new harbor in Alaska with six thermonuclear devices. Although the 1958 proposal met enough resistance from scientists and Natives to expire in 1962, it represented, in Teller's words, "the great art of geographic engineering."[13]

Teller's comment in a commencement speech at the University of Alaska–Fairbanks links the 1950s to the preceding century. Project Plowshare, the AEC's general rubric for ideas about atomic ditch digging, can best be understood as recent installments in a long effort to make the American West more productive for wetland agriculture and more comfortable for new settlers. The three million residents of greater Phoenix may not require oxygen tanks like astronauts on the moon, but they depend on artificial air—or at least on air cooled artificially with the help of electricity from huge hydroelectric dams. The lucrative farms of the Imperial Valley depend on water from the western slope of the Rocky Mountains, captured by dams and doled out by political agreement. The sprawling farmlands of California's Central Valley depend on irrigation water from the Sierra Nevada and on the draining of a vast inland sea. Los Angeles struggles to survive in a location that simultaneously lacks enough "tame" water for households and industry and suffers from too much "wild" water during every heavy winter rainstorm. The bill to deal with each of these problems has totaled in the hundreds of millions of dollars, with security not assured by engineering systems that reach hundreds of miles.

These twentieth-century examples are recent installments in landscape-modification efforts that reach back to the nineteenth century. Americans have long desired to adapt the arid American West for behaviors and uses developed for the humid shores of the North Atlantic, and they've depended on the federal government to take the lead. Federal expeditions mapped and surveyed the West with increasing scientific accuracy: John C. Fremont from 1841 to 1854, surveys of four transcontinental railroad routes in the mid-1850s, post–Civil War surveys led by Clarence King, George Wheeler, Ferdinand Hayden, and John Wesley Powell under the auspices of the War Department and Interior Department. Geologists and topographers mapped land forms and rocks, and assessed economic opportunities, laying the scientific and political foundations for the United States Geological Survey, established in 1879. Land-grant universities worked to improve and adapt agricultural practices, even while boosters touted the myth that rain would follow the plow onto the high plains. Forest Service scientists in the early twentieth century tried to understand the cycles of forest growth and began to argue the merits of wilderness preservation.[14]

Out of this pursuit of science, and in step with it, came the testing and utilization of technologies to massively transform the western landscape. In every case, a utopian vision of expanded economic opportunity contended with land speculation and insider profiteering. The first transcontinental railroads in the 1860s and 1870s followed routes that federal survey parties had roughed out before the Civil War. The Panama Canal, begun in 1905 and completed in 1914, satisfied a vision of progress that dated to the mid-nineteenth century and promised to build great cities on the Pacific Coast.

And there was the challenge of rearranging freshwater—the central necessity in the economic conquest of much of the West. In some places there was too much, and the environmental history of large sections of western Oregon and central California is the story and consequences of draining and drying marshlands for farming.[15] Elsewhere, water was scarce rather than abundant. In 1902, Congress established the Reclamation Service to bring irrigated agriculture to dry valleys—in effect, to reshape the arid West to the expectations of the humid East. Behind the law was what William Cronon has called the "reclamation dream," a moral vision in which water would transform the desert into a new Promised Land. For the previous generation, irrigation canals had been community projects or business ventures, limited by the ability to raise the money for projects whose payoffs were far in the future. Now the profits from sales of public lands in sixteen western states would go into an "arid land reclamation fund" to pay for federal water projects. Roosevelt Dam on the Salt River in Arizona soon sped the growth of Phoenix. Arrowrock Dam on the Boise River, the world's tallest in 1915, transformed southern Idaho from desert to farmland.[16]

Reclamation Service projects set the stage for even more massive water engineering. The 1930s brought dam projects to harness each of the great rivers of the West for electricity, navigation, and irrigation. In a nation beaten down by the Great Depression, there was deep appeal about making "green pastures of plenty from dry desert lands," as Woody Guthrie would sing in "Pastures of Plenty." The construction of Boulder (now Hoover) Dam on the Colorado River caught the national imagination, as workers raised a huge wedge of concrete in the reverberating heat of the Black Canyon. Fort Peck Dam on the Missouri River, 3.7 miles across, was the largest earthfill dam on the continent. Photographer Margaret Bourke-White caught the dam, its builders, and their dream of a better life in a photo essay on "Mr. Roosevelt's New Wild West" for the first issue of *Life* magazine in November 1936. Grand Coulee Dam on the Columbia River went operational in 1941. In the words of Guthrie, hired to immortalize the Bonneville and Grand Coulee dams, "From the rising of the river to the setting of the sun / The Coulee is the biggest thing that man has ever done."[17]

The great dams of the 1930s ushered in another half-century of hydraulic engineering. Dozens of new dams impounded the Columbia, Missouri, Colorado, and Sacramento Rivers. Massive tunnels under the Front Range of the Rockies diverted the melting snow of western Colorado to the lawn sprinklers of Denver, while Lake Powell stored other West Slope water for the Southwest. The California Water Project and the Central Arizona Project fed southern California and southern Arizona with aqueducts hundreds of miles long. The goals remained economic development and the "eastern-forming" of the West for green lawns and water-intensive farming—and served to give plausibility to even more far-reaching ideas about the possible transformation of ecosystems beyond the surface of the Earth.

The Ethics of Terratransformation

To "terraform" a planet is to make it habitable by unassisted human beings. A habitable planet has to have an appropriate atmospheric pressure, the proper atmospheric composition, and the right range of surface temperatures. Humans cannot breathe in an atmosphere that is too thin, and they would be crushed by one that is too heavy. If there is not enough oxygen, we would suffocate; if too much, we would oxidize spontaneously. A livable temperature span is somewhere between Lapland winter and Libyan summer. Terraforming has been the premise for uncounted numbers of stories and novels since Olaf Stapledon suggested the idea in 1930 in *Last and First Men* and Jack Williamson coined the term in the early 1940s. Many of the stories that followed focus on technical questions involved in manipulating a planet's own resources or bringing materials from elsewhere: Might we liberate water from beneath the surface of Mars or import it in the form of water-ice asteroids nudged to intersect the planet? Could we seed a world with hearty plants to add oxygen to the air? Could we lower the temperature of Venus with colossal orbiting sun shades?[18]

The connection to the historic West is clear. Photographer Laurie Brown, poet Martha Ronk, and essayist Charles Little have titled a book of photographs of the bulldozed landscape of southern California *Recent Terrains: Terraforming the American West* (2003).[19] Her sweeping panoramas place regiments of earthmovers and legions of houses against the long, low horizon. They resemble Chesley Bonestell's planetscapes and rover-eye views of the Martian surface. Novelist Kim Stanley Robinson, author of science fiction's most sweeping exploration of planetary modification, lives in Davis, California, in the center of California's reengineered landscape and home to the land-grant university created for Californians to make money from newly useable land. He can see the ironic pleasures of the transformed landscape on a warm summer day: "Into the street. Winding village lane, flanked by flowers and trees. Terraforming at its finest: flat desert valley, now teeming with plants from all over the planet."[20]

As Robinson well knows, the history of landscape change in the American West suggests the need to approach terraforming with caution. One of the central themes of recent environmental history has been the repeated surprises that nature springs on scientists and engineers. Natural systems are complex, and often chaotic in the technical sense of responding in hard-to-predict ways to very slight changes in initial conditions. Because the systems are very, very difficult to describe and model in terms simple enough for policy decisions, many interventions go wrong, even with the best of intentions. Flood control efforts in Southern California repeatedly go amiss. Forest managers throughout the Pacific Northwest misjudge the effects of cutting and timber management, while the region's great dams surprise the communities that consume their electricity by destroying salmon runs despite remediation efforts. Smoky the Bear notwithstanding, fire suppression in the forests postpones and sometimes exacerbates fires rather than eliminating the danger.[21]

In the largest theoretical frame, natural ecosystems are resistant to the desire for comprehensive control. The postmodern critique is that big systems—like the dozen big Columbia and Snake River dams—can never be planned with enough nuance to account for every consequence. They are all examples of the "Project of the Enlightenment," the mistaken expectation that human society can be rationally comprehended and improved as a whole. James Scott's *Seeing like a State* (1999) examines and indicts an impressive variety of comprehensive social and economic engineering efforts, from Soviet collectivization and China's Great Leap Forward to Brasilia. The common failing is to attempt too much, and without adequate feedback from actual effects on the ground.[22]

Simultaneous with this practical critique has been an ethical reaction that revalues the natural for itself. Even as private utilities and governments were building ever more massive projects, the post–World War II West was spawning environmentalist reactions—moral visions of a "green" or natural West that have clashed with economic and engineering approaches. The responses can be as mild as the advocacy of xeroscaping and xeriscaping in Arizona cities, as straightforward as building sustainability goals into public policy, as comprehensive as questioning the validity of altering natural systems for human use, as extreme as ecoterrorism. Edward Abbey's popular novel *The Monkey-Wrench Gang* (1975) presented antidevelopment vandals as freedom fighters on behalf of the landscape. From Robinson Jeffers to Gary Snyder, many poets of the western landscape have argued the moral primacy of nature. By the 1990s, the Pacific Northwest was the home for an Old Growth Religion that saw logging not just as a mistake, but as a sin. Other environmentalists argued for the end to irrigated agriculture and seriously suggested breaching or abandoning some of the great dams on the Colorado and Columbia-Snake River systems.

In parallel, science fiction writers have examined questions about the ethics of environmental interventions. Do natural systems have moral claims? Do humans have responsibilities to preserve the prehuman Mars? There has long been science fiction that warns about the unexpected consequences of human interventions in poorly understood planetary ecologies—the story of rabbits in Australia rewritten. The last two decades, however, have brought more stories that extend the question: not only whether we know enough to adapt other worlds to human needs, but whether we should, even if we could.

Gregory Landis, in "Ecopoesis" (1997), imagines a Mars that has been bypassed by human users, leaving it open to be transformed as a sort of work of ecological art into an environment not for people, but for anaerobic bacteria. It was not human-centered terraforming, said the global engineers, but ecopoesis, the establishment of an ecology. "They looked down with contempt on unimaginative humans who believed that humans were the pinnacle of creation . . . They believed that once life, however primitive, could establish a toehold on Mars, it would adapt to its environment and flourish, and someday evolve. Not to make a copy of Earth but something indigenously Martian." But this moral stance runs into another problem: The transformation of Mars "spawned debate across Earth and cis-lunar space: Was this the greatest feat of engineering in history, or was it a crime against nature?" The chief engineer was brought to trial in Geneva on the question "Do Rocks Have Rights?" That is: "Can it be a crime to destroy an ecosystem that contains no life? The trial took three years, and ended in a hung jury."[23]

Kim Stanley Robinson has also tackled the ethics of environmental change in his trilogy about the settlement of Mars, *Red Mars* (1993), *Green Mars* (1994), and *Blue Mars* (1996).[24] The books constitute a single densely written novel of the settlement of the red planet over two centuries ("a triple decker in the old style," says the author[25]) that transposes many of the problems of the American West to a new setting. They start with one hundred settlers, divided equally among Americans and Russians, and trace two centuries of settlement, environmental change, social change, and politics.

Robinson uses the science fiction gimmick of longevity treatments to maintain the members of the "first hundred" settlers through these two centuries, allowing him to encapsulate changing ideas and values within the lives of individuals.

Robinson is a Californian, raised in Orange County and living in Davis. He has commented: "I think of myself as a Californian writer more than I do a science fiction writer, and would be happy to be grouped with the California writers. To be grounded in that way, even regionalized, would be a very good way of giving some physicality or heft to the inclination of science fiction to be otherworldly by being set in the future."[26] Out of this background comes his strong moral-aesthetic appreciation for environments with minimal human alteration, whether Mars, Antarctica, or high mountains in North America and Asia. To open an anthology that he edited of science fiction stories about back-to-nature utopias, he turned to Gary Snyder, a western visionary whom Robinson lists as a favorite poet. "Tomorrow's Song" celebrates the vanishing of the American state and the return of North America to biological rhythms and values.[27]

As the American West has been, the Martian frontier is projected to be a place of often rapacious resource development. The theme of conquest, which is central to recent western history writing, takes the form of the conquest of nature. The first settlers—a hundred carefully picked Russian and American scientists and technicians—begin with exploration and road building. Subsequent settlers construct high-speed transit lines, build dams, and dig mines. They tap geothermal heat, pump out aquifers, and seed bioengineered plants to add weight, heat, and oxygen to the Martian atmosphere. With no building codes or environmental regulations in place, large corporations dig and run, build company towns on the cheap, and play workers of different nationalities against each other. Like the mountain West, Mars is an urban frontier of gateway cities and production cities from which miners and eventually agriculturalists spread outward: Sheffield stands in for a port city like San Francisco, Burroughs for an industrial city like Denver, Serenzi Na for a mining town like Butte, Bradbury for small agricultural cities like Grand Junction.

The titles of the three books—*Red*, *Green*, and *Blue Mars*—trace the success of terraforming through massive engineering interventions to raise the ambient temperature and atmospheric pressure, to bring water to the surface, and to introduce plants and animals bioengineered from Earth originals. There is careful and fascinating detail about the terraforming process—options, choices, setbacks, side effects, accomplishments. The technical dimension is reminiscent of the cetology and whaling lore in *Moby-Dick*, and Robinson himself argues that "there is no intrinsic reason why scientific detail cannot be as interesting as the stage business of a chase scene."[28]

The history of the American West is testimony to the momentum of engineering technology, the easy step from "can do" to "should do." So too is Martian history. The power and nearly inexorable appeal of terraforming technologies are similar to the American impulse to apply more and more technology to capture and deliver western water. In fact (the twentieth century) and in fiction (the twenty-second century), we see the ramping up from smaller to larger projects, the aesthetic attraction of the technical intervention, the promise of better life, the opening of land to settlement and use. A handful of scientists start the process without the agreement of their colleagues among the first hundred because they want to see whether their ideas work. Technical papers at a terraforming conference decades later morph easily into grant applications from ambitious scientists.

The terraforming project brings out contrasting environmentalisms of preservation and utilization. The ideas of western irrigation utopians like William Smythe echo in the American advocates of use. They find allies among the Russians, who are also development advocates, reflecting their own national history of intensive exploitation of Siberia and central Asia. New Martians "naturalize" the transformation by thinking of Mars in terms of western landscapes and settlement change. Settlers reproduce the flora and fauna of a southwestern canyon in a Martian valley that is tented to hold in atmosphere. On a planetary surface that has never before supported human beings, say the terraformers, there is no way to deny that "wilderness" and other concepts through which we understand the physical settings of human life are socially constructed.[29] At one point of a debate over the future of the planet, scientist Sax Russell argues that "the beauty of Mars exists in the human mind. Without the human presence it is just a collection of atoms. . . . It is we who understand it and we who give it meaning."[30] He thus enters a debate that has divided the environmental movement between those who see wilderness as a transcendent entity that stands apart from human activity and those who argue that wilderness is a concept that only has existence if humans define it.

We also hear the voices of the preservationists who try to think like a marsscape. These are characters who share Robinson's own awe at the planet depicted in NASA photos: "this most amazing landscape . . . everything on a giant scale, in general two magnitudes larger than the corresponding Terran feature."[31] One character "humanizes" Mars by devising the areophany, a "landscape religion, a consciousness of Mars as a physical space suffused with kami, which was the spiritual energy or power that rested in the land itself."[32] Ecologist Ann Clayborne, the most committed advocate for an unchanging Mars, counters that most of the settlers "value consciousness too high, and rock too little. We are not lords of the universe. We're only one small part of it. We may be the consciousness of the universe, but being the consciousness of the universe does not mean turning it all into a mirror image of us. It means rather fitting into it as it is, and worshiping it with our attention."[33]

The trilogy returns again and again to the argument between Sax and Ann, who articulate the intellectual rationales for the "greens" who advocate the transformation of the planet and the "reds" who want to preserve the landscape and geological record. Slowly but surely, the atmosphere thickens, bioengineered plants and animals spread, and released water forms seas and oceans. At the extreme, the reds spawn an ecoradical "Mars First" movement of sabotage, taking Ann as their increasingly reluctant symbol. Greens struggle with balancing gradual and rapid change, partial and complete transformation. As Robinson explores these positions, the books become something of a philosophical novel in the style of Thomas Mann in addition to retaining their close attention to character and politics (a topic to be explored in Chapter 5). Robinson presents both sides eloquently and sympathetically, mirroring his own internal debate: "I'm very ambivalent myself. I think Mars right now is such a magnificent place, that you don't need to terraform it to make it sublime and wonderful. So I have teeter-tottered between red and green, which has been one of the energy engines for writing such a monster."[34]

The story draws to a close with reconciliation, and an implicit plea for compromise in the American debates about wilderness. The vertical scale, thin atmosphere, and limited sunlight of Mars allow division of the planetary surface into lowlands and highlands. The Martian constitution that the settlers and their descendants eventually adopt (at the beginning of *Blue Mars*) has an entire article on "The Land" to balance its article on "Individual Rights and Obligations." It states that "The primal state of Mars shall have legal consideration, and shall not be altered except as part of a terraforming program dedicated to making the surface of the planet survivable by humans up to the six-kilometer altitude contour. Above the six-kilometer elevation the goal shall be to keep the surface as close to its primal condition as possible." Other sections specify maximum air pressure, carbon dioxide content, ocean levels, and procedures for the introduction of new species. It is as if the protection of Yellowstone and Big Bend, the Mojave and Denali, had been added by amendment to the U.S. Constitution.[35]

Sax and Ann themselves slowly move from their original extremes toward a middle point that recognizes the validity of areoformation, or careful change that balances the primacy of the marsscape with the requirement of a living ecology. They end *Blue Mars* as household companions and lovers, living in a Martian city on the shores of a huge crater-filling sea. In the last section, a very old Ann joins a party of friends on the beach, experiences a near brush with a heart attack, and looks around one more time—at happy children and at the planet: "She lifted her eyes to the hills west of the sea, black under the sun. The bones of things stuck out everywhere. Waves broke over the sand in swift lines on the beach, and she walked over the sand toward her friends, in the wind, on Mars, on Mars, on Mars, on Mars, on Mars."[36]

Tyranny and Terraforming

Terraforming raises political as well as philosophical questions. Most terraforming projects are envisioned to require generations and centuries of careful work and gradual change, raising the question of how a society can keep large numbers of people engaged in a hard project that will only pay off for their grandchildren or even their great-great-grandchildren. Will the mobilization of labor and capital require slavery and tyranny, or will democratic processes be adequate to keep people devoted to the task?

To look back again to the American West, one of the most obvious requisites for landscape modification has been a powerful alliance of government and capital. Congress offered railroad companies the natural landscape itself, in the form of land grants, and the corporate promoters mobilized eastern and European investors to build transcontinental and feeder lines. It also required capital to take advantage of irrigation and drainage projects for ranching and farming, to reach and cut the forests of the Pacific Northwest, to follow deposits of copper and silver into the Earth and smelt the ores into useable metals. By the start of the twentieth century, big business dominated the western economy—the Southern Pacific Railroad and Miller and Lux land empire in California, Anaconda Copper in

Montana, Weyerhaeuser in Washington, Rockefeller and Guggenheim trusts in Colorado. U.S. senators dangled from the hip pockets of corporations. Nevada was a great "rotten borough" at the beck and call of Southern Pacific railroad bosses.[37]

Historian Donald Worster has taken a step back from the specifics of the "Battle for Butte" and the efforts of California Progressives to fight the railroads to the idea of "oriental despotism" introduced a half-century ago by Karl Wittfogel. Looking at societies in Mesopotamia, India, China, and pre-Columbian America, Wittfogel argued that despotic governance had emerged in "hydraulic societies" that depended on large-scale irrigation works, which required the continual mobilization of labor for construction and maintenance. Water control and distribution spawned authoritarian centralized empires and sprawling bureaucracies, both deeply hostile to change.[38] In *Rivers of Empire* (1985), Worster borrowed and adapted the idea for the western United States, contending that the need to mobilize large amounts of capital for western water projects created an undemocratic—even despotic—alliance of big government and big business.

Poul Anderson's 1954 story "The Big Rain," set on Venus during the process of terraforming, fits the narrative of hydraulic despotism. The work seems to stretch on forever as unexpected feedback loops are leading to diminishing returns from the huge investment. Nevertheless, the goal is to trigger the Big Rain by catalyzing the release of chemically bonded water. The ten-year deluge is intended to push the planet toward earthlike conditions. In a hundred years, there might be easily habitable areas; in five hundred, the planet may be a paradise. To make this happen, Venus has evolved into a police state where even marriages are arranged in the interest of the project. Anderson's protagonist, a secret investigator sent from Earth, muses: "The essential ethos of Venus was, indeed, different from anything which existed on Earth. It had to be, the landscape had made it so. Man was necessarily a more collective creature than at home. That helped to explain the evolution of the peculiar governmental forms and the patience of the citizenry toward the most outrageous demands."[39] Workers live for the future generations, not for themselves. They dream of the Big Rain without really believing it will improve their own lives. In the following exchange with the Venus woman who's been designated his wife, the earthman comments on the way in which the state exercises its hegemony by linking popular ideology to engineering goals.

"Venus is your god. This is a religious movement you have right here, with a slide rule in its hand. . . ."

"You're a funny one," she said uncertainly. . . ."After the Big Rain, things will be easier. It'll be—" She struggled through vague memories. "It'll be the Promised Land."[40]

Pamela Sargent, working a generation after Poul Anderson, has dealt with the same big question, giving a compelling and nuanced depiction of the political requirements of terraforming in *Venus of Dreams* (1986), *Venus of Shadows* (1988), and *Child of Venus* (2001).[41] The books follow several generations of one family from Earth to Venus to participate in the ongoing Venus Project. Sargent has commented that the trilogy was inspired by Thomas Mann's *Buddenbrooks* (1901), the classic novel of a bourgeois family in a changing world: "I wanted to write a story about a family, a realistic book about the decline of the society they knew."[42] Indeed, the books use the family saga to comment on issues of political power and control.

Because of the close timing and the symmetry of numbers, comparisons between Sargent's trilogy and Robinson's Mars trilogy are inevitable. At first glance they seem to embody the pop psychology distinction that "men are from Mars, women are from Venus," coined originally to differentiate styles of communication.[43] When Robinson writes about Mars, he writes about individuals without families (or very tenuous ones), about abstract philosophies of environment, about civic life, economics, and governance. When Sargent writes about Venus, her subjects are successive generations of young women struggling to find their own voices and purposes, family obligations and constraints, and the daily rounds of household life. Beyond these differences, however, are many similarities that make the two trilogies complementary. Both cover the span of several centuries. Both are interested in character and show a high regard for the work of ordinary people—scientists, engineers, construction workers—who turn grand schemes into realities. Both texts are hard science fiction that plays by the rules of physics, and both authors build their stories within the physical constraints of their planets. As Sargent has noted, knowledge about conditions on Venus was growing rapidly as she was writing, forcing her to give more and more attention to the specifics of terraforming itself, and never allowing her to let it fade into a briefly sketched background.[44]

When *Venus of Dreams* opens, the Venus Project is already several centuries old. After the devastation of the Resources Wars, Earth is united under an Islamic world government. The Islamic heartland of western Asia is the center of power. The different monarchies into which the world is divided run local affairs and follow their own religions, but under the firm guidance of the Council of Mukhtars, enforced by a world spanning information network and by counselors whose "suggestions" about career tracks and political opinions cannot be successfully ignored. Three hundred years earlier, the Mukhtars had launched the terraforming of Venus not only for its practical potential, but also as a way to unite the Earth around a common goal and distract attention from inevitable economic and social adjustments at home.

The project, vast in physical and temporal scale, dwarfs puny projects like the Great Wall of China and Egypt's pyramids. Pioneers on Mars might walk on the surface with adequate protection from their first landing and hope to live there unassisted within a century or so. Facing a far more ferocious planet, pioneers on Venus have to work for transformation that may take a millennium. The Venus Project began with the construction of a giant Parasol floating in orbit between Venus and the Sun, shielding the planet from radiation and starting a gradual process of cooling a surface that had been hot enough to melt lead. Hydrogen from Jupiter was added to the atmosphere in a steady stream to combine with Venusian oxygen into water. Genetically engineered algae were seeded into the thick clouds to slowly convert the sulfuric acid that spiked the atmosphere into iron and copper sulfides. The second stage was the construction of artificial platforms to float high in the atmosphere. Balanced on great tanks of helium, covered with soil, and sealed from the elements, these ten Cytherian Islands, in place by the start of the first book, stretch several miles across and provide the living space for tens of thousands of workers who pursue the continuing transformation of the atmosphere. The third stage, just implemented as *Venus of Dreams* begins, is the erection of domed settlements on the surface itself. After centuries of work, "the Venus of the past existed more in memory than in reality; the Venus of the future, that green and fertile planet that would become a second Earth and a new home for mankind, was still a dream."[45]

The plot dynamic of the three novels is generational conflict. Strong-willed mothers try to bind their children to the way of life to which they have committed themselves, while strong-willed children break away to follow different dreams, with painful consequences for all. *Venus of Dreams* follows Iris Angharads from a young child growing up in the narrow-horizoned matriarchy in rural Nebraska through her heroic self-sacrifice to save the Venus Project. As a teenager, she earns the opportunity to leave home to study to be a Venus specialist. She dedicates her life to preparation on Earth and then leaves to work on one of the Islands. Meanwhile, she is as blind to her son's disinterest in the project, and his plans to abandon it, as her mother was to her own disinterest in carrying on rural life.

Venus of Shadows and *Child of Venus* continue with the next three generations. *Shadows* centers on the life of Risa Liangharad, the daughter of the martyred Iris. Risa grows up with a fierce commitment to the project and the idiosyncracies of its society. She follows her impulse for control by rising to political power within the local councils that settlers have recently been allowed. But she is betrayed in turn by her daughter Chimene, who starts as a spoiled brat and grows to be the dangerous leader of a cult of Ishtar that worships the emergent spirit of Venus. The new religion challenges the secular and scientific culture of the project and acquires increasing political influence, driving Risa from power and leading to a coup and countercoup that eventually destroys Chimene and puts the Islands back under the direct control of Earth. *Child of Venus* examines the fourth generation's Mahala Liangharad, who grows up under the stern determination and direction of her grandmother Risa. The book follows her pathway through schools, thwarted ambitions, a visit to Earth, and finally to a berth on the first starship launched from the solar system—effectively the first possible escape from the despotism of the Mukhtars.

The family saga, examining the difficulty of passing beliefs and commitments from one generation to the next, encapsulates the fundamental political issue that Sargent poses. "What reasons would people have for undertaking this centuries-long endeavor, even if I assumed it would become technically feasible?" she asks in an "Author's Afterword" to *Venus of Shadows*. The answer, given in an interview: "You'd have to be driven, even obsessive, to take part in such a vast project."[46] Within the family, psychological needs translate variably into religious fervor, secular utopianism, and the simple desire to belong, but even one of the characters most devoted to the project looks around at workers new from Earth and "wondered if they could sustain that hope during the years of work ahead." Even Mahala thinks back: "We lived there in order to stake a human claim to that world, but a heretic might have said that we were prisoners, living our lives out in those enclosed places solely to make a point, to insist that Venus would eventually become habitable, whatever the obstacles that lay ahead."[47]

But channeling these needs is the global dominance of the Mukhtars, who hold out the Venus Project as "Earth's glorious destiny."[48] The Mukhtars carefully monitor public opinion through a global computer network and quickly squelch anyone who questions their plans. Every citizen receives periodic audiences with a counselor, who uses feel-good language to keep people in line. Only a fool who wants to be effectively written out of society ignores a counselor's suggestion about schooling or career choices. Your record from earliest schooling follows you through life. Mahala knows that "it always came back to that in the end, serving the Project."[49]

The project also serves the Mukhtars as an escape valve for Earth's dreamers and malcontents. Places on the project are doled out as rewards for making it through the Darwinian application and selection process. Scientists and engineers for the project are the most successful students at special academies (this is how Iris wins her way from Nebraska to the Islands). Ordinary workers are chosen from applicants who make their way to a handful of spaceports and wait, sometimes for years, in guarded camps where only the strong survive.

On the Islands and in the Domes, the Mukhtars rule through their bureaucracy of administrators and counselors. At the climax of *Venus of Dreams*, they crush what amounts to a Venusian independence movement. In *Venus of Shadows*, they dole out small fragments of autonomy, allowing Risa to rise within the network of district councils, but they are quick to pull back authority when they dislike the choices that are being made. After the revolt, they do grant a larger measure of autonomy, but they retain absolute control over the flow of workers and resources from Earth. By keeping the Venusian population small, the Mukhtars make immigration from Earth a privilege while limiting the capacity of the Island and Dome dwellers to fend for themselves. The people of Venus worry about news from Earth, because a small shift of power on the Council of Mukhtars can have huge consequences for the project. "Any changes among the Mukhtars make things more uncertain for us," Risa comments.[50]

The Mukhtars remain a high-tech tyranny from beginning to end of the trilogy. Their purpose may be lofty—to make the Venus Project the moral equivalent of war—but it is not reached through the consent of the governed. Earth's rulers treat people as "pawns" and wield "the power, and maybe the inclination, to manipulate people as if they were pieces of a larger game."[51] They do not merely stifle dissent, but manage over the course of generations to build a commitment to the Venus Project into everyone's structure of assumptions and belief. The result is social stability at the price of obsession. This is a form of hegemony as analyzed and described by political theorists such as Louis Althusser and Antonio Gramsci, who argued that power operates most effectively when it turns citizens into "good subjects" who internalize the values and beliefs that cause them to serve the interests of the powerful without considering alternatives.

Engineering Dreams

Terraforming stories are part of the science fiction tradition of science puzzles. Many science fiction writers, from Hal Clement in the 1950s to Vernor Vinge in the 1990s, have speculated about the types of life that might develop under different planetary conditions such as extreme gravity or extreme fluctuations of heat and cold. The interest lies in anticipating and appreciating the ways in which the author works through the logical consequences of the initial conditions. Terraforming approaches the puzzle from the other direction, exploring the logical requirements for human adaption of initially hostile environments. Any good terraforming fiction has to take the principles of physics, biology, and ecology very seriously, and it is possible to write a fascinating terraforming story or novel that essentially ends with the mastery of technical challenges.

The idea of terraforming is thus, at its heart, an "engineer's dream." Willy Ley, the German émigré to the United States who became one of the leading popularizers of science and space travel in the 1940s and 1950s, is best known for his book *The Conquest of Space* (1950), which brought a plausible scenario for exploring the solar system to thousands of coffee tables. But he also wrote *Engineers' Dreams* (1954) to describe schemes for transforming the Earth by draining the Mediterranean Sea, flooding the Sahara Desert, towing icebergs to water dry lands, and similar vast efforts. Terraforming Mars or Venus is the same sort of grand dream, and Ley's work shows the continuities between earthly engineering, space travel, and extraterrestrial engineering.[52]

The trilogies by Robinson and Sargent that I've highlighted try to make the science and engineering as plausible as possible, but they are just as interested in settlement as in engineering. Similarly, the reclamation dream of the American West was not so much about engineering itself, or its environmental consequences, as about the social possibilities and problems that engineering promised to open up. For U.S. history, these human implications are the focus of the critique found in recent environmental and economic history. For science fiction, these are the questions that turn science projects into novels.

In a future sequence of development, terraforming is the prelude to settlement—just as railroads and irrigation works preceded the settlement of Idaho's Snake River Valley or Colorado's western slope. The next two chapters pursue the narratives of settlement. "Johnny Appleseed, John Wayne, and Homesteading on the Extraterrestrial Frontier" follows future farmers. As in American regional literature, these are stories that use changes in the land as background and metaphor for the conflicts of successive generations. The focus is local, on farms, families, and small towns. "Little House on the Big Planet," we might also call it. "Frontier Democracy" follows with the questions of social and political change. What happens as isolated farmsteads grow into communities, as little towns become cities, as settlers cease to identify themselves as Terrans and come to see themselves as people of Mars or Tau Ceti Four, as citizens rather than settlers?

4 Johnny Appleseed, John Wayne, and Homesteading on the Extraterrestrial Frontier

The colony was made up of homesteaders and townies. The townies worked for the government and lived in government-owned buildings. . . . But most of the colonials were homesteaders and that's what George had meant us to be. Like most everybody, we had come out there on the promise of free land and a chance to raise our own food.

—Robert Heinlein, *Farmer in the Sky* (1950)

Johnny Appleseeds

Ray Bradbury and Robert Heinlein define opposite poles in postwar science fiction. Bradbury made and sustained his reputation as a stylist who crafted small stories with big emotional wallops. He has published only one science fiction novel—*Fahrenheit 451* (1953)—but many collections of loosely connected stories that wander back and forth among science fiction, fantasy, and nostalgic realism. Heinlein started with space adventure stories for *Astounding* but soon learned how to sustain longer narratives in more than two dozen novels for adult and juvenile readers. He liked problems in physical and social engineering, and protagonists with can-do values. In his literary heritage are bits of the Tom Swift books mixed with Jack London's politically charged romances. Bradbury's contrasting model was the connected stories of Sherwood Anderson's *Winesburg, Ohio* or the miniature narrative poems of Edgar Lee Masters.

Beneath their stylistic choices, however, Heinlein and Bradbury had much in common. Both writers harked back to middle western childhoods, but their ideas about the future drew as well on their first-hand experience of California during its great transformation during and after World War II.[1] In the later 1940s, each made crossover sales to mainstream magazines that were helping their readers understand the age of galloping technological change. In their distinct voices, Heinlein's and Bradbury's mass market stories evangelized for the high frontier of space exploration and its power to redeem or rescue a troubled and threatened world.

In so doing, each writer at the same moment found room for a Johnny Appleseed figure in a story of extraterrestrial pioneering. Heinlein's *Farmer in the Sky* (1950) and Bradbury's *The Martian Chronicles* (1950) both feature characters who reenact the story of John Chapman. It was certainly more than coincidence. Americans had been working hard to recover or create regional folk heroes since the boom in folklore studies in the 1930s. The ability to identify American virtues with larger-than-life figures was a way to emphasize national distinctiveness and unity. Nazis might have had Thor and Odin in their attic, but Americans had Paul Bunyan, Pecos Bill, and Johnny Appleseed.[2] In 1948, Walt Disney studios had released a nineteen-minute *Johnny Appleseed* animation with Dennis Day voicing the character and singing "The Sun, and Rain, and an Apple Seed."[3]

Bradbury's version is elegiac. "The Green Morning" is the ninth of the twenty-three loosely overlapping stories and vignettes that constitute *The Martian Chronicles.* Nearly all of the stories, set from 2030 to 2057, examine the effects of Mars landings and settlement on individual Earth people (and occasionally on the dying Martians themselves). In effect, they are thought experiments about the ways that middle-class Americans of the 1930s and 1940s might respond to an actual frontier.[4]

"The Green Morning" zooms in on Benjamin Driscoll, who has spent the previous month planting trees across the landscape of Mars, digging holes, dropping in seeds, and bringing water from the canals: "The thing that he wanted was Mars grown green and tall with trees and foliage, producing air, more air." Fair enough. Bradbury postulates a red planet with atmosphere that is breathable but painfully thin, and Driscoll's self-appointed mission is to hurry its thickening as a sort of single-person terraforming team. His goal is practical, to provide the oxygen that feeds warm fires and eases straining lungs. "'That's what I'm here for,' he muses. 'In school they told a story about Johnny Appleseed walking across America planting apple trees. Well, I'm doing more. I'm planting oaks, elms, and maples, every kind of tree. . . . Instead of making just fruit for the stomach, I'm making air for the lungs.'" And on Bradbury's mythicized Mars, dedication brings success. Driscoll wakens to a green morning. His seeds are now great trees, grown "as tall as ten men . . . nourished by alien and magical soil and, even as he watched, throwing out new branches, popping open new buds."[5]

Heinlein offers a very different Johnny in the stony new fields of Ganymede. It's Johann Schultz, a farmer from Earth who is determined to transform Jupiter's third moon into a breadbasket for the solar system. To some settlers he seems like a crank: "Johnny Appleseed. That's what everybody calls him in town," says the lazy and scheming Mr. Saunders. "He's nuts. You know what he did? He gave me a handful of apple seeds and acted like he had handed me the riches of Solomon."[6] Bill, the teenage narrator of *Farmer in the Sky*, knows better. Papa Schultz is a good and generous neighbor. Bill has seen Schultz's single apple tree, heard how he had persuaded it to grow, tasted its fruit—Winesaps this year, with Greenlings and Rome Beauties to come—and received a gift of seeds with suggestions about where and how to plant.

Johnny Appleseed is the harbinger of agricultural settlement, and both writers place their stories directly in the tradition of the American farming frontier as it has been embodied in popular memory. The colony ships in *Farmer in the Sky* are the *Mayflower* and the *Covered Wagon*, and Bill carefully calculates that the trip from Earth to the Jovian moon will be three days shorter than the Pilgrims' original crossing of the Atlantic. "The Wilderness," toward the end of *The Martian Chronicles*, begins in Independence, Missouri, one of the jumping-off points for the Oregon Trail. Women whose husbands are already on the red planet recall the American past as they wait to follow: "Is this how it was a century ago, she wondered, when the women, the night before, lay ready for sleep, or not ready, in the small towns of the East, and heard the sound of horses in the night and the creak of Conestoga wagons ready to go. . . . Is this then how it was so long ago? On the rim of the precipice, on the edge of the cliff of stars. In their time, the smell of buffalo, and in our time the smell of the Rocket. Is this then how it was?"[7]

The Johnny Appleseed legend grew out of the early settlement of Ohio in the nineteenth century, where John Chapman was a successful orchardist, but the idea of tree-planting as a civic cause originated west of the Missouri River, where natural tree cover was scarce. Arbor Day got its start in Nebraska in the 1870s as easterners reacted to the treeless prairie. The Nebraska legislature made it official in 1885 when the practice of tree-planting as a good deed was spreading to other states. What is now Nebraska National Forest originated a century ago in efforts that planted 20,000 acres of ponderosa pines on the barren Sand Hills. In the Dust Bowl years of the 1930s, westerners learned to plant shelter belts of trees to protect farmsteads and hold soil. Bradbury thus transported a western tree-planting impulse to Mars.[8]

The homespun image of Johnny Appleseed, and his western imitators, is a good entry into the homesteading theme in science fiction. Homesteading is a particular facet of the complex processes by which agriculturalists settle "empty" or underdeveloped territories, whether the prairies of North America or the imagined planets of science fiction, and it is a process with deep resonance in American history and national identity. Homesteading is settlement of new farms by individual families or small groups who hope first to be self-sufficient and then to raise crops and livestock for the market. As a topic of fiction, it has usually centered attention on individual character and family dynamics.

In the United States, homesteading is both a general settlement pattern and a very specific practice that followed passage of the Homestead Act in 1862. The Oregon Trail pioneers whom Bradbury evoked in the preceding passage found their Willamette Valley farms first and then figured out how to obtain title (eventually involving special Congressional action). The 1862 law, however, offered 160 acres of the public domain to anyone who would cultivate and live on the land for five years. The timing coincided with the push of agriculture into the Great Plains (the Homestead National Monument is in Beatrice, Nebraska) and into fertile valleys tucked among the western mountains, making the Homestead Act a key tool for developing the western half of the nation. Much of the West's economic history revolves around the inducements of the 1862 legislation and later modifications that adapted the terms to the region's dryer lands.

A focus on individual homesteading families, however, looks at the second installment of the settlement process. Settlers relied on their own pluck and luck, but they also depended on railroads, grain elevators, irrigation systems, and town merchants with stocks of seed and machinery—in short, on the infrastructure of regional development. In the same way, homesteading in science fiction stands in clear contrast to terraforming novels that retell the "modern" story of big science and state action on behalf of big goals. As Kim Stanley Robinson and Pamela Sargent highlight in their trilogies about the settlement of Mars and Venus, the big questions of terraforming have to do with public purpose and public action: What goals are worthy of the state? How can the costs and benefits of economic change be fairly allocated? How can large-scale action be sustained over time? But the unearthly landscape, whether previously terraformed or directly (luckily) habitable by human beings, can also be the setting for small-scale stories of individual and family settlement and adaptation. These are homesteading stories that draw on the rich experience and mythology of the American farm-making frontier. Terraforming narratives look from the top down, from the broad problems of technology and organization to the roles and conflicts of individuals within the big picture; they're about power and politics. Homesteading narratives start literally from the ground up, considering the ways that individuals respond to deliberately chosen new places and how they do—or don't—work together among themselves and with their neighbors; they're about families and neighborhoods.[9]

This chapter examines homesteading as one of the many and often conflicted stories that Americans have developed behind the facade of "high frontier." The discussion starts with a simple and positive vision that reproduces and adapts ideas found in nineteenth- and twentieth-century fiction and civic discourse about the economic and political possibilities of the West. The next two sections look at more complex and often less hopeful understandings of homesteading futures, first with texts from the 1960s and 1970s, and then with texts from the 1990s. The treatment thus moves from straightforward and celebratory ways in which homesteading narratives are written onto the future to more ambiguous and questioning stories that reflect Americans' increasing ambivalence about aspects of their past.

O Pioneers!

For the United States, homesteading history can be seen as starting with the spread of English-speaking settlers into and beyond the Appalachians in the later eighteenth and early nineteenth centuries, if not with the even earlier movement of Spanish-speaking farmers into the upper Rio Grande valley of New Mexico. However, homesteading is described and imagined most extensively and vividly for the central prairies, Great Plains, and western mountains roughly from the 1850s to the 1910s. We can note in this regard that Laura Ingalls Wilder started her sequence of books with a little house in the big woods of the upper Great Lakes region, but that it was the little house on the prairie that made it to prime-time television. Out of this experience developed a common homesteading narrative with two prominent elements. The first is the challenge of learning to live off a strange land. The second is the problem of generational change as children prove better able than parents to learn and adapt to the new environment.

Most American homesteading stories start with the dangers and inhospitality of the physical setting. Think about some of the defining stories of the prairies and plains penned in the later nineteenth and early twentieth centuries. They are filled with drought, blizzards, grasshoppers, and sheer physical discomfort. Hamlin Garland's *Main-Traveled Roads* (1891) is filled with the crushing work of farm life and "the barn yard's daily grind."[10] The immigrant Norwegian-Dakotans of Ole Rolvaag's *Giants in the Earth* (1927) deal with isolation and desolation, insect plagues, and endless winter. Jules Sandoz, as his daughter Mari Sandoz recounted in *Old Jules* (1935), brought his new wife to a dank sod hut where water and bugs dripped from the roof.

Recent writers who have revisited the homesteading narrative keep the same troubles in mind as physical challenges that must be controlled and overcome. The intrepid heroine of the movie *Heartland* (1980), crafted by screenwriter Annick Smith from the 1910 diaries of Elinor Stewart, finds Montana a place of blizzard and cold. Jane Smiley includes drought in the troubles facing the Newton family in 1850s Kansas in *The All-True Travels and Adventures of Lidie Newton: A Novel* (1998). Molly Gloss subjects her lonely woman homesteader in *The Jump-Off Creek* (1989) to bears, blizzards, and back-breaking hard work. Lydia Sanderson came to Oregon from Pennsylvania "seeking the boundless possibilities that are said to live on the frontier." The claim that she's bought has nothing but a rat-infested cabin. The rain pours down, and cattle mire themselves in the boggy creek bottom. Windstorm and ice kill and scatter her livestock: "Crossing the field with the empty kettle, she fell on the ice and sat there crying dryly, tiredly. But she got up after a while and went on the rest of the way, because the goat was bawling, thirsty, waiting for her."[11]

But as Willa Cather reminds us, to homestead successfully is to learn to *understand* the land and natural processes that they face. *O Pioneers!*, published in 1913, is Cather's first great novel, and the one book that more than any other represents the homesteading story as understood in American culture. The book spans twenty years in the life of Alexandra Bergson and uses her story to dramatize the transformation of Nebraska from frontier to community. Alexandra grows up on the Nebraska prairie, turns the family homestead into a prosperous farm, and becomes a mainstay of a maturing agricultural region. The novel's first section is "The Wild Land." Here, in the early years of settlement, the place itself takes on active character as a "wild old beast" that resists human agency: "In eleven long years John Bergson [Alexandra's father] had made but little impression upon the wild land he had come to tame. It was still a wild thing that had its ugly moods . . . Mischance hung over it. Its Genius was unfriendly to man."[12] This is the harsh landscape of failure and doubt: scorching sun, bitter winters, misadapted crops, and worn-out pioneers.

Alexandra sees it differently. She grows up with the country and comes to love it. The spirit of place speaks differently to her: "When the road began to climb the first long swells of the Divide, Alexandra hummed an old Swedish hymn. . . . For the first time, perhaps, since that land emerged from the waters of geologic ages, a human face was set toward it with love and yearning. . . . Her eyes drank in the breadth of it, until her tears blinded her. Then the Genius of the Divide, the great, free spirit which breathes across it must have bent lower than it ever bent to a human will before."[13] The new partnership of place and pioneer equates to progress; grinding isolation gives way to singing telephone wire, dilapidated shacks to neatly painted houses, hills of dry grass to rich fields.

Homesteading narratives are also family stories. Later in *O Pioneers!* Cather has one of the characters muse: "And now the old story has begun to write itself over there. Isn't it queer: there are only two or three human stories, and they go on repeating themselves as fiercely as if they had never happened before, like the larks in this country, that have been singing the same five notes over for thousands of years."[14] Those same five notes are the tensions of fathers and sons, mothers and daughters, brothers and sisters. *O Pioneers!* and *My Ántonia* (1918) are both about daughters who guide and grow beyond their immediate families. Mari Sandoz had to escape from the fierce monomania of Old Jules before she could write about him. Even Mary O' Hara's *My Friend Flicka* (1941) is about father and son more than boy and horse.

Homesteading stories thus deal with folks whom writer Wallace Stegner calls "placed" people, the newcomers who "stuck" on their new lands to establish what historian Walter Nugent defines as "Type II" frontiers. These are frontiers of agricultural settlement by families, where there are close ties between farmers and the small towns that serve them, where newcomers work hard to establish schools, churches, and fraternal organizations and other social institutions, and where levels of violence are low. They contrast with the "displaced" people of "Type I" frontiers who travel from one locale to another to harvest easily accessible natural resources. These are boom-and-bust frontiers that attract disproportionate numbers of young men who are rough, edgy, and often violent. Examples include California mining, Northwest logging, Alaska fisheries, and, in the imagination of the future, asteroid mining.[15]

Robert Heinlein—who imagined a Type I frontier in the asteroids in *The Rolling Stones* (1952)—neatly encapsulated the two homesteading themes in *Farmer in the Sky*. Heinlein is in many ways the quintessential American science fiction writer, and this relatively early novel for young people reaffirms the farming frontier as a source of positive values. First published in installments as "Satellite Scout" in *Boy's Life*, the national magazine for Boy Scouts, the book focuses on high-school-age Bill, whom we've already met. It starts in an overcrowded California, where 60 million people depend on a fragile system of nuclear powered desalination plants and "a million other gadgets."[16] Faced with constricting opportunities, Bill, his father, and new stepmother and stepsister emigrate to Ganymede in the company of 6,000 other settlers.

The family's goal on Jupiter's third moon is to become homesteaders. The Colonial Commission has done the basic terraforming to provide a thin but breathable atmosphere, but it is up to newcomers to build a new society. Those who want to become farmers, like Bill and his father, can "prove" a homestead, transferring a nineteenth-century term to the twenty-first century. As with U.S. settlers after the Homestead Act of 1862, they can earn title to a future farm if they cultivate and live on it. The first steps are to crush the rocky surface into soil with special machinery—in effect, using the "plow that broke the rocks." Hard work turns boulders successively into rocks, gravel, and powder, which can then be seeded with "good black soil from earth," carefully sterilized and then reseeded with "bacteria and fungi and microscopic worms."[17] Like much Golden Age science fiction, much of the fun comes from imagining technical details, as the problems of earthside soil conservation, a major issue of the middle decades of the twentieth century, are inverted into moonside soil creation.

Bill and his father don't work in isolation, for this is the frontier as Americans want to remember it—a place of sturdy yeoman farmers who happily cooperate through voluntary association. Dad earns money in town as an engineer while Bill apprentices to neighbor Johann Schultz to learn the art of moon farming. Schultz is generous with his experience and his resources, showing once again that "pioneers need good neighbors." There is a house-raising scene straight from American frontier mythology, when Bill's Boy Scout troop and his father's coworkers pitch in to turn a pile of stone blocks into a dwelling, while the women cook wholesome food for the crew. This is what Ganymedians do; Bill has already participated in six house raisings himself because "you can't do it alone."[18]

When a moonquake strikes soon after, the whole community pulls together in the rescue operations and rebuilding.

Pioneer grit has its rewards. Within two years, "you would never have known anything had happened. There wasn't a wrecked building in the community . . . and the town was booming."[19] After the disaster, Bill is more determined than ever to stick it out rather than return to Earth for college. "I'm not going home, if I ever do, until I've licked this joint."[20] He sees his future in the new land, quite consciously on the model of the nineteenth-century frontier. While overcrowded Earth moves toward war over scarce resources, the colonists will be increasingly self-sufficient. Looming wars on Earth will pass them by as Ganymede builds its own strength and looks outward to even newer frontiers—much as the United States watched nineteenth-century wars among European powers from across a wide ocean. The lesson is straightforward: America's westward movement worked once, and it can work again in new circumstances.

In the years since Heinlein mapped the idealized homesteading frontier onto Ganymede, a number of science fiction writers have continued to utilize the standard homesteading themes at something like the same face value. Their work taps widely shared American values and assumptions, but it has not substantially advanced the genre beyond the 1940s and 1950s.

Given science fiction's adventure story roots, it is no surprise that stories about the settlement of new planets repeatedly revisit the problem of the harsh land as pioneers try to cope with ecologies that they do not completely understand, and that fight back. The challenge can be simple inhospitality, with a Ganymede moonquake the equivalent of a "blue norther" blizzard on the Great Plains. Unexpected beasts can lurk in the jungles and swamps, raiding crops and animals like swarms of earthly grasshoppers, rearing up to kill unsuspecting settlers on exploring jaunts. Allen Steele's 2002 planetary settlement novel *Coyote* brings a set of political refugees to a new planet where they have to get crops in for survival, learn the weather, and cope with food shortages. The land surprises them in the form of large, fast predators that cross emu and velociraptor. But hardship breeds courage and pulls the entire colony together. The flowery language and sentiments of satisfaction are much like the reminiscences of aging pioneers looking back on the exciting days of first settlement: "they'd endured the extremes of climate, suffered through deprivation and loss, overcome hardships that might have broken lesser men and women. . . . they'd found something within themselves that many of them probably didn't know was there: a spirit unwilling to surrender to anyone or anything."[21]

More interestingly, crisis may arise from a mistaken intervention in the new ecology in ways reminiscent of American ecological disasters such as crowding the northern plains with far too many cattle to survive the severe droughts and snows of the 1880s or plowing beyond the line of adequate rainfall in the 1890s. The science fiction variations are endless, for readers and writers are well aware of the notorious examples of ecological disruption on Terran frontiers, as well as the scientific implications of the "Columbian exchange" between the ecologically isolated eastern and western hemispheres, with its massive trading of crops, animals, and deadly diseases.[22]

A good example is the first human colony on Avalon (Tau Ceti Four) as detailed by Larry Niven, Jerry Pournelle, and Steven Barnes in *The Legacy of Heorot* (1987) and *Beowulf's Children* (1995). Two hundred carefully selected colonists have settled comfortably on a large, apparently safe island off the main continent. The ecology seems simple. Apart from equivalents of grass, trees, birds, rodents, and freshwater fish, the planet appears largely a blank slate that is open to earthly crops and animals. Indeed, it seems a paradise: "Golden fields. Silver rivers. . . . Year-round water supply and fertile croplands. . . . a beautiful place to start a new world, lovely enough to make him feel . . . almost at peace."[23]

We know that the picture is too perfect to be true. The authors set up the first novel as an intellectual puzzle requiring scientific detective work, for readers can guess that an ecology with so few occupied niches is unstable. The colonists soon encounter implacable, carnivorous killing machines that they call "grendels" and learn how to kill them—only to discover that they have made their situation even more perilous.[24] By killing off the adult grendels on the island, they allow the thousands of harmless fish creatures ("samlon") to grow into grendels themselves. Only the presence of adult grendels, who devour each other's young, had prevented a grendel population explosion. It is as if slaughtering the buffalo has opened the way for saber-toothed tigers to spring up in their place.

The story is quite exciting, because Niven, Pournelle, and Barnes are good action writers who follow the thriller model in which the colonists defend their settlement, are overwhelmed, save themselves at great cost, relax after defeating the monster, and then find that it's back! However, the authors' real interest is the hard science fiction challenge of building a scientific puzzle and laying down clues for the reader. They layer on interpersonal conflicts to keep the plot moving, and the climax is a classic defense-of-the-fort scene, but the novel is really about the process of learning a new land. The lesson for the reader, as well as the colonists, is to question assumptions. Their puzzle involves biology rather than physics or engineering, the mainstays of Golden Age science fiction, but the instructional spirit is the same.

In *Beowulf's Children*, the first children of the colonists are coming of age. Chafing at their parents' hard-learned caution, they establish their own beachheads on the mainland. They think that their parents are like Europeans in the new world, strangers in a new land, while they see themselves as native Avalonians: "They could not own the land, but they could be a part of it."[25] But the children too are confounded, because the mainland has new ecological tricks. They think they know all about grendels, but they encounter new types in new places, and they suffer serious casualties from the planet's equivalent of killer bees, which swarm every fifty years or so. It is another "Avalon surprise" because the life cycle of the bees is tied to weather changes, which are tied to sunspot cycles. Again, there is plenty of intergenerational conflict to push the plot, but the heart of the book is setting and resolving a mystery.

In Marta Randall's *Journey* (1978), in contrast, the generational conflict is the story. Randall prefaces the novel with Cather's passage about "the same five notes." Like many homesteading stories, *Journey* is about generations on the land. It pulls together many of the threads of the planetary settlement story, such as struggles for economic stability and the growth of communities, but its central concern is not the science of survival. The landscape reads easily, without mistakes and misunderstandings, for Aerie is a remarkably benign and fertile planet just waiting to produce a marketable crop. Instead, the "old story" that interests Randall is stress and adjustment within families, as telegraphed by the 1978 paperback cover, showing overlapping faces of parents and children, and the front-cover blurbs: "a human drama of passion and power" and "an epic novel of the last frontier."[26] Among western American fiction it has something in common with Ivan Doig's novelization of his Montana family in *English Creek* (1984) and *Dancing at the Rascal Fair* (1987) or with Annie Dillard's fine historical novel *The Living* (1992) about generations on the shores of Puget Sound.

The plot is driven by father Jason Kennerin's love of the land, his ability to pass that love to his "dutiful" daughter Quilla, and the inability of his two sons to share the same commitment. Jason is a remittance man par excellence, whose family wealth allows him to buy the entire planet of Aerie sight unseen, but one who works at making it a new home. He experiments with crops, works with the sentient natives to develop a shared agricultural economy, and builds an estate and a family, two goals that are identical in his mind:

> This—the land—that doesn't change. You put work and love into it, and it gives you food and fruit and flowers and beauty. . . . Making things grow—the importance of that doesn't change. I mean, things change, sure, but their importance—what they mean—that doesn't change much. Sunlight, the earth, water, children. Making life.[27]

As the Kennerins find a place for their planet in the larger economic and political system, a town grows at the foot of the hill below their house: dirty streets are paved, the one-room school becomes a four-story edifice, utility systems replace water hauled in buckets—all in roughly the same ten- to twenty-year time frame that saw the transformation of raw settlements like Bismarck, North Dakota, or Cheyenne, Wyoming, into respectably pretentious towns. Meanwhile, Jason's children take on familiar family roles. The eldest daughter Quilla is a match for Alexandra Bergson. She's a bit plain-looking, intense, and intelligent; she steadily takes on responsibility from her parents and becomes the colony's general manager, and consensus queen at her father's death. One of her brothers parallels Alexandra Bergson's friend Carl Linstrum. Carl leaves Nebraska for Chicago, only to find that jobs in the city are all alike, while Quilla's brother is a restless romantic who gets into space as an apprentice on a cargo ship, then officers a freighter. He may cut a romantic figure when he returns to visit, but he soon finds that space piloting is routine work and each space port much like every other. The younger brother cannot make his family match his ideal and therefore learns to manipulate his environment. Exiled from Aerie for abusing the natives through scientific experiments, he becomes a highly skilled physician and researcher. But in the end, he tires of his life and comes home to try to make the best of what he still thinks of as *his* planet and *his* family—the prodigal returned, and the family trying to work out its future with economically successful homesteading as a backdrop.

Questioning a Myth

In the 1960s and 1970s, in counterpoint to standard retellings of the homesteading narrative, some writers began to question and undercut the popular story as a model for the future. Along with a number of other writers who were a couple decades younger than Heinlein and Bradbury, Ursula K. Le Guin and Philip K. Dick pushed the boundaries of the genre. Their generation in science fiction explored substantive topics—gender roles, drugs, and sometimes rock and roll—that had largely been kept under wraps in the hard science fiction of the 1940s and 1950s. They tested innovations in narrative form and style. And they wrote about homesteading in ways that questioned simple stories of success through perseverance.

In so doing, their fiction paralleled postwar historical writing that was probing beneath the surface of the western myth to find uncomfortable and incongruous realities, a mismatch between dreams and realities. Novelist Wallace Stegner and historian Walter Prescott Webb documented the fundamental inhospitality of the arid West and the problems that arose when eastern expectations came westward. In Webb's memorable phrase, much of the American West was a "perpetual mirage" that defied eastern farming practices and technological solutions such as dry farming and irrigation. Literary scholar Henry Nash Smith, in one of the most influential works of post–World War II scholarship, analyzed the many ways in which the dream of a welcoming, gardenlike continent had misdirected both political decisions and popular culture. Indeed, these scholars argued, expectations of individualism ignored the deep dependence of western settlers and communities on outside institutions.[28]

In Ursula K. Le Guin's 1974 story "The Eye Altering," in contrast with Randall or Niven, Pournelle, and Barnes, the process of learning a new planet has been abstracted into metaphor. The settlers on New Zion find the light and landscape's brown, purplish, and dark red colors ugly: "Dirty colors, the colors you got when you scrubbed your watercolors too hard."[29] They are aliens to the new environment, and they depend on special enzymes to enable their bodies to metabolize the native foods. But one of the Zion-born, sickly since his birth, decides to forgo the medication and take his chances with the local flora. His decision turns out to be correct, showing that many of the planet-born have suffered not from Zion itself, but from their loving parents' efforts to treat them as Earth-born.

For Le Guin, with her family background in anthropology, the frontier story is ultimately about the cultural gap between pioneers and natives. To her very simple "technical" plot, metaphorical as it is (there's no attempt to suggest a physical mechanism), Le Guin added a second layer of adaptation. Genya, the young man who experiments with local diet, is also an artist who has skillfully painted portraits and other pictures that the first generation can see and appreciate, but he now starts to paint Zion as it looks in its muddled ugliness; as he works, he comments that he is "just beginning to learn to see." But when one of his pictures of Zion is hung in the common room, where the older settlers are most at home, they see it as a beautiful countryside from Earth. It is still the same picture, but the Earth-born realize that young people who have adopted and adapted to Zion see their surroundings as a beautiful landscape: "It's here. Zion. It's how Genya sees it. With the eyes and the heart. . . . How do we know what a child of Zion sees? We can see the picture in this light that's like Home [Earth]. Take it outside, into the daylight, and you'll see what we always see, the ugly colors, the ugly planet where we're not at home. But he is at home! He is!"[30]

Where Le Guin was interested in cultural change, Philip Dick saw the frontier controlled by the inescapable power of capitalism and consumerism. Neither *Martian Time-Slip* (1964) nor *The Three Stigmata of Palmer Eldritch* (1965) is about homesteading per se. The former explores some curious propositions about the nature of consciousness, and the latter uses its plot as an occasion for eccentric musing about the nature of God. Nevertheless, Dick set all of *Time-Slip* and a substantial chunk of *Stigmata* on the surface of a cynically conceived red planet whose social and economic life subverts the values of dedication, family, and neighborliness that lie at the heart of the homestead myth.

The Three Stigmata of Palmer Eldritch imagines a Mars of unrelieved bleakness. The planet is essentially a penal colony, peopled by homesteaders who have been drafted into their new lives. Their situation is like trying to set up farming in the very worst of the Dust Bowl. Newcomers may start off trying to farm, but their machinery quickly fails in the never-ending dust and Martian rodents eat the crops that haven't shriveled. The only rational response is despair: "On all sides of him their abandoned, decaying gardens could be seen and he wondered if he would soon forget his. Maybe each new colonist had started out this way, in an agony of effort. And then the torpor, the hopelessness, claimed them." On this squalid frontier, the settlers learn to hate the land, not to love it. They huddle in tiny groups in subsurface hovels that they give names like Chicken Pox Prospects. There is no second generation to take over, only furtive, sordid sex and a super-LSD that lets members of a group share the experience of inhabiting a set of dolls and their miniature dollhouses—to be Barbie and Ken for a day. A marsscape of dead fields, abandoned machinery, and rotting supplies is a stand-in for the universal failure of the frontier ideal: "He knew from edu-tapes that the frontier was always like that, even on Earth."[31]

Dick was correct that homesteading, viewed realistically, is a hard fit with American narratives of growth, for close examination of the historical experience shows as much disaster as triumph. Settlement from the eastern United States has repeatedly washed across the high plains into the Rocky Mountains, lingered for a decade or two, and then washed back. One generation of failure began with the Homestead Act of 1862, expanded with the first transcontinental railroads, and crashed in the drought and depression of the 1890s. More generous land laws and European hunger for American grain during World War I attracted another ambitious generation, who hit trouble in the 1920s and disaster in the 1930s. World War II, farm subsidies, and energy exploration subsidies fueled a third generation of ambition that crested and crashed in turn in the 1980s and 1990s.

Towns grew, perhaps even prospered, but they also failed. From the Texas Panhandle to the Dakotas, the region is one of declining agriculture, aging population, and few in-migrants.[32] Just as the western American mountains are specked with the ghost town remnant of the mining frontier, the plains are slowly taking back small farm towns while regional centers struggle to keep young people from the attractions of Denver, Seattle, or Minneapolis. Some areas actually peaked in population in the 1890s, others in the 1940s or 1950s. Jonathan Raban has chronicled the process of ambition and decline in eastern Montana in *Bad Land* (1996) and Larry McMurtry fictionalized the experience in *The Last Picture Show* (1966). William Least Heat-Moon has explored the thinning human imprint in central Kansas in *PrairyErth* (1991). Geographers Frank and Deborah Popper aroused consternation and fascination when they noted that 388 western counties in 1980 supported fewer than six people per square mile, the shorthand for frontier conditions. Their proposal—really a metaphor—was to slowly return unneeded lands to a preagricultural ecology as a Buffalo Commons.[33] The made-up title *Pilgrims without Progress*, the banned book that supposedly encompasses the Martian settlement experience in *Stigmata*, would not be a bad summary for much of homesteading history.

Martian Time-Slip describes a superficially more successful Mars, but one in which the hopes of a family frontier have given way to the worst of 1960s suburbia, with many of the details taken directly from the popular suburban critique of the 1950s and 1960s.[34] The Martian homesteaders/householders that we see might as well be in San Bernardino County. They use water from the Martian canals for gardens rather than commercial agriculture. Husbands have second jobs as machinery repairmen or black market merchandisers while wives carry on sexual affairs in the afternoons. There are ads for automatic farm tractors, but no picture of how they might be used. There is also agribusiness, represented by a "ranch" in an area purchased by a Texas oil tycoon and administered by Texas (but, joke on Texas, it is really a dairy farm).

Meanwhile, the way to make money is land speculation. The father of one of the homesteaders arrives unexpectedly from Earth with plans to buy land in the arid FDR Mountains: "It was the last gasp of hope springing eternal in the old man; here there was land selling for next to nothing, with no takers, the authentic frontier which the habitable parts of Mars were patently not." In fact, the father is not a deluded romantic but a shrewd insider, attracted by an inside tip about a planned government facility that will cause the value to skyrocket. He wouldn't need his son's warning: "Don't commit yourself, because it's a known fact that any Mars real estate away from the part of the canal network that works—and remember that only about one-tenth of it works—comes close to being outright fraud."[35]

Dick's 1960s Mars novels are satirical assaults on postwar American culture, with similarities to Kurt Vonnegut's *Player Piano* (1952) and Frederick Pohl and Cyril Kornbluth's *Space Merchants* (1953) and *Gladiator-at-Law* (1955), but they are also critiques of the nation's past. They are positioned both chronologically and conceptually between the historians and critics of the 1950s, who pointed out the misunderstandings inherent in the agrarian myth, and those historians of the 1980s and 1990s who emphasize conquest, environmental devastation, and the corruptive effects of land monopoly. Dick's version of homesteading coincides with the ideas of several writers who have pointed out that the enterprising family of the homesteading West was caught from the start in a web of political and economic institutions beyond its control. If it existed at all, the agrarian family utopia of nineteenth-century American aspiration and twentieth-century nostalgia was, at most, a brief moment in a process dominated by big institutions and capital.[36]

Inventing New Stories

The writers whom I have examined so far worked with the assumption that high homesteading is possible, even when they highlight the human costs. In contrast, Kim Stanley Robinson, Jonathan Lethem, and Molly Gloss have offered science fiction that addresses the same broad topic of agricultural settlement but steps outside the standard narrative. Writing in the 1990s, they anticipated and responded in different ways to William Kittredge's challenge to invent new stories that move beyond the simple pioneer imperative to claim and own new territory.[37] The three following examples render the settlement narrative more complex and more realistic. It is not that Robinson, Lethem, or Gloss are necessarily more negative or pessimistic than earlier writers (it is hard to beat Philip K. Dick for a black view of the future), but that they are more willing to address both the ambiguities of homesteading and its larger contexts.

Kim Stanley Robinson, in *Blue Mars* (1996), revisits the question of learning the land as a writer very aware of the contemporaneous wave of environmental activism and analysis. This third book in the Mars trilogy is set at a time when terraforming has made the red planet marginally habitable. It includes an extended episode in which one of the central characters takes several years off to cultivate a desolate piece of the marsscape, exploring the possibilities for the individual (that is, homesteading) that the vast scientific and bureaucratic project of terraforming has made possible. Where Niven, Pournelle, and Barnes made Cather's "wild beast" literal and Le Guin used it as a springboard to think about the conditions of cognition, Robinson understands it as both natural system and metaphor. The "genius of the divide" is what Nirgal seeks to understand : "Only the tiniest part of the basin would be his farm. . . . It wouldn't be self-sufficient, but it would be settling in. A project. . . . He would be an ecopoet."[38]

Nirgal, given one of Mars's many names, is one of the first people born on the red planet. He encompasses the ways in which humans relate to their new planet. He grows up in a maverick community of idealists who are trying to create a natural alternative to the initial high-tech settlement. He wanders the planet as a young man, interests himself in politics, and helps to negotiate Martian autonomy from Earth. He then drops out of public life to come to terms with his own maturity and mortality, looking more and more closely at the planet itself as the source of his identity before deciding on his homesteading experiment. The remainder of the episode traces years of detailed landscape modification *and* Nirgal's effort to inhabit the place fully—to think like a marsscape. By the time Mars reclaims the tract through a massive dust storm, Nirgal has become a true native of the new land. Growing in understanding of the detailed character of his place in ways that match the "practice of the wild," as argued by western poet and essayist Gary Snyder (whom Robinson greatly admires), he has imagined a new story, even if it was one that could not overcome the dust storm that eventually buries his homestead and brings the episode to a close.

Nirgal's years in the small, high basin acknowledge the social as well as ecological complexity of homesteading.[39] The episode begins and ends with community, not isolation. Below the ridge is a Tibetan-Martian settlement whose residents are happy to have him as a distant neighbor and help him get started. Nirgal is a loner but not a hermit. He puts in stints of work with construction crews in a nearby city and manufactures blimpgliders as a cottage industry, making monthly trips to sell his latest work. He calls up other settlers for advice and entertains visitors.

The homesteading episode fails, but the overarching narrative of Mars is human success. Nirgal's work is part of an optimistic endeavor. His public role changes as he deliberately becomes more marginal to the changing tides of Martian politics, but his personal drive is always to encompass the planet, to understand it in broad sweep and in detail. In his way, he is working out the family issue that has been with American settlers since the Massachusetts Puritans had to think up the Halfway Covenant: How does the second generation shape its own future while remaining true to the vision of original settlers? For Nirgal, it is necessary to understand the land before he can work out his own answer, which involves an eventual return to engage the changing Martian society.

Jonathan Lethem's *Girl in Landscape* (1998) moves in very close parallel to *Farmer in the Sky*. Written nearly fifty years later, and for a quite different audience, it shares episodes, scenes, and situations. Lethem takes the strangeness of high homesteading seriously and has an interest in the theme of generational transition—but with a vastly different tone and approach. Heinlein wrote from an era of technical and social optimism, Lethem with a voice of ironic doubt. The former repeated the modern story of progress and contained generational conflict *within* that story, whereas the latter explored the postmodern doubt that any social solution can suffice.

In the one-sentence capsule, *Girl in Landscape* has the same plot as *Farmer in the Sky*. A family migrates from a troubled and overcrowded Earth to a new planet, settles in the countryside, and experiences challenges that leave the teenaged protagonist chastened but ultimately determined to make it as a founder of the society. Lethem's characters understand the planet as a "frontier," themselves as "homesteaders," their task as "breaking new ground" and "tam[ing] the wilderness." But everything else is undermined or reversed from Heinlein. The protagonist is a thirteen-year-old girl, Pella

Marsh, rather than a boy. Her mother dies and the remnants of her family are dysfunctional and apathetic, not cohesive and supportive. The new planet feels like exile: "The family was moving to a distant place, an impossible place. Distance itself haunted them, the distance they had yet to go."[40] It is not empty but inhabited by the sad remnants of a race that had once built huge arching structures. The challenges are social, sexual, and spiritual, not technological and economic. Disaster strikes from within rather than from without. The ending is resigned determination, not determined optimism.

The Marshes are the third family and the fourteenth to seventeenth humans in a valley settlement a day's journey from the port. One of the problems about homesteading here is that there is really nothing to do—no technical challenge. Familiar crops from Earth can be grown with difficulty, but there is no reason to bother. The ancestors of the native Archbuilders have left behind a ubiquitous plant whose tubers can produce the equivalents of potatoes, vegetables, cake, and meat. Mostly the women cook, the men sit around and talk, and the kids wander the valley and hills. If they had to leave Brooklyn, Pella wishes they had at least stayed in "Southport, the older, bigger town, where there were doctors, stores, a restaurant . . . she already wished they lived there instead of here, in the new settlement without even a name, this place on the edge of nothing."[41]

The Archbuilders hover in the background. Those who interact with the settlement are feckless and childlike in curiosity. They join the children's lessons and hang around the general store until kicked out, like deracinated Indians at a trading post. They've lost the capacity or desire to construct the great arches that make the planetscape into a version of Monument Valley: "The settlement was at the farthest edge of a basin ringed by crumbled arches. Eroded spires that rose a thousand feet into the air. Fallen bridges, incomplete towers, demolished pillars. The valley was a monumental, roofless cathedral with only the buttresses intact, and the calm purple-pink sky of the Planet of the Archbuilders glowed like stained-glass windows between these vast ruined frames."[42]

The novel is driven by Pella's sexual awakening and her struggles to understand her sexuality in a social vacuum. This central tension comes directly from the classic western movie *The Searchers* (1956), in which John Wayne searches compulsively for young Natalie Wood, who has been abducted by Indians. Lethem himself speaks of his "obsession" with that movie and its details of presentation. The book, with its bleak tone, also comes from Lethem's years in California and "that we've-reached-the-end-of-the-world" thing.[43] Pella is the Natalie Wood figure, abducted spiritually rather than physically. Her mind begins to resonate with the planet. She finds a hiding place in the hills where she dreams or goes into fugue states in which she takes on the point of view of ubiquitous small creatures like "quicksilver giraffes" that scurry inside and out, allowing her to secretly observe other people. She has become literally a girl *in* the landscape, not simply set against it but merging with it.

Both the novel's title and its development thus respond to the importance that Jane Tompkins places on landscape as a defining feature of the American western novel and movie. The western desert (or the wide open spaces of the Planet of the Archbuilders) places human beings directly in nature. Mary Lawlor similarly emphasizes the horizontality and openness of the settings for many western stories. In turn, science fiction extends that openness to infinity, from cold desert surfaces of the Moon or Mars to the wide open spaces of entire galaxies. The western plains and desert are thus made boundless and their possibilities and dangers extended to the ends of the imagination.[44]

The self-sufficient, arrogant, and planet-wise rancher Efram Nugent is the stand-in for the movie's Ethan Edwards, the monomaniacal character played by John Wayne. It's easy to hear John Wayne's voice in Nugent's dialogue and mannerisms, to see Wayne's silhouette when Nugent is introduced standing against the skyline or described as physically imposing: "Possibly any space he inhabited was his, the way he moved his shoulders to carve the air."[45] Nugent's obsession is to maintain the separation between the two peoples. He's been on the planet for seven years, can speak one of the natives' many languages, and can work with them. But he also holds these remnants of the race in contempt: "I think we ought to draw a line around this town we're starting here, Marsh. Make it a *human* settlement, a place where kids are safe. . . . I'm just talking about moving them out of our settlement. They don't care. They've got plenty of other places to wander around. A whole ruined planet for them to gawk at and wonder what the hell happened to their civilization."[46]

Nugent "searches" for Pella by keeping track of her movements and by playing on her growing sexuality to pull her back to human society. He seeks out her hiding place physically and spies on her dreaming body. His physical and moral presence upsets and attracts her. She wants his notice, angling for an invitation to his house, where she tries to come on to him (further confusing her and demonstrating his power over her). *His* sexuality, in the end, is his downfall. In the final crisis of sexually driven violence, Pella falsely but plausibly accuses him of rape in order to save one of the natives. One of the other teenagers then shoots Efram to death.

In the crisis, the ideas of town and family both collapse. The "might-be-town" shrinks rather than grows: "The spaces between things were growing instead. The silences." The only woman with domestic skills can scarcely hold her family together, let alone knead together a fragmented community. Individual pain and passion triumph. "There is no town, Pella thought. There never was one. There was only Efram and whatever he wanted. . . . Families that weren't in a town than wasn't."[47] The settlers return to Earth or flee into the outback, leaving Pella to rename it for her dead mother and start it over again. She is a survivor, who endures and carries on, but with the parental generation fled from the story. To adapt another phrase from Willa Cather, if there is to be a history of *this* country, it will surely be in Pella's heart and nowhere else.

In stripping away the surrounding society and leaving an isolated protagonist, Lethem's work has similarities to that of Douglas Coupland, another writer of the same generation who treads the line between mainstream fiction and science fiction. The twenty-somethings of *Generation X* (1991) have deliberately isolated themselves from families and meaningful careers on the low-rent side of Palm Springs. In *Girlfriend in a Coma* (1998), Coupland uses the device of a mysterious plague that kills off everyone except one small clique of thirtyish slackers, who have to contemplate what to do with the next fifty years of their lives (after they've watched all the available videos). Although Pella's specific circumstances are very different, she finds herself making decisions about her own future in virtually the same isolation in which the male hero of the classic western often finds himself.

Lethem thus situates himself in contrast to Kim Stanley Robinson as well as Robert Heinlein, for Robinson is a cautious utopian. Both in his Mars trilogy and his earlier semiutopian *Pacific Edge* (1990), he embeds his characters in communities and civil societies, as the next chapter discusses in more detail. To be successful is to make the thoughtful compromises that are necessary when individuals work together to construct communities, something that Nirgal understands even in his years as a loner.

Robinson takes the political process seriously and his most admirable characters are politically active, balancing their own desires against those of others. His preferred society in both trilogies manifests the "wise provincialism" that nineteenth-century philosopher Josiah Royce saw as the middle ground between radical individualism and corporate dominance.[48] Lethem's version of politics is Pella's failed and foolish father, defeated on Earth and unable to find an outlet for his "committee-chairing" skills in the intensely individualized and ego-driven community of his new home. The novel progressively strips away family members and community members as characters die, flee, or withdraw into catatonia. Only Pella is left, and only Pella's hard-won understanding and individual determination will be able to prevail on the homesteading frontier.

In contrast to Lethem but similarly to Robinson, Molly Gloss offers a complex homesteading story in which the answer to individual doubts is community, not radical individualism. She also places the homestead narrative in a larger chronological frame by showing that the real drama may be in the decision to emigrate rather than the result. In *The Dazzle of Day* (1997) she takes on the steep challenge of injecting drama into Quaker decision-making practice—a far cry from the cardboard characters that Dick put through plots of corporate manipulation and individual greed. The bulk of the novel takes place on a generation ship toward the end of its long voyage from Earth to a new planet, but Gloss subverts the most common version of this setting by showing a society that has grown stronger and more cohesive over the generations rather than falling into anarchy, thus entering a plea for the power of social connections in a strongly individualistic genre.

Dazzle is a homesteading story in which life on the outward trail is more important than the arrival. The novel opens with a single chapter in which a member of a Quaker settlement in Central America struggles with the sadness of embarking on the great journey to the stars.[49] It ends centuries later with another short chapter in which one of the planet-born generation encounters the new planet's ferocity and danger and takes it all for granted as the conditions of life. In between, the body of the novel centers on the immigrant ship *Dusty Miller* as it nears the new planet and its passengers try to decide whether it is habitable. In other words, the generations that interact directly in *Journey*, *Beowulf's Children*, *Girl in Landscape*, and "The Eye Altering" are drawn apart from each other in time and in place.

Because *Dazzle* is a novel about a community making up its mind, the plot line is about the struggle of the colonists to decide what to do about the new planet. They send probes and debate the findings that show a stormy, subarctic land that may barely be survivable. A manned reconnaissance ends with two of four explorers dead and the planet's inhospitality highlighted. The interstellar voyagers talk and set up committees, hear reports, and talk some more. Their ship may, just barely, have the capacity to seek out a new star system, but hopes and fears come to revolve around *this* one ball of rock and ice. Gloss takes the deliberations seriously—both the contrasting attitudes and ideas that the participants bring and the Quaker process through which insights are aired and a larger sense of the community emerges.[50]

Once the transfer has been made, the concluding chapter echoes Le Guin and Robinson, for new generations learn the planet in ways that the shipborn cannot. "My mother has an old, religious reverence for books," muses one of the new generation. "My mother's understanding of this world, even after seventy years, is intimately linked to the fusty smell inside the covers of the books. . . . Mine is in the waxy panes of riverine ice, in the smell of a mouse's old bones and the spiny rustle of a ring-eye's nest. The landscape we inhabit as children, inhabits us."[51] It is a quasi-mystical sense of place, perhaps related to the altered seeing of Le Guin's short story and the deep landscape immersion of Nirgal, but it is also a fearsome understanding that takes stress and storm, disaster and death as parts of everyday experience. Indeed, the very wildness of the planet which so disturbed the star-born and pushed the first explorer into mental collapse ("'There was a wind!' he said wildly, as if that explained everything.") becomes an essential for the planet-born ("The weather rode very slowly across the grass . . . I suppose that was the first time I heard the earth speaking.")[52]

Uniquely among the writers considered in this chapter, Molly Gloss has written both historical fiction and science fiction about homesteading, and *The Dazzle of Day* reflects that dual understanding. It is the most complex of the texts I discuss because it critiques one historical moment—homesteading—by inserting it into larger processes of historical change. For Gloss, homesteading is a story of tensions between mobility and community. She writes within a long historical literature that sees the democratic experience rather than continental abundance as the determining national experience. In particular, a number of western historians emphasize the transfer of ideas and institutions from East to West, the continual reestablishment of values and institutions, and the hard-won formation of civil communities from individuals and families.[53] She wants readers to understand the story of homesteading not as the achievement of an end state but as one part of a larger process, directing our attention to the longer histories of prelude and consequence of which the crafting of family farms is only a brief stage.

Science fiction writers, historical novelists, and historians are tilling the same ground as critics of the American past. They have been moving toward similar understandings of the national experience—as embodied in the history of the West—whether by reevaluating historical sources or reflecting on standard narratives in fictions of the future. As this analysis has tried to show, science fiction homesteading stories are most challenging when they step beyond the frames of adventure tale and family saga to place homesteading within larger narratives of economic development and cultural transfer. Academic historians who have taken on this task are often grouped as practitioners of a "new western history." There is no similarly convenient term for writers as disparate in specific interests and sensibility as Philip K. Dick and later Kim Stanley Robinson, Jonathan Lethem, and Molly Gloss, but they are participants in the same debate about the underpinnings of one of the prominent American creation stories.

5 Frontier Democracy

There is no end in politics, only process. The curtain may come down on individuals, and even on societies and cultures, but the flow of human history moves on and we make new associations and try on new forms of politics. It's an off-center wheel, always turning, always bumping along.
—Greg Bear, personal communication, June 12, 2003

It's more history, more trouble, between us and any decent society.
—Kim Stanley Robinson, quoted in David Seed, "The Mars Trilogy: An Interview" (1996)

Everything is political in one way or another.
—Octavia Butler, quoted in Marilyn Mehaffy and AnaLouise Keating, "Radio Imagination" (2001)

Before the Revolution

Ursula K. Le Guin's story "The Day before the Revolution" (1974) is as superficially unexciting as science fiction gets. It follows the daily routine and thoughts of Laia Osaieo Odo, an old woman living out her life in the company of younger colleagues. She wakes from a dream of her younger years, stares morosely at her dried-out skin and knobby veins as she struggles stiffly from bed, struggles to take more than a few bites of breakfast, labors to climb the steps back to her room—they've been a problem ever since her first stroke. "Her right hand tingled. She scratched it, and then shook it in the air, spitefully. It had never quite got over the stroke. Neither had her right leg, or right eye, or the right corner of her mouth." She tries to work, but her thoughts wander back to her long-dead husband. She meets with some visiting young people, tries to pay attention to the news of a rapidly gathering revolution, and then dies:

> She waited her time, managed to get up and, for all her clumsiness, to limp away unnoticed among the people busy with their own planning and excitement. She got to the hall, to the stairs, and began to climb them, one

> by one. "The general strike," a voice, two voices, ten voices were saying in the room below, behind her. "The general strike," Laia muttered, resting for a moment on the landing. Above, ahead, in her room, what awaited her: The private stroke. That was mildly funny. She started up the second flight of stairs, one by one, one leg at a time, like a small child. She was dizzy, but she was no longer afraid to fall. On ahead, on there, the dry white flowers nodded and whispered in the open fields of evening. Seventy-two years and she had never had time to learn what they were called.[1]

The revolution is the old woman's revolution. She has been working for this day for her entire adulthood, enduring years of incarceration, writing *The Prison Letters* and *The Analogy* in the hope of forging a society without government. She lives in one of hundreds of Odonian Houses whose residents practice and preach the principles of cooperation and mutual aid. The movement that she and her husband served with their lives has taken on its own momentum into a cascade of change, but she remains an inspiration and an icon for the new generations.

"The Day before the Revolution" appeared in 1974, the same year as *The Dispossessed*, Le Guin's novel about the Odonian utopia as it might develop several generations after Odo's life and death. The book won both Hugo and Nebula awards for best science fiction novel of 1974. "The Day before the Revolution" won the Nebula Award for best short story of 1974 and has been widely anthologized. Published when the social hopes of the 1960s were slowly sinking into the morass of Watergate, it inspired some readers as a reaffirmation of the possibility of forging a cooperative world.[2] Le Guin was also one of the key writers who brought the concerns of the new feminism into science fiction, and her story played two cards at once, identifying a woman as the prime mover of political change and portraying that woman realistically: old physically as well as mentally, proud, self-centered, a bit vain, and still devoted to the cause.

The story carries another point that science fiction writers and readers also needed to hear. Political change, Le Guin tells us, is a long process. Political action arises from community needs and can give new meanings to community. It results from the steady work of thinking, arguing, organizing, demonstrating, lobbying, and voting, not from neat behind-the-scenes maneuvers or the brave deeds of individual heroes. It takes a long time and lots of hard work to bring equitable order on new frontiers; it takes patience to construct utopia. Indeed, *The Dispossessed* itself suggests that no utopia can survive in a steady state, for even self-conscious anarchists fall into rigidities of belief and institutions that need to be continually challenged and rethought.

Twenty years after Le Guin published her story, Greg Bear mirrored its message with the last section of his Nebula-winning novel *Moving Mars* (1993). The novel's action concerns a movement for Martian independence from Earth, and it takes the process of politics very seriously. We follow its central character, Casseia Majumdar, from haphazard revolutionary student to skilled constitution writer and vice president of the new Martian republic, then to repudiated leader as the dialectic of politics consumes its own. Long after she has been deposed, imprisoned, and then released with apologies by a new government, she's an object of pilgrimage. "A straight, proud, stocky woman with wispy grey and black hair" who pursues her own scientific research, she is annoyed at news that the new administration plans to erect a statue in her honor, for she knows that communities are built through sustained, shared work, not by the deeds of heroes.[3]

Both Le Guin and Bear address the basic problem of governance and politics: How can we coordinate the actions of strong-willed individuals to get benefits of cooperation without repression of difference and originality? They also give a common answer that good government requires an active and permanent civic life, an insight that reinscribes the republican values of community-serving politics that many founders of western states tried to incorporate into their new governments. Science fiction writers over the past half century have been drawing on the western American experience to offer increasingly sophisticated ideas about these issues. In the next section, I contrast the antidemocratic assumptions of Golden Age science fiction with more recent work that has taken seriously the role and process of formal constitution making in protecting democratic communities. The following section examines how writers have been drawing on the long line of religious and secular utopias and community experiments to imagine the obstacles and possibilities of deliberately reconstituted Wests. The final section frames some of these utopian fictions as efforts to imagine societies rooted in the "wise provincialism" of community building animated by a sense of place.

Coups or Constitutions

John W. Campbell, the editor of *Astounding Science Fiction* (later *Analog*) from 1937 to 1971, would have made a great host for call-in talk radio. Like many of the voices that fill truck cabs and echo through construction sites, he was quick with words, opinionated, and skilled at finding holes in ideas that he didn't like. Like most radio hosts, he was also an increasingly strident libertarian. Especially in *Analog* editorials in the 1960s, he argued that people are inherently unequal in abilities, and therefore in their capacity to govern themselves. Again and again, he tried to puncture what he saw as Great Society platitudes and advocated government by the capable. These would be the engineers and scientists who understand how the world really works ("God Isn't Democratic") or the men and women who had proved their abilities by economic success ("Constitution for Utopia").[4]

Translated into hard science fiction, Campbell's assumptions placed engineers, scientists, and visionary entrepreneurs at the center of the action. Ignorant or venal politicians who cater to the masses hold them back. So do bureaucrats who try to stifle initiative with endless rules and regulations. At best, politics and government provide good foils who add some rudimentary plot tension in what are basically puzzle-solving stories ("If only they'd let us work," laments the prototypical hero). At worst, the stories become platforms for right-wing diatribes and free-market evangelism.

The Campbellian contempt for democratic processes was ready made for exciting stories with masterful heroes, and it has taken science fiction a long time to shake off its influence. Everyday politics and grassroots political life are conspicuously absent in many of the genre's classics. Golden Age writers frequently treated the processes of governance as nothing but top-down and behind-the-scenes manipulation. The general public is in the hands of propagandists and skilled press secretaries, wire pullers and masters of back-room deals, secret agents and leaders of revolutionary cells. A. E. Van Vogt in *The Weapon Shops of Isher* (1951) described a world in which superior beings provide superadvanced weapons to individual citizens so they can defend themselves against the state, which is assumed to be undemocratic, unresponsive, and oppressive. Isaac Asimov's Foundation series imagined a galaxy as a huge puppet whose strings might be manipulated by a single, brilliant psychohistorian. Robert Heinlein explored different facets of the elitist model from the 1940s to the 1960s: futuristic espionage and counterespionage in *Beyond This Horizon* (1942), politics as public relations in *Double Star* (1956), and Leninesque revolution in *The Moon Is a Harsh Mistress* (1966).

Double Star is a good example of science fiction that treats politics as manipulation. The plot elements are thoroughly of the 1950s, drawing on the new crafts of market research and public opinion polling, the proliferation of advertising, and fresh memories of fascist propaganda. The novel tells of Lorenzo Smythe, a washed-up actor who is recruited to stand in for the kidnapped leader of the solar-system-wide Expansionist Party. The handful of party leaders who arrange the impersonation expect it to last only a few days, until "John Joseph Bonforte," former supreme minister and now leader of the opposition, can reach Mars to be adopted into the Nest of Kkkah, thereby becoming a Martian as well as a human being and forging an important political alliance. But the deception stretches over additional days and then weeks. Smythe deals with the press, delivers campaign speeches, and leads the Expansionists to victory over the narrow-minded Humanity Party. Readers are not surprised when Bonforte dies from the mistreatment he suffered during his kidnapping and Larry Smythe steps permanently into his role, becoming Joe Bonforte, the new head of government and humanity's leading statesman for the next quarter century.

There is much to like in *Double Star.* Despite his later reputation for right-wing politics, Heinlein makes the Expansionists the expression of moderate liberal "one world" values of 1950s America. Like a latter-day Adlai Stevenson, both Bonfortes favor economic opportunity, free trade, investment in science, cooperation among the home planet and its colonies, and full political rights for all intelligent beings, including those funny-looking Venusians and smelly Martians. Nevertheless, the novel pokes fun at the processes of democracy. Smythe has never voted before signing on for the impersonation. He instantly converts from his vague Humanity Party leanings after seeing the forceful logic of Bonforte's speeches. He trusts one political insider for all his cues. Back-room deal making and a few fine speeches win the pivotal election. Government itself is a huge impersonal machine that runs itself while the political insiders are enjoying a game: "It's the only sport for grownups" says one.[5] And, of course, the very premise of the story turns politics into a big practical joke.

Ten years later, Heinlein offered a different take on politics as conspiracy. *The Moon Is a Harsh Mistress* tells the story of political change via revolutionary coup. As we've seen in Chapter 2, the novel depicts the twenty-first century moon as an analogy of the industrializing mining frontier. Resistance to the power of the Lunar Authority begins when workers try to protest unfair economic arrangements. After company goons break up a mass meeting in the fateful year 2076, however, the rebellion falls into the hands of a self-appointed revolutionary cell led by the brilliant Professor

Bernardo de la Paz with the help of computer troubleshooter Manuel Garcia O'Kelley, beautiful and fiery Wyoming Knott (don't think of trying the obvious nickname!), and a sentient computer known as Mike. Working behind the scenes, they organize other revolutionary cells, massage public opinion, and turn three million Lunies into an effective resistance movement. Much of the fun comes from watching de la Paz maneuver Lunies and ground pounders alike.

Heinlein's most direct comment on the political process is the Ad Hoc Congress for Organization of Free Luna, a constitutional convention that convenes after the colonials have declared independence. Despite keying the date to the American Revolution, he has little tolerance for the sorts of debates and compromises that actually forged a new nation. O'Kelley complains that "our biggest headaches were self-appointed statesmen," but Bernardo de la Paz corrects him.[6] The purpose, says de la Paz, is to divert the "yammerheads" and keep them out of the way of the revolutionary coterie who are planning the necessary political and military strategies. The whole affair is arranged so that the delegates will never get anything done, with ineffective chairmen, committees with conflicting jurisdictions, and plenty of time for empty speech making—and not a James Madison in sight.

In contrast to Heinlein's cavalier dismissal of politics on the high frontier, Americans in the nineteenth-century West actually took constitutions and constitution making very seriously, working within political traditions brought from older communities. The first generation of Anglo-American settlers in Colorado or California or Oregon were immediately aware of the need for self-government. They quickly established a basic social contract to protect people and property. Prospectors established extralegal miners' assemblies and mining districts in gold rush districts to record and adjudicate prospectors' rights to their individual finds. Agricultural settlers in early Colorado organized claim clubs for the same purpose. People's courts tried to protect life and property by apprehending and trying criminals before the establishment of formal courts.

As rapidly as possible, western settlers moved to create formal governments. Nineteenth-century Americans enjoyed politics as a spectator sport as well as serious business, and the history of the West is full of ad hoc assemblies that devised territorial governments or provisional states and tried to convince Congress to ratify their actions. As David A. Johnson has shown, members of constitutional conventions in places like Oregon and California were ordinary citizens who understood the need to balance competing interests in order to open opportunity for individuals.[7] The results could be impressively progressive—voting rights for women in Wyoming, a unicameral legislature in Nebraska, populist leanings in Oklahoma (which had a large, homegrown socialist movement).

Greg Bear's *Moving Mars*, published a quarter century after Heinlein's tale of revolution, constructs a Martian future that comes much closer to this western American experience. Indeed, Bear wrote in deliberate contrast to Heinlein's model of manipulative politics.[8] The book opens with a half-baked coup attempt that fails—a direct argument against the likelihood of Heinlein's oh-so-easy Lunarian revolution. As a vote on a new, centralizing Mars constitution nears, the University of Mars expels 80 percent of its students in order to forestall political demonstrations. Casseia Majumdar, a government and management major, is among those "voided" from the university. She joins a hastily improvised student revolt that tries—and fails—to seize control of the university. She comes out of the experience with her future salvaged but with cynicism about the egotistical, manipulative leaders who had incited the other students: "my fresh young idealism waned rapidly, replaced by no wisdom to speak of. . . . My youthful ideals had been trodden on none too delicately, and I didn't know what to make of it."[9]

Then follows the personal and political maturation of Casseia Majumdar, a rare example of a science fiction protagonist who wants to study political theory and public administration rather than to follow a technical or scientific profession. About a hundred pages into the five-hundred-page book, Cassie has a family showdown about her continuing interest in government and politics. Her mother, in particular, has never approved of the political process. Cassie's grandmother "had left the Moon in protest when it reshaped its constitution, and her daughter had retained a typical Lunar sense of rugged individualism. . . . Still, if I wanted to study state theory and large-scale govmanagement, she would go along, after voicing a quiet, polite protest." In effect, Cassie's mother takes the position of many traditional science fiction fans who might automatically reject the political realm, while Cassie speaks for a more sophisticated viewpoint.

> "I've put up with your eccentricities," [her mother] said with a lift of her chin and a stretch of her neck, "because we try to encourage independent thinking in our young folks. But I honestly never thought I'd see a daughter of mine go into politics—"

"Govmanagement," I amended.

"For a career," she said. "I'm put off by it, of course, but I'm also intrigued. After a few years studying the Council, what can you teach *me* when we argue."[10]

The central challenge for twenty-second-century Mars is to find an acceptable way to coordinate the extended families that dominate Martian society and economic life. Somewhat akin to closely held corporations, these family-business units have been accustomed to working flexibly under a set of accepted customs. Powerful interests on Earth, however, want a strong central government that will bring Mars more closely under its economic and political control. Bear traces this issue through a sequence of untenable compromises, double-dealing, and economic pressure from Earth to a declaration of independence and a constitutional convention that is the intellectual focal point of the novel.

In effect, the question is what to do with success. After overcoming the physical and technical challenges of finding and developing resources, how can a society make the transition to a stable and sustainable economy? The answer requires economic adjustments on the scene, but also a reallocation of power. Initial development is always dependent on external sponsorship and capital, and those external interests have to be recognized without stifling local independence. In the American West, those interests included the federal government, eastern railroads and corporations, and European bondholders. For Mars, the same forces work through the central Earth authorities.

Cassie herself is a central figure in the constitutional process. She works for months to forge a basic agreement on the procedures and goals of a constitutional assembly, which finally convenes in the debating chamber of the University of Mars. Thereafter follow weeks of exhausting negotiations:

> We all walked a tortuous path, preserving privileges here, removing them everywhere, listening patiently to anguished appeals, working compromise after compromise, yet never—we hoped—compromising the core of a workable democratic constitution. The birth cries of the new age were the voices of dozens of women and men, talking until they were hoarse, late into the night and early in the morning, arguing, cajoling, persuading."[11]

Bear describes the issues and compromises in substantial detail that copies the American model. There are to be executive, legislative, judicial, and extraplanetary branches. Districts will have substantial autonomy, but the economy will run with a central bank and common currency. There is a bill of rights. No district that ratifies the constitution can later withdraw from the Federal Republic of Mars. Martians debate and finally ratify by a two-to-one margin. Cassie becomes the first elected vice president: "Beyond any doubt, I was now a politician."[12] Her realization is rueful but not unhappy, for she realizes that she has the kind of political talents that her new nation needs. Compared to Smythe/Bonforte, these are the talents of leadership and negotiation, not deception and role-playing.[13]

Kim Stanley Robinson also places constitution making at a crucial point in his Mars trilogy. Slowly but surely, the books test different sorts of figures as the creators of a new Mars. Charismatic utopians, skilled scientists and engineers, lonely explorers, and fanatical environmentalists all have their moment of prominence in the story and influence on the future of Mars. But the heroes at the end are the community builders—not the loners and roamers, but the ones who understand the need to create the institutions that balance the desires of individuals and the needs of the community. The trilogy directly challenges the frontier metaphor. The Earth-held idea that Mars is a social safety valve acts as an exogenous force driving the story. Mars offers a symbolic (even if impractical) release for an Earth collapsing from environmental stress. Crowded countries put in their claims for Martian land and resources, and illicit immigrants arrive despite official quotas and limits, for "millions on Earth wanted to come to Mars, to the 'new frontier,' where life was an adventure again." Everyone knows that another planet cannot really relieve pressure at home, but home governments are unwilling to give up the fiction. As the settlers move toward a first revolution, one of the Martian leaders notes the problem: "Did you see that program aired on Eurovid about all the open land on Mars?. . . It was like a real estate ad." The reference looks back directly to the booster literature with which railroad companies and state governments attracted settlers to the Great Plains and mountain states.[14]

The safety valve fails on both demographic realities (the mismatch between tens of thousands of immigrants and billions on the home planet) and on cultural conflict. Visions of inventing a new Martian culture from scratch or blending the best from Earth into a new amalgam crash against the persistence of cultural differences among immigrants from Switzerland and India, the United States, Arab nations, and many other cultures. Here is the theme of convergence from the new western history, an exploration of the ways in which a "white" frontier (pioneered in this case by Americans and Russians) is complicated by the arrival of immigrants from very different cultures, just as the presence of native peoples and the arrival of Latinos, Chinese, Japanese, Filipinos, and many others has complicated the development of an Anglo-American West. The planet is linked inextricably to the history of Earth, becoming a social battleground where multinational immigration reproduces old ethnic identities and cultures in desperately pure forms.

Questions of resource use and community come together in the relations between Earth and Mars, metropolis and colony. Central to the action is the clash between local autonomy and the domination of outside capital and corporations, another central issue in the development of the American West.[15] Beyond the direct tensions of capitalists and workers, Robinson argues that the global and local are interdependent because local opportunities are always embedded within larger structures. Mars cannot exist without a viable Earth.[16] The societies are linked through history, heritage, and information exchange. The web of economic and cultural connections remains too strong to allow isolated purity. As Americans discovered after 1783 and again after 1815, the web of connections that tie new settlements to their places of origins are not easily severed or ignored.

In fact, heroic individualism is replaced not by utopian experiments but by the merits of civic life. Robinson's alternative for Mars is also the great alternative for understanding western America: frontier as community building. The course of the Mars books problematizes end-state utopias (this is also why the Russian model drops away). The future must be found in the unruly and morally complex processes of community making, not in intellectualized schemes. We have, I think, a fictionalized version of Stanley Elkins and Eric McKitrick's meaning for Frederick Jackson Turner's frontier in the challenges of working together. Elkins and McKitrick, who wrote in the 1950s, gave new life to the idea of democracy as a function of the frontier by examining World War II boom towns, where the necessity of building community from scratch forced residents to pool energies and work together. There are also echoes of Robert Hine's argument that western Americans have most effectively built cohesive communities when they enjoy a common sense of place.[17]

Red Mars (1992), the first volume of the Mars trilogy, pivots on political revolutions. By positing a "first hundred" settlers equally divided among Russians and Americans, Robinson can use two structuring narratives from nineteenth- and twentieth-century history. One is the promise and problems of socialist revolution. The second is the possibilities and processes of community building in new lands. The first is the big, dramatic framework. The second underlies Robinson's projections of the evolution of everyday life on the high frontier. Both metaphors tie the hypothesized history of Mars to repeated falls into history—the failures of Russian socialism and French revolutionary utopianism, the transformation of New England between the 1630s and the 1680s, Utah from the nineteenth to the twentieth century, or any new place that wriggles free from the static idealism of its founders.

The first revolution fails in 2061 (the Martian equivalent of Russia in 1905) but the second succeeds in 2127 (think 1917), when the oppressive regime is under external stress from ecocatastrophe on Earth. But history in the Mars narrative is always conditional and mutable. It is made through the articulation of ideas, public debates, power plays, assassination. It is never final, balanced between structure and agency, culture, politics, and economics. It is "whole, nonrepeatable, and contingent."[18] By *Green Mars* (1994) and *Blue Mars* (1996), the increased complexity and density of cultures, institutions, and "history" make action more problematic and complex. The heroes are now the builders and state makers, the architects of viable governments, and by implication the scientists who help to create an inhabitable Mars. No single narrative can now contain the multifarious history. The model of the Russian revolutions drops away, for no simplifying theory works, in favor of Madisonian political compromises. The meat of the process of community formation is engaged conversation, engaged politics.

The key event is the establishment of formal government after the successful breaking away from Earth control. The constitution makers struggle to reconcile respect for cultural peculiarities with universal rights, hoping at best for "a lot of different cultures coexisting."[19] Nadia Chernyshevsky, introduced as the builder of engineering works in the first book, emerges as the builder of constitutions and as the story's new hero. She shares the role with Maya Toitovna, a woman of enormous personal magnetism who begins as Nadia's opposite—a manipulator of sexual liaisons for personal influence—and ends as a devoted organizer of political change.

The pivotal figures of the political struggle are John Boone, the politically savvy leader of the first Americans, Nadia, and eventually Maya.[20] These are the people who talk. The true solution is to build civil society through conversation. Mars at its best, says critic Carol Franko, is "an argumentative and interdependent confederation of diverse communities."[21] Boone seeks utopia through dialogue, and the speech in which he sums up his ideas about forging a new Martian society pulls together thoughts and suggestions that he has picked up in years of conversation. Nadia and her supporters seek stability through negotiation. They work the hallways during political meetings and do the hard work of community organizing. Maya helps to organize the successful revolution and then works quietly to get the government going without interfering with Nadia's leadership. Franko references literary theorist Mikhail Bakhtin and the literary-linguistic idea of "dialogism," in which meaning emerges from the continual interaction among people, their words, their actions, and their unspoken ideals.[22] In Bakhtin's view, novels establish their worlds by setting multiple voices in interaction, allowing their characters to form new meanings from the play within and between persons and words. De Witt Douglas Kilgore has a similar reading of the Mars trilogy that emphasizes the creation of a "heterotopia" that challenges the white male, bourgeois narrative that dominates solar system futures. Heterotopia, as the word implies, is participatory and multicultural, inviting of repeated redefinition.[23]

These are the reasons that the constitutional convention sets the tone for the third volume and functions as the intellectual climax of the trilogy, bringing together issues of political economy with environmental and scientific issues raised by terraforming. The debates, and their strategic positioning (comparable to the role of the constitutional debates in *Moving Mars*), allow Robinson to highlight the merits of democratic political interchange. The document, he says through the words of Martian historian Charlotte Dorsa Brevia, was "not to be a static 'final law' wherein all social contradiction was resolved forever, but rather to be a template to structure argument, and a spur to justice. . . . The constitution was, to my mind, written to give people a sense that their management of their affairs was in no way 'natural' or written in stone; laws and governments have always been artificial inventions, practices, and habits. They can change, they have changed, they will change again. That being the case, there is no reason not to try to change them for the better."[24]

Robinson's emphasis on the importance of civic life takes a concrete expression in his favorable view of life in maturing Martian cities. He portrays urbanization as a natural and positive outcome of settlement, a rare judgment in much science fiction. The cities that develop around the new inland seas are places of apartments, sidewalk cafés, and promenades that evoke a Mediterranean ambiance. The crater rim cities are a cross between Italian hill towns and American Midwestern college towns, certainly two of Earth's most attractive environments. The proximity of other people allows the development of what political scientist Robert Putnam calls social capital—the low-key bonds of trust that develop from shared activities and shared spaces. In one telling passage, Robinson describes one of the first hundred as she reflects on the interaction between the big events of political revolution and the pleasures of everyday life: "They lived in a third-floor apartment . . . and on evenings warm enough they often ate down at tables in the courtyard and talked with their neighbors, played games, did handiwork. It was a real community, and sometimes Maya would look around her at the people in it and think here was a historical reality that would not ever be recorded in any way: a good solid neighborhood, with everyone doing their work . . . in which an individual family made sense as part of a larger whole that was not easy to characterize."[25] Even the fiercely intellectual and independent Ann Claybourne ends the trilogy embracing community and friends.

Left Coast Utopias

If one route to community is the imperfection of political compromise and constitutions, another is the option of intentionally building communities on new principles. In the 1970s and 1980s, many Americans learned to use "intentional community" to describe everything from a hippie commune to a group of people carefully living according to an intellectually coherent program. The latter, of course, is what advocates and critics usually refer to as a utopia. Several western writers of science fiction have explored the possibilities and problems of intentional communities. This section, for comparison and consistency, examines California futures imagined by Ernest Callenbach, Octavia Butler, and Kim Stanley Robinson. Their novels offer three approaches to utopia—as an admirable end state, as a successful model created out of deep struggle, and as a "pocket utopia" that is constantly in need of care and updating. Each picture is more complicated, provisional, and realistic than the one before. In particular,

Butler and Robinson present fictional arguments for democratic utopias that are works in progress rather than realizations of blueprints handed down by a single big thinker. In so doing, they offer a complement to the preceding discussion of politics as a sequence of tentative compromises that gradually include more participants and points of view.

These new Californias are firmly rooted in the region's history, for the western frontier and then the regional West have been the preferred location for Americans to build utopia. Puritan Massachusetts and Quaker Pennsylvania were both religiously driven experiments in community making. Nineteenth-century utopians, motivated both by secular and religious visions, planted most of their communities within a hundred miles of the westward moving settlement frontier.[26] The frontier offered relatively cheap land, physical isolation, and, ideally, social and cultural elbow room. Before the Civil War, this meant places like Tennessee, Ohio, Indiana, Iowa, and Texas. The Mormons, perhaps the most successful and persistent of nineteenth-century utopians, tried two locations in Missouri and Illinois that were not adequately isolated from hostile neighbors before finding a location with plenty of room around the edges on the far side of the Rocky Mountains.

In the late nineteenth and twentieth centuries, the wide spaces and relatively sparse settlement in much of the Rocky Mountain and Pacific West continued to attract utopians. Land in desert valleys and cutover foothills remained affordable, and the same sorts of locations had few nosy neighbors to poke into unusual lifestyles and property arrangements. Historians have chronicled religious settlements and socialist experiments as alternatives to the economic polarization of corporate capitalism.[27] Over the past generation, the Northwest and Southwest have been preferred sites for countercultural communes, survivalist enclaves, white racist settlements, and protocities directed by religious figures such as Bhagwan Shree Rajneesh (in Oregon) and Elizabeth Clare Prophet (in Montana).[28]

Just as new Martians try out old Earth-based ideologies and religions in a new setting, Americans have long projected political and cultural hopes on the West in forms that range from geopolitical boosterism to communitarian experiments. And we have been particularly eager to burden California with often contradictory roles as arcadia, utopia, and featured player in the collapse of civilization.[29] Science fiction is a natural extension of such western discourse, reinscribing the hopes and fears that shaped stories of the nineteenth- and twentieth-century West onto new places and times.

The simplest approach to utopia is to focus on results rather than process, to describe the good society in its steady state. Among the fictions about the western American future, the most influential such exercise is Ernest Callenbach's *Ecotopia: The Notebooks and Reports of William Weston* (1975).[30] Sometime, not too far into the book's past, Northern California, Oregon, and Washington have seceded from the United States to pursue an ecologically sustainable future, with lots of "soft energy," free bicycles, cooperative economic arrangements, cool, misty forests, spiritual respect for the landscape, gender equality, and good sex. The story is told—as are many such depictions of end-state utopias—through the diary entries and news dispatches of a visiting U.S. journalist. In one sense, it is Berkeley and the Bay Area of the early 1970s writ large. It is not a sophisticated future, but it was telling and popular and sold more than 700,000 copies.

Criticized for assuming a revolution rather than demonstrating how a "green" nation might come into being, Callenbach followed in 1981 with *Ecotopia Emerging*.[31] The revolution, however, remains a thought experiment rather than an exploration of the real ambiguities of political action: A high school student invents an improved photovoltaic cell and decides to make it available to everyone; her mother organizes "cancer commandos" and the greens organize as a political party; a bit of nuclear blackmail leads to a peaceful parting of the ways. In short, Callenbach comes off more like Heinlein than he would probably like, accepting the standard science fiction premise that political change requires only a few individuals to push in just the right place.

The utopian community that Octavia Butler envisions for the same landscape as *Ecotopia* is far more ambiguous and problematic. The community—then movement—of Earthseed emerges slowly and painfully as its founder Lauren Olamina simultaneously thinks through its possibilities and tries to build an actual community in the northern coastal mountains of California while American society dissolves into near chaos. Butler has traced the story of Olamina and Earthseed in *The Parable of the Sower* (1994) and *The Parable of the Talents* (1998), which won the Nebula Award as best novel. As critic Jim Miller notes, Earthseed is "a constantly evolving body of thought and action" whose end results are clear neither at the start of *Sower*, when fifteen-year-old Olamina gains her first insights, or the end of *Talents*, when she sees spaceships lift from Earth to realize her vision of seeding the stars.[32]

Parable of the Sower starts in 2024 with a dystopian Los Angeles that reflects Butler's own experiences of home—and the environment that spawned the Rodney King beating in 1991 and the subsequent riots at the verdict in 1992. Central government in the United States is weakening. Hundreds of thousands of Angelenos have become an underclass, living in shantytowns, scratching, thieving, and killing for survival. Fifteen-year-old Lauren Olamina has grown up in a suburban cul-de-sac whose racially heterogeneous residents have protected themselves against social collapse by walling their neighborhood for protection (see Chapter 6 for more on Butler's future Los Angeles).

Out of this chaos, Lauren begins to develop the idea of Earthseed. After a drug-crazed mob burns her neighborhood and kills the rest of her family, she heads north with the hope to reach Oregon, "where water isn't such a problem and food is cheaper."[33] She follows Route 118 (the Ronald Reagan Highway) to Route 23 to reach the ocean near Ventura, then heads north to Salinas, inland through Sacramento, and northward again. At the same time, she continues to expand the Earthseed philosophy and to gather together a handful of other refugees, mixed in race, class, and gender. They come together for mutual support and protection on the road and stay because of the growing force of Lauren and her ideas. They settle on land in Humboldt County owned by one of the refugees. The furrowed, green hills are classic hippie country/utopia country. "This is a ridiculous place to build a community," Lauren says. "It's isolated, miles from everywhere with no decent road leading here, but for us, now, it's perfect."[34] At the end of the first book, the diverse group of individuals has developed through its struggles into something of a political collective that presents an alternative to broken capitalism.[35] Butler names the community Acorn and ends the book with the parable from Luke about the seeds that fell on stony ground and the seeds that fell on fertile ground.

The slow and halting emergence of Acorn shows that Butler finds process more interesting than result. The experience of the refugees also reflects Olamina's Earthseed philosophy: God is Change and "exists to be shaped."[36] By embracing change, people can themselves change god, meaning that humans have a role in constantly reshaping their own destinies. Lauren Olamina's own goal is to reach beyond the present to envision and preach a human destiny in exploration of the stars. As Tom Moylan puts it, "she looks at the suffering of her family and others and decides that they could one day benefit from her version of a materialist and activist spirituality that seeks to regain control over society in the name of a transcendent yet still secular purpose."[37]

Earthseed starts small and rooted in its troubled times, building one, then a few other small communities in which people can take charge of their own lives and relearn the responsibilities of community. *The Parable of the Talents* moves to a future in which Earthseed communities have grown and developed. In line with the Earthseed vision, the movement is not monolithic. Butler has commented that these are "*multiple* communities, self governing and supporting, but also interactive with each other," again emphasizing the importance of active participation in shaping the structures of communities.[38] The book gives us lots of continuing social and political nastiness in the 2030s. While Christian fundamentalists and moderate reformers battle over the future of the United States, however, Earthseed trains its young people to serve the internal needs of the communities. Lauren Olamina becomes more fixed on the transforming prospects of human movement outward and upward. *Talents* ends with a flashforward to 2081 and the launching of the first Earthseed colony into space, leaving behind the messy, detailed, and practical work of community making for a vision of apocalyptic change.

A further complicated version of utopia as process is Kim Stanley Robinson's Three Californias trilogy.[39] Written in the 1980s, the books imagine three very different futures for Orange County. *The Wild Shore* (1984) describes a village climbing back to tribalism after the neutron bombing of the United States. The historical record is truncated, and the survivors are too busy toiling for food and shelter to sift historical fact from fiction. The Southern California of *The Gold Coast* (1988) is a straight line projection of an overcrowded "condomundo" where alienated young people do designer drugs with eyedroppers, drive automobiles with electronic guidance systems, and toy with terrorism against the transnational corporations that twist their coils around every activity. In *Pacific Edge* (1990), the alternative is a federation of ecologically sensitive communities organized around the "small is beautiful" precepts of Ernest Schumacher and the principles of social ecology and mutual aid articulated by political philosopher Murray Bookchin.[40] Americans have used the political process to gradually rein in corporate America and focus self-government at the local level, although each community remains part of a larger world economy.

Robinson builds in specific continuities across the three books, a characteristic that he reinforces with a reference in *Pacific Edge* to Lawrence Durrell's Alexandria Quartet of novels that retell the same story from four points of view. Like much historical writing, the stories are grounded on the importance of place—a particular stretch of coast from Point Dana to San Onofre, the ridges and canyons that trail off the Santa Ana Mountains. The protagonist in each is a young man who matures, in part, by attracting and then failing to hold a strong woman. Each book makes it clear from the roster of characters that Orange County in the twenty-first century will be as much Latino as Anglo. The character Tom Barnard appears in each book at the end of a very different but logically derived life. The storyteller of *The Wild Shore* and the diary keeper of *Pacific Edge*, he ends his life in *The Gold Coast* in a nursing home, reminiscing to occasional visitors. And the books share an explicitly historical motif of digging up the past. Each opens with a group of friends wielding shovels—trekking to abandoned San Clemente to loot a grave for imagined treasure in *The Wild Shore*, digging beneath the street for the fun of discovering relics of the twentieth century in *The Gold Coast*, cheerfully sharing required community work on a street project in *Pacific Edge*.

The trilogy is a set of variations on the common trope of "seeing the future in California." An imposing scholarly literature that examines the ways in which greater Los Angeles served through the twentieth century as the summary or shorthand for the American future, "the mystic writing pad for forecasts both delightful and dismal" in Kerwin Klein's apt phrase. More than half a century ago, Carey McWilliams argued that California was twenty years ahead of the rest of the nation. Los Angeles, claimed Neil Morgan in 1960, was "the center of gravity in the westward tilt" that was creating the America of tomorrow in the West of today.[41] In recent years, yet another scholarly generation has declared greater Los Angeles as the prototype for the twenty-first-century city. A "Los Angeles School" of urban studies now argues that the SoCal metropolis manifests a new, postmodern urban form and dynamic. As argued by Allen J. Scott, Michael Dear, Edward Soja, and others, this is a metropolis whose flexibility and decentralization exemplifies not the past but a coming future. And it is a metropolis where Orange County may seem to express the newest of the new as a postsuburban exopolis that can only be understood through fragmentary snapshots.[42] The county's popular image of political conservatism and frantic consumption (as in the television series *The O.C.*) in fact collides with its growing ethnic pluralism and political competitiveness.

Place—the Orange County setting—thus matters as the key to the trilogy's impact as well as serving as a factor in each narrative. It seems unlikely that a Fort Wayne trilogy or a Preble County, Ohio, trilogy, no matter how carefully done, would attract the same readership. As Robinson has agreed, Orange County's role as an "awful paradigm for the future . . . could not be replaced by just any American city or suburb."[43] All three of Robinson's futures gain resonance as subtle departures and challenges to the standard dystopian California of *Blade Runner* (1982) and the fictional variations on a Los Angeles apocalypse that Mike Davis summarized in *The Ecology of Fear* (1998).[44] Davis roots his dark vision in *City of Quartz* (1992) in the economic failure of his southern California hometown of Fontana. In contrast, Tom Barnard in *Pacific Edge* explicitly identifies the California of *his* childhood in the 1980s as a "pocket utopia."

> California when I was a child was a child's paradise, I was healthy, well fed, well clothed, well housed, I went to school and there were libraries with all the world in them and after school I played in orange groves and in Little League and in the band and down at the beach and every day was an adventure, and when I came home my mother and father created a home as solid as rock, the world seemed solid! And it comes to this, do you understand me—I grew up in utopia.
>
> But I didn't. Not really. Because while I was growing up in my sunny seaside home much of the world was in misery, hungry, sick . . . I had been on an island. . . .
>
> And if—if! if someday the whole world reaches utopia, then that dream California will become a precursor, and sign of things to come, and my childhood is redeemed.[45]

To get to that dream is to engage in politics, for the challenges and mechanics of democratic self-government set another theme that cuts across the three books. Taken together, the books are an examination of how history might happen as well as what history might mean. *The Wild Shore* contrasts local town meeting democracy with a strong-man government that emerges from the ruins of San Diego. The second and third books describe unsuccessful and successful ways to undercut the military-industrial complex. *The Gold Coast* comes closest to incorporating Orange County's popular image of political conservatism, military dependence, and mindless consumption.[46] Several of the characters rebel against the narrow horizons, but efforts at resistance are little more than slapdash terrorism that turn out not only to be ineffective but also to be corrupted by corporate power. The final book, *Pacific Edge*, takes a very different approach by foregrounding the processes of representative democracy—lobbying, bargaining, the use and abuse of bureaucratic rules to advance local interests. In the background narrative, improvements have been achieved incrementally, with political mobilization and organizing over many decades. In the intense local debate over developing a portion of the town's remaining open space, change again comes by increment through lobbying and votes in the town council.[47]

Pacific Edge thus sees utopia as "the process of making a better world, the name for one path history can take, a dynamic, tumultuous, agonizing process, with no end."[48] This preferred Orange County is achieved through legislation. The participants reflect the county's actual ethnic variety rather than its all-white image and represent the possibility of building coalitions across ethnic boundaries. Political participation matters, the process is more important than the end state, and victories can be real, even if small and sometimes morally ambiguous. In Robinson's view, "utopia has to be rescued as a word, to mean 'working towards a more egalitarian society, a global society.'" Utopia is "a road of history, something we are working within."[49]

Wise Provincialism

Pacific Edge, at least in part, is an argument for the "wise provincialism" advocated by American philosopher Josiah Royce (1855–1916). A child of Gold Rush California and one of the first graduates of the new University of California, Royce spent most of his adult career teaching at Harvard as a colleague of William James and later Frederick Jackson Turner. His ideas about politics and society, however, were deeply rooted in his understanding of California's formative decades (just as Robinson has been shaped by the character and feel of the Pacific West). Royce viewed that history as a great struggle between unchecked individualism and the moderating power of community. His solution to social disorder was to emphasize the importance of "wise provincialism" as the counter to "the brutal freedom" of the pioneers. Provincialism—loyalty to places and communities and the opportunities they may offer to all members—arises from the continued interactions of people and nature (or, Forty-Niners and the California frontier in the example that Royce studied). Community does not just happen; it has to be constructed, tended, and valued. "We are all but dust save as this social order gives us life," he wrote at the end of his history of Gold Rush

California. "If we turn again and serve the social order, and not merely ourselves, we soon find that what we are serving is simply our own highest spiritual destiny in bodily form."[50]

Royce's vision resonated—perhaps unexpectedly—with that of his colleague Fred Turner. Contrary to the easy opinion that Turner celebrated the frontier in all its excess, his model held the hope of promoting democratic virtue and community values alongside individual initiative. As the nation developed, Turner wrote in 1903, the watchword of the frontier became "a steady increase of the social tendency" and a "growing magnitude of social achievement." Fifty years later, historians Stanley Elkins and Eric McKitrick restated the civic impacts of the frontier. The challenges of problem-solving and community-making in new settlements, they argued, demanded wide participation, cooperation, voluntary association, and support for public institutions. Far from undermining the civil community, the frontier balanced individual competition against the needs of the larger group. As Alexis de Tocqueville had observed, westward expansion reproduced egalitarian and participatory communities across the continent. Indeed, Americans settled the West not as individuals but as members of interlocking communities.[51]

Wise provincialism is the message of *Pacific Edge*, and it is also at the center of Ursula K. Le Guin's curious and challenging novel *Always Coming Home* (1985).[52] The book tells about the Kesh, an agricultural people living in the Valley of the Na River in northern California. They are a people in an alternative timeline, "who might be going to have lived a long, long time from now." Le Guin's California has been shaped by geological upheaval. Volcanoes have erupted. Tectonic plates have slipped and shaken. There are lands at a distance that were poisoned by radioactivity or chemicals, but the new California is the creation of the Earth itself: "There had been some very large and recent events on the geological scale . . . all of which had, among other effects, left most of what we know as the Great Valley of California a shallow sea or salt marsh, and brought the Gulf of California on up into Arizona and Nevada."[53]

Le Guin has a deeply felt sense of place, and her affection for the northwestern quadrant of North America is a constant substrate for her books. From maps that Le Guin carefully provides, we see that the Na Valley is a version of the Napa Valley (indeed, its chief product for trade remains wine). The setting allows the author to revisit the landscape where she spent summers as the daughter of a Berkeley anthropologist and a writer. Indeed, the land is lovingly depicted as "austere . . . generous but not lush," where long, dry summer turns suddenly into wet, foggy winter, a land whose people intimately learn its meadows, rivers, roads, hills, and canyons. A resident of Portland for nearly forty years, she set *The Lathe of Heaven* (1971) in that city and drew the landscapes of other books from the wider Northwest—the Oregon desert for *The Tombs of Atuan* (1971), the islands, shores, and fjords of Puget Sound and British Columbia for the maritime world of the several Earthsea tales.[54] Her descriptions of place echo Robinson's equally affectionate depiction of Orange County's mountains and canyons, which serves to ground the *Pacific Edge* community.

Always Coming Home is not a traditional novel with a unified plot. Instead, Le Guin gives us a potpourri of anthropological data. One of the voices is an archeologist from even further in the future, or perhaps from "outside the world," as the Kesh refer to the social order that preceded theirs. There are poems, songs, legends, and fables of the Kesh, drawings of artifacts, descriptions of burial customs, musical instruments and food, a glossary, charts showing the "lodges" and "societies" through which the Kesh sort themselves, and other such chunks of data. There are also stories recounted by different members of the Kesh, about daily lives and adventures. It is unlikely that any reader has opened the book, started with the three introductions, and read straight through to the glossary and final poem. It is designed for sampling, as one might wander through the collections of a museum.

The Kesh are a deceptive people. They seem to be—are—tribal and spiritual. Their lives are regulated by clans and septs and totems. They are literate, but they prefer to describe the world through recited poems and parables. Ritual, ceremony, and dance are important. They make no distinction between human and natural history. They seem in some aspects a sort of hippie feminist commune who've worked out the problems of sharing and responsibility, or, in another view, a people who follow a blend of European folk wisdom and Native American spirituality. Coyote figures in one of their origin stories, and Le Guin has commented that "Native American literary texts . . . served me as an unfailing inspiration for an ethic and aesthetic native to the western American earth."[55]

But the Kesh are not isolated and ignorant; nor are they always nice. Their young people sometimes wage unnecessary, deadly wars against their neighbors. Some Kesh are richer and some are poorer. They make careful and selective use of complex technologies to support their misleadingly simple lives. They have maps of the world and know where their valley lies, although few are interested in anything beyond their future California. They operate a railroad, but with wood-burning steam locomotives. They also can communicate with the "City of Mind," a vast complex of computers that has taken on a life of its own and exists in 11,000 nodes scattered around the globe.[56] Nevertheless, these complex technologies are not central to the lives of the Kesh; they are tools like any other, to be used in the real work of inhabiting their place consciously and carefully.[57]

Le Guin contrasts the Kesh with the Condor people through the narrative of Stone Telling, a young Kesh woman who goes to join her Condor father far to the north. Stone Telling's story is by far the longest segment of the book, and the part that reads most like a conventional quest narrative. She travels to meet her father, is taken into his city and household, learns to deal with new customs, comes to realize that her new home is inferior to her old, escapes, and returns to her original town. She, and we, learn that the Condor people are devoted to war and conquest. Nomads from the east, they have come to California as conquerors. Their society is rigidly divided among warriors, workers, serfs, and women, with the elite living in a sterile "City" rather than natural towns. With fierce insistence on individual status, they can manage war but not politics. Their society eventually collapses under the burdens of waging war and trying to reconstruct superweapons like tanks and airplanes with plans from the computer network but without an adequate industrial base, a fatal example of their inability to temper their competitive individualism with the compromises of political debate. They embody the wrong way to construct a lasting society, and the valley people decide in retrospect that "the Condor people seem to have been unusually self-isolating; their form of communication was through aggression, domination, exploitation, and enforced acculturation. In this respect they were at a distinct disadvantage among the introverted but cooperative peoples native to the region."[58]

Le Guin's preferred alternative of political action comes in a shorter story segment about "The Trouble with the Cotton People." For many years, the people of the Na Valley have traded wine for cotton grown at the southern end of the Inland Sea. Recently, however, the quality of the cotton has plunged, causing the Kesh to reduce their wine shipments and then to send emissaries south, where none of them has visited for forty or fifty years. When the delegation finally arrives, after some mild adventures on their voyage, they engage in talk, and more talk, and more talk. The cotton people harangue the Kesh about reducing the wine shipments and sending back the shoddiest goods. The Kesh then compliment the Cotton people, never complaining about the inferior product but leaving openings for explanation. It goes on for one, two, three, four days, until the cotton people slowly reveal that they've been having troubles with drought and excess salinity. After a week, they renegotiate the contract with some compromise on both sides. The cotton people, it turns out, are "not unreasonable, except in . . . being ashamed to admit they have had troubles," and successful politics is about finding common ground, no matter how long the search may take.[59]

Always Coming Home embodies ideas that Le Guin previously outlined in her essay "A Non-Euclidean View of California as a Cold Place to Be." That essay critiques the common European and American approach to utopia as an end state to be reached by a linear string of decisions. Instead, she proposes a utopia of process, a yin utopia to contrast with the "big yang motorcycle trip" of progress. We might reach such a state that "we would do well to find a rock crevice and go backward" to find roots in the land and to seek the Spirit of Place. A yin utopia would be like the Pacific Northwest, "dark, wet, obscure, weak, yielding, passive, participatory, circular, cyclical, peaceful, nurturant, retreating, contracting, and cold."[60]

Successful politics for Le Guin, as for Robinson, is thus an expression of culture, depends on community, and works through talk. The Kesh share their obligations to their common homeland, and they treat other groups such as the cotton people with the respect they expect for themselves. In Le Guin's work, the Kesh contrast not only with the Condor people but also with the isolated individuals in *Searoad* (1991), a set of stories about the late twentieth-century Oregon coast which shade into magical realism. When they wash up at the literal edge of the world, the characters in *Searoad* find that the frustrations of everyday life lead to failures of communication between wife and husband, parent and child, lover and lover, and things end with a sigh in the muffling mist. *Always Coming Home* takes on the same details of everyday life but explores the multiple possibilities and failures of communication as the tools for constructing a viable society. *Searoad* starts with the impersonality of the landscape: "The rain women are very tall; their heads are in the clouds. Their gait is the pace of the storm-wind, swift and stately. They are tall presences of water and light walking the long sands against the darkness of the forest. They move northward, inland, upward to the hills. They enter the clefts of the hills unresisting, unresisted, light into darkness, mist into forest, rain into earth."[61] *Always Coming Home* ends with people in place:

> There is a valley, high hills around it.
> There is a river, willows on its shores.
> There are people, their feet are beautiful,
> dancing by the river in the valley.[62]

6 On the Urban Edge

> *The west side [of South Comb Two] looked out across the old communities of Inglewood Culver City and Santa Monica, now covered with great reddish brown slashes as the old city was leveled and new combs encroached upon shadow. . . . Here and in the stabilized deep sunk pads of Malibu was where the notyetchosen waited for vacancies within the combs.*
> —Greg Bear, *Queen of Angels* (1990)

> *The city was like a great mind, a matrix of ideas, concepts pressed into concrete and asphalt, and he was the center of consciousness traveling that mind, touching first on one idea—one location in the city—and then another, the street addresses laid out in orderly array, one leading to the next, like the pathways of free association.*
> —John Shirley, *City Come A-Walkin'* (1980)

San Narciso, California

Political experiments may be attempted most easily when the slate is blank or the landscape is empty—on new planets in need of a constitution, in utopian communities tucked somewhere in the hills. But political ideas and institutions face their greatest challenges in great cities—those intense concentrations of people and activity that require constant adjustments among the rights and needs of their residents. The western conception of public life comes out of cities, from the *polis* of the Greeks and the *civitas* of the Romans. We have seen that Kim Stanley Robinson offers a positive take on Martian urbanization, but what about places closer to home? What potentials and problems do science fiction writers find in the western supercities of San Francisco and Los Angeles? What sort of futures have they envisioned, especially those writers who have grown up as part of the urbanization of the West or observed its cities at first hand?

One of the latter is Thomas Pynchon, whose slim novel *The Crying of Lot 49* (1966) is a headlong rush through the California of the mid-1960s. Pynchon crafted an intricate architecture of commentary and epistemology and overlaid it with a thick stucco of literary and historical allusions. The book revels in the everyday detail of California's cold war communities. It also imagines that a secret society might run a shadowy alternative postal system outside the view of the state. For literary critics, the book is a delightful stew of ambiguities that fuel endless interpretive arguments.

First—and perhaps foremost—*Crying* is a giddy satirical take on California places and people. The scenes stretch from a Tupperware party to a motel swimming pool, from subdivisions to suburban industrial parks. The heroine, Mrs. Oedipa Maas, encounters a grand range of California types. Among others are a right-wing conspiracy nut who thinks that John Birchers are communist dupes, a swastika salesman with a great business in Orange County, an experimental theater director, an aspiring rock band, a hip professor, protohippies in Golden Gate Park, defense engineers who congregate in a nerd bar where the jukebox plays the music of Karl Heinz Stockhausen, and a private security force of "one-time cowboy actors and L.A. motorcycle cops."[1]

Pynchon's fiction is also a meditation on the problems of communication. The action begins with a letter informing Oedipa that she's been named executor for the estate of Pierce Inverarity, a Southern California investor and real estate developer who is also her former lover. She relocates temporarily from northern California to the Southern California city of San Narciso, where she slowly discovers the extent of his investments. She also begins to encounter and trace the presence of an alternative postal system: What's its true name (WASTE? Tristero?)? Does it trace back to medieval Europe, or is it a practical joke by Pierce Inverarity? Is it benign or malevolent? Is it a set of secret revolutionaries or a passel of extortionists? Described in loving, parodic detail is a play within the novel, a gory renaissance revenge drama called *The Courier's Tragedy* that may or may not concern the mysterious postal system. Oedipa tries to find out by tracing down a variant passage through multiple scholarly editions derived from obscure manuscripts, an enterprise that graduate students in English can especially appreciate. She is continually frustrated by her failure to resolve the ambiguities, even at the book's end, which leaves Oedipa and readers both waiting for the outcome of an auction (the "crying of lot 49").[2]

With one foot firmly on the everyday ground of urban California and the other planted in a parallel universe of satiric excess, *The Crying of Lot 49* joined a long-running debate about the urban future of the American West. Despite the dominant imagery of Klondikers, cowboys, and homesteaders, the West has always been a region of cities. A century ago—in 1900—more than half of all Californians and more than a third of Coloradans, Washingtonians, and Montanans already lived in cities. By 2000, metropolitan areas accounted for more than 80 percent of the residents of California, Washington, Texas, Colorado, Arizona, and New Mexico and more than 70 percent of Utah, Hawaiʻi, and Oregon. Eight of the nation's ten fastest-growing metro areas in the 1990s were in the West, led by an explosive 83 percent growth in boomtown Las Vegas. The region's ten largest urban areas in 2000 had 49,568,434 people by official count—53 percent of the entire West.[3]

If the West is now a set of supercities scattered across sparsely settled countryside, writers who deal with the regional future have to factor in its cities and city life. The implication of the census numbers, as Pynchon knew as early as the 1960s, is that suburb-packed and fast-growing Southern California *is* the western norm, and, by extension, the norm for its nation. This is what Oedipa realizes as she explores Southern California and its multitude of real estate developments: "San Narciso had no boundaries. No one knew yet where to draw them. She had dedicated herself, weeks ago to making sense of what Inverarity had left behind, never suspecting that the legacy was America."[4]

The Crying of Lot 49 is thus a skewed fictional contribution to the vigorous ongoing enterprise of reading the future from Los Angeles. Many commentators have taken L.A. to be the representative city for the later twentieth century—the example that succeeds Manchester, England, Paris, and Chicago.[5] Visitors after World War II called it a "leading city" or "the prototype of the supercity," or even the "ultimate city." Journalist Richard Austin Smith thought that it was "emerging as the forerunner of the urban world of tomorrow." Richard Elman traveled to the Los Angeles suburb of Compton "with the thought in mind that this was the future . . . what lies in store for all of the new suburbs of all the big cities of America." From Frenchman Jean Baudrillard to American Fredric Jameson, sophisticated cultural critics have offered Los Angeles as a prime exhibit for what is wrong (and occasionally right) about American cities, and as a warning for the twenty-first century.[6]

Intellectuals by the 1960s were staring down their noses at a place that was on the pivot of change. Southern California was still riding a wave of popular appreciation as a potential paradise. The aerospace industry was booming. New suburbs such as Lakewood may have been monotonous and all white, but they were also peaceful and affordable.[7] The California university system was opening opportunity for everyone. Disneyland was new, and the surfing subculture was being discovered and popularized. Young people elsewhere in the United States knew the region for the beaches where Gidget, Annette, Frankie, and California girls all hung out.[8] But 1964 brought the free speech movement in Berkeley, 1965 saw the rebellion in Watts, and 1967 ushered in the Summer of Love in San Francisco. Critics would soon be describing Los Angeles with references to the dark dystopia of *Blade Runner* (1982), the violent alienation of *Falling Down* (1993), and the new noir of *L.A. Confidential* (1997).

So *Crying* appeared at a point of overlap and conflict between different ways of imagining Southern California, allowing Pynchon the full enjoyment of ambiguity, challenging Californian self-satisfaction but also delighting in the surface glitter and giving the state a place of importance. In joining this tangled discourse, he certainly incorporated the common critique of Los Angeles as repetition, a place that endlessly recycles standardized urban components into many, many San Narcisos. At the same time that Pynchon was dreaming up his thickets of allusions and wordplay, historian Robert Fogelson was completing a history of Los Angeles with the title *The Fragmented Metropolis* (1967).[9] Its only pattern, according to another overwrought observer, has been "helter-skelter" growth into a "noncity" or "nowhere city"—"topless, bottomless, shapeless and endless . . . random, frenzied, rootless, and unplanned." There is no center to the Southern California metropolis through which Oedipa moves, only fragmented scenes that are connected by highways, much like the landscape fragments and disconnected scenes of the film *Pulp Fiction* (1994). And there is no deep identity to San Narciso itself: "Like many named places in California it was less an identifiable city than a grouping of concepts—census tracts, special purpose bond-issue districts, shopping nuclei, all overlaid with access roads to its own freeway."[10]

By the 1990s, as we've noted, some observers were making a virtue from necessity, seeing greater SoCal as the model of the new postmodern metropolis where cityscape, economy, and society are fragmented, flexible, fluid, not so much formless as constantly in re-formation.[11] The region is indeed multicentric and multicultural. Los Angeles does have a downtown, despite rumors to the contrary, but its economy has been driven by widely dispersed industrial clusters—aircraft production in the San Fernando Valley and the southwestern side of the city, entertainment production in Hollywood and Burbank, clothing and jewelry clusters near downtown, old manufacturing in a corridor leading south from the center, and half a dozen distinct high-tech clusters.[12] Los Angeles is a "new Ellis Island," receiving tens of thousands of Latino and Asian immigrants each year. In 2000, according to the U.S. census, just over half of the region's 17 million people described themselves as non-Latino whites, and 47 percent of adults regularly spoke a language other than English in their home.

In its obsession with information, order, and entropy, *Crying* ultimately anticipates the excitement of the "L.A. school" rather than repeating the complaints of East Coast journalists. Pynchon steps beyond demographic trends and social critique to understand cities as great machines for facilitating and channeling—and frustrating—communication. This is exactly what cities are, of course: complex networks of places and institutions whose fundamental purpose is to bring people and ideas together. Tristero's posthorn symbol is chalked on San Francisco sidewalks, scratched on the back of a bus seat, stitched on gang members' jackets, tacked on a Laundromat bulletin board, tucked under the pillars of an elevated freeway. As she tracks clues through the city, Oedipa works through a long inventory of transportation. As she walks, rides city buses, haunts the airport, and hops a lift on a jitney, her actions not only refer to Tristero's role as a communication system but also refer back to the West's historic reliance on transportation innovations, from the Pony Express and transcontinental railroad to automobile freeways. Oedipa sees San Narciso, the quintessential suburb of Southern California and Inverarity's biggest development, as pure communication system and one—via computers—anticipating the future: She "looked down a slope, needing to squint for the sunlight, into a vast sprawl of houses. . . . The ordered swirl of houses and streets, from this high angle, sprang at her now with the same unexpected, astonishing clarity as the circuit card had."[13]

Embedded in its cultural critique and its own version of sociological science fiction, the novel also suggests multiple readings of urban California that resonate in science fiction views of the near future. In each case, these approaches highlight the continued importance of place in spite of the pressures of placelessness expressed in the anti-California critique. The next section examines how the possibilities of American culture are projected onto the future of Greater San Francisco. In contrast, the section that follows it shows how dangerous economic and social trends that seem to be shaping and undermining American cities are extended into the future of Southern California. The concluding section explores one of the ways that the possibilities of cybernetic technology itself are extrapolated into a world of cyberplaces that look a lot like bits and fragments of real cityscapes.

Just like 1967?

Pynchon's Southern California is generic—and fake. For the most part it is filled with physically indistinguishable commercial strips, ranch houses, and the YoYoDyne factory where employees serenade their company to the borrowed tune of the Cornell University alma mater. When its builders try something different, all they can think of is to imitate other places. Inverarity's Orange County development of Fangoso Lagoons is city as theme park long before cultural critics adopted the metaphor. Fangoso "was to be laced by canals with private landings for power boats, a floating social hall in the middle of an artificial lake, at the bottom of which lay restored galleons, imported from the Bahamas . . . real human skeletons from Italy; giant clamshells from Indonesia—all for the entertainment of Scuba enthusiasts."[14] It's an amalgam of a gated golf course development and Venice Beach, two of Southern California's instant substitutes for an organically evolving community.

Kim Stanley Robinson's view of Orange County's downward spiral in *The Gold Coast* (1988) has a similar commentary. The twenty-something characters who populate the story have few long-term goals. They party, do drugs, and work jobs that may be socially useful, such as emergency medical rescue, but that promise little for a career. One way they search for a more authentic existence is through clandestine archeology, digging up artifacts from old streets and abandoned gas stations to literally reconnect with the mid-twentieth-century past. The Southern California of the 1960s—the exact era in which *Crying* is set—becomes the golden age to which the tawdry present cannot compare.

Oedipa's Bay Area, in contrast, is detailed and specific. Her wanderings through Berkeley and San Francisco take her to actual places: Shattuck Avenue, Telegraph Avenue, and Sather Gate; the Fillmore neighborhood, Golden Gate Park, Howard Street, the Embarcadero. Passing in the background are people with real lives, energies, and problems: student protesters, overworked cleaning people, gang members, drunken derelicts. Just as popular prejudice would have it, Los Angeles is placeless, but San Francisco is a place.

William Gibson agrees about the very concrete differences between north and south. *Virtual Light* (1993) and *All Tomorrow's Parties* (1999) are near-future crime stories. Their central characters are transplants to California: failed cop Berry Rydell is from Tennessee, bicycle messenger Chevette Washington from Oregon. As they travel between the two California supercities, they presumably judge them as unbiased outsiders. In fact, both novels derive from a short story written for a San Francisco Museum of Modern Art exhibition on "Visionary San Francisco," and they have an unabashed northern slant. When Chevette first sees Los Angeles, her description is like San Narciso in a nutshell: "It sure didn't feel like San Francisco. She felt kind of two ways about it. Like it was just this bunch of stuff, all spread out pretty much at random, and then like it was this really big place . . . and all this energy flowing in it, lighting things up." In contrast, San Francisco is detail and small scale and organic growth. Chevette as a bike messenger has to know her city intimately—the different streets, different buildings, patterns of vehicular and human traffic, shortcuts and danger zones.[15]

Rydell draws the same sort of contrasts. In *All Tomorrow's Parties* he muses that "San Francisco and Los Angeles seemed more like different planets than different cities . . . something that went down to the roots." Previously, in *Virtual Light*, he discovered on his first visit that "Downtown San Francisco was really something. With everything hemmed in by hills, built up and down other hills, it gave Rydell as sense of, well, he wasn't sure. *Being* somewhere. Somewhere in particular. . . . Maybe it just felt so much the opposite of L.A. and that feeling that you were cut loose in a grid of light that just spilled out to the edge of everything. Up here he felt like he'd come in from somewhere."[16] What San Francisco offers is therefore that sense of place that nearly all western literature highlights. Los Angeles is an abstraction, an endless grid with no content of information, and a place that Rydell knows through anonymous hotel rooms and indistinguishable minimarts. San Francisco is not necessarily safer or more comfortable, but it is a city where the details of streets and neighborhoods make a difference.

The most arresting element of the city is the San Francisco–Oakland Bay Bridge, a spontaneous squatter town that has accreted after a quake rendered the bridge unusable. This is neighborhood difference taken to the extreme, even in highly differentiated San Francisco. Over the years, the squatters have built and bolted and glued all sorts of secondary structures to the frame of the bridge, created their own social rules, and managed their own barter economy. There has been no plan, just the synergy from individual actions and choices. The inhabited bridge has "a queer medieval energy," a description that links the improvised community to Lewis Mumford's celebration of the medieval commune as an alternative to the industrial city. The bridge has become a physical expression of the social variety that fuels creativity:

> Its steel bones, its stranded tendons, were lost within an accretion of dreams: tattoo parlors, gaming arcades, dimly lit stalls stacked with decaying magazines, sellers of fireworks, of cut bait, betting shops, sushi bars, unlicensed pawnbrokers, herbalists, barbers, bars. Dreams of commerce, their locations generally corresponding with the decks that had once carried vehicular traffic; while above them, rising to the very peaks of the cable towers, lifted the intricately suspended barrio, with its unnumbered population and its zones of more private fantasy.[17]

The bridge is a place of art and creativity as well as a social escape valve. At night it glows with scrounged and recycled lights. To a Japanese anthropologist, it is a place of discovery and magic: "Fairyland. Rain-silvered plywood, broken marble from the walls of forgotten banks, corrugated plastic, polished brass, sequins, painted canvas, mirrors, chrome gone dull and peeling in the salt air." Gibson thus situates the bridge as a continuation of culturally daring San Francisco. Chevette's friend Tessa, a cinematographer from L.A., loves the bridge because it is "interstitial," a word that Gibson consciously takes from the trendy realm of cultural studies. Another character describes it as an "autonomous zone." It functions like the urban Bohemias of earlier centuries, the places "where industrial civilization went to dream." It is populated by a cross section of the bad and the good, drug addicts and thieves, but also eccentrics and dropouts and artists. It is a metaphor for the excitement and risks of art. "The bridge is no tourist's fantasy," Chevette thinks. "The bridge is real, and to live here exacts its own price."[18]

San Francisco as the nurturing environment for creativity is also the theme of Pat Murphy's postholocaust novel *The City, Not Long After* (1989).[19] A few decades after a plague has wiped out most of the American population, San Francisco is the home to a few hundred survivors who grow a little food, scavenge materials to trade with farmers from Marin, and do public art. Something about the city turns the most unlikely individuals into artists who paint vast neo-Mayan murals over the Transamerica building, fill Market Street with metal figures that mutter to each other in the wind, and turn the streets of Pacific Heights into a huge maze of colored glass and mirrors. One of the characters "organizes" dozens of San Franciscans to repaint the Golden Gate Bridge in multiple hues of blue. Out of the amalgam of art and night and fog, the spirit of the city shows itself to characters in need as angels and spirit guides. The art installations and the aura of the city help the residents fight off an invasion by a tin-pot dictator who has already conquered Sacramento and Modesto and wants to add San Francisco to his empire.

This vision of San Francisco recognizes the city's historic role as cultural center for the West Coast. The city attracted Bohemian writers and artists in the early twentieth century, followed by experimental poets and the City Lights crowd after World War II. Across the bay, the University of California was the only major West Coast university until the broadening of higher education during and after the war. Sexual tolerance and cultural venturesomeness led to the ferment of the 1960s, with radical politics, hippies, psychedelic rock, and the Haight, followed in turn by the commercialized artistic explosion of the dot-com multimedia boom in the 1990s.[20] This outline narrative of San Francisco culture may not necessarily match realities, for the Bay Area is the historic command center of California capitalism, while levels of cultural production by writers, artists, musicians, and designers in Los Angeles are certainly larger in dollar volume and number of people involved. Nevertheless, according to urban economist Richard Florida, the San Francisco region ranks first among U.S. metropolitan areas on a composite "creativity index" and sixth on a more specialized "Bohemian index"—and ahead of L.A. on both counts.[21]

The near-futurists of cyberfiction, in short, are not careful students of sociology and economics. Instead, they adopt the cultural projection and prejudice that sees Los Angeles as generic, repetitive, and inauthentic but San Francisco as real and fundamentally *spirited*. What culture Los Angeles has, say the critics from the left, is market driven. It builds fortunes, and it serves to justify the excesses of capitalism. Its practitioners, says Mike Davis, are mercenaries. In the San Francisco ambiance, in contrast, advertising firms and dot-com entrepreneurs can pass themselves off as multimedia artists. The single-phrase take on Los Angeles is defense workers; for San Francisco, it's groovy artists. It may not be the real San Francisco, but it's fun to imagine.

The Excluded Middle

Pynchon's San Francisco is vibrant, but his Los Angeles is a place that is losing its civic heart. The California shaped by Pierce Inverarity's real estate impulse was either cheap motels or guarded developments, with no common ground or opportunities for social interaction of dissimilar people that sparks new ideas and social directions. Late in her travels of discovery, Oedipa muses about "a set of possibilities . . . that had conditioned the land to accept any San Narciso among its most tender flesh without a reflex or a cry." The result is reduced possibilities: "She had heard all about excluded middles; they were bad shit, to be avoided; and how had that happened here, with the chance once so good for diversity?"[22]

The "excluded middle" is a strong metaphor. In logic it is the argumentative fallacy of stating a question with only two answers in order to force a particular choice, even though many alternatives may actually be available. As applied to urban development, it implies the shrinking of the middle class as a few lucky individuals climb to wealth and the rest sink into poverty. As Oedipa notes, it also implies racial and ethnic segregation and the loss of the social and cultural diversity that generates new ideas.

The polarized and decrepit Los Angeles of Cynthia Kadohata's *In the Heart of the Valley of Love* (1992) is a case in point.[23] Francie, the protagonist, is nineteen years old in 2052, but she lives in an aging city. With her parents dead of a wasting disease that is a metaphor for cultural malaise and economic decline, she's living with her aunt in a run-down Los Angeles bungalow and working for the family's financially marginal delivery service. As her aunt's life falls apart, Francie strikes out on her own to live in tacky apartments, work odd jobs, and attend community college. Her life is a series of ordinary events and small crises. She endures an auto accident, gets fired as a waitress, investigates stories for the college newspaper, goes to unsuccessful parties, finds a boyfriend, gets a tattoo. Francie and her friends are constantly driving across town, but they usually find that one nondescript location doesn't offer much more than another—much like Maria Wyeth in Joan Didion's novel *Play It As It Lays* (1970).

Francie's Los Angeles is leading the downward spiral of the American economy. A new highway system, intended originally to relieve the old freeways, looms unfinished over the landscape, started "before everything ran out of money, back at the beginning of the century." American banks are bailing out of the city, and "hardly anybody was as rich as they'd once been." While Francie lives off her dead-end service jobs, her acquaintances make do with petty crime and an off-books barter economy. The family house, bought by her great-great-grandmother, is now "in a section of town largely abandoned by anyone who mattered to the country's economy." Riots are spreading across the nation, and Francie sometimes wakes to the smell of burning buildings not too many blocks away. Meanwhile, upscale cemeteries maintain armed security guards and the people of "richtown" (her term for places like Brentwood) are increasingly moving to "camps," communities "enclosed by high metal fences and guarded by uniformed, armed men and women."[24]

Kadohata's previous novel dealt with Japanese Americans struggling to reintegrate themselves into American society in the 1950s. For this second book, she imagines a young Japanese American woman in the midfuture rather than the near past. There is nothing comprehensive about her portrayal of America in the 2050s, for Kadohata is more interested in character than the sort of detailed extrapolation found in much science fiction. She posits unimpressive technological changes: Foamite floors are soft and warm, and a pipeline from Alaska helps relieve water rationing, but people still wait at bus stops, use TV remotes, put out newspapers on paper, and wait in line at City Hall. Parking fees remain the biggest student issue at the college. Indeed, the lack of fundamental change is a central part of the message. Fifty years hence, Los Angeles is exhausted, a pale reflection of the more exuberant twentieth century. The city—not to say the nation—is now incapable of reforming itself. Francie's coming-of-age search is not to find where she fits in this fragmented and enervated society, with its vanishing middle class, but to determine whether she is actually "alive"—capable of choosing alternatives and shaping herself by moral choices.[25]

Greg Bear's *Queen of Angels* (1990) is set in nearly the same future time/place (Southern California in 2047). Unlike Kadohata's literary excursion into science fiction, *Queen of Angels* fits comfortably in the genre. Bear's version of Los Angeles is far more technologically charged and strange. His Asian American protagonist, Mary Choy, gets a genetic modification treatment that changes her entire skin color, not a mere tattoo. The novel has a strong plot line organized around a murder mystery (Choy is a police investigator), rather than Kadohata's disconnected vignettes. And the city itself is much younger and stronger, radiating energy and a sense of action:

> Los Angeles was a glory at night. Mary had read once that only a young civilization wasted its light by throwing it into empty space. Earth's young cities still did just that. . . . Canted mirrors reflected light, their edges lumed by warning beacons. . . . streets blazed forth in orange and blue and homes sprinkled white and blue like earthbound stars. . . . Nothing in a city like LA ever stopped; whole communities always active doing thinking.[26]

But Bear's L.A. is still divided between haves and have-nots. The favored residents of Southern California live in vast high rises that stretch along the shoreline and expand ceaselessly into old communities like Inglewood and Culver City: "Viewed from the sea California's southern coastline resembled the wall of a vast prison or some gaily colored wrinkle of basalt cast up by the earth, cooling into cubes and tubes and hexagons and towers filled with lemmings gathered from around the world." Lemmings, of course, are mindless conformists as they migrate en masse. Migrating lemmings presumably plunge westward into the sea off Europe, just as rich Americans are piling up on this western edge of North America. Less successful Californians who can afford only the old twentieth-century neighborhoods live literally and metaphorically in the "shadows." Even the old elite neighborhoods like La Jolla are now relegated to shabby gentility, and "the once ubiquitous doctors and lawyers and heads of corporations had decades before abandoned their beachside palaces to move into the central luxuries of the monuments."[27] There is no problem distinguishing winners from losers, nor leaders from the people consciously out of step with the future.

The exclusion—or extinction—of the middle class that Pynchon, Bear, and Kadohata all note is a central point of contemporary social critiques of Los Angeles. Coming soon to Southern California, or already arrived, say novelists and social scientists alike, is the deeply divided metropolis of global capitalism. Urban sociologists such as Saskia Sassen in *The Global City* (2001) and Manuel Castells in *The Information City* (1997) see the global market sorting the world into winners and losers—among nations, within nations, within cities. The metropolitan command centers of the international economy, they argue, are increasingly bifurcated societies in which a growing servant class tends the needs and wants of the bankers, advertising executives, consultants, and corporate executives who run the world. What's disappearing is an urban middle class. Local businesses fall to global franchises, routine white-collar jobs evaporate, and neighborhoods become either derelict slums or protected enclaves of privilege.[28]

This analysis has been notably applied to Los Angeles by Mike Davis. His *City of Quartz: Excavating the Future in Los Angeles* (1990) and *The Ecology of Fear* (1998) are bitter indictments of the ways in which the large land owners and their hangers-on have shaped the metropolis to their own benefit and to the detriment of everyone else. The founding dynasty of greater Los Angeles, associated with the *Los Angeles Times*, banks, oil companies, and land speculators, presided over "one of the most centralized—indeed, militarized—

municipal power structures in the United States. They erected the open shop on the bones of labor, expelled pioneer Jews from the social register, and looted the region through one great real-estate syndication after another." In the last half century, horizontal growth and the rise of entertainment, aerospace, and electronics industries have fragmented the single power elite, but the result is more of the same: "Darwinian place wars as new centers and their elites, from Century City to Orange County's Golden Triangle, have challenged the squirearchy of Downtown L.A." In the process, Southern California's poor have become more diverse—Asian and Latino as well as Anglo American—but remain under the thumb of the wealthy.[29]

The physical result of unequal power, says Davis, is the creation of Fortress L.A. In the San Fernando Valley, the middle class tries to defend its status by protecting home values and neighborhood exclusivity with every political tool available. The Los Angeles Police Department helps by barricading off poorer neighborhoods to halt drug sales. On the south side of the city, police department helicopters hover over the poor neighborhoods of South Central and play their searchlights along its mean streets, while police ground forces mount search-and-destroy operations against gangs and drug houses. Meanwhile, "the carefully manicured lawns of West Los Angeles sprout forests of ominous little signs warning 'Armed Response!' Even richer neighborhoods in the canyons and hillsides isolate themselves behind walls guarded by gun-toting private police and state-of-the-art electronic surveillance." Downtown high rises give cold shoulders to the surrounding city, and every tiny detail of design—down to bus stop benches—drives the public out of "public" space. "Welcome to post-liberal Los Angeles, where the defense of luxury lifestyles is translated into a proliferation of new repressions in space and movement."[30] A bitterly witty diagram in the *Ecology of Fear* puts the pieces together in a parody of standard sociological models of urban form: In place of downtown, working-class zone, and middle-class suburbs are "natural" districts labeled Neighborhood Watch, Narcotics Enforcement Zone, Prostitution Abatement Zone, Med-Fly Quarantine Zone, Urban Simulator, and Toxic Rim.

The bifurcated city that social analysts described for the 1980s and 1990s has also been the template for the future Los Angeles. It is part of the background for Kadohata and Bear. It has been in the foreground of William Gibson's version of Southern California, which comes straight from Mike Davis. In Gibson's books, and others, science fiction's dominant take of the future of SoCal is a series of contrasts between the "street life" of minimarts and the self-contained high rises and gated suburbs that were increasingly a prominent part of the frenzied Southern California real estate scene at the end of the twentieth century. Neal Stephenson in *Snow Crash* (1992), for another example, anticipates a city of burbclaves, each of which hires mercenaries from major firms like WorldBeat Security, claims national sovereignty, and enters into security treaties with neighboring burbs. "Under the provisions of The Mews at Windsor Heights Code," says a Deputy of Metacops Unlimited who has just snared a skateboarder trying to get into a gated burb, "we are authorized to enforce law, national security concerns, and societal harmony" on the territory of White Columns. The skateboarder has run afoul of "a treaty between The Mews at Windsor Heights and White Columns" that "authorizes us to place you in temporary custody until your status as an Investigatory Focus has been resolved."[31]

"Fortress L.A." becomes literal in *Oath of Fealty* (1981) by Larry Niven and Jerry Pournelle. After a massive super-Watts riot has devastated South Central Los Angeles, European money has funded the construction of Todos Santos, a vast city under a single roof. Modeled on the arcologies (massive, self-contained superbuildings) proposed by visionary architect Paolo Soleri, Todos Santos is two miles square and rises a thousand feet from the ground.[32] At the time of the story, sections of the framework are still being filled in with apartment modules. Its population stands at 247,453, close to the design goal of 275,000. The arcology functions under the jurisdiction of Los Angeles, but just barely, using its huge economic clout to fend off most rules and regulations. It has made itself an integral part of the metropolitan economy through its purchases and by building its own subway that makes its three-mile-long shopping mall the downtown for all of L.A.[33]

So far, so good, but Todos Santos is also a virtual city-state and fiercely defended territory. Outsiders can spend their money at the mall, but they can't penetrate any further without passing thick security checks. A wide surveillance zone where grass has grown over the bones of the old neighborhood reaches out from its walls. Beyond the green moat are block after block of "shabby houses and decaying apartments . . . a mockery to city government . . . houses filled with families without hope living on welfare—and on the leavings from Todos Santos."[34] Service entrances bear large signs reading "IF YOU GO THROUGH THIS DOOR YOU WILL BE KILLED," warnings that are enforced (reluctantly) with poison gas. The plot revolves around efforts by environmental radicals to disrupt and sabotage the "termite hill" and its fierce, successful response.

Niven and Pournelle, who have a reputation as extreme right-wingers, are actually more thoughtful than the thimble-sized plot suggests. They understand that Todos Santos is a utopian experiment as well as a technical marvel. Because the story is told from the point of view of the capsule city's supersmart managers, readers want their self-defense to succeed. But the authors also understand that the arcology is like an elite private school that skims off the best, brightest, and most suitable applicants and leaves the rest of Los Angeles outside. The ecoradicals have a point: it consumes far more resources per capita than does a normal city. The idealistic deputy mayor of L.A., who serves as the "worthy" antagonist, argues that Todos Santos is inexorably turning its back on common responsibilities, leaving the civic "middle" under more and more stress as fewer resources are available for social equity. He is, in effect, the voice for the Great Society, while Todos Santos epitomizes the privatizing ideology launched in the Reagan years and carried forward by George W. Bush.

Todos Santos offers a conception of community that seems antithetical to the values of the libertarian authors. Outside is the world of amoral competition, crooked corporations, corrupt politicians, and ordinary people trying to survive among predators. "Isolation is what we're selling," says one of the leaders. People come to get away from crime and bureaucracy, to get independence. Inside is a world of shared values and expectations. "A hundred thousand eyes," muses an opponent, "but they're all looking inward. No privacy at all, and no interest in what goes on out here."[35] Todos Santos folks are low-key and trusting because they all share the same goals. People are polite. Informal mores and customs are more important than formal rules—a sort of idealization of small-town solidarity. It is "a city at peace with its police force. *Our* guards, *our* police, holding *our* civilization together." Is it an anthill, a utopia, or a commune with the petit bourgeois in place of hippies?[36]

The fortress is equally literal in Octavia Butler's *Parable of the Sower* (1993), where the extinction of the middle plays out in fire and blood. I've already discussed Lauren Olamina, the book's central character, as the founder of a utopian experiment. Here we return to the earlier part of her story as she grows up in a collapsing Los Angeles, the social baseline that helps to explain her fierce desire to build a welcoming community. In 2024, the internal combustion era is over, with rusting vehicles cannibalized for metal and plastic and three-car garages turned into rabbit hutches. In this quiet apocalypse, potable water costs more than gasoline. To be clean is to make a target of yourself, so "Fashion helps. You're supposed to be dirty now." A money economy survives, but barter is taking its place. The shrinking middle class holds on and hopes for better times, but even police protection has become fee for service. Foreign corporations are buying up the United States and turning Americans into agricultural slaves or white-collar debt peons in defended enclaves. Teenaged Lauren Olamina, the book's central character, muses about the new economy:

> Maybe Olivar is the future—one face of it. Cities controlled by big companies are old hat in science fiction. My grandmother left a whole bookcase of old science-fiction novels. The company-town subgenre always seemed to star a hero who outsmarted, overthrew, or escaped "the company." I've never seen one where the hero fought like hell to get taken in and underpaid by the company. In real life, that's the way it will be. That's the way it is.[37]

Middle-class families live in constant fear inside walled suburban cul-de-sacs. Adults venture outside on jobs or errands, but only in daylight and always on watch: "That's the rule. Go out in a bunch, and always go armed."[38] Lauren's walled street of eleven houses is somewhere in the San Fernando Valley, a sad survivor of the valley isolationism described by Mike Davis. The whole community learns to handle guns; the only safe respite from the tiny community is a group excursion for target practice in the surrounding ravines, where they are likely to encounter feral dogs and human corpses. As far as possible, Lauren's neighbors live to themselves, growing as much food as they can, home-schooling each other's children, acting as a volunteer fire department and security watch, worrying whether scarce water will continue to flow. The mutual trust that comes so easily in wealthy and secure Todos Santos is a hard-won necessity, all the more valuable and all the more fragile.

Lauren's neighborhood, and others like it behind their own one- and two-block walls, are squeezed between the privileged and the desperate. The rich live in protected communities or mansions protected by many walls, while the poor squat in burned-out houses. On a group expedition out of the neighborhood, Lauren sees the contrast: "Up toward the hills there were walled estates—one big house and a lot of shacky little dependencies where the servants lived. . . . we passed a couple neighborhoods so poor that their walls were made up of unmortared rocks, chunks of concrete, and trash. Then there were the pitiful, unwalled residential areas . . . squatted in by homeless families with their filthy, gaunt, half-naked children." And it gets worse further up into the brown California hills: "There are always a few groups of homeless people and packs of feral dogs living out beyond the last hillside shacks. People and dogs hunt rabbits, possums, squirrels, and each other. Both scavenge whatever dies."[39]

As Lauren comes to realize, her community is staring into the abyss. The older generation hopes that things will get better, get back to normal, but she knows better. Her brother runs away to a short life of robbery, drug dealing, murder, and then his own death. Her father never returns from one of his weekly trips outside the wall. Thieves grow bolder, scaling the wall and cutting the lazor wire, first to strip the gardens, then to ransack houses. Invaders set one house on fire to distract neighbors while they pillage the others, exercising one of the few ways that they can exert any power: by making others as miserable as they are. Three years after the story opens—it's 2027 and Lauren is now eighteen—the community dies in a night of riot and fire, murder and rape. She escapes by luck, returning in the morning to a neighborhood of ash-covered bodies, a host of tattered strangers plundering the ruins and stripping the dead. With the two other survivors out of dozens of neighbors, she salvages what she can and starts the long trek north that will be the road to her new, hard-won, and tentative utopia.

These several books offer contrasting evaluations of the global city of rich and poor. For Niven and Pournelle, whose background is the successful middle class of military-industrial California, the bifurcated city offers a potentially stable solution to urban disorder in the form of the ultimate gated community. Kadohata sees a metropolis in gradual decline, holding together in the center but fraying at the edges of the social fabric. Butler's city is a disaster zone, where minority residents who have done the right thing—climbed into the middle class—find success yanked out from under them. The plight of her family repeats and intensifies the dilemma of African American workers who gained good jobs in the Bay Area and Los Angeles defense industry during and after World War II, only to see the jobs vanish to suburban industrial parks and technology campuses.[40] The only escape that the system offers, and which Lauren rejects, is a virtual reenactment of slavery in the service of the global elite.

City Come A-Walkin'

In *Crying*, communication systems are a metaphor for the course of a life. And they're a mixed metaphor, because Pynchon moves back and forth between images drawn from physical and from electronic systems. He uses a railroad system for life choices made—"Along another pattern of track, another string of decisions taken, switches closed"—and to be made—"She stopped for a minute beside the steel rails . . . knowing as if maps had been flashed from her on the sky how these tracks ran into others, others, knowing they laced, deepened, authenticated the great night around her." A page later, he describes the same options as a binary code. Oedipa pictures her life as "walking among the matrices of a giant digital computer, the zeros and ones twinned above, hanging like balanced mobiles right and left, ahead, think, maybe endless."[41]

If a city, like San Narciso, has the clarity of a circuit card, then the reverse may also hold. For many science fiction writers, the computerized connections that leap across space look like cities. Invisible networks and information nodes may substitute for the traditional connections of spatial proximity and place. Nevertheless, action has to *take place* before it can take on the trappings of fictional narrative. It has to occur in some specific setting where the circuit or the cyberworld functions like a city.

In the case of John Shirley, the city is San Francisco. When Shirley wrote *City Come A-Walkin'* (1980) in the late 1970s, he was as far into the punk scene as you could go and still produce a coherent novel: rock musician, omnipresence in the underground scene in Portland, wild man, writer. William Gibson has called him "cyberpunk's patient zero, first locus of the virus" of hot-edged, plugged-in science fiction.[42] There's a lot to dislike in the book: violence to pump up the plot, long chase scenes to fill out the pages. But there is also a compelling metaphor . . . idea . . . extrapolation. The tall figure in trench coat, hat, and shades that comes walking into Stuart Cole's down-market club in San Francisco is the City, the overmind and avatar of San Francisco itself.

> Cole [stepped outside and] listened to the city, sifting noises. He watched, sorting impressions. What he was looking for was there. It was the presence of the city, the gestalt overpattern uniting its diversity, the invisible relationship between the broken glass in the gutter and the antenna on the limousine. . . . The presence was there, outside. But the personality, the sense of willful intelligence supporting the hum of city activity . . . was indoors, embodied in a man waiting in Cole's club.[43]

Shirley is not the only genre writer to personify San Francisco. Pat Murphy's San Francisco in *The City, Not Long After*, as we've seen, has a spirit that manifests itself through art. There is also a *genius loci* in Fritz Leiber's *Our Lady of Darkness* (1978), a novel that rests on the margin between science fiction and dark fantasy of the sort associated with H. P. Lovecraft and later Stephen King. Its down-market protagonist, a hack writer eking out a living in a low-rent apartment in the posthippie city, slowly realizes that the unconscious dreams and fears of San Francisco's tangled population, concentrated by the very weight and mass of the physical city, are manifesting themselves as a dark, foreboding presence. The plot intertwines with the protagonist's efforts to understand what's happening and to connect the menacing presence to a century-old book called *Megapolisomancy*, in which an imagined student of the occult propounded the theory that monster cities through time have generated dangerous side effects. Now, in the Megapolitan Age, when the world is building dozens of Babylons and Romes, "disastrous blights" of "electro-mephitic city-stuff" have the potential to enshroud and control the people of fog-bound San Francisco and other great cities. The author, reports the protagonist,

> is very much concerned about the "vast amounts" of steel and paper that are being accumulated in big cities. And coal oil (kerosene) and natural gas. And electricity too, if you can believe it—he carefully figures out just how much electricity is in how many miles of wire, how many tons of illuminating gas in tanks, how much paper for government records and yellow journalism. . . . But what he was most agitated about was the psychological or spiritual (he calls them "paramental") effects of all that stuff accumulating in big cities, its sheer liquid and solid mass.[44]

In contrast to the spirit of urban darkness, whose status Leiber deliberately leaves ambiguous, John Shirley's cyberpunk city has the active reality of an artificial intelligence. Shirley starts with the premise, embedded in Cole's musings, that "the city was like a great mind, a matrix of ideas, concepts pressed into concrete and asphalt" and expands the simile into a reality. Where better to explore this conceit than a place whose "fulltime residents have such a strong sense of home in their city; some of them are fanatics about it." Like Leiber's dark lady, City draws energy from both the psychic activity of "hundreds of thousands of very fallible people" and the vast electronic flows of the metropolis along its "electrical neural channels, the interlinked buildings and the loci, the nexus." He—it seems to be male—takes human form at night, communicates over televisions during the day, and is able to control the networks of wires and pipes that constitute the infrastructure of the city. Shirley depicts the gritty San Francisco of seedy rock clubs, porn shops, and cheap apartments and makes its avatar a manipulative, seductive, and dangerous tough guy—a literal cybernetic punk. It sucks Cole into its schemes to fight the tide of suburbanization that would undermine the concentration of energy that keeps it alive and ends up a "beautifully verminous, sweetly squalid, supple but hard-edged *presence*" that trades blow for blow with the mob.[45]

City Come A-Walkin' uses the specificity of San Francisco to explore the idea of a cyber *place*. John Shirley imagines the Internet assuming its own life, but not as one of those commonly depicted abstract artificial intelligences whose distribution over a number of computers renders it colorless and immaterial. Instead, "City" draws on the flux of data and energy to materialize as a human figure—an AI taking on an avatar in the real world rather than a real person taking on an avatar in the metaverse. It uses the resources of its place to manifest as a recognizable big-city badass that/who embodies one important dimension of the historical San Francisco.

Shirley's San Francisco shows two sides in ways that neatly match Martin Green's argument that romances are stories of margins and edges. Stuart Cole runs a barely respectable nightclub in a dangerous corner of town. The action contrasts the worlds of day and night, the visible city of streets and apartments with the invisible city of subterranean conduits, wires, and pulses of energy. The story is rooted in the edgy artistic city of "good" San Francisco, but it also shares some of the menacing shadows, crime syndicates, and social divides of "bad" Los Angeles. The science fiction film *Blade Runner*, made in 1982, two years after publication of Shirley's book, is notoriously a dystopian view of future Los Angeles. It is set in a Southern California from which light has vanished into the ambiance of a noir movie; the climactic scene takes place in the darkly lit Bradbury Building, one of the architectural gems of downtown L.A. But Philip K. Dick set his 1968 novel *Do Androids Dream of Electric Sheep?*, from which the movie was taken, in a San Francisco where fallout plagues have substantially reduced the population and left a city where much of the suburbs are abandoned and many center-city buildings have only one or two occupied apartments among their many.[46] Presumably the filmmakers decided that a downbeat movie and San Francisco didn't go together, but Shirley appreciates Dick's take and knows that the historic and real San Francisco has always had darkness as well as delight.

Beyond Shirley's vigorous metaphor, another implication is clear. Cities are, and will be, systems for creating and ordering information. For Oedipa

Maas, San Narciso and San Francisco are sets of signs that need to be read and decoded. For Gibson and Murphy, San Francisco is a source of and synonym for ideas in motion, a supersized switchboard that is a compelling analogy for the global information network itself. It is also a place where information can be used to good ends. In *Androids*, Dick uses the palatial St. Francis Hotel as the site for an illicit sexual encounter between an android trying to pass for human and the bounty hunter who is tracking other androids. In *The City, Not Long After*, however, the same hotel is part of the network of old spaces that have been reclaimed for art, a place where the female protagonist is slowly able to meet other people, to heal from trauma, and to accept human relationships of friendship and intimacy.

If future San Francisco figures as a real city, where the possibilities and dangers of new ideas are in constant tension, Southern California appears in one science fiction book after another as *stalled* information. Kadohata's protagonist Francie works for a time on her campus newspaper, but the barriers of social class prevent her from using information as effectively as she hopes; she and her friends live beneath the notice of the city's global elite. In *Parable of the Sower* and *Oath of Fealty*, Los Angeles is a system of social relationships set off by stone and concrete, human capacities divided by walls and wire. It is a future in which the possibilities of the American West seem to be freezing into social immobility, where the possibilities of democratic exchange and civic life have been shut off for good.

7 Information Everywhere: Pacific Destinies in the Twenty-First Century

The announcer called out Hackworth's flight [by airship from Shanghai] . . . San Diego with stops in Seoul, Vladivostok, Magadan, Anchorage, Juneau, Prince Rupert, Vancouver, Seattle, Portland, San Francisco, Santa Barbara, and Los Angeles.
—Neal Stephenson, *The Diamond Age* (1996)

We spent a lot of time together that weekend—Bruce [Sterling] and his wife, Nancy, my wife, Edith, and I, Bill Gibson, and various other friends, mostly in the Sterlings' garage apartment, surrounded by Japanese pop music and Bruce's carnivorous plants. We talked a little about literature . . . but mostly we talked about rock and roll, MTV, Japan, fashion, drugs, and politics.
—Lewis Shiner, "Inside the Movement: Past, Present, and Future" (1992)

Console Cowboys

What sort of future is filled with console cowboys and street samurai? In science fiction, it's the information-rich world of intense twenty-first century capitalism imagined by the so-called cyberpunk writers of the 1980s and 1990s. In the backstory against which many of these writers draw their neon-buzzing pictures of things soon to come, it's a world that revolves around the Pacific Ocean and assumes the interpenetration of North American and Asian cultures and economies. It's a world in which empire has taken its course westward from continental America to the rim of the Pacific, where Paris is quaint but Singapore is the future, where the troubled future of California stands for the future of the American experiment.

Console cowboy is a coinage of William Gibson in *Neuromancer* (1984), the most influential book of science fiction's cyberpunk subgenre. In the novel, it applies to Case, a burned-out but still skilled computer hacker. He's a tough guy, not a nerd—a computer punk rather than a wimp.[1] In the international culture of the late twentieth century, *cowboy* became the shorthand term for people who make their own rules and do as they please. The cowboy is a loner who ignores bureaucracies, laws, and cautious advice. At the same time, as Lewis Shiner and others point out, the "console cowboy is a direct linear descendent of the western pulp heroes. His is an adolescent male fantasy to ride unfettered on the consensual range of the matrix, to shoot it out with the bad guys, and finally to head his chrome horse off into a sunset the color of a dead television channel."[2]

Street samurai also comes from *Neuromancer* in the person of Molly, a former prostitute who physically reconstitutes herself as a killer with mirrored eye replacements and cybernetic augmentation. She is an outlaw who wants to bring down the corrupt cybercorporate system. *Street samurai* became a general science fiction term for street fighters and enforcers with biological modifications, synthetic muscles, and electronically enhanced reflexes. Within a decade, Neal Stephenson offered his own satirical science fiction take on the concept in *Snow Crash* (1992), in which lone wolf hero Hiro Protagonist lives in a suburban California storage unit and has attained great skill with his two authentic samurai swords.

The two terms—*cowboy* and *samurai*—also represent the two-way traffic in economic power and cultural icons between the United States and Asia. American culture has deeply penetrated Japan since the postwar occupation. Japan and Okinawa have been essential bases for the projection of American military power in Asia, and Japanese foreign policy has been autonomous only within broad parameters set by the United States. At the same time, Americans since World War II have had a persistent fascination with forms of self-discipline in Asian cultures, from tae-kwan-do to Zen Buddhism. The street samurai image is one more way in which Asian culture comes to America. It quickly entered the world of video games, where the Japanese influence on popular culture is both broad and deep—from Pokemon to pornography—if a bit off the screen for connoisseurs of high culture.

Science fiction that builds on this cultural crossover is one expression of the great transition of American history from an Atlantic to a Pacific era, and the consequent need, in Wallace Stegner's words, to engage a "different and larger universe."[3] The western margin of the United States has long represented a national future in both promotional and imaginative writing. As Henry David Thoreau famously commented in 1851, his feet always took him westward when he stepped out for a walk, for "the future lies that way and the earth seems more unexhausted and richer on that side."[4] In one perspective, science fiction has been directly extending this long narrative of the American nation and its western slope. Americans have seen commercial possibilities in the Pacific since the 1790s.[5] The expansion of national boundaries to and into the Pacific was a major goal of foreign policy leaders from Thomas Jefferson to Theodore Roosevelt, and the assertion of military and economic influence was an equally important theme for the ensuing century. Science fiction about the Pacific future, whether explicitly or implicitly, operates within this story of ambition, expansion, and challenges. Both in direct story lines and in the background assumptions about the shape the world will take, speculative novelists extend the trends and concerns of the American past into the future.

But this science fiction update on the American expectation of a westward-moving empire also complicates the positive narrative of continental expansion with some troubling twists. A number of western science fiction writers who have revisited the trope have approached the turn of the twenty-first century by applying a regional polish to the cutting edge of a new information age. Old and revised visions of a Pacific future have come together to form the underpinning for a group of science fiction writers who are often grouped as "cyberpunk" and "nanotech" speculators. The result is an updating of the American expectation of westward moving empire, but in new forms: a world economy run by Asian nations rather than the United States, a political realm of cybernetic anarchies and autocracies rather than an empire of freedom and prosperity.

This science fiction vision is also situated within the shorter historical context of fifty-year waves in the capitalist economy. Since the eighteenth century, global capitalism has advanced in long cycles of technological innovation, production, and consolidation. In each long wave, certain nations and regions have taken the economic lead—Britain with the great expansion of steam power in the early nineteenth century, for example, or Germany and the United States with the great expansion of chemical and electrical industries in the later nineteenth century. The most recent complete cycle began in the 1940s, fueled the prosperity of postwar North America, and crashed in the mid-1970s. It drew its power from the mass marketing of automobiles, consumer appliances, and housing and the creation of electronics and aerospace industries. Its most impressive regional effects were the rise of Japan as an automobile and consumer electronics powerhouse and the headlong growth of California and the metropolitan West, with Los Angeles leading the way in aerospace and the Bay Area leading the electronics industry.[6]

Coming out of this regional social and economic milieu, cyberpunk writers have been fascinated with the possibilities of the *next* long wave of economic change, which may have begun in the 1990s with the explosion of computational capacity and rapid spread of mobile personal electronics. The frequent science fiction speculation is that the current wave of change will confirm and expand the world role of the Pacific economy. Drawing out possibilities from new electronic and biological information technologies, they depict an early twenty-first-century world that functions under the control of giant corporations and pivots on Pacific nations.[7]

As the term *street samurai* suggests, cyberadventure action is big-city action, and the subgenre offers a distinct view of an urban future as well as a Pacific future. Cyberpunk characters would be very much at home in John Shirley's dark-edged San Francisco, but not in Pat Murphy's sunnier version, Butler's downward-spiraling Los Angeles, or Niven and Pournelle's stasis-locked version of metropolitan development. Instead, their Tokyo and San Francisco offer the frantic pace of a Hong Kong gangster movie. Their cities are places of motion, change, and opportunity that are exciting and deadly at the same time. Going back to nineteenth-century commentators who tried to make sense of the new cities of the industrial revolution, these writers see the metropolis as the locus of the best and worst of human possibility, the place where chaos can be simultaneously creative and destructive.[8]

In this chapter I explore these science fiction takes on the postmodern world of information intensive space-time compression. My overall point is that cyberpunk writing can be viewed as a specific expression of the society and culture of western America, writing that looks forward by drawing on historically embedded ideas about the relationships between the United States and the Pacific world. The next two sections introduce cyberpunk writing in more detail and examine the ways in which William Gibson, the best known among these writers, depicts a pan-Pacific world. The following sections root different visions of the future in American ambivalence about Asia. In one, the Pacific and East Asia are the logical next target for American expansion. In the other, Asia is a threat to the United States—from fears of Asian immigration and the Yellow Peril to speculative futures in which political control runs eastward from China or Japan rather than westward from North America.

So What's This Cyberpunk Stuff?

Neuromancer is the book that kick-started cyberpunk as a miniature publishing phenomenon. Gibson's novel is a story about flawed individuals trying to redeem themselves within the context of a high-tech underworld. The action starts in Chiba City in the Tokyo Sprawl. Its opening line set the tone of electronically mediated menace: "The sky above the port was the color of television, tuned to a dead channel." Gibson, who had never visited Japan, took Chiba's street names off a Japan Air Lines calendar and imagined the city as a kaleidoscope of shifting impressions—lights, signs, bars, shops, busy people, furtive people, dangerous people. It is a North American's reaction to the intense *concentration* and *difference* of metropolitan Japan.[9] It is city as jungle, city as "nighttown" (as in Gibson's 1981 story "Johnny Mnemonic," where Tokyo's Night City is the playground for outlaws), city as inscrutable surfaces as in the film *Lost in Translation* (2003).

Bruce Sterling's anthology *Mirrorshades* (1986), with short stories by Sterling, Gibson, Pat Cadigan, Lewis Shiner, John Shirley, Rudy Rucker, and several others, tried to define the boundaries of the field. Sterling's preface is the most frequently quoted manifesto. He roots the cyberpunks firmly in the literary practice of science fiction but celebrates the influences of low-brow consumer culture. Their common characteristic and contribution, he argued, is to integrate "the realm of high tech, and the modern pop underground," an integration that was the "decade's crucial source of cultural energy." It combined, he claimed, "visionary intensity" with attention to cultural minutiae and "willingness to carry extrapolation into the fabric of daily life."[10]

Sterling's self-promotion aside, the early cyberpunk fiction of the 1980s is a circumscribed subgenre in which the plot lines and sensibility of the down-and-out detective story are used to tell stories that posit direct machine-brain interactions that often lead to ventures or adventures in virtual realities. The heroes are computer hackers, weary cops, marginal musicians, and tough young women who are wise to the ways of the street. Their opponents are corrupt executives, mobsters, crooked cops, and psychopathic enforcers. There is careful attention to the details of daily life: language, fashion, architecture, drugs. The telling is always fast-paced. And the lines blur. Some of the human protagonists are cyborgs with physical and neural enhancements. Sometimes the computer network spawns its own self-aware intelligences. A more expansive version in the 1990s added nanotechnology and the manipulation of biologically coded information to electronic data systems. The shared interest is to explore the implications of information-based or programmable technologies in the near future.

The cyberpunk world is one of big cities and glaring skylines, ubiquitous convenience stores and old factory districts, corporate towers, California beach houses, and sleazy squats in semitropical slums. Protagonists clash in bars, back alleys, and abandoned warehouses in the urban relics of the Rust Belt, London, Los Angeles, San Francisco, Tokyo—and also in virtual realities where their avatars stalk through simulacra of Venice, Mexico City, and totally imagined places. Writers blend their ideas about the potential of information technologies with a hard-driving rock-and-roll sensibility and nighthawk visions of urban life.[11] Cyberpunk cities are fast-paced and often dangerous to individual characters, but they are also *the* places to be because they're at the center of economic and social change.

The excitement with which these writers face the near future may be celebratory or fearful. Cyberpunk often stands accused of swallowing the "bright lights, big city" mentality of the 1980s in one gulp with all the "Reaganesque hype and Ramboesque aggressiveness."[12] In these versions, it highlights slam-bang action cowboy protagonists. However, it may also see the new technologies as leading to corporate-fascist social manipulation or control by the machines themselves, as in the films *The Matrix* (1999) and *Minority Report* (2002). In other versions, it may see the merger of human being and information machine as liberating and transcendent, opening opportunities for self-actualization and expanding the capacities of human beings to a new stage.[13]

The influences on this sort of cyberpunk are many. Literary cousins and progenitors include William Burroughs and Philip K. Dick, with their marginal heroes and interest in altered states of consciousness, as well as Don DeLillo and Thomas Pynchon, whose novels walk the edge between the mainstream and the fantastic. More direct influence comes from Dashiell Hammett, James Cain, and Raymond Chandler, and their noir approach to crime novels and movies, which is closely associated with California.[14]

The outpouring of consumer technotrash inspires cityscapes and backgrounds. The revival of American superhero comics in the 1970s and 1980s contributed. So has the vast body of stylized Japanese manga comics, with their simply drawn, brightly colored characters. Indeed, the reciprocal influence between American and Japanese popular culture is a fascinating subject in itself. Japanese monster movies of the 1950s, depicting Godzilla, King of

Monsters, and his various opponents, were a way for Japanese to struggle with the horrors of World War II and earn some money from the American taste for science fiction. The huge Japanese animation, or *anime*, industry that emerged after the war drew on Disney style and American pulp fiction and B movies, but it quickly developed a distinctive aesthetic and interlocking products—comic books, movies, TV series, video games, spinoff toys—that made fortunes for Sony, Nintendo, and other companies. Anime entered the United States in the 1970s and 1980s as the obsession of a subculture of nerdy young men (just like early science fiction) but turned mass market with computer games and the Internet in the 1990s. Pokemon, which began as a children's game for handheld computers, grew into a marketed phenomenon that made the cover of *Time* magazine.[15] If Lawrence Ferlinghetti could fix on "A Coney Island of the Mind" as a metaphor for the experience of post–World War II America, the writers of the 1980s, 1990s, and beyond have explored a "Ginza—or Las Vegas—of the Soul."

William Gibson's Pan-Pacific World

Idoru (1996), the sixth novel by cyberpunk science fiction star William Gibson, blends three plot lines. One is the story of Chia Pet McKenzie, a fourteen-year-old from Seattle whose devotion to the Asian pop music group Lo/Rez takes her adventuring to Tokyo to check out troubling rumors. Chia gets pulled into a second high-energy story line about data theft and betrayal among American, Japanese, and Russian criminals. Hovering in the background is a moral tale about the meanings of celebrity, as a computer-generated singer first becomes a popular culture idol *(idoru)* and then takes on a life of her own. *Idoru* retains the gangster movie elements and fast plot that earned the "punk" part of cyberpunk, but it also has touches of humor that are rare in the subgenre.

Gibson published *Idoru* fifteen years after he burst onto the science fiction scene with a handful of brilliant short stories, followed by the Sprawl series, which comprised *Neuromancer* (1984), *Count Zero* (1986), and *Mona Lisa Overdrive* (1988). Gibson and his work quickly became the public face and epitome of cyberpunk. Gibson, raised in South Carolina, Arizona, and Virginia, moved to Canada in 1968 with the acquiescence of his draft board and ended up in Vancouver, where he earned a B.A. in English from the University of British Columbia. He then decided to try writing rather than graduate school. He entered the field of science fiction at the same time that Vancouver was turning cosmopolitan: "My wife was born in Vancouver and we moved out here in 1972. . . . At that time Vancouver was a kind of backwater. . . . In the meantime it has become sort of post-modern Pacific-rim and an endlessly expanding urban scene." Vancouver was indeed becoming a multicultural city, where 25,000 Asian immigrants were arriving annually by the early 1990s and only 60 percent of residents used English as a first language by 1991. It was a setting that made Pacific futures central to Gibson's speculative imagination.[16]

Gibson has described his intentions as mixing elements from a Velvet Underground album, from Alfred Bester's breakneck-paced science fiction classic *The Stars My Destination* (1956), and from mainstream novelist Robert Stone's *Dog Soldiers* (1974).[17] This last is worth some attention. Stone's admirable book anticipates cyberpunk settings as it careens through the settings of the emergent Pacific Rim economy circa 1970—from Vietnam to the East Bay to the American Southwest and Mexico. In its transpacific world, Samoan immigrants muster out of the Coast Guard to work for the petty gangsters, San Francisco flight attendants smuggle pot from Bangkok, East Indian women spin topless in seedy bars, Japanese military brides work for Filipino dentists, and the outlaw hero draws inspiration from Native American warriors and East Asian warrior religion.

Stone's characters are people who cross borders, and Gibson—himself an expatriate—has made boundary crossing a central feature of his fiction. Chia certainly lives and moves in a world of fluid and permeable boundaries. She lives in Seattle but spends much of her time with an online fan club whose members live as far away as Houston and Mexico City. When she reaches Tokyo, she first stays with a member of a Japanese counterpart club, but she meets with the whole club through computer-generated avatars (which allow, for example, chubby teenagers to appear glamorous). The real and virtual worlds interpenetrate most completely through the holographic "person" of Rei Toei, the *idoru* who interacts with the flesh-and-blood world. The singer Rez eventually tries to "marry" Rei Toei and live with her online in a virtual world that mimics part of old Tokyo.

Many of the other characters in the novel also embody literal crossings of national and cultural borders. Chia has a Canadian father and an Italian immigrant mother, who chose the name Chia Pet because it sounded melodious to someone with little English. The computer and media technicians who work for Lo/Rez are Japanese Americans, who've come to Tokyo via Tacoma or San Francisco. Rez himself is half Chinese and half Irish. He starts his career in Taiwan, is based in Tokyo in *Idoru*, and is touring by train through the whistle-stops of Siberia in the sequel *All Tomorrow's Parties* (1999).

Gibson's work bounces back and forth across the continents, but it always seems to pivot on the Pacific. Tokyo lies at the center of the world's transportation and communication networks. *Mona Lisa Overdrive* opens in Tokyo's Narita Airport before switching back and forth among London, California, and New Jersey, with action driven at full tilt by Japanese *yakuza* feuds. *All Tomorrow's Parties* opens with squatters in the dark corners of the Tokyo subway system, one of whom is also plugged into commanding knowledge of the global communications matrix. That character remarks that "It's all going to change. . . . We're coming up on the mother of all nodal points. I can see it, now. It's *all* going to change."[18] Gibson thus places Tokyo, of all possible points in cyberspace, as the center of the future.

The backdrop of these stories is the cross-fertilization of American and Japanese popular culture. Bruce Sterling has noted that "there's a voracious appetite for American popular culture in Japan; they feed on it" and that "they know everything about us and we know almost nothing about them." Gibson was similarly struck by the influx of Asians into Vancouver in the 1980s—both Hong Kong Chinese looking for a Commonwealth refuge to hedge against possible absorption by the People's Republic and Japanese students and tourists wanting to learn English and explore North America: "Vancouver is a very popular destination for Japanese tourists," he commented in 1990. "There are special bars here that cater exclusively to the Japanese, and almost no one else goes into them because the whole scene is too strange."[19]

Asian customers were indeed big business in western American tourist destinations in the 1980s and 1990s. In 1990, 2.8 million Japanese and 1 million other Asians visited the United States for business or leisure; by 2000, the figures had grown to 4.8 and 2.9 million. Many of the visitors were bound for California (which received $15 billion of international tourism spending), Hawaiʻi ($7.5 billion), and Nevada ($2.8 billion).[20] Hawaiʻi, already a pan-Asian state that developed with the help of Japanese, Chinese, Okinawan, and Filipino immigrants, has been pushing its role as a bridge for business and information exchange between Asia and America. Honolulu became a major tourist destination for newly affluent Japanese in the 1970s and 1980s. Japanese investors by the end of the 1980s had put nearly $6 billion into Honolulu real estate, including many second homes. Los Angeles and San Francisco were close competitors for Japanese travelers.

So too, Gibson builds that fascination into his fictions. In *Mona Lisa Overdrive*, Kumiko Yanaka "knew the Sprawl [the Northeastern United States] from a thousand stims; a fascination with the vast conurbation was a common feature of Japanese popular culture."[21] In *Idoru*, the Western World in Tokyo is a nightclub decorated with a Sherman tank. Chia encounters a group of Japanese skateboard punks who call themselves the Oakland Overbombers, after a California soccer club. Culture also goes the other direction. Chia's devotion to Lo and Rez stands in for the two-directional flow of popular culture.[22]

Pacific Visions

William Gibson is not the only cyberpunk writer to lean heavily on Pacific Rim settings. Since the 1980s, stories about the social and economic consequences of cybernetic and molecular information technologies have seemed to find a natural setting in San Francisco, Los Angeles, Seattle, Vancouver, Shanghai, Singapore, Saigon, Tokyo. Pacific cities become cosmopolises, where Asian, American, and Russian corporations, mafias, money launderers, police forces, outlaws, and innocents are caught in a competitive whirl of individuals and nations. These are cities where the instant transfer of information accelerates the pace of human life, and they are the places where Americans negotiate their individual and collective futures.

For many speculative writers, this Pacific future is positive and promising. The Pacific is a region to be engulfed in an ongoing westward movement that will take American influence and economic connections into and across the ocean. Given the private character of computerized information exchange, and writing in the aftermath of the Vietnam war, they emphasize the business connections rather than government, diplomacy, and war. These writers may write noir novels whose plot lines depict the details of those connections as criminal and corrupt, but their overall stance is to place America and Americans as dominant participants in the transpacific world.

Such descriptions of transpacific commerce, investment, and settlement reach far back in American geopolitical dreams. For politicians from Thomas Jefferson to William Seward, continental expansion was a step toward larger westward reach. Hawaiian adventurer George Washington Bates caught the spirit of the project in 1854: "It will not be long before such a mighty tide of wealth will roll between California and the Orient as shall render the Pacific the 'highway of nations' on a grander scale than the Atlantic is now. California will sit as empress over the Pacific."[23] In fact, the actual results of commercial dreams in the nineteenth century were limited. There was plenty of long-distance interaction, but relatively few people involved in the trade in sea otter furs, in whaling, in transpacific gold rushes that sent prospectors back and forth among California, Australia, and Canada, or in the promotion of island agriculture. Geographic visionary William Gilpin might have dreamed of a "Cosmopolitan Railway" that would outdo the Union Pacific and Central Pacific by crossing North America, spanning the Bering Strait, and plunging westward through Siberia to China and Europe, but there was no transpacific telegraph cable until 1903, thirty-seven years after the transatlantic cable.[24] Ambitions took on new life with the new century. California-based history publisher Hubert Howe Bancroft summed a century of armchair ambition in *The New Pacific* (1900). He ended his boosterish inventory of western resources with the ancient trope of the westward course of empire and the newer American trope of searching for new frontiers. The twentieth century, he proclaimed, would be the century of the *new* Pacific, with North Americans shouldering aside tired Europeans and the wealth of the Pacific surpassing that of the Atlantic. The vision was one of classic liberalism, with free trade in goods and ideas lifting the strongest individuals and nations to success:

> The far west facing the far east, with the ocean between, have lain hitherto at the back door of both Europe and America. Now by magic strides the antipodal No-man's-land is coming to the front to claim a proper share in the world's doings. . . . We have no longer a virgin continent to develop; pioneer work in the United States is done, and now we must take a plunge into the sea. Here we find an area, an amphitheatre of water, upon and around which American enterprise and industry . . . will find occupation for the full term of the twentieth century, and for many centuries thereafter. The Pacific, its shores and islands, must now take the place of the great west, its plains and mountains, as an outlet for pent-up industry. Here on this ocean all the world will meet, and on equal footing, Americans and Europeans, Asiatics and Africans, white, yellow, and black, looters and looted, the strongest and cunningest to carry off the spoils.[25]

Bancroft's peroration was tied to a specific moment. In the single decade starting in 1898, the United States annexed Hawai'i and parts of Samoa; fought the Spanish-American War and acquired the reluctant Philippines through four years of colonial war; declared an open-door policy for trade with China and intervened during that nation's Boxer Rebellion; mediated an end to the Russo-Japanese war; and started work on the Panama Canal (it opened in 1914). In turn, West Coast cities anticipated an explosion of trade when the new waterway tied the Pacific and Atlantic worlds. Journalists penned stories about "The Coming Supremacy of the Pacific" and "The Momentous Struggle for Mastery of the Pacific."[26] Civic leaders staged international expositions with transpacific themes: The Lewis and Clark Centennial Exposition and Oriental Fair in Portland (1905), the Alaska-Yukon-Pacific Fair in Seattle (1909), the California-Pacific Exposition in San Diego (1915), and the Panama-Pacific International Exposition in San Francisco (1915).

A quarter century later, the Golden Gate International Exposition in 1939–1940 outdid them all as a sort of apotheosis of American-Pacific expectations. Its 17 million visitors received an art deco introduction to the Pacific Ocean as an American lake. The style was "Pacific Basin," an amalgam of Incan, Cambodian, Malayan, and Thai elements laid on with Hollywood exuberance. Towers of the East cast reflections on the Lake of All Nations. Pacific House sheltered a relief map of the bottom of the Pacific Ocean and six murals by Miguel Covarrubias on themes of Pacific culture. Outside, visitors watched Pan Am's China Clipper take off for Asia, little expecting that the U.S. Navy would soon purchase the site to augment the Bay Area's naval facilities for war with Japan.

As Bancroft had implied, the United States in the late nineteenth and early twentieth centuries faced competition for Pacific islands and coastal ports from Britain, Germany, France, and Japan, even as rivalry from Spain and Russia receded. Military strategist Alfred Thayer Mahan argued that a maturing nation would naturally turn to the Pacific world after settling the North American continent, for to do otherwise would stunt its national growth. Brooks Adams urged the expansion of Anglo-Saxon civilization across the Pacific as a necessary step in national progress and survival.[27] Three generations later, as the long multiphased war for dominance in the western Pacific that lasted at least from 1937 to 1974 moved to its inconclusive end, the U.S. economy grew stronger ties to Asia. With the lifting of national quotas for entry to the United States by the Immigration Reform Act of 1965, Asian immigration climbed to over 2 million in the 1970s, 2.8 million in the 1980s, and approximately 3 million in the 1990s. Trade with Japan, South Korea, Taiwan, Thailand, Hong Kong, and then China itself burgeoned in the last decades of the century. The value of U.S. commerce across the Pacific passed that across the Atlantic in the very early 1980s, a milestone that finally realized the boosterish expectations from the Panama Canal, and four of the ten leading U.S. trading partners in 2003 were Asian.

This is the old *and* new context in which science fiction writers have anticipated the opportunities of twenty-first-century Asia, seeing the Pacific Rim as the source of scientific change and economic growth. Bruce Sterling, for one example, depicts Singapore as outdoing American cities in all their high rise grandiosity and economic capacities. "[Singapore] was like downtown Houston. But more like Houston than even Houston had ever had the nerve to become. It was an anthill, a brutal assault against any sense of scale. Nightmarishly vast spires whose bulging foundations covered whole city blocks. . . . Story after story rose silent and dreamlike, buildings so unspeakably huge that they lost all sense of weight." Since Sterling wrote, Kuala Lumpur and Taipei have outdone Singapore, Houston, and Chicago by erecting (in turn) the world's tallest building. The new high rise metropolis of East Asia—Singapore, Shanghai, or someplace else—is a huge information transfer system. "It's a wind-up city, this place. Full of lying and chatter and bluff, and cash registers ringing round the clock."[28]

Linda Nagata is another writer who has found it natural to look westward. Born in California, raised on Oahu, and resident on Maui, Nagata thinks naturally in terms of American-Asian connections. Her *Limit of Vision* (2001) concerns an artificial life-form that develops the capacity to assemble itself like coral into a great variety of intelligent organisms. The bulk of the action is set in the Mekong Delta of South Vietnam, whose government is able to stave off American pressure for most of the book. The key characters are a Hawaiʿi-based American researcher and a young, English-speaking Thai journalist who stumbles on the story that the life-forms have escaped the laboratory. By mediating Asian and western ambitions and cultures, she is a cultural hybrid who reflects the hybridity of cyberpunk itself—as well as the blending "mongrel" culture of Pacific basin gateways and control centers.

The fascination with East Asia appears again in Pat Cadigan's *Tea from an Empty Cup* (1998). Although the key action of this cyberspace detective story takes place on the Net, the physical base for the cops is California. There are more boundary crossers among the key characters, who include a Japanese American woman and an entertainer whose heritage mixes Japan and Mongolia. The fashion is now for whites to make their features more Asian. The book opens with an encounter between a young American and a Japanese hustler selling a virtual experience program that allows trippers to visit virtual cities, with virtual Tokyo at the top of the list, much desired but as hard to get into as a trendy nightclub: "You keep thinking that way, you're never gonna get into Tokyo. They're gonna see you comin' and send you to Chinatown with the rest of the tourists. With my package, you really *will* be Japanese." A bit later, the allure of virtual Tokyo reappears: It's "coming soon, to a hotsuit near you. 'Sposed to be the next big hot spot. They say it's gonna make the Sitty [virtual New York] look like Sunday afternoon in Nebraska, with these parts you can access only if you're Japanese or a convincing simulation."[29]

To return to Gibson, Kumiko, daughter of a *yakuza* overlord, is hustled off to London for her safety at the start of *Mona Lisa Overdrive.* London is dynamic and interesting, but "it isn't Tokyo." It is the past rather than the future. In England, fragments of the past are meticulously preserved in "the very fabric of things, as if the city were a single growth of stone and brick, uncounted strata of message and meaning, age upon age." The London economy endlessly recycles antiques and junk as "a major national resource." In Japan, Kumiko continues, the same rubbish is dumped into Tokyo Bay as landfill for the expansion of the city.[30] There is an element of truth to this characterization, for Tokyo is indeed rebuilt on the ruins of the 1923 earthquake and 1944–1945 firebombing and built anew on made land. But Gibson is after more, the sense that the Japanese are a society that—like Americans—happily plow under their past in the pursuit of the future.

Eastward the Course of Empire

"Westward the course of empire takes its way" is an ambiguous slogan. It can imply inevitable U.S. westward expansion across North America, then into and across the Pacific. But it might also suggest that the locus of power that had moved from Europe to America might move again from the United States to East Asia. As historian Andre Gunder Frank argues in *Re-Orient* (1998), the Pacific might be the future, but it might turn out to be a future that is Asian rather than American. His thesis is that China and South Asia have been the center of gravity in the world economy for most of the past two millennia, with the recent rise of Europe and North America the result of short-term factors. For the coming century, he sees the rise of Japan, the Asian "tiger economies," and China as a natural rebalancing of the world system.[31]

Frank's sweeping revisioning of world history introduces the flip side of the Pacific vision. The Pacific may be a realm of American opportunity, but the economic expansion of East Asia may also tilt the balance of power the other direction. Americans may find themselves bought out, overwhelmed, invaded, and colonized by Asia—an alternative future that runs through a wide spectrum of science fiction. China is the new technological leader in Greg Bear's *Queen of Angels* (1990) and Paul McAuley's *The Secret of Life* (2001). Agents of the New Hong Kong space habitat are drugging and abducting San Francisco workers in Richard Paul Russo's *Carlucci's Edge* (1995), and the city's Asian Quarter is the most vibrant and most threatening part of the city, revisiting the cultural construction of Chinatown as a danger zone where anything goes.[32] Kim Stanley Robinson took the reversal even further. In *The Wild Shore* (1984) he imagined a future in which Japan quarantines the United States after it is devastated by neuron bombs. Japanese space satellites spot and destroy efforts to claw back from a village/barter economy, Japanese naval vessels patrol the Southern California coast, and Japanese tourists make clandestine landings at San Clemente to gather American artifacts.

Neal Stephenson similarly imagined a future Vancouver as a cosmopolitan city that is controlled by Asian money. The Nipponese and the Hong Kong Mutual Benevolent Society have acquired "Old Vancouver's pricier and more view-endowed precincts," while "Hindustan had a spray of tiny claves [short for *enclave*] all over the metropolitan area." This is a city remade by imported money and immigration, creating "the sheer maddening profusion of the place, each person seemingly an ethnic group of one, each with his or her own costume, dialect, sect, and pedigree."[33] The description is a direct reflection of Vancouver's transformation after 1980 from a small, provincial, oh-so-English city into a commonwealth cosmopolis, with new communities from the Caribbean, South Asia, and especially China. Many Hong Kong families bought Vancouver real estate as a safe haven, often tearing down 1920s pseudo-Tudor houses to build what indigenous Vancouverites called "monster houses," and Hong Kong investors rebuilt much of the 1986 World's Fair site with wafer-thin high rises.

Cyberpunk science fiction developed at a very specific historical moment in the 1980s. Just as the United States realized its century-old ambition for a Pacific economy, fear of Asia, represented most obviously by Japanese industry, took one of its periodic upswings. Capital-rich Japanese corporations were buying West Coast real estate and pasting the names of Japanese banks and zaibatsu onto Los Angeles and San Francisco high rises, causing a sort of mini panic and some substantial Japan bashing. Japanese direct investment in the United States jumped from $4.2 billion in 1980 to $83 billion in 1990. In comparison, U.S. direct investment in *all* Pacific nations rose from $30.1 billion to $77.3 billion in the same decade.[34] The U.S. trade deficit with Japan and other Asian countries was rising at the same time that the American economy was coping with the trauma of deindustrialization. Japanese opinion makers were agitating to break free from close connections with the United States in books such as *The Japan That Can Say No* at the same time that American economic commentators were warning of the Japanese juggernaut.[35]

Such concerns about the Asian influence on the West Coast reach back to anti-Chinese agitation that began as early as the 1860s and 1870s and to anti-Japanese sentiments of the early twentieth century. Americans worried about economic competition, and they projected fears of social disorder and disease onto neighbors from Asia.[36] They not only legislated against the Asian menace but also stoked their antipathy with apocalyptic novels. Pierton W. Donner in *The Last Days of the Republic* (1880) feared invasion by Chinese hordes who would overrun the continent and raise the standard of the emperor over the Capitol. For Homer Lea in 1909, the newly ascendant Japanese were the threat that required an expanded military establishment. In *The Valor of Ignorance*, he mapped out how Japan might successfully seize Hawaiʻi and the Philippines, land at Gray's Harbor on the Washington coast to conquer the Northwest, and continue by taking San Pedro and then San Francisco itself. In 1915, J. U. Giesy in *All for His Country* depicted a Mexican invasion that would draw off American forces, opening California to invasion from Japan, with house servants as a fifth column. By 1921, when Peter Kyne published *Pride of Palomar*, Mexicans were in good graces again, with Bolsheviks in Siberia now the distraction from the Japanese threat to California.[37]

Not all was fear, however. An aesthetic fascination with things Chinese and Japanese ran counter to the Yellow Peril literature. Artists and designers learned from East Asian painting styles, and they drew decorative motifs from traditional Chinese and Japanese art and crafts. Missionaries brought back collections. European and American writers set dramas in East Asian locales. Museums of East Asian art appeared in Pasadena, California, and Eugene, Oregon. The ambivalence was clear in the 1930s. At the same time Pearl Buck was depicting a noble and sympathetic China in *The Good Earth* (1931), Buck Rogers was battling future Mongol invaders in the comic pages and movie serials

The ambiguity continued after World War II. In the "orientalist" manner analyzed by Edward Said for European understanding of West Asia,

Americans looked across the Pacific and saw what they wanted to see. Japan was both chrysanthemum and sword, in Ruth Benedict's famous formulation. It was the despised attacker of 1941, a land of subhuman vermin whom Americans hated far more than German Nazis.[38] But it was also the home of Zen Buddhism, tea ceremonies, and fascinating new cinema. West Coast painters such as Mark Tobey and Morris Graves were deeply influenced by Japanese art. Gary Snyder and other poets absorbed influences of Buddhism and brought a new sensibility and sensitivity to place into West Coast writing.

Philip K. Dick's alternate universe novel *The Man in the High Castle* (1962) is a fascinating example of the positive take. He depicts a world where Germany and Japan won World War II. Now, in 1962, Germans control the eastern United States and Japan directs a puppet government for the Pacific Coast, with the Rocky Mountain states as a small, independent enclave. The Germans have been energetically rebuilding New York and Baltimore and reconstructing the economy in a sort of Speer Plan for the defeated people, meanwhile deporting and exterminating every American Jew they can find. San Francisco apparently fell without becoming a battlefield. It remains undamaged, while the culturally sensitive Japanese try to mitigate the worst impacts of vicious German racism. They cherish the peacefulness that they have brought to the Pacific Coast ("completely different from—back there"), treasure artifacts from prewar America such as Colt revolvers, and see a Mickey Mouse watch as "most authentic of dying old U.S. culture, a rare retained artifact carrying flavor of bygone halcyon day."[39]

But another thirty years, and attitudes shifted again. In the 1990s, the Asian menace took new life in popular culture, reflecting fears of economic eclipse by Japan. The movie *Rising Sun* (1993), based on a best-seller by Michael Crichton, opens with the kinky murder of a white American prostitute in the board room of a Japanese corporation. The combination of economic threat and sexual menace harkens back to the most virulent anti-Japanese agitation of the 1910s and 1920s, and it takes the combination of Japan expert Sean Connery and L.A. cop Wesley Snipes to solve the mystery. *Strange Days* (1995) is a science fiction film in which virtual reality pushers sell memory chips with other people's experiences to information junkies who congregate at the Retinal Fetish nightclub. The Asian villains are a variation on the nineteenth-century fear of the corrupting influence of Chinese opium dens, and the American tendency to transfer fears of disease onto racial minorities.

This long, contradictory dance of attraction and repulsion is the context for two very different books, William Gibson's *Virtual Light* (1993) and Neal Stephenson's *Snow Crash* (1992). The former is a tightly conscribed effort to link cyberpunk tropes to a traditional crime novel plot (failed policeman redeems himself). The latter is a panoramic, satirical portrait of new social and cultural patterns for the twenty-first century. But both embody the casual assumption of Asian expansionism and American weakness, and both depict a West Coast economy that will be thoroughly penetrated by Asian investment.

Berry Rydell, the cop in *Virtual Light*, works for a private security firm that is owned in Singapore and works in tight alliance with Chinese capitalists. Greater L.A. is littered with "fallen-in edge-cities" from the implosion of European money. Meanwhile, Hong Kong interests have bought up a large chunk of San Francisco's Embarcadero to build Container City, a vast shopping mall large enough for entire container ships to moor under its roof and sell merchandise straight off the deck. In the sort of role commonly played by the United States in the later twentieth century, Japanese peacekeeping forces are busy putting down the South Island Liberation Front in New Zealand in another inversion of the relationship between indigenous rebellion and neocolonial enforcer. The plot revolves around the theft of a pair of high-tech sunglasses that transmit visual information directly to the brain (hence the wearer sees with "virtual" rather than real light). The glasses in question, snatched on a whim by bicycle messenger Chevette Washington, contain Chinese plans for a vast reconstruction of San Francisco with huge multiblock buildings, just as the Chinese have previously remade Tokyo after the "Godzilla" earthquake.[40] When Chevette clicks the glasses on, "She was facing the city. . . . 'Fuck a *duck*,' she said, these towers blooming there, buildings bigger than anything, a stone regular grid of them, marching in from the hills. Each one maybe four blocks at the base, rising straight and featureless. . . . Then Chinese writing filled the sky. . . . The Chinese writing twisted into English. SUNFLOWER CORPORATION."[41] For San Francisco, a city with a fetish about its skyline, marching monster buildings is an especially disturbing image that implies the destruction of American cultural difference by Asian capital—yet one more inversion of the common complaint about the Disneyfication of global culture.

Neal Stephenson's California is far more fragmented and satirical than Gibson's. The landscape is dotted with self-protected burbclaves while international franchises act as sovereign nations. Indeed, the U.S. government is now just one among many franchises. The feds are less powerful and technically sophisticated than Mr. Lee's Greater Hong Kong, a chain of mini-mart outposts that double as fortified safe houses. Mr. Lee's co-owns UCLA with the Japanese in a satiric extension of Los Angeles real estate fears.

Snow Crash embodies the cultural cross-fertilization of Asia and America in the character of a Japanese rap artist who starts a U.S. tour with a vastly ill-advised concert to an audience of skateboarders who are into heavy metal. In the following verses from his multipage rap, Stephenson includes many references to Japanese power—not only to samurai swords but also to the Greater East Asia Co-Prosperity Sphere, the Japanese term for the economic and political empire that was their goal in World War II.

> I'm Sushi K and I'm here to say
> I like to rap in a different way. . . .
> The Nipponese talking phenomenon
> Like samurai sword his sharpened tongue
> Who raps the East Asia and the Pacific
> Prosperity Sphere, to be specific.
> He learn English total immersion
> English/Japanese be mergin'
> Into super combination
> So can have fans in every nation.[42]

Sushi K may be little threat to U.S. rappers, but the novel also embodies American fears of Asian hordes. The Raft is an accretion of derelict ships from junks to supertankers, strapped into a single floating world and carrying hundreds of thousands of passengers. It circulates around the rim of the Pacific with the prevailing currents, moving north from the Philippines along the coast of Asia, around past Alaska, down the coast of the Americas, and back across the South Pacific. Most of its people are refugees from Vietnam, China, and Korea. When it gets to California, it functions like an invasion fleet whose description recalls the greatest excesses of Yellow Peril fiction:

> It will shed much of its sprawling improvised bulk as a few hundred thousand Refus cut themselves loose and paddle to shore. The only Refus who make it that far are, by definition, the ones who were agile enough to make it out to the Raft in the first place, resourceful enough to survive the

agonizingly slow passage through the arctic waters, and tough enough not to get killed by any of the other Refus. . . . A new wave washes up onto the West Coast every five years or so . . . owners of beachfront property in California have been hiring security people, putting up spotlights and antipersonnel fences along the tide line, mounting machine guns on their yachts.[43]

The world of Stephenson's next book, *The Diamond Age*, is even more fragmented. Asian societies have coalesced into expansive economic enterprises on the model of the overseas Chinese. Western societies have divided among a multitude of phyles, globe-spanning voluntary associations that are part tribe and part nation and that interact by the rules of the Common Economic Protocol.[44] There are Mormons, Afrikaners, Maoist Senderos, the Distributed Republic (computer jockeys), Jesuits, Heartlanders (from the United States), Tutsis, and hundreds of others, but the great phyles are Atlantis, Nippon, Han (China), and Hindustan. Most of the western phyles are second and third rank. Only Atlantis, a neo-Victorian phyle that offers loyalty to Queen Victoria II, is the semiwestern heir of nineteenth-century Anglo-American business values and drive. Otherwise, the power relationship of the nineteenth and twentieth centuries is inverted.

The neo-Victorians are experts in nanoengineering of products at all scales. Two of their largest companies manufacture artificial land with nanotech. Their new places are strategically located in the global-Pacific economy to be the equivalent of "blessed places like Tokyo, San Francisco, and Manhattan . . . each new piece of land possessed the charms of Frisco, the strategic location of Manhattan, the feng-shui of Hong Kong, the dreary but obligatory lebensraum of L.A." The choice of cities is deliberate: one Atlantic and three Pacific. This is a world in which the European frontier of North America, South Africa, or Australia has passed into history. "It was no longer necessary to send out dirty yokels in coonskin caps to chart the wilderness, kill the abos, and clear-cut the groves; now all you needed was a hot young geotect, a start matter compiler, and a jumbo Source [for the raw atoms needed for nanotech assembly]."[45]

The book reverses the normal American expectation that the United States is superior or preferred to Asia. All of the border crossers choose Asia over the United States. One of the leaders in the neo-Victorian meritocracy was born in Korea, raised in Iowa, became a nanotech whiz in Minneapolis, and then joined Atlantis to live adjacent to Shanghai. One of the judges of the Chinese Coastal Republic, consisting of Shanghai and adjacent trading zones, is a former Chinese American hoodlum from New York who has become a convert to the social discipline of Confucianism, and one of his assistants has emigrated from Austin, Texas. Another central figure is John Hackworth, a neo-Victorian engineer who is promoted from San Francisco to Shanghai after inventing chopsticks that play advertisements while you eat. He had enjoyed San Francisco "and was hardly immune to its charm, but Atlantis/Shanghai had imbued him with the sense that all the old cities of the world were doomed, except possibly as theme parks, and that the future was in the new cities, built [by nanotechnology] from the bedroom up one atom at a time."[46] Old city, in this case, means European and American cities, not Asian.[47]

The secondary plot line revolves around the assertion of Chinese nationalism against western interests. The center of the action is Shanghai. The city itself is divided into a Chinese Coastal Republic, where the historic Bund is a vast shopping street with western and Japanese stores, and a small, traditionally governed enclave of the Celestial Kingdom. Adjacent are the western phyles residing on a large nano-built island, which use the Coastal Republic to access a huge Chinese interior that is still a great market for consumer goods. Chafing under western technical and economic domination, China is seeking to develop its own technology that is more in tune with the essence of Chinese society (it does so, in part, by messing with John Hackworth's brain and causing him to design needed technologies—the tertiary plot line for this complex book). At the end, a new manifestation of Righteous Fists of Harmony (Boxers) sweep aside the warlords of interior China and drive the foreigners out of Shanghai in a variation on the cultural revolution. In so doing, they pave the way for China to adopt productive technologies suitable to its needs and to cut itself off from dependence on the West. The end result is the twenty-first-century negation of the Pacific ambitions that animated Americans through two previous centuries.

Pacific Present/Pacific Futures

Because writers such as William Gibson, Bruce Sterling, and Neal Stephenson incorporate so much of the surface glitter of the late twentieth century, it is easy to argue that they are representing and fictionalizing the present rather than seriously projecting the future.[48] David Brande, for example, argues that cyberpunk simply reflects the actual structures of late-stage capitalism, with its commodification of culture and breakneck market turnover of products and cultural icons. Fredric Jameson offers a similar critique in *Postmodernism, or The Cultural Logic of Late Capitalism* (1991), arguing that cyberpunk functions as realism for a fragmented society. Many cyberpunk writers are kaleidoscope makers who collect bits and pieces of the world around them and recombine them in startling and telling ways. Gibson supports the view by noting that one of the inspirations for *Neuromancer* was the video arcades along Vancouver's Granville Street. He has described his work as "stitching together all the junk that's floating around in my head," mental junk that he accumulates by browsing thrift shops for entertainment, and comments, "When I write about technology, I write about how it has already affected our lives; I don't extrapolate in the way I was taught an SF writer should."[49] Bruce Sterling argues that "it's a moral and ideological necessity for SF writers to develop a portrait of a future we might actually be living."[50]

Cyberpunk is thus fascinated with the surfaces of North American culture and consumption, and it finds that culture in purest form in California. Because California epitomizes the consumer-goods culture of the postwar decades, cyberpunk writers can use it as the source for both the physical and virtual goods in the next economic era. The relentless focus on consumer items in *Snow Crash*, where fast pizza delivery is satirically presented as a crowning achievement of the American economy, is another reflection on the West Coast milieu. Stephenson and Gibson both give mini-marts a place in future L.A. that is even more prominent than they now occupy.

The best cyberfiction also revels in the intense depiction of very specific settings. Even if cyberwriters accept the postmodern argument that there can no longer be a single comprehensive territorial map, they still describe very particular here-and-nows. The title of Bruce Sterling's *Islands in the Net* (1988) seems to refer to a set of purely abstract spatial relationships, but the islands are literal as well as metaphorical places. Every computer has to have a physical home and a set of safeguards to protect it from sabotage, riot, and insurrection. These homes include real islands that are described in vivid detail: Galveston Island is surrounded by a sea "like slate-green gumbo"[51] with hurricane detritus buried in its beach; Grenada's airport has faded travel posters in Japanese; Singapore contrasts the old town of low warehouses with wooden shutters and ceiling fans with the new town of towering banks.

Sterling, Gibson, and others have taken to heart the admonition of Robert Venturi, Denise Scott-Brown, and Stephen Izenour to learn from Las Vegas. They use strong visual images to picture neon cityscapes full of blaring advertisements, street vendors, bars and shops, and crowds. There is loving attention, as Dani Cavallero writes, to "detail and assemblage. . . . The aesthetic and psychological impact of their sprawling megalopolises derives from both a keen eye for the minutiae of settings and architecture and a concern with the multifarious ways in which these fragments coalesce."[52] We can see Gibson's transformed Bay Bridge, with its fantastic lights and glittering surfaces, as a squatter-town equivalent of the Las Vegas Strip.

Because of their interest in these surface manifestations of contemporary society, cyberpunk writers are sometimes treated as apologists for capitalism who are trying to substitute a distinct new frontier myth for a familiar old one. In Brande's critical view, for example, Gibson turns the old, deluding myth of a physical frontier into a new myth of endless opportunity in a marketplace of information. The actual content of much of the work, however, offers little support for this assertion. Critics who call Gibson and others cheerleaders for high-tech corporatism are confusing the genre conventions of the hard-boiled crime story with the actual contours of the imagined future. Cybernetic anarchies and digitally enhanced corporate autocracies are scarcely the equivalent of the idealized frontier of mountain men and homesteaders. Console cowboys reach back to the nineteenth century for their name, but they're outlaws, not herdsmen, and they live off the leavings of the corporate world. The electronic compression of time and space makes individuals more dependent, not less so, on large institutions and on each other.

Equally important for the effect of these stories is their incorporation of the bright, superficial spirit of Japanese pop culture alongside that of California pop. Manga comics, video games, and anime drawings and movies are boldly and sketchily outlined, brightly colored, and fast-paced. It is a style that seems equally suited for quick adventure stories and for pornography—Godzilla meets American pulp fiction, pin-up girl meets video game. The style has influenced American pop artists, illustrated novels, and movies, and has begun to penetrate mainstream media. The recent made-for-America television show *Cowboy Bebop* (1998), for one example, is animated science fiction set in 2071 that is drawn in the unmistakable anime style. A crew of bounty hunters careen from adventure to adventure in the spaceship *Bebop*, whose name presumably symbolizes the American readiness to improvise. It is an example of the multidirectionality of cultural penetration, with Japanese appropriating American tropes and imagery and repackaging them in Japanese style for the American market.

Beyond their interest in the ephemera of the present day, cyberpunks have been as excited about the possibilities of new information technologies as Golden Age science fiction was about space travel. As *predictive* speculation (never actually the strong point of science fiction), cyberpunk has engaged the implications of the economic long wave that took off in the 1990s after two decades of global political and economic adjustment that began around 1974. The drive wheels of this next capitalist transformation are thought to be vastly powerful technologies of data storage and transmission via electronic and biological means. Because much of the base for this cycle developed in the California and Japanese electronics industries, it has seemed plausible to project its future in the same settings—hence the strong affinity of cyberpunk and nanotech stories for the people and places of the Pacific Rim.

There is also a deeper historical context. Cyberpunk juxtaposes the 2010s and 2020s with the 1960s and 1980s, but it also draws on narratives of western America that span the last two centuries. Just as predictions for the next long wave can be optimistic or pessimistic for Americans, these longer stories include both positive narratives of national progress and expansion and fearful visions of racial defeat. In Stephenson's imagination, the West Coast becomes a tired and mildly quaint backwater, playing the same role in the future as England does in our present. In Gibson's future (and in Nagata's and Sterling's), North America remains an active equal with East Asia.

In sum, we need to understand cyberpunk science fiction in terms of its origins in historical *place* and *time*. Science fiction is often thought to deal with global concerns, with the human future writ large. The novels I discuss in this chapter may be such universalizing efforts to understand the transformations of capitalism in the face of new information technologies, but they are also examples of western American writing. Their authors are trying to understand the changing possibilities and future of Pacific America. Cyberpunks augment the narratives of collapsing community and national exhaustion that see California as the cutting *end* of the American dream. They also celebrate the continued triumph of production and consumption and the capacity of the nation to accommodate recurring waves of technological change.

If we imagine California as a great golden coin, the visions of cyberpunk and communitarian science fiction are stamped on opposite sides. The questions of civic life and public action that engage the writers in the previous chapter are reduced by the prophets of the information economy to law enforcement and organized crime as the sources of order in offline suburbia and online cyburbia. They follow the derring-do of isolated protagonists within massive institutions, rather than building characters who make do within moderate-sized communities. They partake of West Coast exuberance in their storytelling energy and surface glitter, but they also update the American expectation of a Pacific destiny with ambiguous and uncertain judgments.

8 Bigger than Texas! Americans, Our Wests, and Science Fiction

Space is like Texas, only bigger.
—Thomas Disch, *The Dreams Our Stuff Is Made Of* (1998)

The school session when I was seven there was this unit . . . about the early frontiers, the ones way back on Earth, while the Europeans were conquering everybody else, before the real frontiers out here even started.
—John Barnes, *The Sky So Big and Black* (2002)

Woody and Buzz

Sheriff Woody is the big toy in Andy's room. He enforces law and order and leads the other toys: Mr. Potato Head, Slinky Dog, T. Rex, and the rest of the toy box. He knows that he's Andy's favorite, but the world turns upside down on Andy's birthday. One of the gift boxes contains Buzz Lightyear, Space Ranger. Now two heroic action figures are competing for Andy's time. Woody can talk when Andy pulls the string in his back, but Buzz has batteries and buttons to push. It looks like no contest. The new eclipses the old; the future trumps the past.

Toy Story (1995) was an extremely successful children's movie. It skillfully advanced the style of computer-based animation that has become the industry standard. It is also a metaphor for this book. Woody and Buzz start off as rivals for Andy's attention. When they find themselves lost and threatened outside the house, however, they learn to work together, for they embody the same heroic character traits in different guises. Their adventures include a perilous visit to Pizza Planet, a space-age theme restaurant that's full of science fiction games. Its contorted shape and bright lights mimic the "googie" architecture of drive-in California and firmly places the toys' story in the future-focused West.[1] When Buzz falls into despair on discovering that he is only a toy and not a real Star Ranger, Woody brings Buzz out of his funk and masterminds their escape. It's the Western action figure who gives meaning to this fantasy world, just as Western narratives provide basic formulas for writing about a future where Star Command battles the evil Emperor Zurg.[2]

But Buzz is essential for reaching the future. The two toys discover that they've been left behind as Andy's family moves to a new house. They try to catch the moving van with the technology of the present, in the form of a toy car, only to be stranded with exhausted batteries. New technology saves the day. The two toys launch themselves into the air with a rocket, and Buzz deploys the folding wings in his spacesuit to glide back to Andy. Cowboy and space ranger have learned to cooperate. The metaphor can't bear a whole lot of weight, of course, but the new understanding between Woody and Buzz is a bit like the way that stories of the western American past and future have come to work together, with science fiction incorporating tropes and stories from the western past and dressing them in spacesuits.

Always Going West

History may not repeat itself, but American science fiction writers have certainly repeated history. Golden Age science fiction emerged in the 1930s and early 1940s when *The Decline of the West* seemed to be a real possibility as well as the translated title of Oswald Spengler's pessimistic book about the twilight of Europe. Writers could absorb Spengler's speculations about the imminent collapse of European culture, study the first volumes of Arnold Toynbee's sweeping account of the rise and fall of civilizations, and watch H. G. Wells's version of decline and renewal in *Things to Come* (1936) on the silver screen.[3] Isaac Asimov, writing in the 1940s, modeled his Foundation trilogy on the decline of the Roman Empire (as understood in popular culture) and then found Toynbee's *A Study of History*. James Blish had Spengler in mind while developing his Cities in Flight stories about a collapse of civilization and the escape of entire cities with antigravity devices. Donald Wollheim, a writer and editor from the same clique of Futurians as Blish, later described a consensus future, or cosmogony, in which humankind expands to the solar system and then the stars, builds a galactic empire that flourishes and then collapses, endures an interregnum, and rebuilds another civilization.[4] The Renaissance philosopher Giambattista Vico and the medieval historian Ibn Khaldun, with their theories of cycles of civilization and barbarism, were later intellectual discoveries who influenced, for example, Frank Herbert's portrayal of the conflict between the Empire and the nomadic desert Fremen in *Dune* (1965).[5]

Indeed, the collapsed empire is one of the more common science fiction backgrounds. Earth has become a backwater or long forgotten, and people in the isolated colonies on the fringe cope as best they can. Theodore Cogswell's 1952 *Astounding* story "The Spectre General" depicts a forgotten planetary outpost somewhat like a Roman garrison in fifth-century Britain, where a detachment of Imperial Space Marines keeps up appearances even as they forget how to use or repair their high-technology equipment. Other stories of imperial decline revolve around the rediscovery of an Earth that has dropped from memory as human beings have spread toward the galactic core. Andre Norton's *Star Rangers* (1953) starts with a Patrol ship crashing on a world "so near the rim of the galaxy that it had been overlooked—or forgotten—centuries before." The handful of stranded patrolmen stumble on a space port with a building that looks like the sacred Place of Free Planets that stands in Central City. When they investigate, they realize the amazing truth: this is the original of that ancient building and the planet is "Terra of Sol—man's beginning."[6] Now the rangers know why the green of the trees and grass, a shade unlike the vegetation of any other planet, has stirred them so deeply: they have come home at last to the green hills of Earth.[7]

The common American version of postempire stories are postdisaster stories that play off the national fascination with westward pioneering. Indeed, we don't need space travel to find the western past in the American future. Much of our history is animated by exploration, travel, and migration across the continent. We retrace the pathways of Daniel Boone, Lewis and Clark, and Jim Bridger. We trudge behind the covered wagons in the ruts of the Oregon Trail, ride with the pack trains to Santa Fe, marvel over the gritty Mormons pushing their handcarts across the plains, share the terrible excitement of John Wesley Powell's white-water plunge through the Grand Canyon. The landscape is marked with the routes and way stations—Saint Joseph and Independence and Council Bluffs, Fort Laramie, Donner Pass . . . Ho, for California! . . . Pike's Peak or Bust!

These same routes and places that loomed so large in the nineteenth century reappear in science fiction that tries to imagine the *re*discovery and *re*settlement of North America after disaster and depopulation. When society collapses, head *west* to reconstruct it. Some stories explicitly follow a nuclear apocalypse—Leigh Brackett's *The Long Tomorrow* (1955), Walter Miller Jr.'s *A Canticle for Leibowitz* (1959), David Brin's *The Postman* (1985). Other writers sweep the continent clean with plagues (Stephen King in *The Stand*

[1978]) or leave the cause unspecified (Ursula Le Guin in *City of Illusions* [1967]). Whatever the cause, their characters face a continent that has been cleared of most remnants of twentieth-century civilization and a landscape that calls out for journeys, for expeditions, for a new corps of discovery.

The Long Tomorrow (1955) is a postapocalypse novel set eighty years after nuclear war. The United States Constitution now has a Thirtieth Amendment: "No city, no town, no community of more than one thousand people or two hundred buildings to the square mile shall be built or permitted to exist anywhere in the United States of America." Technology has reverted to the level of the early 1800s. The surviving nation is a "wide and cityless land" of farming settlements and trading towns linked by annual trading fairs and steamboats where "only a few old folk could remember the awesome cities that had dominated the world before the Destruction." Now the traders bring stories of "the little shipping settlements and fishing hamlets along the Atlantic, the lumber camps of the Appalachians, these endless New Mennonite farm lands of the Midwest, the Southern hunters and hill farmers, the great rivers westward with their barges and boats, the plains beyond and the horsemen and ranches and herds of wild cattle."[8]

The story begins in the New Mennonite community of Piper's Run in northwestern Pennsylvania. Children learn to read and write, but the available books are carefully hoarded relics from before the war, little used and less understood. Teenager Len Colter has heard stories of Bartorstown, far to the west, where science and learning are alive. After getting hints that Bartorstown is real, Len steals away to find this place of promise. The journey reenacts the nineteenth-century frontier. Len makes his way down the Pymatuning River to the Shenango River, the Mahoning River, and the Beaver River to the commercial emporium of Refuge on the north bank of the Ohio. Here wagon roads from the Great Lakes bring furs, iron, flour, and cheese to exchange for salt beef and tallow from the west, kegs of nails and dried fish from the east, molasses and tobacco from the south.

When the town explodes in violence over one merchant's attempt to build an additional warehouse, and thus breach the size limit on settlements, Len makes a run for it. With the help of Bartorstown agents, he takes a steam-powered barge down the Ohio, upstream into the Mississippi, and then into the wide Missouri. Burning cord after cord of wood to breast the current and navigate the treacherous channels, "for days they wallowed up the chutes of the Big Muddy." The country changes from rolling forest to gray-green plain that seems to "go on and on over the rim of the world." At the mouth of the Platte River, the group switches to mule-drawn wagons for a trek southwestward across the "large and lonely prairie." In the cottonwood groves along the streams are isolated ranches whose residents harvest the great herds of wild cattle. At a rendezvous along the South Platte (where small fur trading posts could have been found in the 1830s and 1840s), they meet other wagons that have come up the Arkansas Valley or eastward over South Pass, following other historic trading routes. Finally their route penetrates through red rock canyons deep into the heart of the Colorado Rockies.[9]

Behind the wall of the Front Range is a forward-looking community built on the past. The mining town of Fall Creek is cover for Bartorstown. Occasional visitors see only an ordinary mountain settlement. They don't know that the pre-Destruction government had built a research facility deep in the mine shafts, nor that technicians and scientists are still tending a supercomputer and trying to find ways to reintroduce advanced technology that will not lead to war. In the 2030s, in short, Len Colter seeks the future in the same way as Americans two centuries earlier, retracing the movement westward to the mountains, valleys, and vastness of the West.[10]

Walter Miller Jr. located the future's refuge and ironic hope in the western desert rather than the mountains in *A Canticle for Leibowitz*, one of the most popular and highly regarded science fiction books of the post–World War II era. Generations after the Flame Deluge destroyed civilization in nuclear war, the monks of an abbey dedicated to the Blessed Leibowitz work tirelessly to salvage books and documents from the old time and carefully copy them by hand. In so doing, they carry on the legacy of Isaac Leibowitz, a scientist-survivor of the holocaust who began to save books from angry mobs. The setting is the dry lands of New Mexico, somewhere in the foothills of the Sangre de Cristo Mountains, where the monks can hope to carry on their work undisturbed.[11]

One more example of the westward quest is *The Stand* (1978), usually classed as horror fiction rather than science fiction. Over a hefty 823 pages, Stephen King sends another small, brave band westward to fight for the future. After plague has killed the vast majority of Americans, a small remnant of humanity come together from scattered points in the Northeast (the escape from Manhattan through a Lincoln Tunnel clogged with corpse-filled cars is a deeply vivid scene). The adventurers (pilgrims, knights errant) work their way westward. They stop first in rural Nebraska and then pause to gather both physical and spiritual strength in the almost enchanted Middle Earth of Boulder, Colorado, where they pause to work with other survivors to reconstitute civil society and get the electricity working.

Before winter falls, a chosen few are on to Nevada for ultimate battle with the forces of darkness, which are thriving in the artificial environment of Las Vegas. The showdown comes in front of the MGM Grand Hotel, where the snake of evil devours itself with the accidental detonation of an atomic bomb. The handful of Boulderites become a sacrifice as the entire false city vanishes in fire. Like true pioneers, all of the people of the Free Zone have been tested and strengthened by their westward journey. They find in the West both an oasis of recovery and the apocalyptic wasteland, the places where the future of the nation and world are to be decided.

In the American cycle of history, these very different books agree, the West is the future. When we anticipate the course of global disaster, we commonly imagine saving remnants surviving in the West or trekking westward to reestablish the American project.[12] In similar fashion, we look west to a cyberneticized Pacific world to find continuities from the present to the near future. And we imagine human expansion into the solar system and galaxy as reenactments of the multiple American experiences of continental expansion, with the various wonders, excitements, sins, and mistakes that this expansion has brought.

Bigger than Texas, More Complicated than California

Nicknames and catch phrases are a great convenience. When applied to people or places, they highlight some essential characteristic and help us tell one from another. Across the American landscape, there's a Motor City, an Iron City, a Rose City, an Emerald City, and a Crescent City, not to mention more than enough Gem Cities and Queen Cities to go around. One city is where the West begins, and another is the capital of an inland empire. One state is Golden, another is a Treasure, one is a Water/Winter Wonderland, and yet another was once Photoscenic, if you can believe everything you read on license plates. Nicknames and slogans in turn can generate their own humor, as with the motto once proposed for Iowa: "Warmer than Minnesota, More Fun than Nebraska."

In the same vein, I'm heading these final thoughts with a new slogan: "The American Future: Bigger than Texas, More Complicated than California."[13] The phrase tries to capture the optimism and excitement about the future than has animated much American science fiction—a future that lies before us even more expansively than Texas. It also highlights the complexity and problems that will lie ahead, a complexity that is previewed by the enormous social variety and cultural tensions of contemporary California. If western American history suggests the promise of escape to new frontiers, it also reminds us of the troubles, costs, and contradictions that will accompany any such futures.

It may seem curious that a literature about the future makes such use of the past, but one function of western tropes and narratives is to give science fiction legitimacy. Since the time of Nathaniel Hawthorne, American writers have worried that the United States lacks the long traditions, layers of history, and embedded social patterns that give depth and resonance to European stories. The nation's short history sometimes caused writers to take refuge in European settings (*The Marble Faun* [1860], *The Wings of the Dove* [1902]). At other times it incited them to invent a past of questionable accuracy (*The Scarlet Letter* [1850], *The Deerslayer* [1841]) or recreate entire subcultures (*Moby-Dick* [1851]). By locating future stories as extensions of American history, science fiction practitioners find one way around Hawthorne's complaint. For many such writers, the development of the American West in the nineteenth and twentieth centuries becomes that historical foundation on which to erect narratives and to imagine the future. The western past, in other words, not only provides conceptual tools for thinking about the future, but it also gives those ideas depth and resonance.

This being said, it is important to remember that simple histories have much appeal. The models that have shaped the common understanding of the American experience have long been linear and progressive. Formed during the age of reason of the eighteenth and early nineteenth centuries, the new nation constructed its institutions as expressions of universal principles. Americans thus internalize a fundamental faith in the progress of freedom, as expressed by political leaders otherwise as different as Theodore Roosevelt, John Kennedy, and George W. Bush. As Louis Hartz noted a half century ago, the United States was born free of feudalism and its cultural and social encumbrances.[14] From George Bancroft in the 1840s to Francis Fukuyama in the 1990s, the liberal state that is open to free expression and free enterprise has been praised as a new site for the birth of freedom.[15]

The nation also absorbed and seemed to justify the Victorian faith in economic and scientific progress as it grew to maturity during the nineteenth century. The application of reason and ingenuity could overcome old obstacles to abundance and make the United States the great expression of scientific engineering and development. The natural richness of the continent, as David Potter pointed out in a classic interpretation, made it possible for Americans to act as a "people of plenty."[16] The settlement of the Mississippi Valley and Far West offered a physical analogy, source, and confirmation of such worldly progress. National leaders like such a positive past because it seems to extend reassuringly into a progressing future, and Americans identify the idea of progress most deeply in their narratives of the West.

As I have tried to show, however, science fiction itself has become more complicated in its utilization of western history, simultaneously accepting and questioning our western stories. If one view of the future in space is "like Texas, only bigger," then another, more interesting view is "like California, but even more complicated"—and that's saying something, because California is already a complicated place. It is a state where ethnic and racial variety is previewing nationwide demographic change, where politics is populist and corporate at the same time, where the information economy has taken deepest root, where breakneck growth in a fragile landscape has presented stark environmental choice—the place that Americans love, and love to hate.

One way to introduce complications is to undercut the imagery and implicit values by showing pedestrian realities behind heroic facades (the Wizard of Oz strategy, to reference another western story). Kage Baker's time travel novels, which take special agents from both the past and future to early California, provide pointed satire. Her books are full of crooks, fools, and ordinary bumbling folks, and they fit with historical novels and movies that have tried to deromanticize the western past, such as Robert Altman's film *McCabe and Mrs. Miller* (1971). In *Sky Coyote* (1999), Baker depicts precontact Indians, along the coast near Santa Barbara, as giggling Valley Girls who think that group sex is a kick. *Mendoza in Hollywood* (2000), set in southern California in 1862, includes a tiny, dusty, impoverished Los Angeles that comes out of south-of-the-border western movies and undercuts the modern supercity. A central character is a California teenager who's a sort of premodern surfer dude.[17]

John Barnes, in *The Sky So Big and Black* (2002), simultaneously questions and uses the idea of frontier values. It follows the story of a Martian ecospector and his fifteen-year-old daughter Terpsichore Melpomene Murray. In the twenty-second century, prospectors who find deposits of methane and water are useful for the terraforming effort, but the easy finds have been tagged, and the Development Corporation is starting to squeeze out the independents. In this background story, the book shares the framework of a vanishing miners' frontier with Larry Niven, Robert Heinlein, C. J. Cherryh, and others. "So there's going to be more and more of us out here," says Teri-Mel's father, "and the big scoreholes'll get found faster, and for the most part, the big wild areas are gonna be overrun in short periods of time, something like I imagine the old gold rushes were a long time back."[18]

However, Barnes plays the vanishing glory days against cynicism about the relevance of the frontier myth. The plot revolves around Teri-Mel's coming of age, and Barnes uses her sarcastic teenage voice as a way to surface ambiguous feelings about "frontier" values. Teri-Mel tries to keep the family business going; she knows that she'd rather be out prospecting than sitting in school. In particular, she hates history class. She comments,

> The school session when I was seven . . . there was this unit (schools are always having units like people have boils) about the early frontiers, the ones way back on Earth, while the Europeans were conquering everybody else, before the real frontiers out here even started. Studying this was supposed to Teach Us Something or Other. They called it "The Frontier Tradition," which was pretty silly because even if the roundings is a frontier, it isn't one like the outback, the West, the New East, or El Norte, or any of the others were.

But there is also value to the actual frontier experience: "RSC [Red Sands City] is getting to be less of a frontier town, just as Mars is getting to be less of a frontier world. There's less ignorance and less crudity than there was, but more bone-deep stupidity out here now."[19] Barnes thus scorns the historical comparison while simultaneously identifying the Martian outback as a *real* frontier, which is a concept meaningful only in comparison with the past. Like her American predecessors, Teri-Mel doesn't much care about history, but she also knows the American frontier is a source of validation for her life—just as it helps validate science fiction futures.

Another skillful challenge to western tropes is Melissa Scott's effort to simultaneously embed and undercut western tropes in *Trouble and Her Friends* (1994) (see Chapter 1). As Scott comments, "what I liked about framing *Trouble* as a western of sorts was the way it set up certain very strong expectations—the solitary gunslinger, the unsympathetic forces of law and order, the showdown—which I could at the same time fulfill and subvert."

The western framework gives the novel a strong structure, but also gives it "extra dimensions by the ways it does and doesn't fit the formula" (this is very similar to the ways that Barnes uses the frontier comparison). As noted earlier, the gunslinger role in *Trouble* is filled by two lesbians rather than one straight but bashful white-hatted man. Scott also sees her story, which emphasizes the ways in which Net users might embody themselves, as questioning the first wave of cyberpunk and its heroes who want to escape their body. In effect, she says, the book challenges the image of the early console cowboys in "the same way that revisionist historians have been reconsidering the western experience."[20]

As I hope the previous chapters have shown, science fiction *has* become more sophisticated in its understanding of western historical narratives as well as the clichés of western writing. Independent, steely-eyed prospectors evolve into female pilots who have to navigate the fine line of professional and sexual independence in a masculinized environment, or into a fifteen-year-old girl (Teri-Mel) who spends much of her time thinking about eligible boys but has moral courage when a crisis comes. Terraforming may initially attract audacious engineers and scientists, but it requires discipline and perhaps even despotism to carry through. Homesteading ends in heartbreak as well as fertile fields. The preservation of political freedom comes only through years of tedious committee meetings, not by heroic revolution, and the best that any one person can hope is to move society one small step toward utopia. The powerful, imperious cities of Los Angeles and San Francisco face problematic futures even as they grow to global influence, and the American dream of a westward empire may begin to fade even as it seems poised to succeed.

We arrive now at a final question. Science fiction may be fun, and it may be increasingly literate, but is it useful in the here and now? Reading science fiction may feed our imaginations about the future, stretching our minds like high school Latin was once thought to do. But can it make us more thoughtful and effective citizens in dealing with the nonimagined world around us? The answer, I think, is yes, for science fiction looks both backward and forward as it recycles and rethinks the older themes and narratives of the American West.

Western narratives are not going to go away. Even if western films and TV series are currently eclipsed by other types of adventure stories, the history of western exploration and settlement still resonate with the broad public. Think about the way that the skillful regional novelist Larry

McMurtry (*Horseman, Pass By* [1961], *Leaving Cheyenne* [1963], *The Last Picture Show* [1966]) turned himself into a *Lonesome Dove* (1985) cowboy book franchise. Stories of cattle drives—and Lewis and Clark, transcontinental railroads, homesteaders, and Forty-Niners—still excite Americans in the present, and they help to structure the ways that we are able to think about the future. Science fiction helps to affirm the continuing relevance of these western stories by incorporating them into the future. In doing this, of course, it adds to its own appeal as a product and commodity of popular culture. It is not that science fiction readers want Louis L'Amour transposed directly to other planets, but many do enjoy the familiarity of frontier stories replayed. The forbidding and frightening future may become more comprehensible with familiar guideposts from a valued past.

At the same time, many writers of the last generation have questioned and transformed these old narrative stories by using them in new ways. Fredric Jameson, in one of the most influential critical essays about science fiction, has claimed that science fiction serves a political function by showing the possibility of different futures.[21] It enables political change by making it possible for readers to see that their own times and circumstances are historically contingent rather than fixed. He argues that historical fiction in the nineteenth century had a similar effect by highlighting the contingency rather than inevitability of the European present. In its encouragement of historical consciousness, such fiction was part of the growing nineteenth-century understanding of history as a story of improvement through conscious choice (rather than endless cyclical repetition or irresistible movement toward the millennium).[22] Science fiction, Jameson says, has now assumed a similar role of embodying and dramatizing the idea of *continuing* historical change and the malleability of the future. Science fiction thus undermines the cultural dominance of consumer capitalism, a role that he applauds from the viewpoint of neo-Marxist political philosophy.

If Jameson's proposition is accurate, then science fiction can make us more historical and therefore more critical in our thinking, and help us to see alternatives to the powerful one-dimensional culture of this (or any) present time. Writers who want to challenge common versions of the western past can utilize western narratives and metaphors to gain attention and to lead readers far enough into their stories to see their variations on these same old narratives and metaphors. To the extent that they turn these old narratives of progress and success into more complex and ambiguous stories, they also remind us of the need to think critically about the nation's established narrative. In the examples I've chosen, the bedrock concern is how to construct an inclusive society in which the civic realm is legitimate and supportive of individuals trying to realize their potential.

Even when it uses and often celebrates the new technologies that are being spawned by global capitalism and big government, science fiction often moves beyond self-satisfaction. It can help us see the present as historical and uncertain, and therefore it can help us to think about alternatives. It does so, however, by placing the present in the middle of this ongoing history that stretches seamlessly from past certainties to conceivable futures. The essence of my argument in the preceding chapters has been the possibilities of retooling the *old* narratives through the science fiction imagination. Writers as diverse as Kim Stanley Robinson and Octavia Butler, Ursula K. Le Guin and C. J. Cherryh, Melissa Scott and Greg Bear, Pamela Sargent and Jonathan Lethem, all show ways that the old narratives can be reconfigured and reanimated. The outlines of mining frontiers and farming frontiers remain the same, as do the frameworks of western democracy and westward empire. But many science fiction writers reinhabit the frameworks in new ways, thinking about ambiguities as well as triumphs and highlighting the necessity for critical citizenship.

If science fiction is a guide, we do not have to repudiate the narratives that have been such powerful nation-builders. Americans—that is, white middle-class Americans like me and many science fiction writers—have not been telling stories that are wrong, just overly simple. We need to understand how to adapt and enrich our western-national stories for new centuries, how to maintain their virtues while making them more inclusive and careful of people and places. In this way, science fiction may offer ideas for recasting historical questions about borderlands, wilderness, and community. It can likewise explore issues that remain current and ongoing concerns for the nation—the balance of individual freedom and civic obligations, the problems with trying to substitute economic growth for social justice, the need for a future in which careers and opportunities are open to talent across the divides of gender, race, and class. If we can live in our present as the richest science fiction inhabits the future, we will be following the advice of Tom Barnard in Kim Stanley Robinson's *Pacific Edge*: "utopia is when our lives matter."[23]

NOTES

Introduction: Launching Pads

1. Samuel R. Delany, *Shorter Views: Queer Thoughts and the Politics of the Paraliterary* (Hanover, NH: Wesleyan University Press, 1999), 343; Thomas Disch, *The Dreams Our Stuff Is Made Of: How Science Fiction Conquered the World* (New York: Simon and Schuster, 1988), 91.

2. Kingsley Amis, *New Maps of Hell: A Survey of Science Fiction* (New York: Harcourt, Brace, 1960), 18.

3. Delany, quoted in Gary K. Wolfe, *The Known and the Unknown* (Kent, OH: Kent State University Press, 1979), 18. Joanna Russ, "Toward an Aesthetic of Science Fiction," *Science-Fiction Studies* 2 (1975): 112–19. Also David Ketterer, *New Worlds for Old: The Apocalyptic Imagination, Science Fiction, and American Literature* (Bloomington: Indiana University Press, 1974), 18–19.

4. Carl D. Malmgren, *Worlds Apart: The Narratology of Science Fiction* (Bloomington: Indiana University Press, 1991). Darko Suvin, *The Metamorphoses of Science Fiction: On the Poetics and History of a Literary Genre* (New Haven, CT: Yale University Press, 1979), used a similar distinction between extrapolation and more freewheeling analogy. Suvin also introduced the concept that the driving force in science fiction is the author's introduction of a *novum*, or "a totalizing phenomenon or relationship deviating from the author's and implied reader's norm of reality" (64). By "totalizing," he means that the novum "entails a change of the whole universe of the tale" and is not simply diverting or metaphorical. Yet another way to put the essential point is from critic Eric Rabkin, who states that "a work belongs in the genre of science fiction if its narrative world is at least somewhat different from our own, and if that difference is apparent against the background of an organized body of knowledge." Quoted in Sharona Ben-Tov, *The Artificial Paradise; Science Fiction and American Reality* (Ann Arbor: University of Michigan Press, 1995), 11.

5. The examples are from Kim Stanley Robinson, *Years of Rice and Salt* (2002); Ward Moore, *Bring the Jubilee* (1953); Philip K. Dick, *The Man in the High Castle* (1962); Len Deighton, *SS-GB* (1978); and Phillip Roth, *The Plot against America: A Novel* (2004). See Karen Hellekson, "Toward a Taxonomy of the Alternate History Genre," *Extrapolation* 41 (2000): 248–56.

6. Kim Stanley Robinson, "Notes for an Essay on Cecelia Holland," *Foundation* 40 (1987): 54; Norman Spinrad, *Science Fiction in the Real World* (Carbondale: Southern Illinois University Press, 1990), 56.

7. Edward James, *Science Fiction in the 20th Century* (New York: Oxford University Press, 1994), 66, 57; Alexei Panshin and Cory Panshin, *World beyond the Hill* (Los Angeles: Tarcher, 1989), 376.

8. James, *Science Fiction*, 109; Tom Moylan, *Traps of the Untainted Sky: Science Fiction, Utopia, Dystopia* (Boulder, CO: Westview Press, 2000), 25–28.

9. Isaac Asimov, "Social Science Fiction," in *Science Fiction: The Future*, ed. Dick Allen (New York: Harcourt, Brace, 1971), 273.

10. Margaret Atwood, interview in the Anchor Doubleday edition of *The Handmaid's Tale* (Garden City, NY: Anchor Doubleday, 1998) 317; and "The Queen of Quinkdom," *New York Review of Books*, September 26, 2002.

11. For example, Suvin, *Metamorphoses*, 16–36.

12. Thomas Disch recalls a noted literary critic who refused the categorization of 1984; to this keeper of the temple, "an accredited intellectual of Orwell's magnitude could not, by definition, have written science fiction." Samuel Delany tells of reducing a bookstore clerk to tears by insisting that Don DeLillo's *Ratner's Star* could be shelved with science fiction. No, no, she cried, he should not insult such a *good* book. Disch, *Dreams*, 4; Samuel R. Delany, *Shorter Views*, 208–9. We can assume that the roll call of such incidents is long indeed. *Ratner's Star* shares its premise with James Gunn, *The Listeners* (1972; fully science fiction), Carl Sagan's *Contact* (1985; science fiction as mass market thriller), and Mary Doria Russell, *The Sparrow* (1996; theological speculation in the clothing of science fiction).

13. Malmgren, *Worlds Apart*, 157; James, *Science Fiction*, 60.

14. Brian Aldiss with David Wingrove, *Trillion Year Spree: The History of Science Fiction* (New York: Atheneum, 1986), 280. This book updates Aldiss's *Billion Year Spree* of 1973.

15. James, *Science Fiction*, 182.

16. Pamela Sargent, interview with Jill Engel-Cox, December 2000–April 2001, available at http://www.sff.net/people/PSargent/interview2002.htm.

17. None of this boundary drawing is to argue that pure space operas can't be entertaining, nor that fantasy is an inferior genre—just different. But such literature requires an entirely different critical and historical approach than I offer here, one that leads readers back to myth, epic poetry, and the universal unconscious in its various guises.

18. The deep background of science fiction can be followed in H. Bruce Franklin, *Future Perfect: American Science Fiction of the Nineteenth Century* (New York: Oxford University Press, 1966), and *War Stars: The Superweapon and the American Imagination* (New York: Oxford University Press, 1988); I. F. Clarke, *Voices Prophesying War: Future Wars, 1763–3749* (Oxford: Oxford University Press, 1992); Everett E. Bleiler, *Science Fiction: The Early Years* (Kent, OH: Kent State University Press, 1991); Thomas Clareson, *Some Kind of Paradise: The Emergence of American Science Fiction* (Westport, CT: Greenwood Press, 1985); Marjorie Hope Nicolson, *Voyages to the Moon* (New York: Macmillan, 1948); Robert Philmus, *Into the Unknown: The Evolution of Science Fiction from Francis Godwin to H. G. Wells* (Berkeley: University of California Press, 1970); Paul Alkon, *Science Fiction before 1900: Imagination Discovers Technology* (New York: Twayne, 1994); James Gunn, *The Road to Science Fiction: From Gilgamesh to Wells*, vol. 1 (New York: New American Library, 1977); Darko Suvin, *Victorian Science Fiction in the UK: The Discourses of Knowledge and Power* (Boston: G. K. Hall, 1983).

19. Other Verne books that are really travel adventures include *Michel Strogoff* (1876) and *The Children of Captain Grant* (1867). Martin Green classifies these and other Verne works as "wanderer stories" and continues the type with *Kim* (1901) and *The Adventures of Huckleberry Finn* (1884) in *Seven Types of Adventure Tale* (State College: Penn State University Press, 1991), 145–62.

20. Richard Phillips, *Mapping Men and Empire: A Geography of Adventure* (New York: Routledge, 1997). Australian adventure stories that range from children's adventures to early feminist reworkings are discussed in Robert Dixon, *Writing the Colonial Adventure: Race, Gender and Nation in Anglo-Australian Popular Fiction, 1875–1914* (New York: Cambridge University Press, 1995). We can note in relation to *Coral Island* that Herman Melville had recently offered his own Pacific castaway stories for adults in *Typee* and *Omoo*. For American readers, the South Seas adventure story continued to thrive in the twentieth century in the books of Charles Nordhoff and James Norman Hall, authors of a trilogy about the mutiny on the *Bounty* and other South Seas books.

21. Roger Nichols, "Western Attractions: Europeans and Americans," *Pacific Historical Review* 74 (2005): 1–18.

22. Dixon, *Writing the Colonial Adventure*, 62. Martin Green, *Dreams of Adventure: Deeds of Empire* (New York: Basic Books, 1979), 38. The books were also a sort of dialectic reaction to the dominance of midcentury English literature by triple-volume novels written by and for women, with the adventure stories claiming a masculine readership for manly tales in which women were only decorations (not unlike much American science fiction). Robert Fraser, in *The Victorian Quest Romance* (Plymouth, UK: Northcote House, 1998), gives a good summary of this publishing phenomenon and offers the term "quest romance" for the genre that others call "imperial romance."

23. John McClure, *Late Imperial Romance* (New York: Verso, 1994), 30–55, discusses Conrad, Forster, and Kipling as artists who undercut the genre and find spiritual strength in the land of the "other." Also see Andrea White, *Joseph Conrad and the Adventure Tradition: Constructing and Deconstructing the Imperial Subject* (New York: Cambridge University Press, 1993). In Kipling's 1888 novelette "The Man Who Would Be King," the adventurer Daniel Dravot loses his life by overreaching ambition and cultural arrogance, and his sidekick Peachy Carnehan barely escapes to tell his tale of a "white" race high in the Hindu Kush Mountains who turn out to be uninterested in being rescued by English adventurers.

24. Thomas Clareson, "Lost Lands, Lost Races: A Pagan Princess of Their Very Own," in *Many Futures, Many Worlds: Theme and Form in Science Fiction*, ed. Thomas Clareson (Kent, OH: Kent State University Press, 1977). Kim Stanley Robinson's *Antarctica* (New York: Bantam, 1998) is a recent science fiction novel that revives the trope of the secret community hidden beneath that continent's frozen surface, albeit with the intent to stimulate ecological thinking rather than Eurocentric dreams.

25. Green, *Dreams of Adventure*; Tom Pocock, *Rider Haggard and the Lost Empire* (London: Weidenfeld and Nicolson, 1993); Wendy Katz, *Rider Haggard and the Fiction of Empire: A Critical Study of British Imperial Fiction* (Cambridge: Cambridge University Press, 1987).

26. Fraser, *Victorian Quest Romance*, 67. Leading science fiction writer Greg Bear recently paid tribute to Conan Doyle, as well as to Lost World movies such as *King Kong* (1933), in *Dinosaur Summer* (New York: Warner Books, 1998). It is set in an alternative past in which the Lost World is real and dinosaurs become circus attractions. By 1947, interest has dwindled and it is decided to return the

remaining captive dinos to their home plateau in Venezuela. Many adventures occur on this reverse expedition of "undiscovery." The characters include a fictional version of Ray Harryhausen, the pioneering movie special effects artist. It is a fun read on many levels.

27. Pamela Sargent, interview with Jill Engel-Cox, December 2000–April 2001, http://www.engel-cox.org/sargent/interview2001.htm.

28. Martin Green, *Seven Types of Adventure Tale* (State College: Pennsylvania State University Press, 1991), 36.

29. Ketterer, *New Worlds for Old*, also associates the sense of wonder with the transformative, mind-expanding actions and moments of the apocalyptic imagination that he finds central to science fiction.

30. Northrop Frye, *Anatomy of Criticism* (Princeton, NJ: Princeton University Press, 1971); Richard Chase, *The American Novel and Its Tradition* (New York: Doubleday, 1957); Harry Levin, *The Power of Blackness: Hawthorne, Poe, Melville* (New York: Knopf, 1958); R. W. B. Lewis, *The American Adam* (Chicago: University of Chicago Press, 1955); Daniel Hoffman, *Form and Fable in American Fiction* (New York: Oxford University Press, 1961); Ketterer, *New Worlds for Old*, 22–24.

31. David Mogen, "The Frontier Archetype and the Myth of America: Patterns that Shape the American Dream," in *The Frontier Experience and the American Dream: Essays on American Literature*, ed. David Mogen, Mark Busby, and Paul Bryant (College Station: Texas A&M University Press, 1989), 15–30.

32. Another writing tradition within the romance is the Gothic tale of confrontation with the unknown or extrahuman. Brian Aldiss derives science fiction from the nineteenth-century Gothic novel in *Trillion Year Spree*, 16–17, 25. He identifies *Frankenstein* as the first self-conscious science fiction novel. David Mogen argues that much of American writing in and about the West is gothic in form and sensibility, and he argues that science fiction derives as a variant of this national-regional genre. See David Mogen, "Wilderness, Metamorphosis, and Millennium: Gothic Apocalypse from the Puritans to the Cyberpunks," in *Frontier Gothic: Terror and Wonder at the Frontier in American Literature*, ed. David Mogen, Scott P. Sanders, and Joanne B. Karpinski (Rutherford, NJ: Fairleigh Dickinson University Press, 1993).

33. Jane Tompkins, *West of Everything: The Inner Life of Westerns* (New York: Oxford University Press, 1992), 70–71; Mary Lawlor, *Recalling the Wild: Naturalism and the Closing of the American West* (New Brunswick, NJ: Rutgers University Press, 2000), 2.

34. Gary K. Wolfe, "Frontiers in Space," in Mogen, Busby, and Bryant, *Frontier Experience*, 256–57.

35. Quoted in Richard Etulain, *Re-imagining the American West: A Century of Fiction, History, and Art* (Tucson: University of Arizona Press, 1996), 93.

36. Krista Comer, *Landscapes of the New West: Gender and Geography in Contemporary Women's Writing* (Chapel Hill: University of North Carolina Press, 1999), 11.

37. Wallace Stegner, *Where the Bluebird Sings to the Lemonade Springs: Living and Writing in the West* (New York: Random House, 1992), 138.

38. Mogen, "Frontier Archetype," in Mogen, Busby, and Bryant, *Frontier Experience*, 16–19.

Chapter 1. Never Final Frontiers

1. For the curious, "pompatus of love," which follows in the lyrics, was taken from a 1954 rhythm and blues song, "The Letter," by the Medallions, where it signified an idealized sex figure. For the derivation, see http://www.straightdope.com/classics/a4_065.html.

2. David Wrobel, *Promised Lands: Promotion, Memory and the Creation of the American West* (Lawrence: University Press of Kansas, 2002).

3. For examples, see Paul Carter, *The Invention of the Future: Fifty Years of Magazine Science Fiction* (New York: Columbia University Press, 1977), 60–72; Wyn Wachhorst, "The Dream of Spaceflight: Nostalgia for a Bygone Future," *Massachusetts Review* 36 (Spring 1995): 7–31; Maura Phillips Mackowski, "The Moon, Mars, and the Imagination: The Southwestern Landscape and the Visualization of Other Worlds," paper delivered to Western History Association, October 2001. The convention for depicting Venus was to copy African or Amazonian rain forests, or perhaps southern Florida before air conditioning.

4. Greg Metcalf, "American Images of Space and the Future as the Final Frontier," in *Possible Futures: Science Fiction Art from the Frank Collection*, ed. Dorit Yaron (College Park: University of Maryland Art Gallery, 2000), 42 51.

5. Kim Stanley Robinson, *Red Mars* (New York: Bantam Spectra, 1992), 40, 183, 245, 261; *Green Mars* (New York: Bantam Spectra, 1994), 364; *Blue Mars* (New York: Bantam Spectra, 1996), 275.

6. Quoted in Gregory M. Pfitzer, "The Only Good Alien Is a Dead Alien: Science Fiction and the Metaphysics of Indian-Hating on the High Frontier," *Journal of American Culture* 18 (Spring 1995): 52.

7. The body of the book concerns the overthrow of the worlds-spanning empire of Eron through heroic subversion, the revolt of the provinces, and pitched battles in a world-sized city. "The Masters of Eron are the mightiest beings in the universe," reads the back of my paperback copy, "a space-traveling race whose advanced technology has won them control of an intergalactic kingdom and the power to stifle all planets under their iron fist." James E. Gunn and Jack Williamson, *Star Bridge* (New York: Collier Books, 1983).

8. John Jakes, *Six-Gun Planet* (New York: Warner Books, 1970); John Boyd, *The Andromeda Gun* (New York: Berkley, 1974). See Robert Murrau Davis, "The Frontiers of Genre: Science Fiction Westerns," *Science-Fiction Studies* 12 (1985): 33–41. Another direct transplantation of the Old West is H. Beam Piper and John J. McGuire, *A Planet for Texans* (New York: Ace, 1958).

9. Ben Bova, *Mars* (New York: Bantam Books, 1992), 4. Bova does not seem to know much about the actual Navajo, describing them as living in pueblos, making pottery and "carpets," and descending from the Anasazi of Mesa Verde.

10. Melissa Scott, *Trouble and Her Friends* (New York: TOR, 1994), 320, 323, 330. Scott modeled her heroine after the trope of the returning gunslinger as part of an effort to explore the "frontier" character of the electronic frontier, as she describes in comments posted on www.pointsman.net/mpage/trouble.html.

11. Paul J. McAuley, *Red Dust* (New York: AvoNova/William Morrow, 1993), 106, 247–48.

12. Gary K. Wolfe, "Frontiers in Space," in *The Frontier Experience and the*

American Dream: Essays on American Literature, ed. David Mogen, Mark Busby, and Paul Bryant (College Station: Texas A&M University Press, 1989), 249.

13. Robert A. Heinlein, *Farmer in the Sky* (New York: Ballantine, 1975) and *Tunnel in the Sky* (New York: Ballantine, 1977), 13–17; Bradbury, *The Martian Chronicles* (New York: William Morrow, 1997 [1950]), 158–59.

14. Beverly J. Stoeltje, in "Making a Frontier Myth: Folklore Process in a Modern Nation," *Western Folklore* 46 (October 1987): 240, makes the same point in slightly different language: "As the last frontiersmen of the West put away their pistols and placed their shotguns on the pick-up gun racks, science and technology gave birth to a new era—the Space Age—which would explore and claim the space above the earth . . . and before our very eyes the covered wagon magically became a space rocket."

15. David T. Courtwright, *Sky as Frontier: Adventure, Aviation, and Empire* (College Station: Texas A&M University Press, 2005).

16. Vannevar Bush, *Science: The Endless Frontier* (Washington: U.S. Government Printing Office, 1945), from letter of transmittal, July 25, 1945, and from President Roosevelt's letter, November 17, 1944.

17. Howard E. McCurdy, *Space and the American Imagination* (Washington, DC: Smithsonian Institute Press, 1999).

18. Susan Landrum Mangus, *Conestoga Wagons to the Moon: The Frontier, the American Space Program, and National Identity* (Ph.D. diss., Ohio State University, 1999).

19. Gerard K. O'Neill, *The High Frontier: Communities in Space* (New York: Morrow, 1977), 274. Also see O'Neill, *2081: A Hopeful View of the Human Future* (New York: Simon and Schuster, 1981) and Harry Shipman, *Humans in Space: 21st Century Frontiers* (New York: Plenum, 1998). See also the chapter "The Domestication of Space: Gerard K. O'Neill's Suburban Diaspora" in De Witt Douglas Kilgore, *Astrofuturism: Science, Race, and Visions of Utopia in Space* (Philadelphia: University of Pennsylvania Press, 2003), 150–85. Ray A. Williamson, "Outer Space as Frontier: Lessons for Today," *Western Folklore* 46 (October 1987): 255–67, cites many examples of politicians and engineers using the frontier analogy: military satellites are equated with forts in the old West; Senator John Glenn describes space as "the modern frontier for national adventure"; the U.S. National Commission on Space in *Pioneering the Space Frontier* (1986) touches base with Columbus, notes the attractions of virgin lands in North America, and states that "the settlement of North America and other continents was a prelude to humanity's greatest challenge: the space frontier."

20. Norman Spinrad, *Science Fiction in the Real World* (Carbondale: Southern Illinois University Press, 1990).

21. For information about these two organizations, see http://www.marssociety.org and http://www.asi.org.

22. The text of Bush's speech can be accessed at http://www.nasa.gov/pdf/54868main_bush_trans.pdf.

23. It's impossible to write about Heinlein without using the word *frontier*. "The Last Frontier: Escape into Space" is a section in H. Bruce Franklin, *Robert A. Heinlein: America as Science Fiction* (New York: Oxford University Press, 1980). "History to Come: New Frontiers" is a chapter in Leon Stover, *Robert A. Heinlein*

(Boston: Twayne Publishers, 1987). "Frontiers of the Future: Heinlein's Future History Series" is David Samuelson's chapter in *Robert A. Heinlein*, ed. Joseph D. Olander and Martin G. Greenberg (New York: Taplinger, 1978); and "Building a Space Frontier: Robert A. Heinlein and the American Tradition" is Kilgore's chapter in *Astrofuturism*.

24. Robert A. Heinlein, *The Green Hills of Earth* (New York: Signet, n.d. [1951]), 37, 51, 168. The stories were published in magazines from 1941 to 1949. The same sorts of western frontier background were still in use fifty years later, as in G. David Nordley's depiction of the opening of a section of terraformed Venus as an Oklahoma land rush: "Some media types were saying that the opening of the Devani Archipelago south of Beta Region was the largest new land rush in the history of the human race," requiring participants to file a claim on a central map and then occupy the parcel by the next sunrise. G. David Nordley, "Dawn Venus" (1995), in *Worldmakers: SF Adventures in Terraforming*, ed. Gardner Dozois (New York: St. Martin's Press, 2001), 221.

25. Heinlein, *Green Hills*, 137.

26. Gregory Benford, *The Martian Race* (New York: Warner Books, 1999), 322.

27. Robert Zubrin, *First Landing* (New York: Ace Books, 2001), 241; Robert Zubrin, "A New Martian Frontier: Recapturing the Soul of America," in *Frontiers of Space Exploration*, ed. Roger Launius (Westport, CT: Greenwood Press, 1998), 152–60; Robert Zubrin and Richard Wagner, *The Case for Mars: The Plan to Settle the Red Planet and Why We Must* (New York: Free Press 1996).

28. Langdon Elsbee, "Our Pursuit of Loneliness: An Alternative to This Paradigm," in Mogen et al., *Frontier Experience*, 31–49; Annette Kolodny, *The Land Before Her: Fantasy and Experience of the American Frontier* (Chapel Hill: University of North Carolina Press, 1984). Robinson's books are *Red Mars*, *Green Mars*, and *Blue Mars*. Sargent's are *Venus of Dreams*, *Venus of Shadows*, and *Child of Venus*.

29. See the editors' introduction to Mogen et al., *Frontier Experience*, 4–8.

30. Samuel Delany, *Shorter Views: Queer Thoughts on the Politics of the Paraliterary* (Hanover, NH: Wesleyan University Press, 1999), 181–83.

31. Wolfe, "Frontiers in Space," 248.

32. Leo Marx, *The Machine in the Garden: Technology and the Pastoral Ideal in America* (New York: Oxford University Press, 1964).

33. David Mogen, *Wilderness Visions: The Western Theme in Science Fiction Literature*, 2nd ed. (San Bernardino, CA: Borgo Press, 1993). The essays in *Frontier Gothic: Terror and Wonder at the Frontier in American Literature*, ed. David Mogen, Scott P. Sanders, and Joanne Karpinski (Rutherford, NJ: Fairleigh Dickinson University Press, 1993), explore American frontier fiction and draw links to evocations in science fiction of the terror and possibility of the wilderness.

34. Frederick Jackson Turner, "The Frontier in American History," in *Proceedings of the Forty-First Annual Meeting of the State Historical Society of Wisconsin* (Madison: State Historical Society of Wisconsin, 1894); Harold Innis, *The Fur Trade in Canada: An Introduction to Canadian Economic History* (New Haven, CT: Yale University Press, 1930).

35. Entry points for the "new western history" include Patricia Nelson Limerick, *Legacy of Conquest: The Unbroken Past of the American West* (New York: Norton, 1987) and *Something in the Soil: Legacies and Reckonings in the New West* (New York: Norton, 2000); Clyde Milner II, Carol O'Connor, and Martha Sandweiss, eds., *The Oxford History of the American West* (New York: Oxford University Press, 1994); Richard White, *It's Your Misfortune and None of My Own: A New History of the American West* (Norman: University of Oklahoma Press, 1991); Patricia Nelson Limerick, Clyde Milner II, and Charles Rankin, eds., *Trails: Toward a New Western History* (Lawrence: University Press of Kansas, 1991); and the essays in a special issue of the journal *Historian* 66 (Fall 2004), written by ten recent presidents of the Western History Association.

36. The phrases come from Theodore Roosevelt, *The Winning of the West*, 4 vols. (New York: G. P. Putnam's Sons, 1889–1896); and Stephen Ambrose, *Undaunted Courage: Meriwether Lewis, Thomas Jefferson, and the Opening of the American West* (New York: Simon and Schuster, 1996).

37. Elliott West, "A Longer, Grimmer, but More Interesting Story," *Montana: The Magazine of Western History* 40 (Summer 1990): 60–76.

38. Walter Nugent, *Into the West: The Story of Its People* (New York: Knopf, 1999); Patricia Nelson Limerick, "Going West and Ending Up Global," *Western Historical Quarterly* 32 (Spring 2001): 5–23. For one of the most imaginative such comparisons, see Kate Brown, "Gridded Lives: Why Kazakhstan and Montana Are Nearly the Same Place," *American Historical Review* 106 (2001): 17–48.

39. Moylan, *Scraps of the Untainted Sky: Science Fiction, Utopia, Dystopia* (Boulder, CO: Westview Press, 2000), 6–7; Edward James, *Science Fiction in the 20th Century* (New York: Oxford University Press, 1994), 96.

40. My project is not a history of science fiction, for which see such books as James Gunn, *Alternate Worlds: The Illustrated History of Science Fiction* (Englewood Cliffs, NJ: Prentice-Hall, 1975); James, *Science Fiction*; and Brian Aldiss with David Wingrove, *The Trillion Year Spree: The History of Science Fiction* (New York: Atheneum, 1986). Nor is it a comprehensive critique, as offered, for example, by Thomas Disch, *The Dreams Our Stuff Is Made Of: How Science Fiction Conquered the World* (New York: Simon and Schuster, 1998). Perhaps the closest to my approach is Kilgore's *Astrofuturism*, which examines the ways in which Americans have used the settings of science fiction to explore issues of racial division.

Chapter 2. Beyond Alaska: Sourdoughs, Lunies, Belters, and Other Tough Guys

1. Gregory Benford, "Dark Sanctuary," in *Matter's End* (New York: Bantam Spectra, 1995).

2. The quote comes from the Amazon.com advertising site.

3. Susan Kollin, *Nature's State: Imagining Alaska as the Last Frontier* (Chapel Hill: University of North Carolina Press, 2001), 28–39; William H. Goetzmann and Kay Sloan, *Looking Far North: The Harriman Expedition to Alaska, 1899* (Princeton, NJ: Princeton University Press, 1982).

4. Kollin, *Nature's State*, 62.

5. Henry M. Stanley, *In Darkest Africa, or The Quest, Rescue, and Retreat of Emin Pasha*,

Governor of Equatoria (New York: Scribner's, 1890).

6. In reality, of course, there were forms of cooperation from the start, quickly followed by investments in railroads and steamboats to ease the journey. For the rigors of travel into the gold country, see Kathryn Morse, *The Nature of Gold: An Environmental History of the Alaska/Yukon Gold Rush* (Seattle: University of Washington Press, 2003).

7. Kenneth Coates and William R. Morrison, *The Alaska Highway during World War II: The U.S. Army Occupation of Canada* (Norman: University of Oklahoma Press, 1992).

8. One of Lolita's last letters to Humbert Humbert reports that she and her husband have a great job prospect in Juneau. Coach Pepper dreams of Alaska as an alternative to the failing town of Thalia, Texas. Kollin, *Nature's State*, 179–80.

9. John S. Whitehead, "Noncontiguous Wests: Alaska and Hawaiʻi," in *Many Wests: Place, Culture, and Regional Identity*, ed. David Wrobel and Michael Steiner (Lawrence: University Press of Kansas, 1997), 315–41.

10. Jon Krakauer, *Into the Wild* (New York: Villard, 1996).

11. Philip Fradkin, *Wildest Alaska: Journeys of Great Peril in Lituya Bay* (Berkeley: University of California Press, 2001); William Lang, "Water Trails," *Pacific Historical Review* 71 (November 2002): 667.

12. A few hours later, the hippies "feed on this new dream, this dream of starting over, of building something from the ground up like the pioneers they all secretly believed they were. . . . One by one they stripped off some garment or charm or totem and flung it into the fire, all the while pledging allegiance to the new ideal, to freedom absolute, to Alaska." T. Coraghessan Boyle, *Drop City* (New York: Viking, 2003), 33, 168, 176.

13. Judith Kleinfeld, message to H-Net Western History List, May 6, 2003. Kleinfeld, *Go For It: Finding Your Own Frontier* (Kenmore, WA: Epicenter Press, 2004).

14. "A Belter's home is the interior of his suit," writes Larry Niven in *World of Ptavvs* (New York: Ballantine, 1966), 72.

15. C. J. Cherryh, *Devil to the Belt* (New York: Warner Books, 2002), 6, 16. *Devil to the Belt* combines two separately published novels, *Heavy Time* (1991) and *Hellburner* (1992). At the beginning of the story, Cherryh sets the scene: "It was a lonely place, this remote deep of the Belt, a place where, if things went wrong they went seriously wrong. And the loneliest sound of all was that thin, slow beep that meant a ship in distress" (6).

16. Larry Niven depicted this sort of Belt culture as background in a series of stories about "Known Space" published in the 1960s and 1970s.

17. Robert A. Heinlein, *The Moon Is a Harsh Mistress* (New York: Tor, 1966), 38.

18. Ibid., 259.

19. Robert A. Heinlein, *The Rolling Stones* (1952; reprint, New York: Ballantine Books, 1977), 158.

20. Ben Bova, *Rock Rats* (New York: Tor, 2002), 17.

21. The term "rock rat" is ubiquitous, from use by Jack Williamson in the 1940s to Jerry Pournelle in the 1970s and Ben Bova in the 2000s.

22. Bova, *Rock Rats*, 69; and Heinlein, *Rolling Stones*, 187–88.

23. Mary Doria Russell, *The Sparrow* (New York: Fawcett, 1996), 123.

24. Eric Kotani and John Maddox Roberts, *The Island Worlds* (New York:

Baen, 1987), 128. Also see Jerry Pournelle, "Tinker," and Brooks Peck, "Stealing a Zero-G Cow," both in *Life among the Asteroid*, ed. Jerry Pournelle (New York: Ace Books, 1992), 22, 183.

25. Jack Williamson, *Seetee* (New York: Jove, 1979), 40, 46. *Seetee* combines *Seetee Shock* and *Seetee Ship*, published originally in 1949–1951.

26. Isaac Asimov, "The Martian Way," in *The Science Fiction Hall of Fame*, vol. 2B, *The Greatest Science Fiction Novellas of All Time*, ed. Ben Bova (Garden City, NY: Doubleday, 1973); quotations from pages 13, 17–18.

27. Kim Stanley Robinson, "Coming Back to Dixieland," originally published in *Orbit* 18 in 1976 and reprinted in *Remaking History and Other Stories* (New York: Tom Doherty and Associates, 1994), 189.

28. Larry Niven, *The Patchwork Girl* (New York: Ace, 1980), 145.

29. Heinlein, *Rolling Stones*, 20, 34, 187.

30. Carlos Schwantes, "The Concept of the Wageworkers' Frontier: A Framework for Future Research," *Western Historical Quarterly* 23 (January 1987): 39–55.

31. Heinlein, *Moon*, 118.

32. For readers in the mid-1960s, the novel had many appeals. The depiction of a successfully engineered revolution meshed with the dreams of the radical far left. At the same time, the libertarian values expressed in the slogan TANSTAAFL ("there ain't no such thing as a free lunch") also gave the book a right-wing appeal. And much of its interest came from the way that Heinlein imagined and characterized a sentient computer, to which he gives a quirky sense of humor. The mid-1960s were a time when many people were fascinated with the possibility that computers might be growing large enough to gain consciousness, and Heinlein's computer has a family resemblance to HAL in the movie *2001: A Space Odyssey* (1968), to the computer that takes over the world in the movie *Colossus: The Forbin Project* (1970), and to the supercomputer in John Barth's novel *Giles Goat-Boy* (1966).

33. Olympus Station is a power satellite orbiting between the Earth and the moon. Allen Steele, "The Return of Weird Frank," in *Rude Astronauts* (New York: Ace, 1995), 50.

34. Allen Steele, *Lunar Descent* (New York: Ace, 1991), 25.

35. Ibid., 43.

36. Laurie Mercier, *Anaconda: Labor, Community and Culture in Montana's Smelter City* (Urbana: University of Illinois Press, 2001); Elizabeth Jameson, *All That Glitters: Class, Conflict and Community in Cripple Creek* (Urbana: University of Illinois Press, 1998); Nancy Taniguchi, *Castle Valley, America: Hard Land, Hard-Won Home* (Logan: Utah State University Press, 2004).

37. Steele, *Lunar Descent*, 265–66.

38. Jack Williamson, "On the Final Frontier," in *Space and Beyond: The Frontier Theme in Science Fiction*, ed. Gary Westfahl (Westport, CT: Greenwood Press, 2000); James E. Gunn, personal communication to author, February 6, 2003. Williamson also earned a Ph.D. in English in the 1950s and taught at Eastern New Mexico University in Portales for two decades. The Science Fiction Writers of America named him a Grand Master in 1975, and he continued to publish fiction into the 2000s.

39. Many pages of plot snarls are unraveled when the adventurers realize that the strange seetee ship is traveling backward in time and causing local

temporal eddies as it goes (thus messages mysteriously arrive before they're sent and casualties from a treacherous attack are discovered before the attack occurs).

40. Williamson, *Seetee,* 9, 12, 15, 56.

41. Ibid., 52–53.

42. The Alliance/Union narrative describes the expansion of humans to space stations around planetless stars, wars of independence (the "Company Wars" that pitted the Merchanters' Alliance against Earth Fleet), and the emergence of a third force in the form of a union of new planetary societies that use cloning and psychological manipulation to construct superpeople. Earth, the Alliance, and the Union develop an uneasy equilibrium that alternates war and diplomacy.

43. Cherryh, *Devil to the Belt,* 132.

44. Ibid., 97, 69.

45. Ibid., 92, 63.

46. For Paul Dekker, the belt was escape from a reputation as a teenage screw-up and a mother who essentially wrote him off.

47. Cherryh, *Devil to the Belt,* 162.

48. Ibid., 26–27, 163.

Chapter 3. Science Projects

1. George Adamski and Desmond Leslie, *Flying Saucers Have Landed* (London: W. Laurie, 1953); George Adamski, *Inside the Space Ships* (New York: Abelard Schuman, 1955).

2. Robert Michael Pyle, *Where Bigfoot Walks: Crossing the Dark Divide* (Boston: Houghton Mifflin, 1995), is a naturalist's take on the implications of the legend. Molly Gloss, *The Wild Life* (Boston: Houghton Mifflin, 2001), is a fine historical novel that incorporates a whole clan of the creatures.

3. Thomas Pynchon, *Vineland* (Boston: Little, Brown, 1990), 305.

4. A growing literature examines the development of the Roswell myth and its remarkable traction within popular culture since the start of the 1980s. See Benson Saler, Charles A. Ziegler, and Charles B. Moore, *UFO Crash at Roswell: The Genesis of a Modern Myth* (Washington, DC: Smithsonian Institution Press, 1997); Robert Alan Goldberg, *Enemies Within: The Culture of Conspiracy in Modern America* (New Haven, CT: Yale University Press, 2001), 189–231.

5. One other link between the West and the science fiction future is astronomy's demand for physical isolation and clear air. This has meant western locations since Percival Lowell observed Mars from Flagstaff, Arizona, at the opening of the twentieth century. In the early twenty-first century, astronomers depended on Lick, Mount Wilson, and Palomar observatories in California, the National Radio Astronomy Observatory in New Mexico, and the complex at Kitt Peak, Arizona. The action in Greg Benford's science fiction novel *Eater* (2000) takes place around the huge observatory complex at the 13,800-foot top of Mauna Kea, Hawaiʻi.

6. Tad Bartemus and Scott McCartney, *Trinity's Children. Living along America's Nuclear Highway* (New York: Harcourt Brace Jovanovich, 1991); Necah C. Furman, *Sandia National Laboratories: The Postwar Decade* (Albuquerque: University of New Mexico Press, 1991); Hal Rothman, *On Rims and Ridges: The Los Alamos Area since 1880* (Lincoln: University of Nebraska Press, 1992); Paul Loeb, *Nuclear Culture: Living and Working in the World's Largest Atomic Complex* (New York:

Coward, McCann and Geoghegan, 1982); and Michele S. Gerber, *On the Home Front: The Cold War Legacy of the Hanford Site* (Lincoln: University of Nebraska Press, 1992).

7. A. Costandina Titus, *Bombs in the Backyard: Atomic Testing and American Politics* (Reno: University of Nevada Press, 1986).

8. Roger E. Bolton, *Defense Purchases and Regional Growth* (Washington, DC: Brookings Institution, 1966); Maureen McBreen, "Regional Trends in Federal Defense Expenditures, 1950–1976," in *Selected Essays on Patterns of Regional Change*, ed. Congressional Research Service (Washington, DC: Senate Appropriations Committee Print, 1977); James L. Clayton, "The Impact of the Cold War on the Economies of California and Utah, 1946–1965," *Pacific Historical Review* 36 (November 1967): 449–73. The expansion of the metropolitan-military complex is the central topic of Roger W. Lotchin, *Fortress California, 1911–1960: From Warfare to Welfare* (New York: Oxford University Press, 1992); Ann Markusen, Peter Hall, Scott Campbell, and Sabina Deitrick, *The Rise of the Gunbelt: The Military Remapping of Industrial America* (New York: Oxford University Press, 1991); Martin Schiesl, "Airplanes to Aerospace: Defense Spending and Economic Growth in the Los Angeles Region, 1945–1960," in *The Martial Metropolis*, ed. Roger W. Lotchin (New York: Praeger, 1984), 135–49; Stephen Oates, "NASA's Manned Spacecraft Center at Houston, Texas," *Southwestern Historical Quarterly* 67 (January 1964): 350–75.

9. Keith McLaughlin, *The Flow of Federal Funds, 1981–1988* (Washington, DC: Northeast-Midwest Institute, 1990); Rosy Nimroody, *Star Wars: The Economic Fallout* (Cambridge, MA: Ballinger, 1988).

10. Clayton Koppes, *JPL and the American Space Program: A History of the Jet Propulsion Laboratory* (New Haven, CT: Yale University Press, 1982); Rebecca Lowen, *Creating the Cold War University: The Transformation of Stanford* (Berkeley: University of California Press, 1997); John Findlay, *Magic Lands* (Berkeley: University of California Press, 1992); Margaret O'Mara, *Cities of Knowledge: Cold War Science and the Search for the Next Silicon Valley* (Princeton, NJ: Princeton University Press, 2004).

11. Peter Goin, *Nuclear Landscapes* (Baltimore, MD: Johns Hopkins University Press, 1991); Peter B. Hales, *Atomic Spaces: Living on the Manhattan Project* (Urbana: University of Illinois Press, 1997); Patricia Nelson Limerick and Mark Kett, "Haunted by Rhyolite: Learning from the Landscape of Failure," *American Art* 6 (Fall 1992): 18–39; Tom Vanderbilt, *Survival City: Adventures among the Ruins of Atomic America* (Princeton, NJ: Princeton Architectural Press, 2002) examines the more general landscape of the cold war, of which the atomic West is a part.

12. Len Ackland, *Making a Real Killing: Rocky Flats and the Nuclear West* (Albuquerque: University of New Mexico Press, 1999); Barton Hacker, "Radiation Safety, the AEC, and Nuclear Weapons Testing: Writing the History of a Controversial Program," *Public Historian* 14 (1992): 31–53; Howard Ball, *Justice Downwind: America's Atomic Testing Program in the 1950s* (New York: Oxford University Press, 1986); Eric Mogren, *Warm Sands: Uranium Mine Tailings Policy in the American West* (Albuquerque: University of New Mexico Press, 2002).

13. Dan O'Neill, "Alaska and the Firecracker Boys: The Story of Project Chariot," in *The Atomic West*, ed. Bruce Hevly and John Findlay (Seattle: University of Washington Press, 1998), 195.

14. Richard Bartlett, *Great Surveys of the American West* (Norman: University of Oklahoma Press, 1961); William H. Goetzmann, *Exploration and Empire: The Explorer and Scientist in the Winning of the West* (New York: Knopf, 1966); Donald Worster, *A River Running West: The Life of John Wesley Powell* (New York: Oxford University Press, 2001); David Emmons, *Garden in the Grasslands: Boomer Literature of the Great Plains* (Lincoln: University of Nebraska Press, 1971); Nancy Langston, *Forest Dreams, Forest Nightmares: The Paradox of Old Growth in the Inland West* (Seattle: University of Washington Press, 1995).

15. Robert Kelley, *Battling the Inland Sea* (Berkeley: University of California Press, 1989); David Igler, *Industrial Cowboys: Miller and Lux and the Transformation of the Far West, 1850–1920* (Berkeley: University of California Press, 2001).

16. Donald Worster, *Rivers of Empire: Water, Aridity, and the Growth of the American West* (New York: Pantheon, 1985); Norris Hundley Jr., *The Great Thirst: Californians and Water, 1770s–1990s* (Berkeley: University of California Press, 1992); Marc Reisner, *Cadillac Desert: The American West and Its Disappearing Water* (New York: Viking, 1986). The reclamation dream was articulated by William E. Smythe in *The Conquest of Arid America* (1899).

17. Joseph Stevens, *Hoover Dam: An American Adventure* (Norman: University of Oklahoma Press, 1988); Paul Pitzer, *Grand Coulee Dam: Harnessing a Dream* (Pullman: Washington State University Press, 1994); Mark Foster, *Henry J. Kaiser: Builder in the Modern American West* (Austin: University of Texas Press, 1989); Woody Guthrie, *Roll On, Columbia: The Columbia River Songs*, US DOE/BP-977 (Portland, OR: Bonneville Power Administration, 1987); Ivan Doig, *Bucking the Sun* (New York: Simon and Schuster, 1996) is an energetic novel about the building of Fort Peck Dam.

18. A guide to optimistic thinking about the science of terraforming is Martyn J. Fogg, *Terraforming: Engineering Planetary Environments* (Warrendale, PA: Society of Automotive Engineers, 1995).

19. Laurie Brown, Martha Ronk, and Charles E. Little, *Recent Terrains: Terraforming the American West* (Baltimore, MD: Johns Hopkins University Press, 2003).

20. Kim Stanley Robinson, "Purple Mars," in *The Martians* (New York: Bantam Spectra, 1999), 433.

21. Stephen Pyne, *Fire in America: A Cultural History of Wildland and Rural Fire* (Princeton, NJ: Princeton University Press, 1982); Jared Orsi, *Hazardous Metropolis: Flooding and Urban Ecology in Los Angeles* (Berkeley: University of California Press, 2004); Blake Gumprecht, *The Los Angeles River: Its Life, Death, and Possible Rebirth* (Baltimore, MD: Johns Hopkins University Press, 1999); Paul Hirt, *Conspiracy of Optimism: Management of National Forests since World War II* (Lincoln: University of Nebraska Press, 1994); William deBuys, *Salt Dreams: Land and Water in Low Down California* (Albuquerque: University of New Mexico Press, 1999).

22. James Scott, *Seeing Like a State: How Certain Schemes to Improve the Human Condition Have Failed* (New Haven, CT:

Yale University Press, 1999); Leonie Sandercock, *Toward Cosmopolis* (New York: Wiley, 1998).

23. Gregory Landis, "Ecopoesis," originally published in *Science Fiction Age* (May 1997) and reprinted in Gardner Dozois, ed., *Worldmaking: SF Adventures in Terraforming* (New York: St. Martin's Press, 2001), 318.

24. Kim Stanley Robinson's Mars trilogy comprises *Red Mars* (New York: Bantam Spectra, 1992); *Green Mars* (New York: Bantam Spectra, 1994); and *Blue Mars* (New York: Bantam Spectra, 1996).

25. Kim Stanley Robinson, quoted in David Seed, "The Mars Trilogy: An Interview," *Foundation* 68 (Autumn 1996): 76.

26. Kim Stanley Robinson, personal communication, August 14, 2001.

27. Kim Stanley Robinson, ed., *Future Primitive: The New Ecotopias* (New York: Tor, 1994); Thomas E. Jackson, "Interview with Kim Stanley Robinson," *New York Review of Science Fiction* 117 (May 1998): 15–18.

28. Jackson, "Interview with Kim Stanley Robinson," 18.

29. William Cronon, ed., *Uncommon Ground: Toward Reinventing Nature* (New York: Norton, 1995).

30. Robinson, *Red Mars* (New York: Bantam Spectra, 1993), 177.

31. Seed, "Mars Trilogy," 75.

32. Robinson, *Red Mars*, 229.

33. Ibid., 177–79.

34. Seed, "Mars Trilogy," 78.

35. Robinson, *Martians*, 271–72.

36. Robinson, *Blue Mars* (New York: Bantam Spectra, 1996), 761. A good discussion of the environmental ethics of the trilogy is Robert Markley, "Falling into Theory: Simulation, Terraformation, and Eco-Economics in Kim Stanley Robinson's Martian Trilogy," *Modern Fiction Studies* 43 (Fall 1997): 773–99.

37. William Deverell, *Railroad Crossings: Californians and the Railroad, 1850–1910* (Berkeley: University of California Press, 1994); James Kinsey Howard, *Montana: High, Wide and Handsome* (New York: Oxford University Press, 1943); Michael Malone, *The Battle for Butte: Mining and Politics in the Northern Frontier, 1864–1906* (Seattle: University of Washington Press, 1981); Gilman Ostrander, *Nevada: The Great Rotten Borough, 1859–1964* (New York: Knopf, 1966).

38. Karl Wittfogel, *Oriental Despotism: A Comparative Study of Total Power* (New Haven, CT: Yale University Press, 1957).

39. Poul Anderson, "The Big Rain," originally published in *Astounding Science Fiction* (October 1954) and reprinted in Dozois, *Worldmaking*, 18.

40. Ibid., 20.

41. Pamela Sargent, *Venus of Dreams* (New York: Bantam Spectra, 1986); *Venus of Shadows* (New York: Doubleday, 1988); *Child of Venus* (New York: Eos, 2001). The gap between the appearance of the second and third books reflects changes in editors and in the business plans of publishers.

42. Pamela Sargent, 1990 NOVAExpress interview, at http://www.engel-cox.org/sargent/interview.htm. Sargent, a sophisticated writer, received undergraduate and graduate degrees from SUNY at Binghamton. Through her novels and several anthologies, she is known as a feminist and an advocate for women within science fiction.

43. John Gray, *Men Are from Mars, Women Are from Venus* (New York: HarperCollins, 1992).

44. Sargent, 1990 NOVAExpress interview.

45. Pamela Sargent, "Dream of Venus," in Dozois, *Worldmaking*, 395. This side story to the narrative of the trilogy clearly summarizes the parameters of the Venus Project.

46. Sargent, *Venus of Shadows*, 642, and 1990 interview.

47. Sargent, *Venus of Dreams*, 534.

48. Ibid., 527; *Child of Venus*, ix.

49. Sargent, *Child of Venus*, 101, 165.

50. Ibid., 58.

51. Ibid., 226, 201.

52. Willy Ley, *Engineers' Dreams* (New York: Viking Press, 1954); De Witt Douglas Kilgore, *Astrofuturism: Science, Race, and Visions of Utopia in Space* (Philadelphia: University of Pennsylvania Press, 2003), 70–81.

Chapter 4. Johnny Appleseed, John Wayne, and Homesteading on the Extraterrestrial Frontier

1. Heinlein was born in Butler, Missouri, in 1907. He attended the U.S. Naval Academy and then lived in California and Colorado after illness in the 1930s cut short his navy career. Bradbury was born in Waukegan, Illinois, in 1920 and moved with his family to Los Angeles in the mid-1930s, where he has lived ever since. Heinlein tended to see the Pacific West as an exuberant realization of the American get-up-and-go that had conquered continental frontiers (e.g., engineer Dan Davis in *The Door into Summer* [1957]). Bradbury's response has been a pained flinch from the cacophony of information-rich cities in favor of a nostalgic recreation of small-town scenery and society.

2. For example, see Daniel Hoffman, *Paul Bunyan: Last of the Frontier Demigods* (Philadelphia: University of Pennsylvania Press, 1952); Robert Price, *Johnny Appleseed: Man and Myth* (Bloomington: Indiana University Press, 1954).

3. In both animated films and live-action television, Disney in the 1950s rummaged through American history for a variety of 100 percent American heroes—Davy Crockett, Mike Fink, Pecos Bill. Neil Gaiman's prize-winning fantasy *American Gods* (2001), which imagines the fate of Old World gods struggling to survive in North America, briefly introduces John Chapman as a mythologized culture hero who complains that upstart Paul Bunyan now gets all the attention.

4. Gary K. Wolfe, "The Frontier Myth in Ray Bradbury," in *Ray Bradbury*, ed. Martin Harry Greenberg and Joseph D. Olander (Edinburgh, UK: Paul Harris, 1980), 33–54.

5. Ray Bradbury, *The Martian Chronicles* (New York: William Morrow, 1997), 101, 102, 106.

6. Heinlein, *Farmer in the Sky* (New York: Ballantine, 1975 [1950]), 148.

7. Bradbury, *Martian Chronicles*, 158–59.

8. In the American Northeast, in contrast, growing conditions are such that much of the once-cultivated landscape has reverted to woods with no special human intervention.

9. Historians have usually approached homesteading through family and community microhistory, as in Merle Curti, *The Making of an American Community* (Stanford, CA: Stanford University Press, 1959); John Mack Faragher, *Sugar Creek: Life on the Illinois Prairie* (New Haven, CT: Yale University Press, 1986); and Dean May, *Three Frontiers: Family, Land, and Society in the American West, 1850–1900* (New York: Cambridge University Press, 1994).

10. Hamlin Garland, *A Son of the Middle Border* (New York: Macmillan, 1917), 376.

11. Molly Gloss, *The Jump-Off Creek* (Boston: Houghton Mifflin, 1989), 168, 185.

12. Willa Cather, *O Pioneers!* (Boston: Houghton Mifflin, 1913), 20.

13. Ibid., 65.

14. Ibid., 119.

15. Walter Nugent, "Frontier and Empire in the Late Nineteenth Century," *Western Historical Quarterly* 20 (Autumn 1990): 393–408; Wallace Stegner, *Where the Bluebird Sings to the Lemonade Springs: Living and Writing in the West* (New York: Random House, 1992), 199.

16. Heinlein, *Farmer in the Sky*, 22.

17. Ibid., 146. The allusion is to the Pare Lorentz documentary film *The Plow That Broke the Plains* (1936), which deals with settlement, the dust bowl of the 1930s, and conservation efforts.

18. Ibid., 147, 150.

19. Ibid., 186.

20. Ibid., 183.

21. Allen M. Steele, *Coyote: A Novel of Interstellar Exploration* (New York: Ace Books, 2002), 376.

22. Alfred Crosby, *The Columbian Exchange: Biological and Cultural Consequences of 1492* (Westport, CT: Greenwood Press, 1972) and *Ecological Imperialism: The Biological Expansion of Europe, 900–1900* (New York: Cambridge University Press, 1986).

23. Larry Niven, Jerry Pournelle, and Steven Barnes, *The Legacy of Heorot* (New York: Simon and Schuster, 1987), 7. "Him" in the passage is Cadman Wayland, the lone military man among the settlers, who has a justified sense of ill ease.

24. The grendels have evolved the capacity to boost their rate of oxidation for short periods, allowing them to move at frightening speed. However, they need to remain close to water so that they can quickly cool themselves after these bursts of energy conversion. On this principle of biophysics turns the defense of the colony.

25. Larry Niven, Jerry Pournelle, and Steven Barnes, *Beowulf's Children* (New York: Tor, 1995), 132.

26. Marta Randall, *Journey* (New York: Pocket Books, 1978).

27. Ibid., 125.

28. Wallace Stegner, *Beyond the 100th Meridian: John Wesley Powell and the Second Opening of the West* (Boston: Houghton Mifflin, 1954); Walter Prescott Webb, "The American West: Perpetual Mirage," *Harper's* 24 (May 1957): 25–31; Henry Nash Smith, *Virgin Land: The American West as Symbol and Myth* (Cambridge, MA: Harvard University Press, 1950), 25–31. The troubled application of one aspect of the myth is the subject of David Emmons, *Garden in the Grasslands: Boomer Literature of the Central Great Plains* (Lincoln: University of Nebraska Press, 1971).

29. Ursula Le Guin, "The Eye Altering," originally published in 1974 and reprinted in *The Compass Rose* (New York: Harper and Row, 1982), 157.

30. Ibid., 166, 169.

31. Philip K. Dick, *The Three Stigmata of Palmer Eldritch* (1965; reprint, New York, Vintage Books, 1991), 142, 159.

32. William Frey, "Three Americas: The Rising Significance of Regions," *Journal of the American Planning Association* 68 (Autumn 2002): 349–55.

33. Jonathan Raban, *Bad Land: An American Romance* (New York: Pantheon, 1996); Larry McMurtry, *The Last Picture Show* (New York: Dial Press, 1966); William Least Heat-Moon, *PrairyErth* (Boston: Houghton Mifflin, 1991);

Deborah Popper and Frank Popper, "The Buffalo Commons: Metaphor as Method," *Geographical Review* 91(1999): 491–510. They point out that the extensive tracts of national grasslands are the result of a similar process after the 1930s.

34. Scott Donaldson, *The Suburban Myth* (New York: Columbia University Press, 1969).

35. Philip K. Dick, *Martian Time-Slip* (New York: Ballantine, 1964), 13, 10.

36. William Robbins, *Colony and Empire: The Capitalist Transformation of the American West* (Lawrence: University Press of Kansas, 1994); Melvyn Dubofsky, *We Shall Be All: A History of the Industrial Workers of the World* (Chicago: Quadrangle, 1969); Mike Davis, *City of Quartz: Excavating the Future in Los Angeles* (New York: Verso, 1990); Donald Worster, *Rivers of Empire: Water, Aridity and the Growth of the American West* (New York: Pantheon, 1985); J. Anthony Lukas, *Big Trouble: A Murder in a Small Western Town Sets Off a Struggle for the Soul of America* (New York: Simon and Schuster, 1997).

37. William Kittredge, *Who Owns the West?* (San Francisco: Mercury House, 1996).

38. Kim Stanley Robinson, *Blue Mars* (New York: Bantam Spectra, 1996), 385–87.

39. As Heinlein does for Ganymede, Robinson offers fascinating details of ecological change. Nirgal builds small dams to trap water and thin soil. Lichen has already colonized the basin, so he sows other seeds and spores and observes which ones thrive. Other modified plants that have been seeded on Mars begin to spread into the basin on the wind. He buys loads of topsoil and earthworms. After worms will come moles, mice, marmots, rabbits. Plants bloom with the new spring. Where Avalonians have to fight to learn, Nirgal simply has to inhabit a place, to experiment and experience. Nevertheless, the planet still fools him, first with a viroid infection that withers the grass, junipers, and potatoes, then with a dust storm that buries the cirque a meter deep. "In time, other winds would blow some of this dust away. Snow would fall on the rest of it. . . . Water would carry the dust and fines away, down the massif and into the world. But by the time that happened, every plant and animal in the basin would be dead." Robinson, *Blue Mars*, 402–4.

40. Jonathan Lethem, *Girl in Landscape* (New York: Doubleday, 1998), 1.

41. Ibid., 62–63.

42. Ibid., 48. Also: "They turned a corner and the view opened before them. A spread of enormous ruins, shapes Pella hadn't seen before, including another intact arch, huge, that framed a lop-sided heart-shaped chunk of sky" (97). Note the emphasis on the big sky, both as a trope of the American Western and because you could no longer go out under the sky unprotected on Earth.

43. Interview with Jonathan Lethem, available at http://www.randomhouse.com/boldtype/0598/lethem/interview.html.

44. Jane Tompkins, *West of Everything: The Inner Life of Westerns* (New York: Oxford University Press, 1992); Mary Lawlor, *Recalling the Wild: Naturalism and the Closing of the American West* (New Brunswick, NJ: Rutgers University Press, 2000), 2.

45. Lethem, *Girl in Landscape*, 112.

46. Ibid., 114–15. The Archbuilders have similarities to the Bleekmen in *Martian Time-Slip*, although Dick's race seem most closely modeled on native Australians.

47. Ibid., 229, 257–58.

48. Tom Moylan, "Utopia is When Our Lives Matter: Reading Kim Stanley Robinson's *Pacific Edge*," *Utopian Studies* 6 (1995): 1–24; Carol Franko, "Working the In-Between: Kim Stanley Robinson's Utopian Fiction," *Science-Fiction Studies* 21 (1994): 191–211; Carl Abbott, "Falling into History: The Imagined Wests of Kim Stanley Robinson in the 'Three Californias' and Mars Trilogies," *Western Historical Quarterly* 34 (Spring 2003): 27–48.

49. There is a significant Quaker presence in Costa Rica drawing on both U.S. transplants and native Costa Ricans.

50. See Michael J. Sheeran, *Beyond Majority Rule: Voteless Decision Making in the Religious Society of Friends* (Philadelphia: Philadelphia Yearly Meeting, 1983). There are close parallels between the depiction of Quaker decision practices and the town meeting politics in Robinson's *Pacific Edge* (1990).

51. Molly Gloss, *The Dazzle of Day* (New York: Tor, 1997), 252.

52. Ibid., 187, 253.

53. Richard White, *It's Your Misfortune and None of My Own: A New History of the American West* (Norman: University of Oklahoma Press, 1991); Robert V. Hine, *Community on the American Frontier: Separate but Not Alone* (Norman: University of Oklahoma Press, 1980).

Chapter 5. Frontier Democracy

1. Ursula K. Le Guin, "The Day before the Revolution," in *The Wind's Twelve Quarters* (New York: Harper and Row, 1975), 238, 246.

2. The story is dedicated "In memoriam Paul Goodman, 1911–1972," recognizing the author of *Communitas* and *Growing Up Absurd* as a strong voice for Kropotkinian anarchism.

3. Greg Bear, *Moving Mars* (New York: Tor, 1993), 497.

4. John W. Campbell, *Collected Editorials from Analog*, ed. Harry Harrison (Garden City, NY: Doubleday, 1966).

5. Robert A. Heinlein, *Double Star* (New York: Doubleday, 1956; reprint, New York: Ballantine, 1986), 199; see also 43–44 and 206.

6. Robert A. Heinlein, *The Moon Is a Harsh Mistress* (New York: Tor, 1966), 202.

7. David Alan Johnson, *Founding the Far West: California, Oregon, and Nevada, 1840–1890* (Berkeley: University of California Press, 1992), is the most sophisticated and detailed study of state constitution making. Spontaneous self-government in Colorado is discussed in Richard Hogan, *Class and Community in Frontier Colorado* (Lawrence: University Press of Kansas, 1990); and Carl Abbott, Stephen Leonard, and David McComb, *Colorado: A History of the Centennial State*, 4th ed. (Niwot: Colorado Associated University Press, 2005).

8. "[Heinlein] also enjoyed some of my books—which I was startled and delighted to discover," Bear has commented. "That encouraged me to go up against some of the conclusions in *The Moon is a Harsh Mistress* by writing *Moving Mars*." Personal communication, June 3, 2003.

9. Bear, *Moving Mars*, 45, 47.

10. Ibid., 98.

11. Ibid., 285.

12. Ibid., 326.

13. In the last third of the book, Bear leaves Cassie as a political leader while the

story shifts toward a crisis of military intervention by Earth, which is not happy with an independent Mars that has its act together. The treacherous attack is blocked only by the fact that Martian scientists have learned to use quantum effects to displace large objects in space. Cassie makes the momentous decision to move Mars to another sun and planetary system entirely, saving Martian society but exposing herself to political repudiation, then to eventual vindication by history.

14. Robinson, *Red Mars* (New York: Bantam Spectra, 1992), 170, 389, 380, 425.

15. William Robbins, *Colony and Empire: The Capitalist Transformation of the American West* (Lawrence: University Press of Kansas, 1994).

16. Tom Moylan, "'Utopia Is When Our Lives Matter': Reading Kim Stanley Robinson's *Pacific Edge*," *Utopian Studies* 6 (1995): 8, 19; Kim Stanley Robinson, quoted in David Seed, "The Mars Trilogy: An Interview," *Foundation* 68 (Autumn 1996), 77.

17. Stanley Elkins and Eric McKitrick, "A Meaning for Turner's Frontier: Part I, Democracy in the Old Northwest," *Political Science Quarterly* 69 (September 1954): 321–54; Robert Hine, *Community on the American Frontier: Separate but Not Alone* (Norman: University of Oklahoma Press, 1985). The Elkins-McKitrick thesis also finds support in studies of everyday life in postwar suburbs, for example Herbert Gans, *The Levittowners: Ways of Life and Politics in a New Community* (New York: Pantheon, 1967).

18. Robinson, *Green Mars* (New York: Bantam Spectra, 1994), 220.

19. Ibid., 337. See the entire section "A New Constitution" in Robinson's *Blue Mars* (New York: Bantam Spectra, 1996).

20. Boone's name is a deliberate reference to American pioneering mythology. Western American mythology is also reproduced in his afterlife. His reputation, after his death, becomes legend and conflates with tales of Paul Bunyan on Mars, who in turn encounters a Martian Big Man a hundred times larger yet than Paul and Babe (see Robinson, *Red Mars*, 386).

21. Carol Franko "The Density of Utopian Destiny in Robinson's *Red Mars*," *Extrapolation: A Journal of Science Fiction* 38 (Spring 1997): 60.

22. Ibid., 61. Mikhail Mikhailovich Bakhtin (1895–1975) was a Russian literary critic and philosopher who worked during the Soviet era. His work first came to the attention of American scholars at the end of the 1960s. There is a substantial enterprise devoted to translating Bakhtin's fragmentary works from Russian and interpreting them in terms of literary theory and epistemology. Bakhtin wrote sympathetically about the historical imagination (e.g., the work of Marc Bloch) and opposed metahistorians like Oswald Spengler, who treated societies as fixed units rather than open and constantly changing constructs. There are interesting parallels between the ideas of Bakhtin and those of political philosopher Jürgen Habermas, who has emphasized open dialogue within a public sphere as the foundation of democratic society.

23. De Witt Douglas Kilgore, *Astrofuturism: Science, Race, and Visions of Utopia in Space* (Philadelphia: University of Pennsylvania Press, 2003), 234–38.

24. Kim Stanley Robinson, "Some Worknotes and Commentary on the Constitution, by Charlotte Dorsa Brevia,"

in *The Martians* (New York: Bantam Spectra, 1999), 280–81. *The Martians* is a potpourri of preliminary stories, sketches for alternative plot lines, and ancillary material for the Mars trilogy that includes the text of the Martian constitution as well as Charlotte Dorsa Brevia's commentary.

25. Robinson, *Martians*, 103, 131, 321, 344.

26. Philip Porter and Fred Lukermann, "The Geography of Utopia," in *Geographies of the Mind*, ed. David Lowenthal and Martyn Bowden (New York: Oxford University Press, 1976), 197–223, define the frontier in standard terms as the divide between areas with more and fewer than six persons per square mile. Also see J. Wreford Watson, *Social Geography of the United States* (London: Longman, 1979), 221–26; Dolores Hayden, *Seven American Utopias* (Cambridge, MA: MIT Press, 1976), 8–13, 362–63.

27. Charles LeWarne, *Utopias on Puget Sound, 1885–1915* (Seattle: University of Washington Press, 1975); Robert V. Hine, *California's Utopian Colonies* (San Marino, CA: Huntington Library, 1953). *Factories in the Field* (1939), one of the seminal books on California by left-radical critic Carey McWilliams, highlighted the Kaweah, Durham, and Delhi community experiments.

28. James Vance, "California and the Search for the Ideal," *Annals of the Association of American Geographers* 62 (May 1972): 185–210; Carl Abbott, "Utopia and Bureaucracy: The Fall of Rajneeshpuram, Oregon," *Pacific Historical Review* 59 (February 1990): 77–103; James A. Aho, *The Politics of Righteousness: Idaho Christian Patriotism* (Seattle: University of Washington Press, 1990); Bradley C. Whitsel, *The Church Universal and Triumphant: Elizabeth Clare Prophet's Apocalyptic Movement* (Syracuse, NY: Syracuse University Press, 2003).

29. Alexander McClung, *Landscapes of Desire: Anglo Mythologies of Los Angeles* (Berkeley: University of California Press, 2000); Mike Davis, *City of Quartz: Excavating the Future in Los Angeles* (New York: Verso, 1991).

30. Ernest Callenbach, *Ecotopia, The Notebooks and Reports of William Weston* (Berkeley, CA: Banyan Tree Books, 1975).

31. Ernest Callenbach, *Ecotopia Emerging* (Berkeley, CA: Banyan Tree Books, 1981).

32. Jim Miller, "Post-Apocalyptic Hoping: Octavia Butler's Dystopian/Utopian Vision," *Science-Fiction Studies* 25 (July 1998): 355.

33. Octavia Butler, *The Parable of the Sower* (New York: Four Walls Eight Windows, 1993), 75.

34. Ibid., 291.

35. Tom Moylan, *Scraps of the Untainted Sky: Science Fiction, Utopia, Dystopia* (Boulder, CO: Westview Press, 2000), 223–45, offers one of the best analyses of Butler's political ideas.

36. Butler, *Sower*, 22.

37. Moylan, *Scraps*, 229.

38. Octavia Butler, *Parable of the Talents* (New York: Warner Books, 1998); Octavia Butler, interview in Marilyn Mehaffy and AnaLouise Keating, "'Radio Imagination': Octavia Butler on the Poetics of Narrative Embodiment," *Melus* 26 (Spring 2001): 75.

39. *The Wild Shore* (New York: Ace, 1983); *The Gold Coast* (New York: St. Martin's Press, 1988); *Pacific Edge* (New York: St. Martin's Press, 1990).

40. Shaun Huston, "Murray Bookchin on Mars! The Production of Nature in

Kim Stanley Robinson's Mars Trilogy," in *Lost in Space: Geographies of Science Fiction*, ed. Rob Kitchin and James Kneale (London: Continuum, 2002), 167–79.

41. Kerwin Klein, "Westward, Utopia: Robert V. Hine, Aldous Huxley, and the Future of California History," *Pacific Historical Review* 70 (August 2002): 467; Carey McWilliams, *California: The Great Exception* (New York: Current Books, 1949); Neil Morgan, *Westward Tilt: The American West Today* (New York: Random House, 1963), 3–12.

42. Allen J. Scott and Edward Soja, eds., *The City: Los Angeles and Urban Theory at the End of the Twentieth Century* (Berkeley: University of California Press, 1996); Michael J. Dear, Greg Hise, and E. Eric Schockman, eds., *Rethinking Los Angeles* (Thousand Oaks, CA: Sage, 1996); Rob Kling, Spencer Olin, and Mark Poster, eds., *Postsuburban California: The Transformation of Orange County* (Berkeley: University of California Press, 1991).

43. Robinson, personal communication, August 14, 2001.

44. Mike Davis, *The Ecology of Fear: Los Angeles and the Imagination of Disaster* (New York: Henry Holt, 1998).

45. Robinson, *Pacific Edge*, 300.

46. Lisa McGirr, *Suburban Warriors: The Origins of the New American Right* (Princeton, NJ: Princeton University Press, 2001).

47. Moylan, "Utopia," 9.

48. Robinson, *Pacific Edge*, 95; Carol Franko, "Working the 'In-Between': Kim Stanley Robinson's Utopian Fiction," *Science-Fiction Studies* 21 (1994): 192; Moylan, "Utopia," 4, 11.

49. Bud Foote, "A Conversation with Kim Stanley Robinson," *Science-Fiction Studies* 21 (March 1994):56; Seed, "Mars Trilogy," 77. It is with this understanding that Robinson would later populate Mars with a wide range of sectarian communities that act as unsuccessful counterpoint to the central politics of nation-building. In the empty marsscape beyond corporate control, and between revolutions, are colonies and communities of Sufis, Baptists, Quakers, and Rastafarians. There are followers of Rousseau, adherents of Fourier, and, in another academic joke, acolytes of Foucault. There are also radical Mars-first ecoterrorists and mystical Mars worshipers in the self-contained community of Zygote, concealed under the south polar ice. None, however, is able to do more than encapsulate a fragment of Martian settlers, and their self-satisfied isolation does nothing for the larger polity.

50. Robert V. Hine, *Josiah Royce: From Grass Valley to Harvard* (Norman: University of Oklahoma Press, 1992), 152. Also see John Clendenning, *Life and Thought of Josiah Royce* (Madison: University of Wisconsin Press, 1985); Earl Pomeroy, "Josiah Royce: Historian in Quest of Community," *Pacific Historical Review* 40 (February 1970): 1–24; Josiah Royce, *California from the Conquest of 1846 to the Second Vigilance Committee in San Francisco: A Study of American Character* (Boston: Houghton Mifflin, 1886).

51. Frederick Jackson Turner, "Contributions of the West to American Democracy," in *Frontier and Section: Selected Essays of Frederick Jackson Turner*, ed. Ray A. Billington (Englewood Cliffs, NJ: Prentice-Hall, 1961), 80. Elkins and McKitrick, "Meaning for Turner's Frontier."

52. The book has attracted much critical commentary. See Donna R. White, *Dancing with Dragons: Ursula K.*

Le Guin and the Critics (Columbia, SC: Camden House, 1999), for a summary.

53. Ursula Le Guin, *Always Coming Home* (New York: Bantam Spectra, 1986), 167.

54. Mona Gallagher, "Ursula Le Guin: In a World of her Own," *Mother Jones* (January 1984): 23–27, 51–53, sets Le Guin firmly in her green and gray city. Le Guin herself has paid quizzical tribute to her Portland neighborhood in *Blue Moon over Thurman Street* (Portland, OR: New Sage Press, 1993), a collaboration with photographer Roger Dorband.

55. Interview with Ursula Le Guin, in Larry McCaffery, *Across the Wounded Galaxies: Interviews with Contemporary American Science Fiction Writers* (Urbana: University of Illinois Press, 1990), 172.

56. Le Guin, *Always Coming Home*, 156.

57. In Le Guin's earlier and more traditional science fiction novel *City of Illusions* (1967), the people of a future North America similarly live a low-impact lifestyle in the forests, but they make use of sophisticated communication equipment, fusion lights, solar-power looms, and other automatic tools for housework and farm work.

58. Le Guin, *Always Coming Home*, 404.

59. Ibid., 153.

60. Ursula Le Guin, "A Non-Euclidean View of California as a Cold Place to Be," in *Dancing at the Edge of the World* (New York: Grove, 1989), 84, 90.

61. Ursula K. Le Guin, *Searoad: Chronicles of Klatsand* (New York: Harper and Row, 1991), 1. Also like *Always Coming Home*, it carefully depicts a very particular part of northwestern America, even including maps of the town of Klatsand in 1906 and 1986.

62. Ursula Le Guin, *Always Coming Home* (New York: Bantam, 1986), 563.

Chapter 6. On the Urban Edge

1. Thomas Pynchon, *The Crying of Lot 49* (New York: Harper Collins, 1999), 49.

2. There are brief but insightful comments in Rosemary Jackson, *Fantasy: The Literature of Subversion* (London: Methuen, 1981), 164–71.

3. Los Angeles, San Francisco–Oakland–San Jose, Dallas–Fort Worth, Houston, Seattle, Denver, Phoenix, Portland, Sacramento, San Antonio. The calculations use the nineteen states of the Great Plains, mountains, and Pacific coasts.

4. Pynchon, *Crying*, 147.

5. Sam Bass Warner Jr., *The Urban Wilderness* (New York: Harper and Row, 1972); James Lemon, *Liberal Dreams and Nature's Limits* (New York: Oxford University Press, 1996); Janet Abu-Lughod, *New York, Chicago, Los Angeles: America's Global Cities* (Minneapolis: University of Minnesota Press, 1999).

6. Jean Baudrillard, *America* (New York: Verso, 1989); Fredric Jameson, "Postmodernism, or the Cultural Logic of Late Capitalism," *New Left Review* 146 (July–August 1984): 53–93.

7. D. J. Waldie, *Holy Land: A Suburban Memoir* (New York: Norton, 1996); Alida Brill, "Lakewood, California: 'Tomorrowland' at 40," in *Rethinking Los Angeles*, ed. Michael J. Dear, E. Eric Schockman, and Greg Hise (Thousand Oaks, CA: Sage, 1996), 97–112.

8. Kirse Granat May, *Golden State, Golden Youth: The California Image in Popular Culture* (Chapel Hill: University of North Carolina Press, 2002); Eric Avila, *Popular Culture in the Age of White Flight: Fear and Fantasy in Suburban Los Angeles* (Berkeley: University of California Press, 2004).

9. Robert Fogelson, *The Fragmented Metropolis: Los Angeles, 1850–1930* (Cambridge, MA: Harvard University Press, 1967).

10. Pynchon, *Crying*, 13.

11. Several recent collections of essays on greater Los Angeles have probed and extended these ideas: Dear, Schockman, and Hise, *Rethinking Los Angeles;* Allen J. Scott and Edward Soja, eds., *The City: Los Angeles and Urban Theory at the End of the Twentieth Century* (Berkeley: University of California Press, 1996); Michael J. Dear, ed., *From Chicago to L.A.: Making Sense of Urban Theory* (Thousand Oaks, CA: Sage, 2002).

12. Allen J. Scott, *Technopolis: The Geography of High Tech in Southern California* (Berkeley: University of California Press, 1993); Greg Hise, *Magnetic Los Angeles* (Baltimore: Johns Hopkins University Press, 1997).

13. Pynchon, *Crying*, 12.

14. Michael Sorkin, ed., *Variations on the Theme Park: The New American City and the End of Public Space* (New York: Hill and Wang, 1992); Pynchon, *Crying*, 20.

15. Gibson, *Virtual Light* (New York: Bantam, 1993), 115, 301–2.

16. William Gibson, *All Tomorrow's Parties* (New York: G. P. Putnam's Sons, 1999), 84; Gibson, *Virtual Light*, 301.

17. Gibson, *Virtual Light*, 25.

18. Gibson, *Virtual Light*, 62–63; Gibson, *All Tomorrow's Parties*, 174, 80–81.

19. Pat Murphy, *The City, Not Long After* (New York: Doubleday, 1989).

20. William Rorabaugh, *Berkeley at War: The Sixties* (New York: Oxford University Press, 1989); Michael Davidson, *The San Francisco Renaissance: Poetics and Community at Mid-Century* (New York: Cambridge University Press, 1989); Lawrence Ferlinghetti and Nancy J. Peters, *Literary San Francisco: A Pictorial History* (San Francisco: City Lights Books, 1980).

21. Harvey Molotch, "L.A. as Design Product: How Art Works in a Regional Economy," in Scott and Soja, *City*, 225–75; Richard Florida, *The Rise of the Creative Class* (New York: Basic Books, 2002).

22. Pynchon, *Crying*, 150.

23. Cynthia Kadohata, *In the Heart of the Valley of Love* (New York: Viking, 1992).

24. Ibid., 2, 8, 33, 124. We can assume that Kadohata, of Japanese American ancestry, picked the term *camp* to recall the internment experience of 1942–1945 and relishes the inversion of the image as the elite pull barbed wire around themselves rather than stringing it around others.

25. Krista Comer, "Western Literature at Century's End: Sketches in Generation X, Los Angeles, and the Post-Civil Rights Novel," *Pacific Historical Review* 72 (August 2003): 405–13.

26. Greg Bear, *Queen of Angels* (New York: Warner Books, 1990), 49.

27. Ibid., 89, 13. Authors are not responsible for their publishers' decisions, but the dust jacket for the hardcover edition of Robinson's *Gold Coast* (1988), which also describes the increasing division of wealth and power in southern California, is a perfect depiction of Bear's L.A.

28. Saskia Sassen, *The Global City: New York, London, Tokyo*, rev. ed. (Princeton, NJ: Princeton University Press, 2001); Manuel Castells, *The Informational City: Restructuring and Urban Development* (Cambridge, MA: Blackwell, 1997); Manuel Castells, *End of Millennium* (Malden, MA: Blackwell, 1998).

29. Mike Davis, *City of Quartz: Excavating the Future in Los Angeles* (New York: Verso, 1990), 110, 111; Mike Davis, *The Ecology of Fear: Los Angeles and the Imagination of Disaster* (New York: Henry Holt, 1998).

30. Davis, *City of Quartz*, 223.

31. Neal Stephenson, *Snow Crash* (New York: Bantam Spectra, 1992), 44. "Your ass is busted," the second Metacop translates.

32. Paolo Soleri, *Arcology: The City in the Image of Man* (Cambridge, MA: MIT Press, 1969).

33. Some readers have complained that Larry Niven and Jerry Pournelle's *Oath of Fealty* (New York: Pocket Books, 1982) is not really science fiction, in that the authors simply posit the existence of Todos Santos without exploring the technological innovations and engineering solutions that might be necessary to hold up such a massive structure, keep the air breathable, regulate the temperature, allow people to move around smoothly, and keep them fed and watered. It is, of course, sociological science fiction from authors usually more interested in technical and scientific extrapolation.

34. Niven and Pournelle, *Oath of Fealty*, 22.

35. Ibid., 323.

36. Ibid., 229, 323, 120.

37. Octavia Butler, *Parable of the Sower* (New York: Four Walls Eight Windows, 1993), 18, 114. For an example of the subgenre that Lauren is referring to, see the movie *Logan's Run* (1976).

38. Butler, *Parable of the Sower*, 8.

39. Ibid., 9, 38.

40. Robert O. Self, *American Babylon: Race and the Struggle for Postwar Oakland* (Princeton, NJ: Princeton University Press, 2003); Marilynn Johnson, *The Second Gold Rush: Oakland and the East Bay in World War II* (Berkeley: University of California Press, 1993).

41. Pynchon, *Crying*, 83, 148, 150.

42. William Gibson, foreword to John Shirley, *City Come A-Walkin'* (New York: Four Walls Eight Windows, 2000). The 2000 edition of Shirley's novel is revised from the first edition published in 1980.

43. Shirley, *City*, 30.

44. Fritz Leiber, *Our Lady of Darkness* (New York: Berkeley, 1978), 12–13, also 64–67.

45. Shirley, *City*, 78, 27, 127, 129, 149.

46. Philip K. Dick, *Do Androids Dream of Electric Sheep?* (Garden City, NY: Doubleday, 1968).

Chapter 7. Information Everywhere: Pacific Destinies in the Twenty-First Century

1. Norman Spinrad, *Science Fiction and the Real World* (Carbondale: Southern Illinois University Press, 1990), 112.

2. Lewis Shiner, "Inside the Movement: Past, Present, and Future," in *Fiction 2000: Cyberpunk and the Future of Narrative*, ed. George Slusser and Tom Shippey (Athens: University of Georgia Press, 1992), 23.

3. Wallace Stegner, *Where the Bluebird Sings to the Lemonade Springs: Living and Writing in the West* (New York: Random House, 1992), 140.

4. Henry David Thoreau, "Walking," originally delivered as a lecture in 1851; available at: http://thoreau.thefreelibrary.com/walking/1-1.

5. For example, David Igler, "Diseased Goods: Global Exchange in the Eastern Pacific Basin, 1770–1850," *American Historical Review* 109 (June 2004): 693–719.

6. The latter point is the underlying argument of Carl Abbott, *The Metropolitan Frontier: Cities in the Modern American West* (Tucson: University of Arizona Press, 1993). A good summary of long wave theory, from its origins with Nikolai Kondratieff and Josef Schumpeter to more recent empirical assessments, is Peter Hall and Paschal Preston, *The Carrier Wave* (London: Unwin Hyman, 1988).

7. West Coast science fiction writers who are definitely not part of the cyberpunk movement share many of the assumptions and tropes of the backstory. They range from Greg Bear, whose work touches the margin of cyberpunk, to Octavia Butler and Kim Stanley Robinson, who otherwise share nothing of the aesthetic and sensibility.

8. For example, George Tucker, *Progress of the United States in Population and Wealth in Fifty Years* (Boston: Little, Brown, 1843).

9. William Gibson, *Neuromancer* (New York: Ace, 1984). In 1984, of course, most North American television sets and other consumer electronics were manufactured in Japan. When Gibson finally visited Japan, it confirmed his fictionalization. "I really loved the place. It was always a completely surreal, wonderfully baffling experience." Available at: http://www.salon.com/weekly/gibson3961014.html.

10. Bruce Sterling, ed., *Mirrorshades: The Cyberpunk Anthology* (New York: Arbor House, 1986), xi, xiv.

11. William Gibson cites Lou Reed as an influence. Female characters channel Joan Jett, not Stevie Nicks. Bruce Sterling describes *Schismatrix* (1986) as "bare bones, like a Ramones three-minute pop song: we're not going to have any pretentious light shades of pale guitar noodling here, it's going to be 'Sheena is a Punk Rocker,' blam, blam, blam, let's move on." In *Across the Wounded Galaxies: Interviews with Contemporary American Science Fiction Writers*, ed. Larry McCaffery (Urbana: University of Illinois Press, 1990), 228.

12. Kim Stanley Robinson, quoted in Edward James, *Science Fiction in the Twentieth Century* (New York: Oxford University Press, 1994), 195.

13. David G. Mead, "Technological Transfiguration in William Gibson's Sprawl Novels: *Neuromancer, Count Zero,* and *Mona Lisa Overdrive*," *Extrapolation* 32 (1991): 350–60. Much literary criticism exists that deals with cyberpunk. See, for example, George Slusser and Tom Shippey, eds., *Fiction 2000: Cyberpunk and the Future of Narrative* (Athens: University of Georgia Press, 1992); and Dani Cavallaro, *Cyberpunk and Cyberculture: Science Fiction and the Work of William Gibson* (London: Athlone Press, 2000). The strongest thread in literary criticism deals with the theme of transcendence, by individuals or by the Net itself, with many bows to the ideas of Donna Haraway from *Simians, Cyborgs, and Women* (New York: Routledge, 1991) and *Modest_Witness@Second_Millenium.Female Man_Meets_OncoMouse: Feminism and Technoscience* (New York: Routledge, 1997).

14. Mike Davis, *City of Quartz: Excavating the Future in Los Angeles* (New York: Verso, 1992). One of the most curious spin-offs is Jonathan Lethem's *Gun, with Occasional Music* (New York: Harcourt Brace, 1994), which follows all the conventions and plot elements of the classic noir detective story. However, it is set in a near-future Oakland of designer drugs and sentient, genetically

engineered animals. The mob enforcer is a kangaroo who throws a mean punch. Unlike most science fiction writers, who are interested in the substance of their future world, Lethem is most interested in playing with the limits of the detective genre.

15. The literature on anime is extensive. A Web site with extensive bibliography is available at http://www.animeresearch.com. Introductions to the genre include Susan J. Napier, *Anime: From Akira to Princess Mononoke* (New York: Palgrave, 2001); and Antonia Levi, *Samurai from Outer Space: Understanding Japanese Animation* (Chicago: Open Court, 1996).

16. William Gibson, in *Northern Dreamers: Interviews with Famous Science Fiction, Fantasy, and Horror Writers*, ed. Edo Van Belkom (Kingston, Ontario: Quarry Press), 89.

17. Ibid., 93. See also Gibson's interview in McCaffery, *Across the Wounded Galaxies*, 137.

18. William Gibson, *All Tomorrow's Parties* (New York: G. P. Putnam's Sons, 1999), 4.

19. Bruce Sterling, interview in McCaffery, *Across the Wounded Galaxies*, 214–15; and William Gibson, interview in McCaffery, 149.

20. *Statistical Abstract of the United States: 2003* (Washington: Government Printing Office, 2003), tables 1263, 1264.

21. William Gibson, *Mona Lisa Overdrive* (New York: Bantam, 1989), 133.

22. She "estimated that no hard copies [of *Lo Rez Skyline*, their first album] would have reached Seattle in time for her nativity, but she liked to believe there had been listeners here even then, PacRim visionaries netting sounds from indies as obscure, even, as East Teipei's Dog Soup." William Gibson, *Idoru* (New York: Berkeley, 1997), 17.

23. George Washington Bates, *Sandwich Island Notes: By a Haole* (1854), quoted in Arrell M. Gibson and John S. Whitehead, *Yankees in Paradise: The Pacific Basin Frontier* (Albuquerque: University of New Mexico Press, 1993), 353.

24. William Gilpin, *The Cosmopolitan Railway, Compacting and Fusing Together all the World's Continents* (San Francisco: The History Company, 1890); Gibson and Whitehead, *Yankees in Paradise*; Jean Heffer, *The United States and the Pacific: History of a Frontier* (Notre Dame, IN: Notre Dame University Press, 2002); Arthur P. Dudden, *The American Pacific: From the Early China Trade to the Present* (New York: Oxford University Press, 1992); Walter MacDougall, *Let the Sea Make a Noise: A History of the North Pacific from Magellan to MacArthur* (New York: Basic Books, 1993).

25. Hubert Howe Bancroft, *The New Pacific*, rev. ed. (New York: Bancroft, 1913), 8, 9, 13.

26. Wolf von Schierbrand, "The Coming Supremacy of the Pacific," *Pacific Monthly* 14 (October 1905): 211–26.

27. Gibson, *Yankees in Paradise*, 373.

28. Bruce Sterling, *Islands in the Net* (New York: Ace Books, 1989), 215, 222.

29. Pat Cadigan, *Tea from an Empty Cup* (New York: Tor, 1998), 24, 73–74.

30. Gibson, *Mona Lisa Overdrive*, 33, 5–6, 131.

31. Andre Gunder Frank, *Re-Orient: Global Economy in the Asian Age* (Berkeley: University of California Press, 1998). Also see Manuel Castells, *End of Millennium*, rev. ed. (Malden, MA: Blackwell, 2000).

32. Richard Paul Russo, *Carlucci's Edge* (New York: Ace, 1995); Greg Bear,

Queen of Angels (New York: Warner Books, 1990); Paul McAuley, *The Secret of Life* (New York: Tor, 2001). See the movie *Chinatown* (1974) and Nayan Shah, *Contagious Divides: Epidemics and Race in San Francisco's Chinatown* (Berkeley: University of California Press, 2001).

33. Neal Stephenson, *The Diamond Age, or A Young Lady's Illustrated Primer* (New York: Bantam Spectra, 1996), 228–29, 246.

34. Heffer, *The United States and the Pacific*, 398–99.

35. Shintaro Ishihara, *The Japan that Can Say No* (New York: Simon and Schuster, 1991); Clyde Prestowitz, *Trading Places: How We Are Giving Our Future to Japan* (New York: Basic Books, 1988).

36. Alexander Saxton, *The Indispensable Enemy: Labor and the Anti-Chinese Movement in California* (Berkeley: University of California Press, 1971); Shah, *Contagious Divides*.

37. Heffer, *The United States and the Pacific*, 184–89; Mike Davis, in *The Ecology of Fear* (New York: Henry Holt, 1998), inventories many examples of Yellow Peril literature.

38. Ruth Benedict, *The Chrysanthemum and the Sword* (Boston: Houghton Mifflin, 1946); John Dower, *War without Mercy: Race and Power in the Pacific War* (New York: Pantheon, 1986).

39. Philip K. Dick, *The Man in the High Castle* (New York: Vintage, 1992), 69, 44.

40. If the information in the glasses falls into the wrong hands, the secrecy necessary for a successful real estate speculation will be breached.

41. William Gibson, *Virtual Light* (New York: Bantam Spectra, 1994), 144.

42. Neal Stephenson, *Snow Crash* (New York: Bantam Spectra, 1992), 135–37.

43. Ibid., 272–73.

44. A phyle was the largest political division of Greek city-states, based on a combination of kinship and voluntary affiliation.

45. Stephenson, *Diamond Age*, 18–19.

46. Ibid., 71. In the book, Hackworth/Hacker functions as an updated technologically facile version of the trickster figure.

47. This is perhaps a joke at the expense of cyberpunk author Bruce Sterling, an Austin resident.

48. James, *Science Fiction in the Twentieth Century*, writes: "It was the 1980s, exaggerated, and not usually extrapolated beyond the twenty-first century. It was urban, run down, yet using the technology of the 1980s with as much insouciance as we use the technology of the 1940s" (194).

49. Gibson, interview in McCaffery, *Across the Wounded Galaxies*, 136, 140, 143; David Brande, "The Business of Cyberpunk: Symbolic Economy and Ideology in William Gibson," *Configurations* 2 (1994): 509–36; Frederic Jameson, *Postmodernism, or The Cultural Logic of Late Capitalism* (Durham, NC: Duke University Press, 1991).

50. Sterling, interview in McCaffery, *Across the Wounded Galaxies*, 225.

51. Bruce Sterling, *Islands in the Net* (New York: Ace Books, 1989), 1.

52. Cavallaro, *Cyberpunk and Cyberculture*, 138. In an article on Watts in the *New York Times Magazine*, June 12, 1966, 34–35, 78–84, Pynchon expressed admiration with the ways that the residents were appropriating the debris and detritus of the riot, one more example of his fascination with the surfaces of popular culture.

Chapter 8. Bigger than Texas! Americans, Our Wests, and Science Fiction

1. Postwar Los Angeles sprouted all-night coffee shops, drive-ins, bowling alleys, motels and supermarkets with bold geometric shapes and glittering surfaces of chrome, glass, and plastic that imitated gull-winged Chevrolets and finned Plymouths. See Alan Hess, *Googie: Fifties Coffee Shop Architecture* (San Francisco: Chronicle Books, 1986); and Robert Venturi, Denise Scott Brown, and Stephen Izenour, *Learning from Las Vegas* (Cambridge, MA: MIT Press, 1972).

2. Disney studios followed *Toy Story* with *Buzz Lightyear of Star Command* (2000), a seventy-minute video in which Buzz takes on the nasty Zurg, as Flash Gordon once took on Ming the Merciless.

3. Spengler's *Der Undergang des Abendlandes* appeared in English in 1926–1928 and Toynbee's multivolume work in 1935. H. G. Wells, *The Shape of Things to Come* (New York: Macmillan, 1933), was the basis for the movie.

4. For detail on the various historical sequences of Asimov, Blish, H. Beam Piper, Poul Anderson, Larry Niven, C. J. Cherryh, and others, see John J. Pierce, *Foundations of Science Fiction: A Study in Imagination and Evolution* (Westport, CT: Greenwood Press, 1987), 210–20. Wollheim's "full cosmogony of science-fiction future history" is quoted in James Gunn, *Alternate Worlds: An Illustrated History of Science Fiction* (Englewood Cliffs, NJ: Prentice-Hall, 1975), 225–26. A broad overview of science fiction approaches to history is Robert H. Canary, "Science Fiction as Fictive History," *Extrapolation* 16 (1974): 81–95.

5. A modern English translation of Vico's *New Science* appeared in the United States in 1948. Ibn Khaldun's massive history of the world from a North African perspective began to appear in translation in the 1950s.

6. Andre Norton, *Star Soldiers* (New York: Baen Publishing, 2001), 401, 410. *Star Soldiers* is a combined republication of *Star Rangers* (1953) and *Star Guard* (1955).

7. "The Green Hills of Earth" is the ballad of the spaceways that Robert Heinlein attributes to the blind poet Rhysling. Earlier I quoted its tribute to the questing, exploring spirit ("The arching sky is calling . . ."), but it ends with a return to Earth: "We pray for one last landing / On the globe that gave us birth; / Let us rest our eyes on fleecy skies / And the cool, green hills of Earth."

8. Leigh Bracket, *The Long Tomorrow* (Garden City, NY: Doubleday, 1955), 14.

9. Ibid., 134, 136, 139.

10. Ursula K. Le Guin took her protagonist on a similar transcontinental trek in her early novel *City of Illusions* (1967). Far into the future, North America has been nearly abandoned by humans, and there remain only scattered, quiet settlements and ruins of older times. The hero Falk, suffering from memory loss, awakens in the eastern forest and heads westward in search of the great city of the Shing, the people who have made themselves the extraterrestrial masters of Earth. His journey retraces the route of nineteenth-century pioneers—and of Len Colter—across great rivers and vast prairies and finally reaches an alien city that soars into the sky on both sides of the Black Canyon of the Gunnison River. Le Guin has commented that writing about

journeys is more fun than writing about places, positioning herself with those many other writers who have constructed their stories out of movement into and across the West. She remarked in her introduction to the 1978 reissue that the pleasure of *City of Illusions* was "the chance to imagine my country, America, without cities, almost without towns, as sparsely populated by our species as it was five hundred years ago. . . . The sense of time, but more than that the sense of space, extent, the wideness of the continent. The wideness, the wilderness" (*The Language of the Night: Essays on Fantasy and Science Fiction* [New York: G. P. Putnam, 1979], 147). Into this setting she places the westward quest, with the future's future to be sought in the same place on which earlier Americans pinned their expectations.

11. Wilderness figures as well in David Brin's *The Postman* (New York: Bantam, 1985). The cover art for the paperback edition encapsulates the westward search for refuge and utopia. The foreground is a sun-cracked desert floor. A ruined highway stretches westward to distant snow-dusted mountains. We Oregonians can picture the scene as U.S. 30, partway from Bend to Santiam Pass over the Cascade Range. In the story, it is sixteen years after nuclear war, the Three-Year Winter, and the rise of feral survivalists—in a word, "The Chaos." Gordon Krantz is a refugee from a U.S. Army that simply dissolved. He treks west across plains and mountains, and he reaches and then crosses the Cascades into the Willamette Valley. The fertile land that pioneers saw as an Eden at the end of the Oregon Trail in the 1840s is still a semi-Eden at the end of a bleak desert journey, a place where Gordon can help survivors begin to rebuild civil society. Purely by accident, he takes on the persona of a U.S. Postal Service letter carrier. By so doing, he taps into latent civic idealism and helps to spark the revival of a democratic polity. In this very different framework of postapocalypse story, Brin places himself with Robinson, Bear, and other science fiction advocates of the civic realm.

12. Some postcivilization stories reverse the direction and go east to find familiar ruins as trick endings. Stephen Vincent Benet's pre–World War II story "By the Waters of Babylon" (1937) uses the ruins of New York, the film *Logan's Run* (1976) an overgrown Capitol building.

13. When Thomas Disch, a distinguished science fiction writer and critic, writes that "space is like Texas, only bigger," he is referring to what he considers a naive view in which "outer space is envisioned as that New Frontier where the indignities of ordinary life—onerous no-future jobs and low status—are to be remedied, as they were by an earlier expansion into the American West." *The Dreams Our Stuff Is Made Of: How Science Fiction Conquered the World* (New York: Simon and Schuster, 1998), 178.

14. Louis Hartz, *The Liberal Tradition in America* (New York: Harcourt Brace, 1955), remains essential to understanding U.S. history, even when modified by an awareness of a persisting "republican" tradition that balanced individualism with community.

15. George Bancroft, *History of the United States, from the Discovery of the American Continent* (Boston: Little, Brown, 1834–1875); Francis Fukuyama, *The End of History and the Last Man* (New York: Free Press, 1990).

16. David Potter, *People of Plenty: Economic Abundance and the American Character* (Chicago: University of Chicago Press, 1954).

17. Kage Baker, *Sky Coyote* (New York: Harcourt, 1999), and *Mendoza in Hollywood* (New York: Harcourt, 2000). Baker was born in Hollywood, worked in the movie industry, and lives in Pismo Beach on the central California coast.

18. John Barnes, *The Sky So Big and Black* (New York: Tor Books, 2002), 34–35.

19. Ibid., 22, 132.

20. Melissa Scott, personal communication, June 1, 2003. Scott, who has a Ph.D. in comparative history, is knowledgeable about history and historiography. Compare her use of Western novel clichés to that of John Jakes in *Six-Gun Planet* (1970), where the planet Missouri is a reactionary utopia that is governed by the ruggedly individualistic code of the West. The protagonist is a cultivated bureaucrat from off planet who finds himself trapped in the town of Shane and facing a possible death threat from a brutal gunfighter. But it turns out that the gunslinger is a robot, and the planet's Old West–ness is programmed and imposed by the reactionary idealists who have molded its society, not a natural expression of undaunted individualism.

21. Fredric Jameson, "Progress Versus Utopia; or, Can We Imagine the Future?" *Science-Fiction Studies* 9 (July 1982): 147–58; Tom Moylan, *Scraps of the Untainted Sky: Science Fiction, Utopia, Dystopia* (Boulder, CO: Westview Press, 2000), 26–27.

22. Jerome H. Buckley, *The Triumph of Time: A Study of Victorian Concepts of Time, History, Progress, and Decadence* (Cambridge, MA: Harvard University Press, 1966); Carl Malmgren, *Worlds Apart: The Narratology of Science Fiction* (Bloomington: Indiana University Press, 1991), 3–6, 175.

23. Kim Stanley Robinson, *Pacific Edge* (New York: Ace, 1990), 181.

INDEX